ROMAN

K. M. Ashman

Published by FeedARead.com Publishing – Arts Council funded
Copyright © K M Ashman

First Edition

A CIP catalogue record for this title is available from the British
Library.

**All characters depicted within this publication other than the
obvious historical figures are fictitious and any resemblance to any
real persons living or dead is entirely coincidental**

Follow Kevin's blog at
http://kevin-ashman.blogspot.com/

Contact Kevin direct at:
KMAshman@Silverbackbooks.co.uk

More Books by K. M. Ashman

Vampire
The Dead Virgins
The Treasures of Suleiman
The Mummies of the Reich
The Last Citadel
Savage Eden

Cover design by R.M. Ashman

Rhys.Ashman@hotmail.co.uk

It was an age of fear, an age of brutality, yet overall, when all is said and done, it was an age of glory.

Prologue

The Roman Province of Picenum - 20AD

Karim stood at the centre of the amphitheatre, every muscle aching as rivulets of blood oozed down his face to drip lazily onto the ever-thirsty sand. Damocles the Greek, his comrade from the Ludus, knelt in the sun-scorched arena nursing a stab wound to his side. An injury received just before he had crushed his opponent's skull under the heel of his hobnailed Caligae in a frenzy of aggression and self-preservation. All around, those who had fought like demons to keep hold of their miserable lives and the faint promise of an elusive freedom lay dead or dying, pathetic victims of gladiatorial savagery.

Governor Sibelus Augusta's birthday celebrations had started earlier that day with an air of frivolity. A troop of travelling dwarves assembled from all over Europe, entertained the crowds with mock battles and raced tiny ponies around the amphitheatre. Oddities of nature rarely seen in Rome, let alone Picenum, paraded around the arena on display. Giraffes strode gracefully around the ring, eye to eye with those in the lower tiers, while giant apes contained within barred crates were wheeled into the centre to be taunted into banging their chests by their keepers. Teams of trainee gladiators followed, fighting violent but non-lethal battles to prepare the crowd for what was yet to come. Throughout the day, the level of passion and violence increased until eventually the faint rhythmic sound of distant beating drums permeated the arena, raising the crowd's anticipation.

The excitement finally exploded when two wooden gates were flung open and a herd of bulls, frothing at the mouth and mad with pain, burst into the arena seeking escape from the torture behind the scenes. This was the Venatio, the brutal spectacle of animal against man in a one sided contest of pain and gore. Another gate opened and ten Bestiarii, well-trained animal fighters, ran forward to screams of approval from the impatient crowds.

As soon as the staged conflicts had ended, criminal classes with little or no training faced exotic animals ranging from tigers from the east and hippos and crocodiles from Africa. At last, the first human blood had been spilt. It was what the mob expected and a simple prelude to what was to come.

The crowd took a well-earned break. It was thirsty work watching so much violence. Vendors in the vomitories offered drinks and sweetmeats for sale, and a column of bare breasted female slaves, bearing baskets of the cooked meat of the recently slain animals, circled the arena throwing chunks into the crowd. Many had brought their own refreshments and picnicked on fruit and cheese, or if they were well off, slabs of cold meat washed down by flasks of tepid wine.

Eventually, the crowd returned to their seats for the late afternoon's entertainment. This was when the real excitement started, and what everyone had been waiting for. Blood and gore, preferably human.

First, to come were Noxii, the criminals condemned to the arena for a wide range of indiscretions punishable by death. Adulterers, escaped slaves, deserters, or simply captured enemy, were made to fight each other to the death for the chance to live another day. Mock battles were staged where soldiers dressed in their finest parade gear, mercilessly cut down unarmed slaves representing the enemies of Rome in lavish re-enactments of famous battles known to the audience,

Condemned women and children were released unarmed into the ring, momentarily relieved at the unexpected freedom, before the snarls of the starving lions brought their short-term life expectancy into sharp and terrifying focus. Finally, the time came that everyone had been waiting for, the main event of the day, the Ludi Gladiatori.

Sixteen highly trained fighters at the physical peak of fitness and ability marched into the arena to the accompaniment of deafening cheers and music. This was what it was all about, the final celebrations for Governor Sibelus Augusta on his fiftieth birthday. A display of gladiatorial magnificence that had been awarded the Emperor's privilege of Sine Missione.

The crowd knew this was a rare occasion and many had travelled hundreds of miles to see a gladiatorial contest where every combatant knew he had to win or die. It was as simple as that. Sine Missione was rarely granted, as the cost of training gladiators was so exorbitant and the compensation you had to pay the opponents camp so high, that only the wealthiest of men could afford to sponsor such games. Luckily, Governor Sibelus was such a man, or at least he portrayed that image. In truth, he was drowning in a sea of debt due to a gambling addiction that threatened to destroy his privileged and influential position.

However, today was his birthday and he had an ace up his sleeve, a gladiator whose name was hardly known in the area. Sibelus was risking everything on this extraordinary man. He had made a huge wager with Gaius Pelonius Maecilius, a recently returned war hero who had retired with a substantial pension and extended lands granted to him by the Emperor in recognition of his lifetime achievement and bravery during twenty-five years of military service.

Privately, Sibelus gloated. What would a mere soldier know about such things? By the end of the day, his debts would be substantially reduced at the ex-soldier's expense. The bet was simple. He had wagered that in the finale, Karim, the jet black Numidian would be the last man alive in the arena.

Pelonius had accepted the wager in a drunken haze, and now three weeks later, having seen the gladiator train, regretted that evening terribly and in particular his love for un-watered wine, the curse that had so often cost him much. However, the die was cast and there was nothing he could do.

Karim had trained as a Provocatores and fought with sword and shield, whilst protected by a breastplate, arm guard and double feathered helmet. Provocatores usually fought each other, but in this instance, they could be paired against other gladiators ranging from the Retiarii, who fought with trident, dagger and net, through to the Hoplomachi, who fought with the standard Roman issue sword, the Gladius and a small round shield.

The bloody conflict started and when the original sixteen had been reduced to eight, the mix was altered by the sudden addition of two chariots bursting unexpectedly into the arena. The chariots were from a different Ludus and each held two more combatants armed with spears. These were the feared Essedarii, and their sole purpose was to kill the remaining combatants.

The home gladiators worked together to bring the chariots crashing down. Spears were driven between spokes and horse's legs cleaved from beneath them with blade or axe. Without the advantage of their chariots, the riders were ineffective and though they put up a frantic defence, they were no match for the local gladiator's overwhelming expertise in the administration of bloody and painful death.

Just when the remaining eight had started to believe they would survive, they were instructed to fight each other. Each exhausted combatant drew on every last ounce of strength and skill, to try and defeat his opponent, each as skilled as the other in their own speciality, until eventually, the evening's extreme activities left two bloody gladiators standing, Karim the Numidian and Damocles the Greek.

Karim looked over again at Damocles. Now it was clear that there would indeed be no Missione and that the governor would make them fight to the last man standing. The Greek was his friend and both had trained together at the Ludus. It was never a good idea to make friends because of the probability that one day you would have to fight each other. However, over the last year, the two had formed a close bond borne out of mutual respect and understanding. Karim realised that despite his friendship, the time had come and they would have to meet each other in the final contest. It was what they trained for, and they both knew they would die in the ring one day Death held no fear for either, but the manner of dying was important. He limped over to the Greek and helped him to his feet.

'Come, friend,' he said, 'we have a corrupt Roman and a bloodthirsty crowd to entertain.'

Damocles looked up at the cheering mob.

'Have they not tasted enough blood?' he asked.

'They are Roman,' the reply came, 'they will never have enough.'

'Then let's give them a finale to remember.'

They walked toward the centre of the arena and stood twenty paces apart, facing the sponsor. Both gladiators dripped with blood, standing proud amongst the carnage that surrounded them, yet gaining strength from the screams and chants of the adoring crowd.

High in the stand, Governor Sibelus and his guests enjoyed the spectacle from their comfortable seats, picking on sweetmeats and drinking the best-chilled wine from the deepest cellar in the governor's villa; an extravagance he could ill afford. Sibelus called for silence.

'Citizens of Picenum,' he announced when the crowd had settled, 'behold your two remaining champions, Damocles of Greece and Karim the Numidian. I think you will agree that the contests have been fair and both have earned the Rudis.'

He caught the eye of the referee, whose impartial pairings had ensured Karim had a favourable draw through to the last two. The official felt no guilt; the two hundred Denarii paid to him by one of

8

Sibelus's henchmen were a year's wages for a minor official and he had a family to support.

The crowd cheered in appreciation. The wooden sword of freedom was seldom awarded and never to two combatants. Sibelus raised his hand, waiting for the crowd to settle.

'Unfortunately,' he continued, 'there can be only one Rudis.'

'Release them both,' someone shouted from the crowd.

Once again, Sibelus raised his hand with a benevolent smile.

'However,' he continued, 'the contest is not yet over.'

Silence fell again and he turned toward the two bleeding gladiators staring up at him from the arena.

'One last contest,' he thundered, 'against a common foe. Survive this and you are both free men.'

Karim and Damocles straightened their tired bodies and held up their swords in acknowledgement. Raising his voice to its maximum, Sibelus turned toward another gate and with his voice echoing around the walls of the arena, called out the final challenge.

'Citizens of Picenum,' he shouted, behold the Gauls!'

The crowd screamed in excitement as two dozen warriors spilled out of the gate into the arena, but then fell silent, confused at the sight before them. These weren't warriors, they were women. Their hair was wild and stuck up into terrifying shapes with horse glue, and their naked bodies were daubed in blue dye. Each woman held a skinning knife and they searched the bloody arena for the targets that held the key to their survival.

The spectators weren't the only ones confused, Gaius Pelonius didn't understand either. He had expected Sibelus to cheat him, but this was completely unexpected. Women or not, their numbers were many and there was a definite chance that Karim could be killed.

'Happy with your wager?' asked the governor, sitting back down alongside his guest.

'Shouldn't I be?' asked Pelonius.

'I don't see why not, the odds are in your favour.'

A horn resounded around the arena, followed by the screams of the women as they rushed toward the two wounded gladiators, both sounds drowned out by the roar of the crowd as the last battle commenced.

Karim braced himself. He had no problem killing women, he had done so many times before, and these women were no different. He prepared himself for the onslaught. Legs, shoulder width apart, knees slightly bent, shield presented, and Gladius held in the attack position. However, the expected impact never came, as the screaming women swerved around him and made a beeline for Damocles. Karim spun around, confused as the screaming mass enveloped his friend, and though many fell victim to the Greek's sword, he was quickly driven to the floor by sheer weight of numbers.

Their jailer had made it clear to the slave women.

'If you kill the white man first,' he had said, 'any survivors will be taken back to their homeland and released. If the black man is killed first, all who survive will be fed to the lions.'

The lie had worked perfectly. As far as they knew, this was the women's only chance to escape the hell of slavery and return to their homelands. Therefore, with false hope in their hearts, they had endured the pathetic attempts of other slaves to make them look fierce with paint and glue, before being herded into the arena.

Too late Karim realised the danger, and roaring in anger, charged forward into the fray, slashing indiscriminately at anything that moved. The women panicked and those hysterical few that were left fled around the arena seeking refuge behind anything they could find. Karim knelt beside his comrade, already aware that it was too late.

Damocles had lost his sword in the onslaught and fallen mortally wounded from multiple stab wounds.

Karim picked up the Gladius and folded the Greek's fingers around the hilt, ensuring the fellow gladiator died with his sword in hand.

'So it ends,' said Damocles weakly.

'You die well, friend,' said Karim, 'I will mark your stone as such.'

'Bury me deep, Numidian,' smiled Damocles, 'that wooden sword was almost mine.'

'You too will soon be free, Greek,' he answered. 'Sleep well.'

Damocles' eyes closed as his life slipped away, his blood greedily soaked up by the floor of the arena.

It was a dishonourable fate for a gladiator to die at the hands of a woman and Karim knew the Greek's shade would wander forever in shame. He gently lowered his friend's body to the floor and stood up to raise his gaze to the heavens, before releasing a primeval roar that chilled the blood of all watching. He turned around with cold murder in his eyes, seeking those responsible for the death of the Greek.

The next few minutes were the bloodiest of the whole day as Karim went berserk. The crowd were frenzied in their enjoyment of the spectacle and screamed instructions to Karim, taking untold pleasure in this unprecedented display of savagery. Finally, Karim stood again in the centre of the circle, Gladius hanging limply from his hand, his head hanging in exhaustion as the crowd threw flowers from the stands.

'Karim, Karim, Karim,' they chanted, over and over again.

Governor Sibelus was beside himself with glee, realising his carefully laid plans had come to fruition. Surely, these were the best games seen in his generation. Even Emperor Tiberius would be impressed. He grinned at the sullen Pelonius and raised his hand for silence, waiting as the bloodthirsty crowd settled again.

'Karim of Numidia,' he began, 'you have…'

Suddenly a woman in the crowd screamed.

'Another!' she shouted. 'One of the heathen still lives.'

Karim spun around, alert to the danger and ran toward the dead horse behind which the barbarian was hiding. Again, the spectators were hysterical as the Gladiator dragged his enemy from the hiding place by her hair. Casting her to the floor in full view of the crowd, he raised his Gladius to administer the decapitating blow, but stopped suddenly, confusion and disbelief in his eyes.

'Do it!' someone screamed.

'What are you waiting for?' cried another. 'Kill the witch!'

Karim placed the tip of his sword under the woman's chin, forcing her to her feet. He had fought in many countries, killing more men and women than he cared to remember, but never had he killed a foe such as this. The terrified woman looked at her executioner, tears streaming through the blue dye on her face, hope dawning in her eyes as she realised she had a chance.

'Please.' she whimpered in her strange language, 'don't hurt us.'

Shaking in terror, she offered him the sackcloth bundle she had been hiding enfolded within her maternal arms, a tiny sleeping baby.

Karim stared at the child, fast asleep in the young mother's arms and lowered his sword, all fury spent. Slowly, he walked back to the centre of the arena.

Someone in the crowd seized the opportunity to restore some sense and started to clap. The rest of the crowd mirrored his appreciation and the applause eventually escalated into wild cheering. Soon the occupants of the amphitheatre were again standing on their feet, celebrating not only the skill and savagery of the gladiator, but also his humanity and mercy.

'Fascinating,' said Sibelus to Pelonius over the roar of the crowd, 'but it matters not, the wager is complete. My gladiator is the last man alive, and in due course, I will make arrangements to receive the deeds of your estate.' He stood to leave.

'Wait,' said Pelonius.

'Is there a problem?' asked the governor.

'The wager has not ended,' said Pelonius quietly. 'There is another survivor.'

'What other?' snapped the governor. 'The Greek is dead and the games are over. Now I must go, for I have a slave to free and a farm to inspect.'

'The child,' shouted Pelonius, not taking his eyes off the terrified girl being led from the arena by two guards.

'What about the brat?' asked Sibelus.

'Is it a boy or a girl?'

'Why would it matter?' asked Sibelus before the light of understanding dawned in his eyes. The bet had been the last male alive, and if the baby was a boy, it could be argued that he had technically lost the bet. He thought furiously. He could order the guard to kill the baby, but without explaining the situation, risked losing the crowds support, defeating the object of the whole Munera.

He stared at the old soldier and calculated the implications. Several respectable citizens had witnessed the wager. The last male survivor in the arena had been the bet. No one had mentioned race or age and many bets were fulfilled on lesser criteria. He could ignore the situation and take the farm by force, but Pelonius enjoyed the favour of Tiberius himself. The governor sat back down, his mind racing.

'Think well, soldier,' he growled, 'I will not bankrupt myself on a technicality. Do not think you will claim any of my wealth due to a heathen's bastard child. I have won this wager and will claim my prize.'

Pelonius had not survived twenty-five years in military service without gaining a serious understanding of tactics himself. There was no way he could embarrass this man and expect to live more than a

12

few weeks; he was too powerful. He knew he had to allow the governor to escape from the wager without losing face, and yet still have a chance of retaining his lands. The governor loved to gamble and though Pelonius had a terrible record when it came to gambling, he realised he had no option but to offer one more bet.

'I have another option for you,' he said slowly, 'a new wager. If the child is a girl, the original agreement stands and my farm is yours.' He turned to Sibelus. 'However, if it is a boy, I will relinquish all claims against you, but will retain my estate.'

'Why would you do that?' asked Sibelus, his eyes narrowing as he realised this was a way out.

'I want the gladiator.'

'Karim?'

'Yes,'

'And all bets will be cancelled?'

'Everything,'

Sibelus stared at Pelonius for a long time. The gladiator was good, but compared against the debt he would owe this jumped up soldier, his value was insignificant.

'Okay,' he said slowly, 'I agree, but on one condition.'

'Name it.'

'As long as I draw breath, you will not give him his freedom or engage him as a gladiator to fight against me. He will remain a slave until the day I die.'

'Agreed!' said Pelonius.

'Then we have a deal.' The governor stood up and without taking his eyes off Pelonius, shouted down to the arena. 'Guard, what sex is the child?'

The soldier strode over to the woman, and after a brief struggle, used the back of his hand to knock her to the floor before lifting the baby up high by one foot.

'A boy,' he shouted back, 'and hung like a mule.'

As Sibelus seethed through a false smile, everyone in the arena laughed.

'Citizens,' he cried out for the last time, 'I have one last decree. In my infinite mercy, I release the Numidian into the custody of my good friend, Gaius Pelonius, in honour of his exploits in the servitude of our Emperor, the glorious Tiberius. Long may he reign.'

'Hail, Tiberius,' roared the crowd, as was their expected duty.

The governor turned to Pelonius.

'He is but one slave,' he snarled, 'I have a thousand.'

The last of the crowd left the arena and Pelonius made his way
down to the arena floor, against the flow of the stragglers walking up
the aisles to the exits. He crossed the bloody sands, now busy with
slaves as they piled up the corpses of horses and humans and entered
the gates of the basement. The cloying darkness stank of sweat and
animals and echoed with the groans of the injured and the dying. Out
of the gloom, he saw an approaching figure and recognised the guard
who had identified the sex of the baby earlier.

'Evocatus!' he called to the old soldier.

The soldier came over to Pelonius and they greeted each other
by grasping each other's forearms, both veterans of the army and full
of mutual respect.

'Hail, Gaius Pelonius,' said the soldier, 'I heard you had
retired. I wager thousands of Gauls sleep better in their stinking beds
knowing you have hung up your Gladius.'

'I don't know about that, friend,' answered Pelonius, 'there
seems to be as much blood spilt here, as there ever was on foreign
soil'.

'Such is the way of the world,' said the guard. 'How can I
help?'

'Where can I find the Numidian?'

'At the end of the corridor,' said the soldier, 'the last cell on
the right.'

'Thanks,' said Pelonius. 'Call around to my estate next time
you are on leave. I have some amphorae of wine that need emptying
and a yearning to relive past glories.'

'Sounds good,' said the guard before adding, 'Pelonius, treat
him well,' nodding toward Karim's cell, 'He is a good man.'

Pelonius nodded and walked down the corridor. He found the
cell easily and watched through the open door for a few moments, as a
female slave cleansed the Numidian's wounds. He was sitting on a
wooden cot and drinking deeply from a jug of wine, the flickering
torch light shimmering on his wet black skin. The gladiator looked up
and the two men's eyes met across the cell floor.

'Do you know who I am, Karim?' asked Pelonius eventually.

Karim swigged more wine, his eyes never leaving those of the
old soldier. He nodded silently.

'Can I come in?'

14

'Why do you ask?' asked Karim. 'Am I not your property?'

Pelonius walked in and sat on a stool opposite the gladiator.

'How do you feel?' he asked.

'I have just killed more than twenty men and women for no reason, except entertainment for a corrupt official and a thousand of his ignorant cronies. How do you think I feel?'

'You are a gladiator. Isn't this what you have trained for?'

'I trained to fight others such as me, not to murder babies.'

'The Governor is not a happy man.'

'I am beyond caring. I have shed enough blood for a hundred men in a hundred lifetimes.'

'So why do you do it?'

'What other option is there? If I refuse, I would be one more piece of meat for the stinking lions that share these cells, and as you pointed out, I am a gladiator. If I let myself die without fighting, my shade will wander as Lemures for all time.'

Silence fell.

'So, am I to be freed?' asked Karim eventually.

'What would you do if you were?'

Karim shrugged.

'Probably get drunk, hurt someone and end up back in the arena as Noxii. Who knows?'

'Then I have a deal for you, Karim,' said Pelonius. 'I cannot free you, Sibelus has ensured that, but I can give you a life away from the arena.'

Karim stared in silence, waiting for Pelonius to continue.

'Just before I came back from Germania,' continued Pelonius, 'I prevented some jumped up officer from being killed in an ambush by Germanic tribesmen. It turned out that he was the cousin of Tiberius. When I returned, I was paraded as a hero through the streets of Rome, and they gave me a farm that takes half a day to ride across.'

'And?' asked Karim.

'I am no farmer, Karim, I am a soldier. If it isn't managed properly, I'll be bankrupt in six months or probably lose it in a crooked dice game to that shit Sibelus. I cannot free you, but I can make you my farm prefect.'

'What do I know about farming?'

'Perhaps nothing, but I have workers who have tilled that land all their lives and we can buy any extra labour and expertise we may need.'

'You mean slaves!'

'We would offer a future that is by far preferable to that offered by the beasts of the arena. You and I are the same, Karim. We know only the sword, but farming is like anything else, and can be learned. What I need is someone who can command respect from my staff and is not afraid to dish out discipline where needed. I also need someone who I can trust. I believe you are that man.'

'You would trust a murderer.'

'I would trust a gladiator.' Again, there was silence.

'If I say no?'

'You can stay here and continue to kill for the entertainment of lesser men, but if you come with me, the work will be hard and the days long, but at least you will have a warm bed at night, food in your belly and a modest salary at the end of each month. The choice is yours.'

'When do you need to know?'

Pelonius laughed.

'Do you really need time to consider, Karim? I am offering you a life of normality and peace against one of death and violence. I have been a soldier most of my life and have killed more men than I care to remember. I know which one is better, Karim. Trust me, there is no contest here.'

Suddenly, a commotion broke out in the gloomy corridor and both men hurried out to see the source. A group of well-armed guards stood in the corridor, as another dragged a woman by her hair from her cell.

'Stop!' shouted Pelonius. 'What is going on?'

'Don't interfere old man,' said one of the guards, 'you no longer serve and have no authority here.'

Pelonius recognised the woman from the arena.

'Where are you taking her?' he asked, his tone a bit calmer, trying not to inflame the situation.

'She has an appointment with Sibelus,' said the soldier. 'After all, she just cost him a lot of money.' The screaming continued as the soldier resumed his task.

'Wait!' shouted Pelonius again, his mind thinking furiously. 'What of the child? Surely he has no use of the baby?'

For a moment, the soldier looked at the woman clutching her baby tightly to her bosom. Sibelus had not mentioned the baby and not even his perverted tastes sank that low. He shrugged.

16

'What of it?'

'I will give you ten Denarii for him.'

'He is not mine to sell.'

'No, but surely he will not be missed. If the governor asks, I will return him to you and no one will ever know of our deal.'

The soldier hesitated.

'Ten Denarii,' repeated Pelonius.

'I don't know,'

'Fifty Denarii,' interjected Karim quietly.

Everyone looked at the gladiator in astonishment.

'Where would you get such an amount?' asked the soldier.

'Being a gladiator is a lucrative career, as long as you stay alive,' said Karim. 'I have won many purses. Most have gone on wine and women but I have some money left. I will pay fifty Denarii for the child.'

The terrified woman looked on in fear. Though she could not understand the conversation, she realised that something important was happening regarding her fate.

'Agreed,' said the soldier finally, 'but if he asks, the child will be returned to me.'

Karim walked toward the woman and spoke gently, indicating she should give him the baby. The woman slowly realised that her future as a slave held little hope; the day's events had proved that. This man had already spared her once and she had no reason to believe he had suddenly changed his mind. Her eyes filled with tears and she held her baby tight for the last time, smothering it with kisses. All present were silent as she said her goodbyes and taking an embroidered leather pendant from around her neck, she placed it around the neck of the baby, tears streaming down her face.

'Enough!' said the guard, 'Sibelus is waiting.'

Karim took the child in his giant hands.

'Prydain,' the woman said through her tears in her strange language, 'Prydain.'

'Prydain,' repeated Karim, 'I will look after him,'

She let the baby go, realising this might be his only chance of survival.

'Let's go,' said the guard and taking her by the arm, roughly escorted her from the cells. This time, she did not struggle.

Pelonius stared at the giant gladiator, the tiny baby seemingly out of place in his still bloody arms. Karim looked at the baby for a long time, before eventually meeting the ex-soldier's gaze.

'Is the offer still open?' he asked.

'Why wouldn't it be?' asked Pelonius.

'Now there are two mouths to feed.'

Pelonius paused, realising just how enormous this man was close up.

'Well, you'll have to work that much harder,' he said, offering his sword arm in the recognised gesture of agreement. Karim grasped the offered forearm in his own hand and sealed the deal.

'I will pick you up from the Ludus at first light,' said Pelonius. 'Be ready.'

'We will,' said Karim.

An hour later, the cells were silent. Any surviving occupants had been returned to their owners and an army of slaves had built a bonfire in the empty arena to burn the corpses from the games. The slave girl was bathing the baby.

'What is his name?' asked the girl quietly after she had laid the baby down to sleep.

'Prydain,' said Karim, 'and it seems our fates are entwined.'

'You intend to bring him up as your own?'

'It would seem so. Indeed this is a strange fate the Gods have set before me. This morning, I thought this would be my last day under this sun, yet here I am hours later, a farmer with a ready-made son. I know nothing about farming, which is a damn sight more than I know about children. This is going to be the hardest challenge I have ever faced.'

He looked down at the sleeping baby. Prydain stirred gently in his sleep, blissfully unaware that less than a mile away in a back room of a palatial villa, his mother was screaming his name one last time before she died at the hands of Governor Sibelus Augusta.

Chapter 1

Britannia 42 AD

'At last!' thought Gwenno, seeing the wagon train exit the woods in the distance. She finished her daisy chain and placed it around her brow before adding a buttercup behind her ear as an afterthought. She jumped to her feet and brushed down her white linen dress. She had nagged all morning to be allowed to wear it for her father's return and her mother had finally relented. Gwenno knew she was very lucky to own two dresses; one wool, like every other female of the tribe and this one, a finer linen toga that her father had traded from one of the merchants on the east coast.

Gwenno loved the dress, and although she knew someone else before her had probably worn it, it was her prize possession. Only the wealthy could afford to have such a garment made just for them and when her father had told her it had cost him a brand new knife, she was overwhelmed by his generosity. It was a very simple summer outfit and the thirteen year old looked beautiful, though it could be said she would look beautiful in anything. Her long blonde hair shone in the sunlight, complimenting the polished bronze Torc around her neck and the silver bracelets adorning both wrists.

'One day,' she had vowed to her mother on many occasions as she grew up, 'my Torc will be gold!'

Her mother had smiled sweetly on these occasions. It was every girl's dream to marry one of the princes of the tribes, but the simple fact was, there were too many girls and not enough princes.

Gwenno waited patiently at the wooden bridge across the man-made moat circling the village until finally, she could contain her excitement no longer.

'Father!' she called loudly and ran down to meet the riders.

'Hello, child,' boomed her father's voice, 'what have I told you about that dress? It is far too short for the company of men.'

'Oh, Tad,' she smiled, 'stop being so old.' Secretly she stole a glance back down the column, wondering if a certain young man had also noticed her pretty dress.

Erwyn dismounted and led his horse by the bridle. Gwenno took his arm and skipped delightedly by his side.

'You have been gone ages,' she said, 'I had almost given up waiting.'

'These days, the Cornovii are far better at hiding their herds,' laughed her father. 'They are learning fast.'

Gwenno looked back to the end of the horse column, seeing the first of the stolen cattle that followed the riders, herded by the young boys who had accompanied the party.

'Did you kill anyone?' she whispered, eyes wide.

'No child, there was no need of any killing.'

'But how did you get so many cattle?'

'Let's just say that they were very understanding of our request.'

Gwenno glanced again at the heavily armed warriors. She had heard rumours of how persuasive her father could be during these trading missions.

'Have you brought me anything?' she asked shyly.

'In the name of Ocelus, child,' he laughed, 'at least let me get home first.'

'Stop calling me child,' she hissed, looking around in alarm to see who had heard, 'I am almost fourteen.'

'You are just turned thirteen and you are still my child.' he chided gently, and picking Gwenno up, swung her around in his muscular arms as his freed horse trotted on through the gates, eager to get back to familiar surroundings.

'Tad!' she screamed in mock anger, yet secretly delighted at her father's affection. 'Stop it!'

'Okay, little one,' he smiled, putting her down gently. 'Wait here, he will be along shortly.'

'I'm sure I don't know what you mean,' she said with a huff and a haughty flick of her head.

'So all this nonsense is for me then, is it?' he asked, looking at the flowers in her hair.

'No!' she laughed, 'Mother has her own flowers for you.' She straightened her crumpled dress and after giving him a big kiss on the cheek, ran back through the gates to wait at the bridge as the rest of the trading party passed.

Erwyn walked through the outlying roundhouses of the protected village. It had spread out over the last two years, as the attacks from neighbouring tribes had eased off and the families had felt more confident in the strength of their warriors. As the clan numbers increased, more roundhouses were being built and the timber stockade that afforded them protection from raiding parties had needed to be increased in size twice in the last year. Swirls of smoke emanated from the conical thatched roofs, as the women prepared evening meals for their families, and grubby children played in the dirt, as they waited for their dinner.

The frames of the roundhouses were made from a circle of poles, sunk deep into the floor, and intertwined with walls of hazel or birch. Their thatched roofs swept down to almost floor level and daubed walls of mud, straw and animal droppings, kept the house cool in the summer, and surprisingly warm in the winter. They had made their houses like this for as long as they could remember and the same construction was used throughout the country.

It was a good time for the Blaidd clan and the Deceangli in general. The ruggedness of the landscape, their willingness to defend their own territory from the other tribes, and the tactical positioning of their hill forts, meant they were seldom troubled by would be invaders. In addition, because of the role they played in protecting the nearby sacred island of Mona, they also enjoyed the spiritual patronage of the all-powerful Druids and the possibility of upsetting the religious sect, meant few tribes were willing to risk their wrath.

Most tribes these days were happy trading with their neighbours or farming their own lands. Conflict was more likely to be between clans of the same tribe, and most of these could be sorted out in the gatherings of elders that met every moon to sort out their differences.

Trading missions were frequent and they rarely ended in quarrels. However, honour needed to be satisfied occasionally, and champions from either side often fought to the death. There was no honour in losing a duel, only in winning.

Throughout Britannia, all the tribes interacted with each other on a regular basis, though little was known about the Silures situated in the south. They were a fierce and uncompromising tribe of mountain warriors, who seldom ventured out of the hills of their own territory and few people were ever allowed in.

Gwydion rode his pony at the rear of the column; the halter hanging loose around his mount's neck. The boy guided his steed with pressure from his thighs, and the animal responded to the slightest touch of the skilled rider. He wore plaid leggings made from coarse wool and a linen tunic, which hung down over his upper legs. A heavy plaid cape hung from his shoulders, fixed at one side with a bronze clasp. His weapons consisted of a sword hanging from a leather belt and a yew bow lying across his lap, ready strung for instant use.

Because of Gwydion's skill with a bow, Erwyn had given him the role of Cefn, an important position that guarded the rear of the column. A group of experienced warriors had turned off the track an hour before, and circled miles back along their route, to lie in ambush on their trail. Any unwary followers stupid enough to think they could catch the Deceangli unaware, would find themselves caught in an onslaught of steel and willow, long before they got anywhere near the village.

The role of Cefn was an honour for Gwydion and he took the position very seriously. If they were attacked, he would be the first to know, and he would sound the alarm to the rest of the clan. Every twenty or so paces, he turned his horse around to stare back down the trail, looking for anything out of the ordinary.

Villagers were already herding some of the cattle into prepared pens and their families, relieved to see them home, greeted the dismounted riders. Gwydion noticed someone waving frantically at the gate and was pleased to see Gwenno waiting to greet him. He started to raise his hand to return the wave, but had second thoughts. His smile changed to a frown and a look of serious concentration appeared on his face.

Just in time, he realised it would do his credibility no good at all for any of the other young men of the village to see him with a stupid grin on his face. This had been his first serious expedition with Erwyn, chief of the Blaidd, and he had his image to think about. Other boys of his age would be green with envy when he recalled the tales of this adventure. Though there had been no fighting, the hardship and subterfuge on the trading trip had been exciting enough for the young man, and he was slightly relieved to be coming home to this familiar place after three weeks of hardship.

'Hwyl, Gwydion!' called Gwenno, greeting the young man in the traditional way.

Although he didn't return the greeting, Gwydion acknowledged her with a nod of his head. Instead, when he reached the gate, he turned his horse for the last time and peered into the distance, making sure Gwenno could see the bow in his hand. She joined him alongside his horse, taking hold of the harness.

'Who are you looking for?' she asked, following the boy's stare.

'Cornovii warriors!' he said.

Gwenno looked startled.

'Cornovii!' she said. 'Are we being attacked?'

'They may have followed us and it is my job to make sure the clan is safe.'

They both stared in silence.

'Are you coming in?' asked Gwenno.

'Not yet, I am the Cefn, it is my job to protect the tribe,' he answered.

'Tell me, Gwydion,' said Gwenno, 'how many warriors do the Cornovii have?'

'Hundreds, perhaps even thousands,' said Gwydion, his stare unrelenting.

'What would you do if they appeared now?'

'Attack them,' he said, sitting slightly higher on his horse in self-importance.

'Then, I think you should come in for a while.'

He frowned and looked down at the girl. She had a wicked grin on her face.

'Why would I do that?' he asked.

'You are going to need a few more arrows,' she laughed and pointed at his quiver.

In his efforts to impress the girl, the quiver had tipped forward and emptied his arrows silently onto the bracken.

'Oh no!' he gasped, frantically looking around to check that no one had seen. He jumped down from his horse and dropped to his knees, repacking his quiver as quickly as he could.

Gwenno joined him, trying her best not to burst out laughing. He counted the arrows furiously.

'Eleven,' he said. 'There is one missing.'

'Is there?' asked Gwenno, a look of innocence on her face.

'Have you got it, Gwenno?' asked Gwydion. 'What's behind your back?'

She walked backwards, a smile on her face.

'Gwenno, give it here,' he said and reached out to grab her.

She skipped out of his reach, revealing the goose-fletched arrow she had been hiding.

'Make me!' she said mischievously.

'Gwenno,' he hissed, 'someone might see.'

'So let them see. I don't care.'

'Gwenno, please,' he repeated, 'it is not good to lose a weapon. If your father finds out, he won't let me go again. You won't tell him, will you?'

Gwenno stopped, and walked toward him.

'What is it worth?' she asked, suddenly serious.

'What?'

'Make it worth my while.'

'How?'

'A kiss,' she said suddenly, shocked at her own audacity.

'A kiss?' he asked incredulously, 'I can't do that!'

'Why not?' she asked. 'No one will know.'

'Gwenno,' he said, 'If your father finds out, he will have me whipped.'

'I won't tell if you don't,' she said, blushing.

'I can't' he repeated, 'I daren't.'

'Huh,' she snapped, 'you're afraid of a little whipping, and you call yourself a warrior? What good would you be against the Cornovii?'

'I am not afraid of anyone,' scowled Gwydion.

'Don't you like me anymore?'

'Of course, I do, Gwenno,' he pleaded, 'but Erwyn is my leader. I will not disrespect him.'

'Not even for me?' she asked. 'Just one little kiss on the cheek.'

Gwydion wanted nothing more than to kiss this beautiful girl, but even though he was a Deceangli, he had been brought up with strict Catuvellauni honour. Just after his birth fifteen years earlier, Gwydion had been fostered out to a different family, as was the tradition in his people. However, in his case, he had not been given to a family within his own clan, or even his own tribe, but had been sent many miles to the east in a conciliatory gesture to seal an uneasy truce between Deceangli and Catuvellauni. Similarly, a Catuvellauni baby had taken his place at the hearth of his own family, and both boys had returned to the clans of their birth at the age of fourteen.

Gwydion had been lucky enough to have been fostered to a family close to the now dead King, Cunobelinus. As well as becoming an expert archer and swordsman, he had also been taught the Roman language by a slave brought back by Gallic traders from the forests of Germania.

Both boys were safe from harm, as long as the truce endured, but had either tribe transgressed the agreed terms, then the Druids would have sacrificed both boys, and a bloody war joined. Luckily, for them, the past fourteen years had been relatively peaceful and both were back where they belonged.

'Do what you will, Gwenno,' he said eventually, 'I will not betray Erwyn's trust.'

'I am glad to hear it, boy,' boomed a voice and the two teenagers spun around to face Erwyn, who had returned to see where they were.

'Give him the arrow, Gwenno' he said, 'and get back to your mother.'

'Sorry, father,' she murmured, looking down at the floor.

'Quick about it,' he ordered.

Gwenno sneaked a wicked smile to the boy before running into the camp, dropping the arrow as she went. Erwyn picked it up and joined Gwydion near his horse. Gwydion stared into the distance, the shame evident in his eyes. After a while, Erwyn addressed him.

'Tell me, boy,' he said, 'why do you favour the bow over the sword when you can gain much more honour in close combat?'

'I do not spurn the sword, Erwyn,' he replied, 'and will pit myself against any man if challenged, but arrows can kill many men from a great distance. Surely, this is a great advantage in battle when the enemy is larger in number?'

'Perhaps so, but how can you take the head of your enemy if you are a hundred paces away? Let me teach you the skills of the double axe. That truly is a warrior's weapon and will gain you many heads.'

'I seek no trophies, Erwyn,' said Gwydion.

'Then, I fear you will gain little honour,' sighed the leader. 'The heads of our enemies bestow much honour on the taker.'

'I am happy with my bow.'

'You proclaim your weapon's virtues, yet allow your arrows to fall like firewood. You even allow a mere girl to take one from you. Is this what you have been taught by those Catuvellauni dogs?'

'It is only one arrow, I have eleven more,' answered the young man defensively.

'Only one,' repeated the warrior. 'Tell me Gwydion, how much do you like my daughter?'

'Err…I suppose…'

'Speak up, boy,' snapped the warrior.

'A lot, Sir,' he said quickly.

'Do you wish to court her?'

'I don't know, I mean, yes Sir, I would like that very much.'

'Tell me, why should I let a man who loses weapons court my daughter?'

Gwydion hung his head and silence fell again. They both knew there was no correct answer to the question.

'You made a mistake today, boy. It will be the first of many, but consider this. Imagine we were under attack and you had already used eleven arrows. Consider further, if an enemy then set his sight on Gwenno and you reached for your last arrow in her defence, what would become of my daughter?'

Gwydion looked shocked.

'I would defend her with my life, Sir,' he said.

'I would expect no less, but for that one lost arrow, the clan would be less one warrior, and I would lose my only daughter.'

Gwydion hung his head again, realising he was being taught a valuable lesson.

'Lift up your head and look at me!' snapped Erwyn. 'You are back amongst the Deceangli now and you bow your head to no man. If you make a mistake, you will take your pain with head held high, do you understand?'

'Yes, Sir,' answered Gwydion, standing upright.

'You have done well these last few weeks and I will not hold this mistake against you. Learn from this and ensure it doesn't happen again. If it does, I will have you beaten in public. Do I make myself clear?'

'Yes, Sir.'

'You have a lot to learn, boy, but today you showed me respect. Take your bow and ensure you become the best you can be. The Deceangli have many warriors who wield sword, axe or spear, but few who are archers. Perhaps you may yet find a role. You may visit my daughter, but you will not walk out alone until her sixteenth year. Is that understood?'

Gwydion nodded, not quite understanding how this had turned around.

'Now, stable your horse and get washed. Tonight, you will eat with us.'

Erwyn turned and walked back into the village nursing a wry smile. The poor boy did not know what he was letting himself in for with his daughter. He knew how tricky she could be. After all, she was exactly like her mother.

Gwydion watched as Erwyn disappeared inside the stockade. He was a bit bemused and not sure what had just happened, but whatever it was, it felt good. He picked up his horses reins and followed in his leader's footsteps.

Chapter 2

Cassus stood naked in the dawn's early light, shivering slightly in the damp morning air. His hands rested on his hips, and his feet were planted slightly apart, the soft loam of the forest edge pushing up between his manicured toes. A day's stubble darkened his strong chin and his sun-bleached hair fell about his shoulders like the mane of a desert lion. His body was muscular, and at twenty-one years old, he was nearing his physical peak. Strong, healthy and perfectly formed, he was a vision of self-awareness that bordered on arrogance as he surveyed the immediate world before him.

In front of him, the fertile hills of the farm rolled serenely away toward the Adriatic Sea, and the slopes were already alive with the estate labour making their way out to the vineyards. Some were family, some were freedmen who took their skills from farm to farm, as the harvest demanded, but most were slaves, bought at the monthly market in Asculum where captured foreigners or disgraced Romans were sold to the highest bidder. If they worked hard and were loyal to the estate they were treated fairly, however, those who rebelled, were lazy, or tried to escape, were severely punished by the farm prefect, and risked imprisonment, beatings, or even death depending on their master's whim.

He recognised the familiar frame of Karim, the ex-gladiator who ran the estate with an unbreakable loyalty to Cassus's family. Karim had become the hardest worker on his father's estate and as prefect, had run the farm with a fair but firm hand. He earned a small income and after he had wed the nursemaid, who helped him raise an orphaned child, had been allowed to build a stone lodge for himself and his family. That child, Prydain, grew up alongside Cassus on the farm, and though they were the same age, the differences in upbringing were obvious. Cassus was well schooled and literate and his clothing was of the best quality. He ate the best food and spent his spare time taunting the workers of the farm.

Prydain, on the other hand, was the son of a slave and worked dawn until dusk in the fields. His clothes were plain and often second hand from the villa. It was a hard existence, yet despite this, he was a proud young man, and over the years, had formed a close yet strained friendship with Cassus.

As a boy, Prydain was often summoned from the fields to play with Cassus. At first, he would just do whatever the spoilt boy demanded, but childhood has a way of bridging gaps of upbringing and soon, they were roaming side by side across the estate, swinging their wooden swords enthusiastically as they fought imaginary battles with invading barbarians.

As the years passed, both boys dreamed of a future in the armies of Rome, though in vastly different roles. Pelonius had already purchased a commission for his son in the Ninth Hispana legion, while the best Prydain could hope for was a place in the auxiliaries. Only true Roman citizens could serve in Rome's legions, but despite this, Prydain was happy. Pelonius had granted Karim his freedom and as Karim's son, Prydain was officially classed as a freeman and could enlist in the auxiliaries.

As they grew older, the relationship changed, and Cassus often took delight in taunting Prydain about the differences between legionaries and auxiliaries. Sometimes, it was all Prydain could do to hold his tongue, but the time was fast approaching when childhood dreams would be put aside and the reality of manhood realised. Word had come to all able-bodied men in the region. The new Emperor, Claudius, had received a petition from a displaced barbarian King called Vericus, asking him to help him regain control in some little known kingdom in the north. Claudius needed an opportunity to prove his greatness to the senate, and this excuse was the one he had been waiting for. The message was sent throughout the empire. Four legions would gather at the assembly point in one year's time and any able bodied man wishing to join them, had to present themselves at the Circus Maximus in Rome by the next full moon to sign up. Rome was going back to Britannia, but this time, they were going to stay.

This was the chance both Prydain and Cassus had been waiting for, and plans were made for them to go to Rome. They would travel together on horseback across the Apennine Mountains, camping as they went, and sign up to their respective unit alongside thousands of other men. At last, the day had come for their journey to begin, and while Prydain had spent his last night at home with his father, Cassus had spent his, drinking and fornicating.

Cassus sensed someone closing in from behind. The scent in the air changed slightly, and the hair on his neck rose as he felt the body of Marianna, the cook's daughter, press gently against his back. She opened the blanket she had wrapped around her, and folded it around the front of Cassus, enclosing them both in a cocoon of soft wool. Her naked skin was warm against his cold back. Marianna ducked her head under Cassus's arm and he held her close to his side, continuing his gaze toward the horizon.

'It's a beautiful dawn,' she said quietly.

'It is,' he responded.

'When will you see it next?'

'Perhaps never.'

'Don't say that, Cassus,' she said. 'You can't think like that. You have to return, I will be waiting for you.'

Cassus smiled.

'Twenty five years is a long time for a woman with your, shall we say, special needs. I can't see you lasting that long. Can you?'

'Stop it,' she said, nudging him in his side. 'You make me sound like an animal.'

'You were certainly an animal last night, as I recall,' he said, wincing at the scratches down his back.

'That was the wine,' she said defensively. 'Anyway, I don't hear you complaining.'

Cassus felt her hand sliding slowly downward from his chest.

'Come back to the fire,' she whispered softly, looking up at him with nut-brown eyes, 'one more time, I promise I will be gentle.' Marianna's hands teased his tired body into the reaction she sought. He turned and pushed her long hair back over her shoulders before kissing her deeply.

'Okay, Marianna,' he said, 'once more, but this time,' he threw off the blanket and picked up her slim body in his muscular arms, 'I'm in charge.' He carried her back to the embers of the fire, their young, naked bodies warming in the rising Mediterranean sun.

Chapter 3

Cassus walked out onto the veranda with his father, Gaius Pelonius Maecilius. The labour of the estate gathered in front of the villa to see the two young men set off to meet their destiny. Two horses, each with side panniers packed with food and wine for the journey, were tied to a rail, waiting to transport them on their journey.

Gaius Pelonius stepped forward and the crowd fell silent. Pelonius was getting old, and his voice was not as strong as it used to be, but despite this, he cleared his throat and spoke clearly.

'As you are aware, this day, my son goes forth to seek his fortune in the service of Rome. We weep no tears for the fate that awaits him, for if he falls, then it is in the service of our Emperor and no Roman can ask for more. No, this is a time for celebration, and in recognition of this momentous day, I wish to make a gift to someone very special. As you know, Prefect Karim has been with me for twenty years. Many years ago, I gave him his freedom, but he chose to stay on the farm. He is not only the prefect, but also my confidante and close friend. He has made it clear that he will not leave this farm until such time as he has paid homage at my funeral or has died waiting. Well, friend,' he looked over at the sombre faced man, 'I am becoming tired and I feel you will not have to wait much longer.'

'You will live forever, Gaius Pelonius,' answered Karim in his deep baritone voice.

'We shall see,' answered Pelonius, 'but before I go to meet my Gods, there is something I want to do for you. These past twenty years, I have witnessed our sons grow up together in a friendship that has made fools of those impostors' race and status. Even today, they set forth on this adventure as one, yet society demands that this is where their mutual journey ends. As a freeman, Prydain cannot join Cassus in the legions of Claudius, and though the auxiliaries are no less important, it breaks my heart to see these two seek different roads.'

Karim's eyes narrowed, realising where this was leading. Pelonius reached back and was given a scroll by his wife.

'Karim, my friend,' he announced, 'I have in my hand a document that I hope will demonstrate my appreciation and respect for you and your family.'

The crowd fell silent as he unfurled the scroll.

'On the first day of the year, as required by the statute of Rome, I registered the occupants of this household in the magistrate's offices in Asculum. On this register, I recorded the names of all my family, as is our due as Roman citizens. However, on this occasion, I also took the opportunity to include the name of Prydain Maecilius. As you know, under Roman law, anybody named in the census who are not already citizens, become so with immediate effect. This scroll, delivered only this morning, is confirmation that the registration has been accepted. Karim, today in front of my family and friends, in the name of the Emperor, I greet Prydain, your son, as a Roman citizen.'

After a moment's pause, the gathering broke out in applause. It was not often that a slave became a citizen in Rome. Pelonius held up his arms to regain the silence.

'Prydain,' he continued, 'as a Roman citizen, you are no longer limited to the auxiliaries. You can join Cassus in the legions of Claudius, but of course, as a citizen of Rome that choice is yours and yours alone.'

Prydain looked dumbstruck. Although, he was already a freedman, the status was still quite low in the eyes of most Romans. However, his whole world would take on a different perspective as a citizen. He was free to walk the streets of Rome, to serve in her armies, or even marry a Roman woman. He could stand alongside any man in any street and talk to him as an equal, open a business in one of Rome's many marketplaces, or even use the public baths around the city without fear of segregation.

Karim looked pleased but not surprised. Privately, Pelonius had already offered him and his son citizenship, but Karim had always turned down the offer. The vast difference in the colour of his skin compared to his adopted son would invite too many questions and probably cause the application to fail. Realising this, Pelonius had taken the arbitrary step of applying in Prydain's name only, knowing that the same doubts were not shared by the young man, and though he was unsure how Karim would react, he needn't have worried. The pride on Karim's face spoke volumes.

'I don't know what to say, lord,' stuttered Prydain. 'It is truly a great gift.'

'The gift is your father's, the freedom is yours. Use it well, Prydain,' he said and turned to face Karim.

Their eyes locked together for a moment before Karim nodded. It wasn't much, but Pelonius knew it meant everything. He turned back to the crowd.

'Enough!' he shouted and turned to face Cassus. 'Travel well, son,' he said grasping Cassus's arm. 'Train hard for your Emperor, fight well for your fellow soldiers and if you should fall, then die well for your name.'

Cassus knew that he would probably never see his father again. They said their private goodbyes the night before and his father had given him a purse of coins for the journey, as well as promissory notes for transport and supplies. This display was for the benefit of the staff.

'My blade will send a legion of slaves to prepare for your afterlife,' he said, and though it was never good to display too much affection in front of others, Pelonius pulled his son to him, hugging him tightly.

'Be careful,' he whispered.

'I will be fine, father,' he answered.

Prydain sat astride his horse, waiting patiently to start the great adventure. Cassus strode down to join him and vaulting onto his horses back, turned to face Prydain.

'Don't think that this makes you my equal,' he said under his breath. 'You were born a slave while I am a freeborn Roman. Never forget that. Anyway, my misguided father has wasted his gift, for there is no need for citizenship in the auxiliaries.'

'Auxiliaries?' said Prydain. 'You heard your father, I am now a citizen of Rome and can join her legions if I so wish.' He paused and stared into Cassus's eyes, 'And that, Cassus, is exactly what I intend to do.'

'Cassus,' glared at him.

'We shall see,' he said and spun his horse to face his father.

'Hail Gaius Pelonius,' he shouted, 'may the Gods grant you immortality,' and kicked his heels in to his horse's flanks to send it galloping down the hillside.

Prydain spun his own horse around and stopped beside the man who had looked after him all his life. Karim grabbed the horse's reins.

'I too have a gift,' said Karim. 'It is from your mother.'

'My mother?' queried Prydain, 'I don't understand.'

'Just before she died she gave me something,' said Karim. 'I have kept it safe all these years but it belongs to you.' He hung the leather thong and amulet around Prydain's neck.

'What does it mean?' asked Prydain, struggling to control his horse as it fidgeted.

'I don't know, but it seemed very important to her. With the God's will, it will protect you. If nothing else; look at it often and think of home.'

'I will, father,' came the response, and they grasped each other's wrists in a final farewell. 'You will be in my thoughts always.'

'And you mine, son,' said Karim.

Prydain's horse was straining to be gone and he turned one more time.

'Hail, Gaius Pelonius,' he shouted, 'provider of freedom, may you live forever.'

Pelonius smiled and watched as the horse finally tore itself free from Karim's grasp to gallop down the track in the wake of Cassus.

The crowd finished their cheering at the departure and returned to their duties. Eventually only Pelonius was left on the veranda. Karim joined him.

'Were we ever so impetuous, Karim?' asked the old soldier.

'Their veins are full of adventure and glory,' said the Numidian. 'Let them enjoy it while they can. They will return to the realms of reality soon enough.'

'That they will,' said Pelonius. 'Will you drink to their future with me?' He indicated a jug of wine on the table.

'I will be honoured,' answered the ex-gladiator and both men sat on the veranda long into the evening, reliving old battles. In truth, there was just a little envy embroidered within the conversations.

Prydain and Cassus travelled westward for several days until they reached the Tiber River. They turned south and followed its banks to the outskirts of the city and realised they were nearing Rome long before they could see any of her famous architecture. At first, Prydain thought it was just clouds on the horizon, but as they neared, it became obvious that it was smoke from the countless cooking fires, hanging in the air above the sprawling city.

Prydain had never been anywhere near the eternal city and had only heard of her splendour, through the gossip in the taverns of Asculum and the tales of the slaves on the farm. Strangely enough, his father, who had spent many years within those great city walls, rarely spoke of his time there. The landscape before them both was far from what they had expected. On the outer limits of the city, extravagant villas dotted the hills, nestling within groves of fruit trees. Nobles spent most of their summers relaxing in their villas, avoiding the oppressive heat and dirt generated by the millions of commoners within the city walls. The villas were impressive, but as they approached the city walls, the more squalid the habitation became.

The two friends stopped outside the roadside inn that bore a name given to them by Pelonius, and Cassus approached the half door, banging on the frame.

'Ave,' he called, 'I seek the one called Marcus.'

A middle-aged man approached the doorway out of the inner gloom.

'Who seeks him?' he asked, eyeing the two strangers suspiciously.

'My name is Cassus and I am the son of Gaius Pelonius Maecilius. I am looking for Marcus. I believe he served with him in the Ninth.'

'Can you prove who you are?' asked the man, eying them suspiciously.

'I can, but my words are for Marcus only.'

The man hesitated and looked around.

'OK,' he said, 'I may be Marcus, but depending on your business, I might not be.'

Cassus smiled. His father had said he would be cagey.

'If you are Marcus,' he said, 'you will know the meaning of this message. My father said to tell you that the tale of you and the red haired Spaniard remains a secret, though he aches to tell the world.'

The man blushed furiously and examined the area around his inn in great detail.

'Quiet!' he hissed. 'What do you know of this thing?'

'Nothing,' laughed Cassus, 'though I would dearly love to know what secret causes you so much embarrassment.'

'It is not for your ears or anyone else's for that matter. Okay, so I am Marcus and I believe you are indeed Pelonius's son. Only that old rogue knows my shame. What does he want? If it is the return of the piebald mare he loaned me, tell him it died soon after and I dispute his claim.'

'Not the mare,' said Cassus, enjoying this man's obvious discomfort.

'Is it the money?' Marcus continued. 'Because if it is, I know I am a few months late, but…'

'Marcus!' interrupted Cassus. 'Relax, I am not here to seek redress of any debt. We need a room for the night and my father said you would accommodate us.'

The relief on the innkeepers face was evident.

'Oh,' he said, 'why didn't you say? Come in, I will get the boy to stable the horses.' With a clap of his hand, a boy of approximately eight years appeared from nowhere and took the reins, leading the horses around the back.

'Come in,' repeated Marcus and unbolted the lower half of the door, standing aside to allow them to enter. They walked into an auditorium leading back to the rear of the house, with niches built into the walls for guests to sleep. An enormous mosaic of coloured stones and marble shards decorated the floor, and with a bit of imagination, Cassus realised that it was a poor representation of a naked woman. Marcus saw Cassus's gaze.

'What do you think?' he asked proudly, 'I designed her myself. Cost me a fortune.'

'Nice,' Cassus lied and followed the old man to a nearby table where they all sat down.

'Water?' asked Marcus, pulling three wooden tankards and a pitcher from a nearby shelf.

'Do you not have wine?' asked Cassus.

'I do, but that is expensive and I am a poor man. These are hard times you understand.'

'Marcus,' laughed Cassus, 'my father has told me much about you. He warned that it would be easier to get blood from a stone, than to expect you to part with anything free. He also said that you were one of the richest men in the region,' he looked around the auditorium, 'though by the state of this place, I am beginning to doubt his words.'

Marcus ignored the taunt and poured three mugs of tepid water.

'How can I help,' he asked.'

'We are on our way to join the army,' said Prydain, 'but we do not enlist for two days yet. We need someone to stable our horses until they can be picked up and we thought we could stay here tonight before travelling into the city tomorrow.'

Marcus nodded slowly,

'That can be arranged,' he said, 'the alcoves are two asses a day, or I have clean rooms available for a Denarii each'

'A Denarii for a room?' coughed Cassus. 'No wonder you are so rich. Perhaps I should inform the authorities about your unpaid debts?'

'Both you and I know that will not happen,' said Marcus. 'If I know Pelonius, his son would have been brought up better than that.'

'You are right,' admitted Cassus, 'I will not betray you, but it was worth a try. I tell you what, you give us a room and good food tonight and my father will call it quits on the Piebald.'

Marcus did some quick calculations in his mind.

'And you will sign something to prove this?' he asked.

'Yes,' Cassus sighed, 'whatever you want.'

Marcus smiled. The horse had been worth ten times that amount.

'Then you have a deal,' he said quickly. 'Follow me and I will take you to your room.'

He left his seat and walked upstairs, showing the two young men to a clean room with two freshly made up beds. They unpacked their travel bags onto a table and Marcus returned with an amphora of wine and a further three mugs.

'Well, how is the old rogue?' he asked, sitting on the edge of one of the cots.

'My father is fine,' said Cassus, 'though he tires easily these days.'

'It comes to us all,' said Marcus. 'All those years of toil in service catches up with you.'

'Did you know him long?' asked Cassus.

'I spent ten years in the same Cohort as him,' said Marcus, 'until I got this.' He uncovered the stump of a severed arm from beneath his clothing, the burn scars of the battlefield cauterisation still evident. 'We saw some scrapes together, I can tell you.'

'I bet you can.'

After a brief silence, Marcus continued.

'So, who are you joining?'

'The Ninth,' said Cassus, taking the offered mug of wine.

'Recruiting again are they?' asked Marcus. 'Good choice and your father's name might even help you out a bit.'

'What do you mean?'

'His name is well known in the Ninth. Even now, twenty years since he left, Centurion Maecilius is a name that is admired throughout the cohorts.'

'Centurion?' gasped Cassus. 'My father was a Centurion?'

'Not only was he a Centurion,' he said, 'but he was Primus Pilus. Didn't you know?'

'My father didn't talk much about his time in the legions,' said Cassus.

'No, perhaps he didn't,' said Marcus. 'By the end of our time, I think we were all glad to see the back of it.'

'What is Primus Pilus?' asked Prydain from his own cot.

'Only the most senior Centurion in the legion,' Cassus sneered. He turned to Marcus, 'He is a freedman,' he explained 'and doesn't know about such things.'

Marcus turned to Prydain.

'The Primus Pilus was in charge of the first Century and overall commander of the entire Cohort during any battle,' he explained. 'You don't get that high without being something special. If he had stayed on after his twenty-five years, he would have been given the position of Praefectus Castrorum, camp prefect. Third in command of the entire legion, but like the rest of us, he just wanted to get his pension and go home. Anyway, enough about us oldies, what do you young bloods intend to do while you are in Rome?'

'We don't really know,' said Cassus, 'but bearing in mind it could be a long time before we have any freedom, we want to make the best of it.'

'Well, you've come to the best place,' said Marcus. 'Do you have money?'

'We do.'

'Then let me enlighten you.'

For the next hour, Marcus gave the enthralled boys the benefit of his knowledge of the eternal city, where to go and where to avoid.

'Avoid fish,' he said on the subject of food. 'We have emptied the sea of fish for miles around and any available will have travelled days to get to the restaurants. Even those who are lucky enough to buy fresh from the river, keep them for their best clients. No, don't eat fish unless you want to spend the next two days on the shitter.'

'I'll bear that in mind,' grimaced Cassus, 'what about the taverns?'

'I'll give you the names of the best,' said Marcus. 'They are a little more expensive, but they don't water the wine.'

'And women?' asked Cassus.

Marcus laughed.

'I wondered when you would ask.' It depends what you are after. You are hardly going to meet and get anywhere with nice girls in two nights, so if it is a relationship you want, forget it. If however you just want some fun, then the options are endless.'

'I hear the best places are the arches beneath the Circus Maximus,' said Cassus quickly. 'It is said you can buy any sort of woman you can imagine there.'

Marcus smiled a grim smile.

'This is true,' he said, 'the diversity and skills of some who lurk in its shadows; especially those of eastern descent are beyond imagination.' He paused, his mind seemingly elsewhere as if recalling a distant pleasant memory. 'However,' he said suddenly returning to the present, 'tread carefully, the streets are dangerous to waifs such as you.'

'We can look after ourselves,' said Cassus defensively.

'No offence, young man,' said Marcus, 'but your inexperience in those streets will shine like a lantern to a moth. Not only are you likely to get a dose of the pox and your purses stolen, but you will probably get your heads caved in for good measure. The pimps in particular are especially vicious down there.'

'I thought the streets of Rome were safe,' said Cassus.

'Safe,' sneered Marcus, 'why do you think I spent my pension on a tavern outside of the city walls? I can look after myself, but even I, after ten years of soldiering across the known world, would rather go back to the forests of Gaul, than walk the streets of Rome by night.'

'What about the Vigils, I thought they policed the streets after dark.'

'It is just as likely to be their clubs that do the crushing as any pimp's cudgel,' said Marcus. 'In fact, most Vigils are in the pocket of the pimps and look the other way for a fee, especially if you are a stranger.'

'So the city is lawless, then?'

'No, not lawless. If there is a fight, there are the Urban Cohorts or the Praetorian Guard who deal with any disturbance. It's just that in the thick of things, one skull looks pretty much like another to those overpaid pompous shits and there is only one winner in those fights. No, the best thing is to avoid them at all costs, and if you can't and end up in front of a magistrate, you had better hope your father is drowning in Denarii or you could end up mining for salt to flavour the Emperor's meal.'

'But we are citizens,' countered Prydain. 'Surely we have rights?'

'Did your fathers teach you nothing?' sneered Marcus. 'One word from a magistrate and you could end up as cat food in the arena, citizen or not. Take my word for it, keep your snotty noses clean, pay your dues and have fun, but for your own sakes, stay away from trouble.'

The two boys looked at each other in concern. Marcus laughed out loud.

'Don't look so worried,' he said. 'All I am saying is to be careful. All taverns have waitresses and most will take great pleasure in relieving you of your Denarii, for an hour or two of their company. Just stay to the ones I recommend and mention my name to the landlord. He will make sure that the ladies in question are clean and reasonably priced.'

'Anyway,' he continued, 'about other matters; where is the Ninth garrisoned at the moment?'

'They have just moved from the Germanic forests to northern Gaul to prepare for the invasion.'

'How do you intend to get there?'

'There's a fleet leaving in a few days taking supplies to General Plautius. We were told we could get on one of the warships.'

'Up the Atlantic coast on a Trireme?' laughed Marcus. 'Interesting choice. Not one I would have made, but you may get there I suppose.'

'What do you mean?' asked Cassus.

'Think about it, our war ships are designed for the calm waters of the Mare Nostrum, yet even here, many struggle to stay afloat. The Atlantic has seas a hundred fold worse and yet you intend to trust your souls to a floating box, heavy with stores in a rabid sea and at the whim of a probably drunken failed soldier at the helm.'

'What would you suggest?' asked Prydain. 'It's a long way to walk.'

Marcus thought for a moment.

'I have an idea,' he said, 'I have to check a few things, but if my timing is right, I have a friend who can take you almost all of the way there in a far safer ship. The only thing is you will have to get to a place called Narbonensis across the Mare Nostrum to board her.

'Why?' asked Cassus. 'Does she not sail from Ostia?'

'Let's just say the captain is not welcome here at the moment,' he said standing up. 'Anyway, I must go, I will have a bowl of hot water sent up so you can wash the road from your faces and then you can join me for a meal before you lay waste to Rome's wine and women. I will have the details of my contact before you leave in the morning.'

An hour later, a quiet knock on the door stirred Cassus from his alcohol induced slumber. The boy who had dealt with the horses stood in the doorway.

'The master said that the Cena will be served in fifteen minutes.'

'Thank you,' said Cassus, and threw a Caligae at the snoring Prydain. 'Wake up Prydain,' he said. 'Come on, food is ready and I'm starving.'

The two boys swilled their faces and wet down their hair before changing their clothes. Cassus donned an expensive blue dyed tunic, while Prydain's was a clean yet greying garment patched with several repairs. They walked down the stairs and the boy directed them into a side room. At the centre was a large wooden table surrounded by eight chairs. Six were occupied and it was obvious that the company were waiting for the arrival of the two young men.

'Ah, there you are,' said Marcus, 'meet my family. This is Maria my wife and her parents from the Bruttium region in the south.'

'Ave,' said Cassus, nodding his head to the guests in greeting.

'Ave.' they responded.

'And these are my children, my son, Titus, and daughter, Aula.'

The children were obviously twins, and approximately the same age as the servant boy standing in the doorway.

'And this one?' asked Prydain.

'Oh, we never got around to actually naming him, we call him boy.'

'I take it he is a slave?' ventured Prydain.

'He is,' confirmed Marcus. 'Maria found him abandoned as a baby at the side of the road and we took him in. Fret not, Prydain, he is well cared for. Many such as he are abandoned everyday by those who cannot afford another child, or have borne the wrong sex to a demanding father. Most perish or are picked up by pimps. He is one of the lucky ones and earns his keep by serving us around the house.

41

Anyway, please sit and join my family in our evening meal. A banquet it may not be, but you will find it honest and filling.'

'We're having meat!' exclaimed Aula excitedly, earning a gentle smile from Maria.

'These are hard times,' interrupted Marcus, repeating what seemed to be his favourite mantra, 'and meat is reserved for special occasions, but today, we have killed a pig in honour of your visit. Never let it be said that my hospitality was refused to the son of an old friend.'

Marcus glanced at Maria who suppressed a self-satisfied smile. Cassus guessed that she had something to do with the decision to kill the pig and if Marcus had his way, they would be eating fruit and boiled barley.

'We are honoured,' said Cassus 'and my father will hear of it.'

'You are more than welcome, Cassus,' said Maria, 'and you too Prydain. Shall we start?' She nodded to the boy and he disappeared through a side door, returning a few moments later, struggling to carry a double handled amphora, closely followed by two more child servants carrying trays of food. The boy poured everyone a tankard of white wine, including the children. This time, the tankards were of silver, and engraved with a detailed hunting scene.

'Beautiful,' said Cassus, examining the craftsmanship.

'A souvenir from Gaul,' explained Maria. 'Marcus bought them when he was in the army. Apparently, they were very expensive.'

'Indeed, 'said Cassus and glanced over at Marcus whose stare silently warned him not to delve too deep into their history. Cassus was well aware that Roman soldiers were often allowed to supplement their pension with whatever bounty they could loot after defeating an enemy and wondered what had become of the tankard's previous owner. Perhaps it was better not to know.

The servants laid a tray of mixed salad in the centre of the table, consisting of crisp lettuce leaves and whole radish, interspersed with green and black olives. The whole thing formed a nest within which, nestled twelve hard-boiled duck eggs. A second tray was added to the table containing two neat rows of Libae, the soft small rolls that were familiar on every table of Rome. A silver bowl completed the meal and Maria triumphantly removed the lid.

'Garum,' she said to the obvious approval of all present.

Each person at the table filled their beaten copper plates with a mixture of salad and eggs, before ladling varying amounts of the thick sauce over their meal as a dressing. The Garum, despite being made from heavily salted and fermented fish entrails, was a particular favourite of most Romans, and was served at most meals.

The starters were soon polished off, and before the main course was brought in, hand bowls were provided to wash their sticky fingers. Ornate bowls of Artichokes, whole cloves of roasted garlic and diced stewed marrow were spread around the table before a wooden platter, containing thick slabs of roast pork was placed in the centre, the steam rising to the beamed ceiling and causing everyone's mouths to water in anticipation.

'Please everyone, help yourselves,' said Maria before casting a disapproving glance over at Marcus, whose eyes betrayed the fact that he was calculating how much all this would cost him.

The main course was delicious and the boys ate ravenously, interspersing greasy mouthfuls with complimentary belches, much to the satisfaction of Maria. As they settled down to the meal, the awkwardness eased and conversation flowed.

'Boy, bring red wine,' called Marcus noticing the tankards were empty. He had seemingly accepted the fact that this was going to be an expensive night and had embraced the occasion fully.

'But I thought you wanted me only use the cheapest,' said the boy, confused at the contradictory instruction.

'Cheapest wine? Don't be absurd,' countered Marcus. 'Bring the best red.'

'But this afternoon you said…'

'Do as you're told, boy,' said Maria gently, cutting off the tirade that was about to follow from Marcus.

'Won't you have more garlic, Prydain?' asked Maria's mother quickly, hoping to cover up the embarrassment. 'It will make you brave when you fight the barbarians.'

'Thank you, I will,' said Prydain, 'though I fear any effect will have worn off by the time we meet the enemy.'

'Oh, why is that?' she asked politely.

'After we reach Gaul, our training will last six months and then we have to get to Britannia. I fear the barbarians will be pacified long before we get there.'

'Don't count on it, son,' said Marcus slurring his words and staring into his wine. He had been drinking heavily since before the meal started.

'What do you mean?' asked Cassus.

Marcus looked up through drunken eyes.

'I'll tell you, shall I?' he said. 'I have never been to Britannia; however, I have encountered barbarians, as you call them, on many occasions. Some may live in huts and some may even benefit from Rome's influence, but others are quite civilized and need no interference from Rome or anybody else come to that. They live in beautiful cities built of stone. They have music, culture, art, all the things we take for granted in Rome.'

'But surely it is in their interests,' said Cassus. 'We are bettering their lives by introducing them to our civilization.'

'Our civilization,' sneered Marcus. 'Some of their cities were old when Rome was still a swamp, yet we march into them and raise them to the ground in the name of civilization. Oh no, it's not in the name of bettering their lives that we kill their men, rape their women and leave their children to starve. It's to line the Emperor's coffers with more gold and silver than even the Gods themselves could use.'

'Marcus, stop it,' interrupted Maria, 'you're drunk.'

'Perhaps I am, but I have seen too many friends fall at the hands of so called barbarians, who by the way, are well trained, well-armed and fierce beyond belief. Then I watch as our armies wipe whole civilizations off the face of the earth in retribution, so I feel that, now and again, I am entitled to get drunk.' As if to emphasise the point, he deliberately drank deep from the tankard.

'So,' he continued, 'fear not that you will miss the fighting, Prydain, for I can tell you there will always be fighting, and when you think you have subdued one tribe, another will rise in their place. And when that country is finally conquered, there will always be another. It seems our glorious Emperor's coffers grow to meet supply.'

'You speak treason,' warned Cassus. 'I would guard your words else you fall foul of the Praetorians.'

'I speak the truth, boy,' said Marcus. 'You seek an exciting life filled with glory and adventure. Perhaps you will find what you seek and I sincerely hope you retire a rich man like your father, but it comes at a price. Yes, there is gold and women, conquests and glory, but there is also fear, pain, blood, and death. I left an arm in the forests of Gaul, and have thanked the Gods every day since that I did, for it got me out of there with my life intact. An arm I can spare, my life is the only one I have. Take it from me, lads, don't take the oath. Get on your horses right now and turn away from Rome and her false promises. Gallop as hard as you can back to your father's farm and

44

live your life picking olives and drinking wine. And if it's money you crave…' Marcus drained the last of the wine from his tankard, red rivulets trickling down his well-trimmed beard. He let out an enormous belch, his eyes struggling to focus before continuing. 'If it's money you want, then abandon your morals, banish your conscience and go into politics. If there is one truth out there that is the same all over the known world, then it is this. There is no such thing as a hungry politician.' Marcus laid his head on his folded arms and the table fell into an awkward silence. Eventually Cassus wiped his hands on a napkin.

'Thank you for a wonderful meal, Maria,' he said. 'If you don't mind, I think we will retire.'

'There's no need to leave just yet,' she said. 'Take no notice of him, he's just a drunken old man.'

'It's not that,' said Cassus. 'We are very tired from the journey and have an early start tomorrow. We only have two days, and would like to see some of Rome before we enlist.'

'I understand.'

'Marcus said we can leave the horses here. I will pay for their grain and my father will send someone to collect them within the week.'

'Of course you can,' she said. 'I will have your beds made up and there will be food waiting for you in the morning, ready for your journey.'

'There is no need…' started Cassus.

'It will take you half a day to reach the city on foot,' she said, 'and I will not see you travel hungry.'

Cassus smiled.

'Thank you Maria,' he said, 'you are truly a wonderful host.'

Maria looked down at Marcus, his head on his folded arms, fast asleep.

'Don't be too hard on him,' she said, touching her husband's head gently. 'He has had a hard time. He hates the inequality of life imposed by those in power, and often wakes up in the night screaming at memories I cannot even imagine.'

'My father speaks very highly of him,' said Cassus gently. 'Do you need a hand?'

'I will be fine,' she said, 'you go to bed, I will have the desert sent up. It is only fruit, but it was picked fresh today. Goodnight, boys and good luck in the future.'

The two young men took their leave and went back to their room, leaving the domestic scene behind them. As they walked up the stairs, Prydain looked over at Cassus.

'What did you think about that?'

'About what?'

'He was quite scathing about service.'

'What does he know? He was no-one of importance,' said Cassus.

'He served for ten years, so he must know something.'

'If you fear service, Prydain, then walk away. No one is forcing you to join. I for one am happy to take Rome's glory to the heathen.'

'I didn't say that,' said Prydain, 'it's just different from everything I had ever thought.'

'Well stop thinking' said Cassus,' all we need to concentrate on at the moment is enjoying the next two days.'

Prydain nodded and they retired to their room, Cassus still clutching a half-full amphora of wine. The following morning, a linen pack containing fruit and the remains of the pork from the previous evening was waiting outside their door. A folded parchment was atop the pack. Cassus opened it up and read aloud the contents.

To Perre, my oldest and dearest friend,

The two unfortunate scoundrels that bear this note are in particular need of your help. If you can help them achieve their goal in my name, I would be eternally grateful. I look forward to exploring the taverns of Ostia with you the next time you are in Rome, though be patient as there are still some in the Vigils who resent your last visit, despite their injuries having healed nicely.

Until next we meet

Marcus.

'Sounds like a character,' said Cassus and placed the note in an internal pocket of his tunic before they both crept quietly out of Marcus's home.

Chapter 4

Gwydion rode along the path, seeking the capital of the Deceangli. Erwyn's directions still clear in his mind.

Erwyn had told him to keep the sea to his right and when he reached the fishing village of Treforum, ask the locals to show him the road. It was well known that there was a great fort not far from the sacred isle of Mona and it was this fort that was recognized as the centre of the Deceangli tribe, but apart from the warriors who had served in the armies of the King, most of the Blaidd had never travelled this far north.

Gwydion had filled out in frame over the last few years and had gained in confidence, as his role within the clan had been cemented. He had spurned the longer sword preferred by the older warriors, preferring the shorter style offered by traders from the east coast, but not happy with the quality, had begged his father, commonly referred to as Hammer, due to his skill as a blacksmith, to make his own bespoke weapon.

On Gwydion's sixteenth birthday, Hammer had called Gwydion to his forge. He pointed to a stone gourd containing molten iron and Gwydion realized that at last, he was seeing the birth of his own sword.

'Give me your hand,' said Hammer, and holding his son's wrist firmly in his own grip, drew a knife across Gwydion's palm, holding it over the forge to allow the blood to drip into the molten steel. He then spent a day forging the blade, steadily adding charcoal to the molten iron to harden the blade, and by repeated beating and quenching, formed a weapon of unsurpassed hardness and quality. To make the hilt, Hammer had made him grasp a rod of hot wax, forming an exact replica of his grip, and a skilled woodsman had carefully carved seasoned oak into the exact shape of his hand, using the wax as a template. The final product was magnificent, lightweight and lethal.

Gwydion had practiced every chance he got against any able bodied man of the village willing to go against him, strengthening his arm, and improving his technique, until eventually he was considered the best swordsman in the village.

Gwydion rode his horse through the outskirts of the coastal town. The streets were alive with sound, smell and colour. Wooden crates of chickens competed with squealing piglets for the attention of anyone wanting to purchase meat that morning. Sooth-Sayers vied for trade, each calling out from the doorways of their huts, promising to tell your future for a few coins and weavers hung out examples of their finest work for passers-by to see. Sailing boats, tied to the wooden jetty, unloaded their hauls from the rich fish beds just outside the harbour, and the smell of freshly baked bread from giant ovens, wafted tantalizingly throughout the village.

Men of dubious honour offered slave girls for pleasure, many cheaper than he would pay for a mug of beer and he paused briefly, wondering if he had enough time to sample their particular wares, but remembering the seriousness of his mission, reluctantly moved on.

Gwydion had been travelling hard since before dawn and eventually pulled up alongside a timber shelter. An old woman stirred a large iron pot hanging from a frame over a fire.

'Hwyl, old mother,' said Gwydion from astride his horse, 'what place is this?'

'You are in Treforum,' she replied, stirring her pot, 'and are welcome as long as your sword stays sheathed.'

'Your pot smells good,' he said. 'What does it contain?'

'It contains whatever you want it to,' she said. 'Pork, mutton, rabbit, you name it, it is in it.'

'Well my belly thinks my throat has had a confrontation with a brigand's blade,' he said. 'How much for a plate?'

'Cawl, bread and beer for just a copper coin,' she said, 'though for a Roman coin, you can eat all your stomach can carry.'

Gwydion's brow furrowed.

'Why would those trader's coins buy me more food than our own?' he asked.

'The Romans bring strange and fabulous things from their far shores,' said an old man, coming out of the hut, 'but they only accept their own coins or precious metal in payment.'

'What do they bring that is so different to what we can grow on our own farms?' scowled Gwydion.

The old woman ladled scoops of steaming soup into a wooden bowl and ripped a generous chunk of bread from a nearby loaf.

'Spices, the oil of the olive, perfumes, fruit and vegetables, the likes of which you have never seen before. You name it, they have it,' she said. 'Even this pot was made on distant shores. If you have Roman coins, you can buy anything.'

Gwydion dipped the bread into the steaming soup, soaking up the rich gravy from around the chunky vegetables and meat.

'You make a hearty Cawl, old mother,' he said, speaking through a mouthful of stew. 'There is nothing wrong with this and I trust the ingredients were out in our own fields just a few days ago. As far as I am concerned, the Romans can keep their spices.'

'Thank you,' she answered. 'You're not from around here are you? Do you have business in the town, or are you just passing through?'

'I am hoping to do business,' he answered. 'I am of the Blaidd, a days' ride south of here.'

'I know of the Blaidd,' said the old man, 'I have had cause to lose out in trade to someone called Erwyn.'

'You and a thousand others,' laughed Gwydion. 'He is a shrewd man.'

'What business do you have?' asked the old woman. 'Perhaps we can help.'

'You may be able to point me in the right direction,' said Gwydion. 'We have lost a lot of foals to the wolves this year, and seek to purchase more horses from the council.'

'Horses?' asked the old man, his eyebrows rising. 'Then I fear your journey will be in vain.'

'Why so?' asked Gwydion, scooping the last of the soup into his mouth.

'The council has claimed all available horses for defence of the territory. Look around you traveller, there are far more people walking these streets than ever before. Yet try to engage them and many speak in foreign tongue.'

'And are they a threat?'

'On the contrary,' he said, 'they may be a drain on resources, but the foreigners are seen as allies. However, their presence here is a symptom of a greater problem.'

'Which is?'

'The Romans. They are refugees from Gaul, Belgica and Germania, fleeing the heel of the legions.'

'There have always been foreigners on these shores,' said Gwydion. 'Why is this different?'

'Think about it,' the reply came, 'if anyone knows the brutality of Rome, these people do, for they have witnessed it first-hand. Word has come that their Emperor has cast a covetous eye on these islands

49

and our foreign friends flee their path, long before the Roman galleys have even caught wind.'

'But I thought that you were happy to trade with the Romans,' said Gwydion. 'Not ten minutes ago you were seeking Roman coinage to engage in trade.'

'This is true, for they are a strange lot the Romans. If you roll over and accept their heel, they bring trade and prosperity, though always on their terms. If you resist, they fall on your cities with fire and steel, sparing no one and turning the rivers red with the landowner's blood.

'Then they have not faced the Deceangli, yet,' said Gwydion, 'we would not roll over so easy.'

'Spoken with the exuberance of youth,' said the old man. 'Trust me, I have witnessed these soldiers operate. They fight as one, unrelenting and with overwhelming force. Nothing can withstand them. No, it is far better to trade with this monster than to fight it. I feel that you will probably see a few more sunsets that way.'

Gwydion drank the last of his beer and wiped the froth from his lips.

'Well, old man,' he said, 'it is just as well that you don't lead our tribe. I would rather have seen my last sunset, than see a thousand under the heel of an oppressor.' He handed the empty cup back to the old woman. 'So,' he said, 'can you direct me to the council?'

The old man turned around and pointed southwest toward a mountain range that dominated the skyline.

'They overlook you as we speak,' he said, 'in the Cerrig on the mountain of our ancestors.'

'And how do I get to this Cerrig?' asked Gwydion.

'Follow the road through the village and into the hills. Do not worry about finding them, they will find you.'

'Thank you,' said Gwydion and mounted his horse again. 'Keep that pot well stocked, old mother,' he said, 'for I will surely tell my fellows to sample its contents whenever they pass this way.' He turned away and trotted up the street toward the hills in the distance.

High above the fishing village, the fort encircled a rocky plateau nestling between two hills. A steep path ensured the approach was easily defended and high walls topped the natural crag, hewn from the very ground upon which the Cerrig had stood for hundreds of years. Entry was gained through a pair of wooden gates, framed within thick walls that channelled visitors into an easily defended corridor.

Gwydion stared up at the awe-inspiring fort in amazement. He had only travelled a short way up the hill before two outlying guards appeared from the undergrowth and demanded to know his business. After hearing his explanation, they escorted him up the Cerrig, passing numerous checkpoints on the way until he stood before the doors of an impressive central hall.

'Wait there,' said the guard and he entered the hall leaving Gwydion outside, guarded by six heavily armed warriors.

Within the hall, six tribal elders sat around a horseshoe shaped table, deep in conversation. In the open end of the horseshoe sat two visitors, each eating a platter of cold meat. The door at the end of the hall opened and the guard walked up to the table, interrupting the argument.

'Sire's' he said, 'there is a Gwydion of the Blaidd outside seeking audience.'

'Can't you see we are busy,' snapped one member. 'Send him away.'

'Who are the Blaidd?' asked Owen, a senior member of the council.

'A client clan to the south,' answered a colleague. 'Loyal to the tribe, but of no great significance. Get rid of him.'

'Sire, he is very insistent,' said the guard. 'He said to give you this.' He placed a golden Torc with a wolf pendant on the table.

'What is it?' asked one of the visitors.

'It is the symbol of the Blaidd,' said Owen, realizing like everyone else that any emissary bearing the symbol of their own clan, could expect audience and hospitality with any other Deceangli. 'We will humour him, send him in.'

The guard left the building as the council stood to stretch their legs, some seeking to warm their backs against the roaring log fire at the end of the hall. A minute later, he returned, closely followed by Gwydion.

'Welcome, Gwydion of the Blaidd,' said Owen. 'You bear your clan's totem. I assume you hold the legal right.'

'I do, Sire,' answered Gwydion, 'I was sent by Erwyn of the Blaidd to conduct business on his behalf.

'I know of Erwyn,' said Owen. 'But I forget my manners, have you eaten?'

'I have, Sire,' he replied, 'though my thirst is great.'

'Then let me serve you,' said Owen, pouring a tankard of beer, 'and after you have quenched your thirst, you can tell us how we can help you.'

Gwydion sank half of the draft in one go, before placing the tankard back on the table.

'Well Sir,' he said wiping the froth from his mouth with his sleeve, 'my initial task was to source twenty horses for my clan, but while passing through the village, I learned that there are none to be had due to the threat of invasion.'

'And?'

'If this is true, Sire, I would seek clarification.'

'Your concern is understandable,' said Owen. 'But worry not, we will send word should a threat arise and you will know in plenty of time.'

'But why then are you securing the horses, Sire?' asked Gwydion.

'And why should I share the Kings business with you?' asked Owen.

'I am sorry if I offend, Sire, I think only of my clan. We will have need of horses, whatever the situation. If there is a threat, then we need to defend ourselves, and if there is not, then I fail to see why I cannot purchase the beasts. I passed many on the farms along the coast.

'They are being sent to Caratacus,' said Owen, 'Cunobelinus' heir, and new king of the Catuvellauni.'

Gwydion nodded in recognition. During his time with the Catuvellauni, he had seen Caratacus on many occasions and he was an imposing man. He looked over to the two Catuvellauni travellers talking quietly together, slightly apart from the others.

'I realize we are at peace with the Catuvellauni, Sire, but surely we should not be selling our resources to another tribe. Horses are hard to come by.'

'Guard your manner, young man,' said Owen, 'despite their birth they still enjoy the safety of our hospitality. We do not sell anything. The horses are given freely in the name of the King.' The rest of the occupants had drawn closer to hear the conversation.

Gwydion drew a purse from his belt and threw it on the table.

'I can pay a fair price with good Khymric gold, Sire,' he said. 'You deny your own people the horses they need, yet give them away freely to your enemies?'

One of the travellers stepped forward.

'You have already stated the answer, young man,' he said in a strange accent.

'And who are you?' asked Gwydion scornfully.

'Hold your tongue,' shouted Owen standing up from his chair. 'You too are a visitor and hold no sway here. You will not question our guests.'

The bearded man held up his hand in a conciliatory gesture.

'It's okay, Owen,' he said. 'If we are to meet this threat as allies, then we must share many things, knowledge as well as horses. I am Rebellon of the Catuvellauni,' he said, addressing Gwydion directly, 'and I speak for King Caratacus. We expect the Romans to send their armies before the year is out and our lands overlook the seas from whence they will come. We intend to meet these invaders and crush them like beetles beneath our feet. Roman traders are one thing; Roman soldiers are another. Even as we speak, riders are travelling between all the clans of Catuvellauni gathering warriors to defend our island. Thousands are gathering at the coast and our villages have been tasked to turn out as many chariots as possible, but therein lay the problem. Chariots we can make. Horses take a while longer.'

Gwydion considered the man's words.

'I hear the Romans are a formidable foe,' he said. 'What makes you think you can defeat them?'

'Because we have done so before,' said Rebellon confidently. 'Twice in the last hundred years, they have dared to wave their swords over our people and twice our tribe has turned them away with steel and willow. This time will be no different.'

'And if you do?' asked Gwydion. 'When it is all over and the blood lust is still high in your warrior's veins, what is to stop you from turning your war chariots against us?'

'We do not covet your lands, Gwydion of the Blaidd,' laughed Rebellon. 'Rest assured you can keep your lung tearing mountains and your foot rotting weather, we have lands enough. What we require are enough of your horses to draw a hundred chariots.'

'And if you fail?' asked Gwydion, his tone a lot calmer.

'If we fail, young man, I fear the loss of two hundred horses will be the last thing on your mind.'

'Enough talk!' interjected Owen. 'You have had your answer, Gwydion, the deal is already done. Rebellion's party will take two hundred horses from the village. Now, we have business to conclude. Be on your way.'

'Wait!' said a voice from the shadows, and a well-built warrior stepped into the light. He was dressed in protective tunic of leather and a fine cape of chain mail hung from his shoulders. He had a sword strapped to his back and a dagger hung from his belt.

'You are a strange one, boy,' he said to Gwydion. 'You come in here, interrupting a meeting of your betters, demanding that we explain ourselves to you. What gives you the right?'

'I only seek to protect my clan and my tribe, Sire,' said Gwydion, 'and if I have offended, then I apologize.'

'And I accept your apology,' said the man, 'but I am intrigued, your tenacity is both admirable and annoying. I don't know whether to enrol you in my army or have you beaten for your insolence. Where are you from?'

'The Blaidd clan,' replied Gwydion.

The amour-clad man, walked slowly around the table, picking up Gwydion's purse as he went.

'I don't recognize the accent. Have you always been with the Blaidd?'

'I was fostered to the Catuvellauni as a child, Sire, and grew up in the court of Cunobelinus, the ward of a Roman slave. Despite my Deceangli bloodline, I still carry some accent.'

The warrior stopped and looked back.

'You were taught by a Roman?'

'Yes Sire, a slave captured in Gaul and sold to Cunobelinus as one of many. They were all sacrificed by the Druids to gain him honour, but her life was spared as she was of particular beauty.

'How long were you in the care of this Roman slave?'

'Fourteen years.'

'Can you speak her tongue?'

'I can, and I also know their writing.'

The man approached Gwydion again.

'I like you, Gwydion of the Blaidd,' he said, tossing the purse up and down in his palm, 'you remind me of myself when I was your age.' Without taking his eyes off Gwydion, he called out across the hall.

'Guard, cut out twenty of the best horses and have them delivered to the Blaidd by nightfall tomorrow.' He tossed Gwydion the purse containing the gold. 'I have no need of your money, Gwydion,' he said, 'but I may have need of someone like you. Now, take your leave!'

'You have the gratitude of my clan, Sire,' said Gwydion and turned to leave. Just as he was about to walk through the door he turned again to face the warrior.

'Forgive me my ignorance, Sire,' he said, 'but you have me at a disadvantage, you know my name, but I know not yours.'

Owen stepped forward.

'Gwydion of the Blaidd,' he said, 'you address Idwal of the Deceangli. Now be gone, for we have business to attend.'

Gwydion was led away to his horse, picking up his weapons on the way, dumbstruck that he had actually just met Idwal, famed leader and true blood warrior King of the Deceangli.

Chapter 5

Cassus knew he was in trouble long before he opened his eyes. Subconsciously, he knew there should be pain, but something told him that if he just stayed still, he wouldn't have to face it. A disgusting smell forced itself through his nose, making him gag and he lay still, not quite sure where he was or what had happened. A distant voice forced its way through his foggy senses.

'Wake up,' said Prydain, 'Cassus, come on, we have to go.'

'Go away,' grunted Cassus, though the words that emerged bore no resemblance to those that were intended.

'Cassus you have to wake up now,' insisted Prydain quietly. When again there was little response, Prydain looked around in desperation, his eyes falling on the water pitcher. Picking it up, he hesitated for a second before pouring the contents over his semi-comatose friend.

The effect was instant, and Cassus would have screamed had his throat not been so dry and his tongue as woolly as a camel's scrotum. He forced himself up off the floor and onto his knees, gasping to catch his breath.

'What the fuck,' he gasped, struggling to form the words.

'Come on!' hissed Prydain. 'We have to be at the circus at dawn, so shift your arse.'

Cassus's brain slowly started to make sense of the whole situation. He put his hand gingerly to his hair. It was sticky and matted to his head. He groaned as he realized the source of the smell. He had thrown up in his sleep and his head was covered in vomit.

'Water!' he gasped.

'I think not,' said Prydain. 'That's good old fashioned puke.'

'No,' he croaked, 'I need water.'

Prydain looked around again, but he had poured the only water available over Cassus. He peered inside the expensive glass jug.

'There's some left,' he said, 'but not much.'

Cassus snatched it from his Prydain's hands, holding it up high as he drained the last few precious mouthfuls.

'Get me more,' he ordered, holding the jug up.

'No time,' said Prydain, 'we have to go.'

'Do as you're told, Prydain,' he said. 'There is plenty of time. The circus is only around the corner.' He pinched the bridge of his nose between his fingers and blew the contents onto the floor,

56

following it up with a drawn back cough to clear his airways. He looked up at Prydain, who was obviously in a state only slightly better than himself. Prydain was wrapped in a garment of fine blue silk that hung down past his knees and gathered in around his waist with his leather belt in an attempt to make it seem as manly as possible.

'Why are you wearing a Peplos?' croaked Cassus, staring at the female garment.

'Oh, you noticed,' said Prydain with a grimace. 'She's got mine on.' He indicated the other side of the room with a nod. 'And I daren't wake her - I don't think we've got enough money left to pay her bill.'

Cassus followed his gaze, his memory still struggling to recall the details. A beautiful woman lay sleeping on a double bed, tangled in the remains of Prydain's ripped toga. Alongside her and dominating the rest of the bed was another figure, hidden beneath an embroidered damask blanket, snoring loudly and completely oblivious to the noise in the bedroom.

'Who are they?' asked Cassus.

'One of them,' said Prydain, 'is a high class whore and the other my dear Cassus, is your new fiancée.'

Cassus looked at Prydain in horror, appalled at the mirth on his face.

'Fiancée,' he said, 'what do you mean fiancée?'

'Easy enough,' said Prydain, 'you were adamant you wouldn't pay good money for a woman, and by the end of the night, there weren't that many left. The only way that one would sleep with you, was when you insisted you were madly in love with her and proposed in front of the whole tavern.'

'Oh shit,' said Cassus, looking back at the pile of tangled cloth. 'What's she like?'

As if in answer, the sleeping figure lifted a hidden leg and let out an almighty fart.

'What do you think?' asked Prydain, trying hard not to burst into laughter. 'Put it this way, Cassus, even Hannibal would have had difficulty getting this one over the Alps.'

'Oh shit!' gasped Cassus again, his stare never leaving the now stirring silhouette of the overweight girl. 'By the God's, Prydain, get me out of here before she wakes up.'

Prydain pulled Cassus up from the floor, turning his head from the smell.

'Don't expect any sympathy from the Gods, Cassus,' he said. 'You smell like Pluto's stinking arsehole.'

Cassus knelt to look under the bed frame.

'What are you looking for?' asked Prydain.

'My tunic,' came the muffled reply, 'it must be here somewhere.'

'She probably ate it,' said Prydain, and they both broke down into fits of giggles, like a couple of schoolboys.

'Cassus?' the overweight girl gurgled as she started to wake. The smiles dropped from their faces. They both stayed frozen to the spot, hoping that their stillness would fool her into falling back asleep.

'Cassus, my love,' she said again. 'Is that you?'

Cassus stood up slowly and stared at Prydain, a look of panic in his eyes.

'Say something!' mouthed Prydain silently.

'Yes, my love?' said Cassus eventually, his eyes never leaving his friend, who now had his hand over his own mouth to stop himself laughing, 'I'm just going to get us a drink of fresh water.'

'Come back to bed,' she said and started to untangle herself from the bed sheets.

'Oh shit,' exclaimed Cassus one more time, 'let's get out of here.'

They both turned to run from the room, getting in each other's way, as they rushed to get through the doorway.

Downstairs, two slave girls were on their knees, scrubbing the tavern floor in the pre-dawn lamp light, cleaning up the mess from what had obviously been a particularly busy night. Anyone else may have stared at the sight as the two young men walked quickly across the tavern, but these girls had seen many things in this dubious part of Rome, and the sight of two men, one in a woman's gown and the other naked expect for a discreetly held sandal covering his modesty raised little interest.

Chapter 6

The recruitment officers at the Circus Maximus had paid them and a thousand others, a retainer of twenty Denarii each to cover travel expenses, and they were informed to be at their training camp in northern Gaul in two months. Cassus and Prydain had found a local fishing boat willing to take them to Gallia Narbonensis, and though the sea was relatively calm, the swell ensured that Cassus spent most of the two days with his head hanging over the rail, retching long gone contents into the blue Mediterranean Sea.

When they finally arrived and asked about Perre, they were told that he was due back in a week, bringing with him a laden ship from the trading ports of Gaul. They relaxed in the sunshine while they waited and enjoyed the hospitality of the locals until a few days later than expected, the biggest trade ship either of them had ever seen, sailed into the port. Compared to the sleek, racing dog profile of a Trireme, this was more reminiscent of a well-fed bull, and obviously much better at withstanding the onslaught of the seas. Teams of slaves unloaded the hold, surrounded by a throng of excited locals, keen to see what was contained on the fully laden ship, even before the crew had had time to rest from their arduous voyage.

Cassus and Prydain shouldered through the crowd, eager to meet the man recommended by Marcus a few weeks earlier. Finally, they reached someone who seemed in charge and asked if he was Perre.

'Me, Perre?' roared the man in laughter,' I think not. You obviously don't know him.'

'Where can I find him?' asked Cassus.

'I don't know,' said the man. 'He was first to disembark hours ago, though I would venture that a good place to start looking would be the taverns.'

'What does he look like?' asked Prydain.

'Trust me, you will know him,' said the man, and turned away, still laughing to himself.

They walked to the nearby town and started asking around the numerous taverns. Despite their concerns, it took less than an hour to locate Perre, though they heard him long before they set eyes on him.

'You cheating sons of pigs,' roared a voice as they approached another tavern. 'Come back here or I'll cut your balls off and turn them into tiny purses for high class whores!'

Three terrified men ran out of the tavern, ducking as a chair passed closely above their heads, followed by the remains of a table. Suddenly the biggest, scariest man, Cassus had ever seen, filled the doorway, throwing a half-full amphora after the rapidly retreating men.

'That has to be him,' said Cassus, and Prydain nodded in silent agreement, overawed at the huge bear of a man in front of him. Perre was enormous. His hair was long and unruly, falling about his head like a thorn bush and his matted beard fell to his chest. He was dressed in woven leggings tucked into knee-length leather boots and his waistcoat, also made of leather, was open, exposing his muscular chest to the world. A belt fell from one shoulder to the opposite waist and contained two skinning knives sitting snugly within inbuilt pockets. Insults followed the furniture until he realized the two young men were watching him.

'Got a problem?' he asked aggressively.

'No, Sir,' answered Cassus, 'we are looking for someone called Perre.'

'Who wants him?'

Cassus gave him the introductory note from Marcus and Perre read it while drinking deeply from another amphora.

'Do you have money?' he asked eventually.

'We do!'

'Good. Can you play dice?'

'Not really.'

'Even better,' he said, his temper receding as fast as it had risen, 'come with me.'

He disappeared into the tavern where staff was busy cleaning up the aftermath of a fight. Perre threw a leather purse onto the table as he passed the landlord.

'Cover it?' he asked as he passed, not waiting for an answer.

'Yes,' sighed the landlord, picking up the purse, obviously familiar with the behaviour of the Gaul.

'More wine!' roared the giant, and sat down in one of the remaining chairs, its legs creaking beneath his weight.

'Dice!' he said, more of an order than invitation.

'We were hoping to do business,' said Cassus.

'Dice first,' said Perre, 'talk later.'

'I'll wait over there,' said Prydain, pointing to the bar. He had little enough money as it was and certainly couldn't risk losing it in a dice game. Cassus, on the other hand, had cashed in one of his father's notes and had money to spare.

'Have a word with your friend;' said the barman quietly, 'it would be better for all of us if he loses.'

'He needs no help from me,' said Prydain, 'his arrogance will ensure a suitable outcome.'

Sure enough, Perre's laughter signalled his luck was in and soon, he had relaxed enough to talk business.

'So, you want to go to Gaul,' he stated eventually.

'We do,' said Cassus, 'and we were told you are the man that can take us there.'

'I could, but why would I want to?' he asked.

Cassus peeled off a one of the promissory notes given to him by his father and laid it on the table.

'Seems a good enough reason,' said Perre. 'Twice as much would be a better one.'

The two men stared at each other before Cassus peeled off another note.

'Better,' said Perre. 'Okay, now we talk. I can take you to Gaul, but there are conditions. First, you look after yourselves and provide your own supplies. I am no nurse maid.'

'To be expected!' said Cassus.

'Secondly, you keep yourselves to yourselves. You don't tell anyone your business and if there is trouble, you are on your own. We will dock in village ports each night and I don't want any unwanted attention from the locals if they found out there were wannabe legionaries aboard.'

'We didn't say we were legionaries,' said Cassus.

Perre sneered.

'It's not difficult to guess, young'un,' he said. 'Your letter is from that rogue Marcus and you want to get to Gaul as fast as possible. Something to do with Britannia, I would wager.'

Cassus stared in silence.

'Don't worry;' said Perre, 'it is the worst kept secret in the known world.'

'But I thought Gaul was safe,' said Cassus, 'Caesar defeated them many years ago.'

Perre laughed out loud again,

'Oh, the tribes are quiet enough when they hear the footfall of six thousand legionaries marching past, but I promise you, most

61

wouldn't think twice about skinning you two alive if they got the chance. After all, you could return in a few years, fully trained killers, so they may as well kill you now. Cuts out the middle man, if you see what I mean.'

'Okay,' said Cassus. 'What else?'

'That's it,' said Perre. 'Just meet me back here in one week.'

'Agreed,' said Cassus, 'but we need to buy some horses and supplies.'

'Buy the horses when you get there', he said. 'In the meantime, take one of your notes to a trader called Sellack in the village. Tell him I sent you and that you are travelling on my merchant. He will give you all you need, though no doubt your purse will feel the pain. We start out at first light seven days from now and I will not wait. Now get out of my sight. There's a pretty barmaid over there who's been staring at me all afternoon.'

He barged past them without another word and made his way over to negotiate with the woman as Cassus and Prydain left the tavern to seek Sellack.

Two months later, they stood on a hillcrest looking down into a cleared valley. They had travelled overland since leaving Perre's ship and headed east toward Belgica, each riding a horse purchased in a local market and leading a shared mule carrying a tent and their supplies. Both the landscape and climate had changed dramatically the further north they had travelled. The temperature had fallen, and being from lands that were baked by the sun most of the year, the two friends struggled with the climate. The addition of two heavy capes purchased from a village en-route, did little to raise their mood. Soon, they had left the coast far behind and the landscape had changed into heavily wooded hills.

'Keep to the road,' had been the instruction from Perre, 'it is patrolled by auxiliaries and you should have few problems. Wander into the forest, and you may not be seen again.'

Rome's influence increased as they neared their goal. More mounted patrols were encountered as they rode alongside the road and after receiving directions, they left the road to follow a winding path up a hill. Eventually, they reached the edge of a cliff overlooking a valley over two miles wide.

Immediately below them was a rambling maze of huts and tents, filling every inch of available ground between the wooded hill and the banks of a winding river. The town was alive with the day-to-day commerce that was the focus of its very existence, and the smoke of hundreds of fires filled the air, as the inhabitants carried out the familiar struggle to survive. Sounds of animals and people echoed up from the valley and the smell of roasting meat wafted past the noses of the dozen or so men who had joined them on their journey.

'I'm starving,' said Prydain. 'We should buy ourselves some mutton.'

However, it was not the smell of meat that caught the imagination of Cassus or even the massive sprawl of the village, but what lay across the other side of the valley.

The river flowed toward the bluff before returning on itself in a giant loop and disappearing into the distance, and on the large knot of land, was the first permanent Roman fort Cassus had ever seen. Despite his inexperience, he could see that the positioning was perfect. It was surrounded by the fast flowing river on three sides and overlooked a large open plain to the fourth. A deep ditch encircled the fort and a single well-guarded bridge approached the only visible entrance. Cassus knew that there would be similar entrances on the other three sides, mimicking the layout that every legionary camp followed, no matter where they were built throughout the empire. The walls, made from quarried stone and cut from the cliff by thousands of Germanic slaves, were topped with a wooden palisade, incorporating fighting platforms and watchtowers. The entire enormous rectangular fort was a fierce statement of intent and a fantastic monument to the might of the Roman army.

Alert guards were visible along the ramparts, looking down with feigned interest, at the activity on the plain beyond the fort's walls, a scene they often took part in themselves and one that they did not envy.

Throughout the plain, instructors were drilling thousands of soldiers in groups ranging in number from ten to several hundred. Centurions barked commands causing large bodies of men to march and turn in unison, instead of the hundreds of individuals that formed its shape. Many more were lined up before poles sunk into the ground, assaulting them with wooden training swords, while others took part in Pilum practise against other squads, their points padded to avoid injury. A channel had been cut into part of the river feeding a man-made lake and Cassus could see dozens of men swimming back and fore across the deep water, an important skill for every Roman soldier.

Prydain pointed to one side and Cassus turned to see a full Cohort of four hundred and eighty men running at double time toward the fort. Each was fully armoured and carried both shield and Pilum. Even from this distance, the pain was clear on their faces, and the commands from the Centurions could be heard across the clearing along with the occasional thwack of Vitis, the vine stick used liberally to reinforce their authority.

The recruits were awestruck. They could never have imagined the sheer spectacle of an entire legion and its auxiliaries all stationed in the same place. Cassus and his comrades dismounted and sat on the cliff edge for an age watching the legion train, each lost in their own thoughts as they anticipated spending the next twenty-five years as part of this machine. Finally, Prydain stood up.

'Right,' he said. 'Pointless putting it off any longer. We've travelled a thousand miles for this, so why wait? He mounted his horse and turned to Cassus. 'Coming or what?'

Cassus mounted his own horse and stared down at the fortress.

'So it begins,' he said, before wheeling away to descend the path to the valley floor far below.

Chapter 7

It had been three months since Gwydion had returned from the Cerrig, and when he had brought back not only the horses, but also the untouched purse containing the gold, he had been given command of ten warriors as a reward, one of ten such bands in the clan.

Autumn had arrived early, and Erwyn had taken a large trading party south to trade for winter fodder from the Ordovices. The trip would take several weeks and involved all of the clan's carts, along with half of the available warriors. All were necessary to protect the bag of braided gold jewellery that they intended to trade.

The clan had been left in the protection of Robbus, Erwyn's brother, and Gwydion had been instructed to patrol the surrounding lands by the temporary leader. They were coming to an end of one such patrol, when, returning to the stockade, they saw two heavily armed riders outside the closed gates.

Gwydion and his group galloped out of the forest to confront the strangers.

'Hold,' shouted Robbus from the wall, realizing that Gwydion and his men had drawn their swords.

Though maintaining their readiness, the riders lowered their swords and encircled the strangers.

'Who are you and what business do you have here?' asked Gwydion eventually.

'We are on the King's business and seek the one called Erwyn,' said the taller man.

Robbus shouted down from above.

'He is not here, but I speak in his name.'

'My words are for his ears only,' he replied. 'We will wait.'

'He could be weeks,' said Gwydion. 'Will your message wait as long?'

The two men looked at each other.

'Perhaps not,' answered one.

'Then you will talk to me,' called Robbus and turned to address those inside the palisade. 'Open the gates.'

Gwydion and his men sheathed their weapons as the gates swung slowly inward. The visitor addressed Gwydion quietly.

'Do you answer to this man?' he asked quietly.

'Until Erwyn returns.' he said. 'It is our way.'

'Okay, we will humour him,' said the stranger and they all wheeled their horses to enter the stockade.

As soon as they entered, Robbus's men disarmed the two visitors and led them up to the largest lodge in the centre of the village. Inside, Robbus was already there along with six fully armed warriors.

'State your business,' said Robbus finally.

'I am Alwood of the Deceangli,' he said. 'We seek warriors for Idwal.'

'Why do you need warriors?' asked Robbus.

'He is sending a fist to aid the Catuvellauni.'

'Why does Idwal send our men to aid our enemies?'

'It pains me as much it does you,' he answered, 'but our King has forged an alliance with Caratacus to turn back the Romans. The Catuvellauni are the first line of defence and seek support from all tribes.'

'The answer is no,' said Robbus bluntly.

'You would deny your king?'

'The Deceangli have not united in battle for years,' said Robbus. 'We are told that the Romans covet our lands and yet our weapons remain un-blooded. Perhaps they do not come after all.'

'They will come,' said Alwood. 'Many years ago, when the Romans last left our soil, they left a client King at the head of the Atrebates. For years, he sold out to the Romans, enjoying their patronage and best trading terms. Often they filled their bellies while neighbouring tribes went hungry, but recently they went too far. The new King, Verica, started to raid Catuvellauni lands using the Roman army as a threat, should they retaliate, thinking they would bend a knee to their rule. He thought wrong. Cunobelinus took the Atrebates lands, burnt their villages and razed their capital to the ground. They will never make that mistake again. Verica himself disappeared and no one knew whether he lived or died.'

'That is until now,' said his comrade. 'We now know he fled to his paymasters in Rome, throwing himself at the feet of the idiot Claudius and begging him for help to regain his lands.' He spat on the floor in disgust. 'Begging a Roman to invade the lands of his fathers. If I ever see him again, I will eat his heart.'

'How do we know this is true?' asked Robbus.

'Even now they gather their legions across the sea. Traders tell us of many ships being assembled on the shores of Gaul, clearing the

66

mountains of trees for miles inland to supply timber for their hulls. They will come, Robbus, it is a fact.'

Robbus leaned forward.

'Why should we leave our villages unguarded?' he asked. 'If the Romans do indeed come, we need to defend Deceangli lands not Catuvellauni. Over half our warriors are in the south and we do not know when they will return. I cannot send what is left to the King and leave this clan at the mercy of brigands and Cornovii raiding parties.'

'You don't have to,' answered Alwood. 'He does not seek a war party, just ten well trained men, and in particular, he wants one man. The one known as Gwydion.'

Gwydion was busy in the stable, rubbing down his horse with a deer-fur glove.

'Hwyl,' came a familiar voice and he looked up to see the smiling face of Gwenno, her arms and chin resting on his horse's back.

'Gwenno,' smiled Gwydion, 'I didn't see you coming. How are you?'

'Oh you know,' she said, 'bored, fed up, almost sixteen.'

'I'd forgotten all about your birthday,' he lied.

'You had better not,' she said in mock anger. 'Anyway, now you are back, I thought we could spend some time together.'

'That sounds nice,' he said. 'What do you want to do?'

'I have it all planned out,' she replied. 'In the morning, we will ride up to big-cat crag and picnic by the waterfall. In the afternoon, you can teach me to use the bow.'

'And in the evening?' he asked.

'We will watch the sun set, and if it is very beautiful, I just might sing for you,' she smiled. 'What do you think?'

'I don't think it sounds like a very manly day,' he laughed, 'and that I will be teased by my comrades.'

'Do you answer to them?'

'Of course not,' he said, 'I am my own man.'

'In that case,' she said walking around the horse, 'there is no reason for you not to join me.'

'You forget one thing,' said Gwydion.

'What thing?'

'Your father may not be back and I will need his permission.'

'Forget my father, Gwydion,' she said, 'there is something you should know.'

67

'Can't it wait?' he asked, 'I have to sort out my horse.'

Gwenno fell silent before pulling him close and kissing him deeply on the lips. Gwydion returned the kiss momentarily, before pulling himself away.

'Gwenno,' he said, 'stop, I don't think we should.'

'It's okay,' she gasped, 'I want to!' She kissed him again.

'Gwenno, no!' he said, pushing her away. 'A few more weeks and you will be my bride, let's not spoil it now.'

'We can't wait,' she said. 'You have to take me now!'

'Why?' he asked, realizing the desperate look in her eyes was not lust, but fear, 'Gwenno, what's wrong?'

She hesitated and her shoulders slumped.

'You should know, Gwydion,' she said, her head hanging down. 'I heard my mother talking to Robbus yesterday. It seems you and I will not be allowed to marry.'

'What?' said Gwydion. 'But it is agreed. Erwyn has given his approval.'

'Erwyn is not here and Robbus becomes my guardian in his absence.'

'Yes, but soon he will return and sense will prevail.'

'I fear it will be too late,' she said, the tears starting to flow. 'I am to be sent away on my birthday.'

'But why?' demanded Gwydion, 'Robbus can't just send you away against the wishes of Erwyn; he would simply bring you back.'

'Not from Mona, he can't!'

'The Druid's isle?' he said. 'Why are you going there?'

'Everyone is worried about the coming invasion and Robbus has asked the Druids for the protection of the Gods. They demanded an acolyte in return and it seems that I am the one.'

'I don't understand,' he said. 'Why would your mother allow him to send you?'

'Since Erwyn has been gone, she has grown closer to Robbus,' she said. 'I fear that he plans to overthrow my father with the blessing of my mother.'

Gwydion looked shocked.

'You must be mistaken,' he said.

'I am not mistaken, Gwydion. Each night she sneaks out to his hut when she thinks I am asleep. Two nights ago, I followed her and heard her rutting beneath his furs.'

Gwydion remained silent. The news of the illicit affair was common knowledge amongst the warriors, and though it was only a matter of time before they were discovered, it was a matter for Erwyn to sort out. However, the possibility of a takeover was a different matter.

'If there is a coup, there will be much blood spilt between the factions,' he said. 'Many in the clan will die.'

'I know, she answered, 'and I think that's why Robbus wants me gone. In case I betray him to Erwyn before he has chance to put his plan into action.'

'Can't you just say no?'

'I am the daughter of a chieftain and still untouched by any man. It would seem that purity is powerful magic for the Druids. Even as we speak, they send a wagon to pick me up. It will be here on my birthday.'

Gwydion's face fell. The Druids were all-powerful and enjoyed absolute respect from every clan. They were the keepers of the magic and the servants of the Gods. They had power of life or death over all tribes and were feared by all. He looked at her in dismay. If the Druids had summoned Gwenno then she had to go. It was as simple as that.

'Then there's nothing we can do!' he said unbelievingly.

'But there is!' she said, her eyes ablaze with hope. 'Don't you see, if you take me as a woman, I will not be a virgin and the magic will be gone. They will leave us alone and we can be together.'

'If we do that, Gwenno,' he said, 'they will kill us both.'

'I don't care!' she said, 'I would rather have one night with you and die tomorrow, than face a lifetime on Mona.'

Gwydion shook his head slowly.

'I can't do that, Gwenno,' he said softly. 'I care not for my life and would die gladly for a night by your side. The Gods know I have waited long enough, but I will not see you killed. You cannot stay here for your life will be in danger whatever happens, and I cannot take you away for our people will need every spear when the Romans come. No, if there is blood to be let, then you should be as far away as possible. At least with the Druids, you will be safe no matter who wins control of the clan. You must go with them and when this mess is over; I will find you and take you far away to start our life together.'

'What will you do while I am gone?' she asked through her tears.

'If needed, my sword will support Erwyn, but I hope it doesn't come to that.'

'Oh, Gwydion,' she cried and collapsed sobbing into his arms. He held her tightly long into the evening until they both lay down to sleep in the hay. It was dark in the hut when Gwydion stirred, awoken by a low call from a comrade outside the hut.

'Gwydion,' the voice said quietly, 'Robbus would speak to you.'

'I won't be long,' he whispered to Gwenno, 'wait here.'

She smiled at him, her tears long dried, and watched as he strode away across the compound to the central hut, not knowing that it was the last she would see of him for a long, long time.

Chapter 8

After arriving at the fort, the names of the recruits were taken, and they had been quartered in tents outside the perimeter until any stragglers arrived. Finally, when it was obvious that there were no more due, they were arranged into groups of eighty, and led into the fort itself. Cassus looked around in fascination, drinking in the atmosphere of the busy legionary camp, but before he could take much in, his group stopped in front of a wooden barrack hut. The timber building consisted of a terrace of twelve rooms fronted by a covered portico, one of many such blocks arranged in a straight line along the inner wall of the fort.

'This will be your barracks for the foreseeable future,' announced the soldier who had led them in to the fort. 'Within its walls you will find twelve rooms. The first belongs to your Centurion, and you will never enter it unless ordered to do so. The next ten are shared between the rest of your Century, eight men in each and at the end, there is a latrine. When you are dismissed, you will each settle in to a room and unpack whatever possessions you carry. Choose your roommates carefully, for this will be your Contubernium, the men you will live and die alongside. Inside the room, you will find the equipment you will be expected to carry on campaign. The heavier equipment will be carried on a mule. Look after the beast well, for if it dies, you will carry the equipment until a replacement can be found. There is a mess hall at the end of the row and there will be a meal served at last light tonight. Your training starts tomorrow. Form up outside this hut before dawn and await further instruction. Are there any questions?'

'What about weapons, sir?' asked one man called Montellus, obviously keen to get stuck in.

'You have not earned the right to bear arms yet. Now if there is nothing else, I will see you in the morning. Dismissed.' The soldier marched away and after a moment's hesitation, the group broke up to hurry inside, keen to see their new home. The men who had joined with Cassus and Prydain since leaving Perre's ship had formed a close friendship and they ran forward to be first in the hut.

'Grab the far end,' shouted Prydain. 'Away from the door, it will be warmer.'

'No,' said Cassus, 'it's next to the shitter, get one this end.'

'Bollocks to that,' said Montellus, 'it's next to the Centurion's rooms and I want to be as far away from him as possible.' They settled for one somewhere near the centre and all piled in, throwing their possessions onto whatever bunks they could.

The room was sparsely furnished, containing four double bunks with a folded horsehair mattress on each, a long table with bench seating on both sides and a stone hearth beneath a shuttered window. An iron grill and a large brass pot sat on the hearth, all of which were intended for communal cooking. A stone grinding mill sat in the centre of the table to prepare barley or wheat for dough, along with eight water flasks, bowls and eating tools, spooned at one end for ladling and spiked at the other for spearing meat. A heavy hooded cloak lay folded on each bed along with two white tunics, a belt, a pair of leather Caligae and two woollen blankets. To one side, another doorway opened into a smaller room containing a second fire slab and a drain hole through the wall.

'Drying clothes and storage,' ventured Montellus when the use of the room was questioned. Already stored in the room were a large tent and a range of tools including heavy axes, spades and saws. A wicker basket contained a range of smaller hand tools including hammers, planes and files along with sewing equipment, a Strigil, the curved tool used for scraping the skin during bathing and a set of grooming tools for the mule. Finally, in the corner, lay a bundle of stakes, each four foot long and sharpened at both ends, the use of which was yet unknown to all members of the Contubernium.

'I suppose we will find out soon enough,' said Cassus as they returned to the bunkroom. 'Come on, let's have a look around the fort.'

'I'm going to find the mule,' said Montellus. 'By the look of that lot in there, we need to make sure we have a healthy animal.'

The following morning, a line of a hundred men stood outside the walls of the fort waiting patiently in the pre-dawn darkness for the day's activities to begin. Each was dressed in a black tunic and wore a simple sword belt complete with a wooden Gladius. These were the training Tessaria, handpicked veterans who had either recently retired from active service, or had suffered some minor injury during service. Some only had one eye, others perhaps a hand or lower arm missing, while old battle wounds disfigured some of the others. They waited patiently to greet their new charges, the civilians that they had been tasked to turn into efficient killing machines over the next few months.

A murmur of sound echoed from within the fort and a double file of nervous recruits marched out onto the training ground. As they emerged, they lined up in groups of eight behind the Tessaria. Each recruit was dressed in a white tunic gathered at the waist with a corded belt. By the time, the sun had cleared the horizon; eight hundred men stood shivering on the plain, waiting nervously to be told what to do next.

The buzz of nervous chatter slowly died as a column of trained legionaries marched out of the fort, perfectly in step, finally halting and turning inward to up face the recruits across the cobbled road. The two groups faced each other, one full of faces alive with anticipation and excitement, the other littered with indifference and contempt.

Eventually, an officer rode a black charger out of the gate. His armour was gleaming bronze and on his head, he wore a glistening helmet with hinged metal plates hanging from the brim. A scarlet red cape hung from his shoulders completing the ceremonial uniform.

He stopped his horse and looked around those who had volunteered for servitude in the legions of the Emperor. Landowners, freedmen and tradesmen stood before him, each with their own reasons to be there. The dross had been filtered out during the recruitment process and for their impudence; runaway slaves who had sought to seek a different fate had been sent to the salt mines. Bankrupts and murderers, seeking refuge from Rome's justice, had been handed over to the magistrates, and the papers of every applicant had been carefully scrutinized for authenticity. Rome didn't allow just anyone into her ranks. Desperate or not, she had her standards to maintain.

The silence was absolute and everyone stared at the impressive officer. At last he spoke, his voice carrying strongly to everyone on the parade ground.

'Citizens of Rome,' he shouted, 'I am your commanding officer, Legate Nasica,' he paused briefly before adding, 'and I salute you.'

A murmur flitted around the recruits before he continued.

'As you have taken the sacramentum to serve Rome, your lives now belong to us. From this day forward your existence will become a blur of training and hardship. There will be pain and misery, but I make no apology, for these are the predecessors of the professional soldier. All your instructors are battle veterans and have been handpicked. Over the next few months, they will train you to the standard I expect, and that standard, is greater than any other legion.'

'You will be expected to march further than you thought possible, your blistered feet pouring with blood, but it is then you will double the distance.'

He spurred his horse to parade slowly along the ranks of the gathered trainees.

'When the muscle in your arms ache to such an extent that you can no longer wield a sword, it is then that you will strike twice as hard. When your back breaks from the burden you carry, and your fellow falls at the wayside, you will take his pack and carry him forward. At the end of the day, when your body is incapable of doing any more and you are physically sick through pain and exhaustion, it is then that you will unpack your digging tools and build the defences. This is what we do. We train hard, for when the training is hard, the fighting is easy.'

'Heed your instructors,' he continued, 'for during this pain, they will be alongside you. Their feet will also blister and their bodies will ache for their blood as Roman as yours. Do this and I promise that you will come out of the other end, a military machine the likes of which this world has never seen before.'

'Before this year is out, Rome will embark on a new campaign in a country as yet unconquered. We do this in the name of civilization, and return a rightful King to his throne.'

'Britannia lays off the coast of Gaul a hundred miles to the west,' continued Nasica. 'We will return this exiled King to his country and spread civilization to his deprived people. The merchants, who already trade there, say that they are truly a barbaric race, worshiping the Gods of the underworld and sacrificing their children in unspeakable ceremonies. We will bring peace and prosperity to this oppressed and misguided people, ending their despicable acts and bring law and order into their miserable lives. Make no mistake, they will resist, for it is said they are a warlike race, but they will be no match for our legions. Some of you will pay the ultimate price, but I promise you this. Your lives will be filled with honour and a comradeship that will stay with you till the day you die.

'So look around you, for you are all brothers and your lives lie in the hands of the man next to you. I leave you in the hands of your instructors and the next time we meet, I will lead you to the shores of Britannia.'

Without another word, he rode his horse back into the fort, closely followed by the armed guard. The recruits started to relax, looking to their Tessaria for direction. They split into their ten training centuries and spread out around the arena to pre-determined training areas. At the orders of one of the Tessaria, Cassus's group rearranged into a large circle for their first lesson as Tirones, trainee soldiers of Rome. Cassus and Prydain talked excitedly amongst themselves. This was it. This was what they had waited for all their lives and the great adventure was about to begin. Gradually the chatter died away and silence fell.

'Get out of my way!' said a quiet voice and some of the recruits shuffled sideways to allow a previously unseen soldier to enter the circle.

The legionary walked slowly around the front rank of the circle, his hand ever present on the hilt of his Gladius as he went, staring each man in the eye as he passed. Dressed in a scarlet tunic and lightly armoured, he commanded respect. Everyone present realized this was an experienced veteran, whom no one should mess with. His tunic was held at the waist with a polished sword belt. His Gladius hung on his right and his Pugio, the narrow leaf-shaped dagger favoured by most legionaries on the left. Though he wore no armour on his torso, his arms were each protected with Manica, the chain mail sleeves designed to protect the forearms from enemy sword thrusts in the heat of battle. Similarly, his legs were covered by sheet metal Greaves, designed for the same purpose.

He made his way to the centre of the circle and stood as if waiting for something to happen. The recruits were deathly silent, totally transfixed by this veteran of countless campaigns and the epitome of everything they hoped to be. Eventually he removed his helmet and cast it aside into the sand and tilting his head back, drew in a lungful of the cold morning air. His bald head shone in the morning sunlight, and his muscular neck sat on abnormally straight shoulders. His face was weathered with one side hanging slightly lower than the other, a by-product of an African cudgel in a long forgotten campaign, and a leather patch covered an empty eye socket. He stared at the circle of men.

'Which of you can handle a sword?' he asked.

When nobody answered, he walked up to the nearest recruit.

'How about you?'

'I am a carpenter, Sir,' said the man, 'I have never handled a sword.'

He looked around the circle again.

'You?' he asked, jabbing his finger into the chest of a giant of a man to the side of Prydain. 'You are the ugliest brute I have ever had the displeasure of laying eyes on. You must have killed a few men in your time.'

'I have also never used a sword,' the man stammered nervously, 'I am a farm labourer, Sir.'

The instructor spat on the floor.

'What is this they give me?' he shouted to the sky, 'I ask for men and they give me babes. What chance do I have?'

He dropped his gaze to look at Prydain.

'How about you boy?' he asked.

Before Prydain could answer, Cassus piped up.

'He is the son of a Gladiator, Sir,' he said, 'and can handle a sword as good as any man.'

The instructor stepped forward until he was close to the much younger man, focussing on Prydain's eyes with interest.

'One blue and one brown,' he said, 'interesting. Few men are blessed with the devil's stare and it is said that those who are, will be destined for greatness or infamy. Which will you be boy?' he asked. 'Hero or coward.'

'Only the God's know,' answered Prydain.

'Perhaps,' said the soldier. 'Let's see if we can get a glimpse of the man you will become, shall we?'

'Which blade?' he asked suddenly, turning away from Prydain and striding back toward the centre of the circle of men.

'Gladius, Sir,' answered Prydain.'

'Gladius,' repeated the instructor with a nod of appreciation as he started to undo the straps on the Manica on one arm. 'And where did you learn this?'

'My father fought in the arenas,' answered Prydain, 'and when I was a boy he taught me to fight.'

'Trained by a Gladiator,' the instructor announced to the circle of men with mock pride. 'Impressive!'

'What is your name, boy?' he asked turning again to face Prydain.

'Prydain Maecilius, Sir,' he said, 'Freedman of the house of Gaius Pelonius Maecilius.'

'Freedman!' he said with undisguised contempt. 'So you were a slave and some idiot not only gave you your freedom, but made you a citizen as well?'

'I have the correct paperwork, Sir,' said Prydain, 'everything is in order!'

'Well, Prydain Maecilius,' said the instructor, 'it just so happens that I too can use a Gladius and would you believe it, I happen to have one right here.'

He drew the weapon from its scabbard and walked over to face Prydain once again. He pressed the blade of the sword against Prydain's throat.

'Lesson one, slave-boy,' he said, 'never, ever, call me sir again. Those officers and politicians, who you address as Sir, are not fit to eat my shit. My name is Remus and my rank was, and as far as you are concerned, still is Optio. From now on, you will all address me by that title. Is that clear?'

'Yes, Sir...I mean, Optio,' came the muted reply.

Prydain's head tilted right back to avoid the point of the blade piercing his throat.

'Is that clear?' screamed the instructor.

'Yes, Optio!' shouted Prydain, his voice echoing around the parade ground.

'Good,' he smiled, revealing a line of broken and missing teeth. 'Now the introductions are over, let's get started.'

He turned around and walked back to the centre of the circle. A slave ran forward and loosened the leather ties fastening the Greaves to his legs and as he did so, Optio Remus undid his remaining Manica. Both sets of armour were cast aside before he drew his Pugio and tossed it next to his helmet. Finally, he stood there, donned in red tunic only, but still holding his Gladius in his hand.

He spun the sword into the air and caught it by the blade, hilt facing away from him. With lightning speed, he threw it like a dagger toward Prydain. It span through the air and embedded itself deep in the sand between Prydain's legs.

'Pick it up!' he ordered.

Prydain picked up the sword, folding his fingers around the hilt as he felt its familiar weight and balance.

'Listen very carefully, Prydain Maecilius, freedman of the house of Pelonius Maecilius,' said the Optio sarcastically, 'you are about to receive your first order from me. If you refuse, I will kill you! If you argue, I will kill you! If you question my order, I will kill you! Do I make myself clear?'

'Yes, Optio,' said Prydain, a look of apprehension creeping into his face.

'Sorry,' said Optio through a sickly smile, 'I didn't quite hear you,' His smile evaporated and he growled the question again. 'Do you understand?'

'Yes, Optio!' roared Prydain again.

'Good,' said the older man his tone instantly placatory, 'then listen very carefully.'

He stepped a pace back and opened his arms wide emphasizing the fact he was totally unarmed and vulnerable.

'Prydain Maecilius,' he said, 'I order you to kill me!'

Chapter 9

Prydain stared at the Optio across the sand.

'What's the matter, slave-boy?' sneered Remus. 'Isn't this exactly what you joined up for? Excitement, adventure,' his voice dropped, 'the chance to kill a fellow man!'

Prydain thought furiously and started to say something before stopping suddenly mid-sentence. Remus's raised eyebrows reminded him of the lethal ultimatum he had just been given. The whole group were silent, eighty trainees and eight instructors, all holding their breath as they waited for someone to make a move. Those at the rear strained to see what was happening over the heads of those in front, each wondering who would move first, the Optio with his arms open wide presenting an easy target, or the recruit standing in shock, the acquired Gladius hanging limply by his side.

'It's very simple,' continued Remus calmly. 'The choice is clear. Kill or be killed. A choice that is faced every day by better men than you, all across the empire. Your life or mine, slave-boy, which do you hold dearest?'

Prydain realized he had no choice. It was obviously a set up designed to show off the instructor's prowess in sword play and he had no doubt that Remus would be able to disarm most men, but Prydain was no ordinary man. Karim had taught him, and everyone knew that Karim had been second to no man in the arena.

He looked down at the Gladius, all Karim's instruction coming back to him. Most untrained men would hack at an opponent, lifting the weapon high and opening up their own torsos for blows to the ribs. But Prydain knew better. The Gladius had been designed for thrusting into an exposed opponent and demanded a different technique. He span the sword in his hand and sprang forward into the stance of one used to handling the Gladius. His feet were placed shoulder width apart, left foot half a step forward of the right.

His body was twisted slightly to the right and he held the Gladius at chest level, pointing toward his opponent. Despite his not having a shield, his left hand was extended forward in a natural defence against any attack that the Optio may bring.

Remus smiled.

'That's more like it,' he said. 'Come on, slave-boy, do your worst.'

79

Prydain inched forward, his Caligae leaving a sandy trail as he edged toward the unarmed instructor. Remus stood his ground, his arms now lowered to his side seemingly totally relaxed, but his one eye firmly locked on Prydain.

After a few tense minutes, Prydain made his move. He feinted with his outstretched left hand as if to strike, but quickly took a giant pace forward onto his right foot, changing the point of attack to thrust his Gladius deep into Remus's unprotected midriff.

Cassus looked down at the body lying on the sun-warmed sand, surprised at the amount of blood that had sprayed out from the wounded man. The rest of the Contubernium stared in awe, not quite believing what they had just witnessed.

Prydain's attack had been perfect. The classic stance, the protecting arm providing the feint before the lightning quick killing blow had been administered. All perfect, all textbook. But textbooks had never faced barbarian swords whilst Remus, on the other hand, was a veteran of countless battles.

At the last second, the instructor had leaned backwards and twisted his body to the left, causing the Gladius to miss his chest by the narrowest of margins. Grabbing Prydain's wrist in his own left hand, he continued to spin his body and lifting his right arm to head level, slammed his elbow backwards into Prydain's face, shattering his nose. Prydain was unconscious before he hit the floor, and as he fell, Remus snapped his forearm over his knee, causing him to release the Gladius, which was back in the instructors sheath before Prydain's head hit the sand.

'I am insulted,' said Remus. 'Is this the best that Rome can offer? Not only did he underestimate me just because I am unarmed, but in addition, he told me exactly how he was going to fight. By telling me a Gladiator had trained him, I knew the style, the tactics and most of all, the result he expected. I deserved better. Know everything there is to know about your enemy. Just because they dress in rags or speak in words you don't understand, do not assume that you are better. As legionaries, you will rarely fight alone. You will advance as one, killing the man to your front and defending the man to your left. As you step over your fallen enemy, you will crush him beneath your heel, leaving no threat behind you. Those that still survive will be finished by the rank behind.'

He walked around the inner edge of the circle of watching men, staring at each in turn.

'You will kill and inflict injury, efficiently, coldly and without remorse. You will show no mercy. You will advance through their lines without stopping, administering death without thought, and when you can kill no more, you will step aside for the man behind you to take your place. By the time I have finished with you, you will be killing machines, cold, ruthless and unrelenting. Yes, the training will be hard, but nothing like that pompous arse said earlier. Oh no, nothing like it at all, for in truth, it will be much, much worse.'

'However,' he continued, 'before we can turn you into these killing machines, we have to lose that farm blubber hanging around your bellies, and there is only one way to do that. With immediate effect, each morning before training starts, every man will run ten laps of the fort. The last to finish will do an extra ten laps along with the rest of his Contubernium. This will be repeated before your midday meal and again at last light.'

'Well, what are you waiting for?' he screamed, and the recruits turned to start on the run, confused and shocked at their brutal initiation into the legions of Rome.

Prydain moaned at Remus's feet, coming slowly back to consciousness. The Optio crouched and lifted Prydain's head up by his hair.

'Broken nose,' he said twisting Prydain's head to examine the damage, 'and a broken arm. Nothing life threatening, so stop your whining. There is a medical room in the guardhouse. Get yourself fixed up and join your comrades on the run.'

He paused and pulled out the pendant from around Prydain's throat. Staring at the design etched on the leather, his brow furrowed as a long forgotten memory struggled to reach the surface. When he failed to recall where he had seen the design before, he let it fall back. It did not matter, if it was important, it would come back to him.

By the end of the first week, the recruit's tunics were ingrained with sweat and they each had a week's growth of stubble on their chins. Everyone stank, as there was only so much dirt that cold water from the horse troughs could remove. On the seventh day, after a particularly gruelling morning, the recruits lay scattered over the sand enjoying a brief respite after a meagre meal of plain dough pancakes and dried dates.

A Tribune came out of the fort dressed in full ceremonial armour, accompanied by three legionaries. Two of the soldiers carried a heavy sack between them, while the third carried a drum.

'Get to your feet,' screamed Optio Remus, jumping up from the sand. 'Form up, three ranks facing me.'

The recumbent recruits erupted into action, knowing that anything less than instant obedience would incur painful retribution. When they were all lined up, Optio Remus called them to attention and the Tribune addressed the men.

'Tirones,' he shouted, 'I am Tribune Mateus and I am an officer of the Ninth. In a few months, we leave this place and march to Britannia. The galleys that Plautius has sent to take you to across the sea approach the shores of Gaul as we speak. The training you have done so far will be as nothing compared to the conflict that is to come. Those who do not heed their instructors will probably die in the first battle, and any turning from the fight, will find their comrade's blades waiting for them.'

'However, we are only interested in commanding men who serve without question, and if necessary, will die for their fellow soldiers. Therefore, I am giving everyone here a last chance to avoid the ignominy and the pain. Anyone wishing to reverse their decision to join the legions can leave right now. You can turn around and cross that bridge with no recriminations. We will even give you money for your trip home.'

The two legionaries tipped out the sack they had carried onto the parade ground and a pile of smaller leather purses fell onto the sand.

'A month's wages if you quit right now, no comebacks,' shouted the Tribune.

A murmur crept through the gathered men. Twenty Denarii to end this nightmare. Some of them had never seen so much money at one time.

'So what is it going to be?' shouted the Tribune. 'Enough money for a month in the best whorehouse in Rome, or a lifetime of pain and fear in a far off cold and God forsaken land? You have a hundred beats to decide and then there is no choice.' He turned to the drummer. 'Begin!' he ordered.

The drummer started beating his drum, each beat approximately five seconds apart, echoing ominously off the fort's walls. Talking erupted in the ranks, every man discussing the options with the one next to him, but still no one moved. Eventually one stepped forward and his move was acknowledged by the Tribune.

'No recriminations?' asked the recruit nervously.

'No recriminations,' answered the Tribune. 'Take your money and leave.'

The disillusioned recruit bent down to pick up a purse from the sand. As he was on his knees, Optio Remus drew his Gladius and placed it under the man's chin, forcing him back to his feet, still clutching the purse. The parade fell silent, waiting for the thrust that would surely end this charade.

'There is just one more thing,' said Remus.

The recruit's face was white with fear.

'Don't you ever let me see you again. Is that clear?'

The terrified man nodded slowly, unable to speak.

'Good,' said Remus and lowered the blade. 'Now, get out of my sight.'

The quitter walked backwards, quickly increasing his pace until finally, he turned and sprinted toward the distant town as fast as his injured feet would allow.

'Twenty five!' shouted the drummer, reporting the amount of beats. The voice seemed to spur others into action, and some ran forward to claim the purses in the sand, avoiding eye contact with the veteran Optio.

'Fifty beats,' shouted the drummer.

More joined the first man and crossed the bridge, clutching their severance pay tightly in their fists. Cassus looked at Prydain.

'I'd take the money if I was you,' he said.

Prydain looked back at Cassus, his nose still swollen from the surgeon's attempts to reshape it with wooden rods inserted into his nasal passages.

'I can't believe you said that,' he said, 'after all these years, you think I would quit?'

'Well it's not as if you exactly fit in here,' said Cassus. 'Look around you. Not many others like you on parade.'

'What do you mean, like me?' asked Prydain.

'You know what I mean?' said Cassus.

'Say it, Cassus, let's get this over with once and for all.'

'Okay, I will,' he said. 'You don't belong here, Prydain. Take the purse and join the auxiliaries. There is no shame in that. Stop trying to be something you're not. Even Remus has taken a dislike to you, at least in the auxiliaries you will feel more at home. There are many like you there.'

'Like me?'

'Yes, you know, freed slaves.'

'I am not a slave,' growled Prydain.

'Not anymore, but these men are freeborn. Don't you see? You don't belong here.'

Optio Remus spotted the two young men talking and approached them, beating the flat of his blade into the palm of his hand, in time with the drumbeats.

'Well, boy,' said Remus, addressing Cassus, 'are you a quitter?'

'No, Optio!' answered Cassus bluntly.

'No, I didn't think you would be, and what about you, slave-boy?' he asked staring into Prydain's face. 'Are you taking the Emperor's hard earned money?'

'Seventy five,' roared the drummer in the background as more disillusioned recruits made the short journey to the payoff.

'Can I speak freely,' asked Prydain, his eyes never leaving Cassus.

Remus grunted his permission.

'In that case, Optio, you can shove the Emperor's money up your arse!'

Remus's expression didn't alter. Instead, he lifted his Gladius and placed the flat of the blade against Prydain's cheek.

'At least you've got balls, slave boy,' he said. 'But balls are not enough. Let's see how long you last.'

'One hundred!' shouted the drummer and the beating drum stopped.

Remus spun around and strode back to the front.

'Close the ranks,' he roared. 'Numbers?'

One of the Tessaria counted heads and ran back to the front.

'Five hundred and seven Optio,' he shouted.

The Tribune nodded to the Optio.

'That's better!' he said. 'You know what to do, take them away!'

84

The end of the first week's training was a huge relief for the remaining recruits and they had been marched to the legion's dedicated bathhouse just outside the fort's walls, to bathe in its steaming waters, heated by their huge subterranean boilers.

After the sweat and dirt of the previous week, it was heaven and the pain of their induction was quickly forgotten as they relaxed in the civilized surroundings. Each was shaved and had their haircut, and after they had dressed in clean white tunics, entered an auditorium to feast on fruit and goat meat. Eventually, an elegant figure came out of the baths draped in a rich red toga and sipping a glass of wine, accompanied by two beautiful women.

'Stand up,' screamed Optio Remus and the recruits sprung to attention. The gathering silenced, staring at the women as the familiar Tribune began to speak.

'Soldiers of Rome,' he began, 'we are not barbarians, we are civilized men, and we will act as such. Yes, you will be driven to the edge of your physical endurance, but when the chance arises, you will be rewarded with the benefits of civilization. No matter how sparse the surroundings, or barbaric the foe, never forget the race which you descend, for we are truly the children of the gods.'

'This week has been but an induction. Tomorrow your training starts in earnest. You have twelve hours leave to do with as you wish. I wouldn't go to the town if I were you, for it is rife with spies and murderers. The women have pox and the wine is cat's piss. I suggest you prepare your equipment and get some sleep. It will be in short supply for the next few weeks I promise you. For those of you that are successful, the next time we meet, you will commence your battle training. He held up his wine glass to acknowledge the ranks and returned to the baths with a smile on his face.

'Pompous arse!' said Cassus through the gritted teeth of his false smile.

'Who is he?' asked Prydain

'The same man who tried to buy us off this morning,' answered Cassus, 'I forget his name.'

'Mateus,' said a nearby soldier, 'son of a senator. Never lifted a Gladius in anger, yet poised to lead a Cohort. It's disgusting.'

'No matter, 'said Cassus, 'come on, let's get out of here. There's not much time and too many women.'

'Where are you going?' asked Prydain.

'Where do you think?' said Cassus, 'the town, obviously!'

'But he said…'

'Bollocks to what he said,' interrupted Cassus. 'He already has his strumpets on call. I haven't seen a naked woman in two months. I'll take my chances?'

Prydain paused.

'No!' he said finally, 'I am going to sort out my kit.'

Cassus shrugged.

'Your loss,' he said and joined his other comrades as they returned to their barracks.

Over the following few days, they were issued with their personal equipment. Assorted armour, helmets and capes were distributed, and a frantic day of swapping and altering ensued, while every man tried to obtain the best fit he could. Clerks ensured they signed for the equipment so the cost could be deducted from their pay, and at the same time, they signed up to their retirement fund and joined a death club, ensuring they would get a decent burial should they fall.

The training was harder than they had ever dreamt possible and every man collapsed each night onto their bunks into an exhausted and dreamless sleep.

Every morning before dawn, they endured their morning run followed by an hour's physical exercise, and after a breakfast of cheese and oatmeal porridge, they had two solid hours of sword practice on the wooden posts with a weighted wooden Gladius. Every man carried out a thousand blows with either hand, repeating the exercise over and over again until they were proficient with both. The instructors side-lined any deemed not to be striking with all their force, while the rest of their Contubernium were made to run ten laps as punishment. Soon every man struck the posts with every ounce of strength they had to stop themselves being alienated by their comrades.

'Forward edge,' shouted Julius, their instructor. 'Head, leg, body, change. Back edge, head, leg, body, change.'

The training continued until the strikes were second nature. Then came the finer points, the high parry, the low parry and most important of all, the killing thrust. Over the days, they combined all the drills until eventually; the Tessaria added a new dimension, the Scutum. It was like they were learning all over again, but this time their balance was altered by the weight of the shields, not only in

86

defence, but also as an attacking weapon, smashing the central brass boss into the enemy faces painted on the wooden pole.

For drill instruction, they marched in formation around the fort, keeping step with everyone else as the pace was called out by the Tessaria, learning the commands they would hear in battle, yet safe within site of the legion's fortress.

The midday meal was fruit and bread, washed down with water from the river before continuing the arduous training. Afternoons consisted of more exercising, more sword practise and more drill, interspersed with wrestling and trials of strength and endurance. All around them, hundreds of other recruits shared their pain, as each was pushed to their limits, learning the basics required to be a legionary. Swimming was a welcome relief from the physical pain, but even there they were required to swim back and fore until exhausted, eagerly encouraged and often rescued from potential drowning by the Tessaria from the comfort of their safety boats.

Those who had been identified as being particularly adept at certain skill were formed into smaller units, concentrating on their own talents. Sagittarii worked constantly with their bows, slingers worked their way through mountains of stones and the better riders were given extra practice with the horses, as though there were dedicated cavalry within the auxiliaries, the legion had their own force of horsemen that were always in need of recruits.

Finally came the evenings and they were worst of all. Every recruit was made to clear a patch of sand and dig a hole in the soil beneath. Dimensions varied, but as long as it was as wide as the digger's outstretched arms, as long as their own body and their head was lower than the pit edge when standing on the bottom, then Julius would be satisfied and the recruit allowed to fill it in. Even though Prydain's broken arm prevented him from digging, he too was kept busy, ferrying leather buckets of water to the thirsty recruits. Soon every man was exhausted and his muscles ached from the constant demanding exercise. It was a task universally hated by the recruits and with little explanation as to the purpose, but it was not until every trench was once more level, were the men dismissed for the night. It didn't take long for them to realize that the more they helped each other, the quicker they could be dismissed and the quicker they could eat.

The evening meal was issued as a pack of uncooked food sufficient to feed eight men. It consisted of a piece of meat, usually pork or mutton, and a basket of barley along with whatever assorted vegetables that were available at the time. Each Contubernium built a fire on their stone hearth and cooked a communal stew in the brass pot to make the meal stretch further.

Every week, the Century set out on a twenty-mile route march to be completed in five hours, and when they could achieve that with ease, they started again, but this time carrying their personal equipment strapped to a Furca, the crucifix shaped pole each soldier carried over his shoulder on the march.

As the weeks progressed, the equipment increased. As well as carrying their Furcas, they wore their Lorica Segmentata for the first time, the upper body armour made from bands of overlapping iron fixed to a leather under-vest. In addition, as their fitness and strength developed, they were issued with their Pilae, Gladii and Scutum and every time the legionaries marched they found it easier, building up their strength, stamina and technique until they could easily achieve the twenty miles in full battle dress.

At last, the constant training and weeks of pain passed and the recruit intake was told to pack up their belongings to parade outside the fort with all their equipment. The men did so eagerly and efficiently, now well versed in the drills and familiar with their kit. The excitement was palpable; for this was the day they would be posted to their Cohorts and started battle training.

Six centuries of men lined up in front of the fort in full battle dress. Their instructors walked up and down the ranks, tightening straps, checking water bottles and generally ensuring that everything was as it should be.

The ranks waited in silence and it seemed to Prydain that the life of a legionary consisted of waiting, rushing and polishing armour. Finally, the same black charger rode out of the gates carrying the Legatus, who had last addressed them, months ago. He came to a halt in front of the gathered men and stared at them for a long time. The difference in sixteen weeks was astonishing. They held themselves more upright and there was an air of arrogance about them as they stared directly to their front, disciplined and attentive.

'Tirones,' he shouted, 'tomorrow, the legion moves into the field to start battle training and I know you are eager to join them. You have worked hard and your instructors tell me you are ready,' he paused, 'But I am yet to be convinced. The men of this legion have fought and died in many campaigns and I would be doing them an injustice if unready recruits were to water their ranks like cheap wine. Therefore, I have a challenge for you. Today you will be given a final task.'

'Oh shit,' muttered Cassus under his breath, 'why do I feel another route march coming on?'

'No problem,' answered Prydain quietly. 'Five hours of hard work and it is over.'

The Legatus continued.

'Each Century will march with full kit to a camp already situated in the hills. Within the camp will be five standards, each bearing a number of a Cohort within the legion. You will return here with a standard, and those who are within the allotted time, will stay together within the Cohort whose standard they bear.' He paused again. 'You will note I said there are five standards, yet there are six Centuries. The Century, who fails to return with a standard, will be split up and shared between the cohorts.'

A gasp rippled through the ranks. No one wanted to be split up from the comrades they had shared the pain of training with. They had become brothers and had always been under the impression they would stay together.

'So your future is in your hands,' continued the Legatus. 'Work hard, and you will earn your standard. Take it easy and suffer the consequences.'

He turned to the six Centurions lined up before their men.

'The standards lie in the fort of Chabal. You can pick your own route. Take them out as recruits, and bring them back as legionaries. You may begin.' With that, he spun his horse and galloped back into the fort.

It seemed that the announcement had a delayed reaction for no one moved for a while. Suddenly the Centurions sprung into life, turning on their squads demanding action. Centurion Severus called his men to attention.

'You heard the officer,' he said, 'this is your chance to earn your own standard, but it will be the hardest thing you have ever done.' As he spoke, Severus stomped back and fore, his voice steadily raising the passion in his soldier's chests. 'Chabal is over twenty miles away, so a return journey is twice as far as you have ever marched before. I am confident that every man here is capable of succeeding in this task, but if we do this, we do it as a Century. Eighty men as one. If we fail, we fail together. There will be no dropouts, there will be no quitters and there will be no failures. We have stuck together throughout your training and we will still be together when we meet the first barbarian spear in Britannia. I am proud of what you have achieved so far and have no doubt that we will return with standard held high. Are you with me?'

'Yes, Centurion,' roared the men in return.

'I can't hear you!' screamed Severus. 'Are you fucking with me?'

Again, the Century roared their agreement, this time their voices echoing off the surrounding hills.

'Tessaria' roared Severus, 'check their kit. Optio, get me a sack of Buccellatum.'

He looked at the retreating columns of the other centuries disappearing into the distance, already started on the race. Within a few minutes, the Century was ready to march, each with an extra ration of Buccellatum, the hard tack biscuit issued to legions on campaign and each carrying an extra water bottle, hastily gathered by the Tessaria from the quartermasters in the fort. Centurion Severus took Optio Remus to one side.

'Chabal camp lies along the road twenty miles in that direction,' he said, pointing at a trail of dust left by the departing centuries, 'but our route lies there.' He pointed upwards at the mountain overlooking the valley to the north. 'The other side of that hill lays a track that leads past the camp. If we can gain the summit in two hours, I reckon we can be there before the others.'

'Our horses will never climb that,' said Remus.

'The horses stay here,' said Severus. 'We march with our men!'

Chapter 10

Gwydion sat huddled in his oiled sheepskin cloak, pushing himself as close to the fire as possible to get some warmth into his freezing bones. All around him were hundreds of similar fires providing the same service to thousands of Catuvellauni warriors, each warming themselves against the bite of the nocturnal temperatures. Spring was still weeks away and though the forest canopy had prevented the worst of the snowfall from reaching the forest floor, it could provide little in the way of warmth or comfort to the waiting army below.

Men coughed and spluttered as they tried to get a few minutes sleep, while others talked quietly, anticipating the forthcoming battle. Gwydion blew on his hands for the hundredth time that night, and looked jealously over to the makeshift tent that contained Caratacus's brother, Togodumnus, and his own King, Idwal. Muffled voices came from within and shadows moved on the hide walls, the imagery projected by the roaring flames within.

The Catuvellauni army was impressive, consisting of over sixty thousand armed men and a thousand chariots. Huge piles of wood were built into unlit bonfires every few miles along the coast, each manned by two men under orders to light the pyre should there be any sight of the invasion fleet. Gwydion had never seen such an army. He was sure the Romans would be crushed like ants when confronted by Caratacus and his hordes. He huddled deeper under his cloak and closed his eyes, not sure, why he was even here. Suddenly, his eyes sprung open, instantly alert.

'I told you,' said a voice behind him. 'A common thief, right here in the very midst of us.'

Gwydion sat up, but remained facing the fire.

'To whom do you direct your insult, sir?' he asked staring into the flames.

'You are the only Deceangli pigs around here, so I guess it must be you.'

'There are no thieves here,' said Gwydion slowly. 'Leave us in peace.'

'Ah, but thieves you are?' said the voice.

Gwydion stood up and turned to face his accuser. In front of him stood five men, led by a man of great stature swigging from a flask of ale.

'And what am I accused of stealing?' he asked.

'It is no accusation,' answered the warrior. 'The evidence is right before our eyes.'

Gwydion looked around.

'I see nothing that has been stolen,' he said.

'Then what do you burn on your fire?' asked the man feigning surprise.

'What?' gasped Gwydion in astonishment. 'It is but firewood?'

'Catuvellauni firewood and I don't recall giving you permission to burn it.'

Gwydion's men stood up in support of their leader, their hands resting on their swords.

'But never let it be said I am not a fair man,' continued the warrior, 'you can keep the firewood for a price.'

'Over my dead body,' said one of Gwydion's comrades and drew his own sword.

'Wait!' shouted Gwydion and grabbed his arm before the sword was fully withdrawn.

'What price?'

'Sensible man,' said the warrior, 'I want that heathen bow you carry.'

Gwydion looked down at the Parthenian recurved bow he had been given by his father.

'That is not going to happen!' he said quietly.

'Then I guess I will have to take it myself,' said the warrior and reaching over his shoulder drew his long sword from the scabbard fastened to his back, closely imitated by his fellow Catuvellauni.

Gwydion's comrades followed suit and all faced each other, the tension rising in the firelight.

'Hold!' ordered a voice, and all men looked up to see Togodumnus watching the confrontation outside the flap of the tent, along with Idwal, King of the Deceangli.

'Brallot, these are our guests,' said Togodumnus. 'Why do you draw your sword, have they borne you insult?'

'Their very presence insults me,' answered Brallot. 'This is our war and we need no aid from Deceangli pigs.' He spat at Gwydion's feet.

'You are a good warrior, Brallot,' said Togodumnus, 'and I know your blade itches to taste blood but let it be Roman blood. These are my guests and I will not allow you to slay the boy.'

'He stole firewood from my pile,' said Brallot, 'and I seek payment.'

'I did not know it was yours,' said Gwydion. 'It was untended.'

'Mine nonetheless,' said Brallot.

Something landed in the thin layer of snow at Brallot's feet.

'Is that payment sufficient?' asked Cody, Gwydion's right hand man.

'What is it?' asked Brallot, his eyes not leaving Gwydion.

'A bracelet,' said Cody, 'Khymric gold.'

Brallot hesitated, and then bent quickly to pick up the bracelet.

'The debt is paid,' he said eventually and sheathed his sword before turning away to leave the clearing.

'Wait!' shouted Cody and the man turned back around to face him. 'You and I still have unfinished business.'

'Which is?'

'You call my people pigs in front of my own King. I demand redress.'

Brallot looked at Togodumnus and the King's brother nodded in agreement. It was a matter of honour.

'I paid you a fair price for your firewood,' said Cody, 'now you must pay me a fair price for insulting my tribe.'

'I am not returning the gold,' said Brallot.

'You can keep the bracelet,' said Cody,' I want something of yours.'

'What?'

'Your head!' said Cody and drew his own longsword.

The men in the clearing gasped and formed a circle. It was a fair challenge, as honour was at stake. A grin spread across Brallot's face and he drew his sword for the second time that night. The surrounding men picked up burning branches from nearby fires to light the circle.

Both swords swished back and fore as the two wary men circled each other, Brallot the experienced Catuvellauni warrior and Cody, a young warrior of the Deceangli. A few heartbeats after squaring up, the forest rang with the clash of steel upon steel as the first blows were dealt.

Brallot launched himself into the attack, raining blow after blow on the Deceangli warrior, the strikes from his broadsword falling thick and fast. His bigger frame and muscular arms meant his attack was stronger and Cody was forced backwards as the seemingly inexhaustible Brallot rained his rage down on the younger man. Gwydion stared in horror as Cody struggled to defend himself, constantly retreating and not landing a single blow in return, but as the minutes passed, he realized that his comrade was not even attempting to return the assault, but was absorbing the frenzy of the attack, deliberately soaking up the ferocity with a mix of patience and technique.

Slowly, the strategy started to tell and Brallot's blows eased in intensity as he strained for breath, his arms weary from wielding the heavy sword. Finally, he stumbled as he missed Cody completely and the young Deceangli took the initiative. Now it was Brallot's turn to retreat, throwing his sword up wildly to parry Cody's counter assault as he stumbled backward, with a look of fear on his face. Despite this, he countered bravely, seizing the opportunity of a mistimed strike by Cody to smash him in the face with the butt of his sword and knocking him to the floor in the process.

He screamed wildly and drove his blade downward to deal the deathblow, but Cody had rolled away, kicking Brallot's legs from beneath him as he went and Brallot fell to the ground, losing his sword in the process. Cody was on his feet above Brallot who lay gasping for air on the floor. He picked up the Catuvellaunian sword, holding it in his left hand.

'Get up!' he said.

'Just do it!' gasped Brallot.

'I will not kill an unarmed man,' answered Cody.

'You have defeated me, I seek no quarter.'

'And I offer none!' said Cody. 'This is yet unfinished!'

Brallot lifted himself to his feet and faced Cody, both men breathing heavily. Cody threw Brallot's sword across to him.

'Like I said, I do not kill unarmed men.'

Brallot caught his sword and stared back at the younger man.

'That was a big mistake,' he said and suddenly launched a huge swing at Cody with unexpected ferocity. Cody ducked instinctively and spinning around, whirled his heavy blade in a wide backhand strike of his own, connecting cruelly with Catuvellaunian flesh.

The surrounding men stared in shock as Brallot's head bounced across the clearing and his dead body fell forward into the snow, the dying heart still pumping blood from the severed arteries. Collectively they looked toward Togodumnus for guidance, all willing to strike down the man who had killed their comrade. Togodumnus walked over to the severed head lying on the floor and stared down for a moment before kicking it into the fire.

'It is done!' he said. 'Return to your fires and take his body with you. Honour is satisfied. He returned to his tent closely followed by Idwal.

The rest of the men dispersed into the darkness and Gwydion wrapped himself in his oiled cape once again, watching the flesh peel from Brallot's head in the flames.

Chapter 11

High above the legionary fortress, Cassus's lungs burned as he pushed himself up the last steep rise of the mountain. Before him lay the summit, a twenty foot rocky escarpment that rose vertically in their path like the palisade upon the fort walls. The Century were spaced out in single file up and over the crag, passing their equipment along a human chain to the top, and as he waited his turn to clamber up the rocks, he stared at the scene far below. From this height, he could see the whole military camp and marvelled at its enormity. Over five thousand troops were stationed within its barricaded walls, and a further four thousand auxiliaries outside in a tented village. The cavalry horses were corralled within fenced paddocks, as were the herds of donkeys intended to carry the legions supplies to Britannia. Cassus realized that this was a rare sight for many soldiers were often away from their legionary headquarters on postings or expeditions, and only the fact that the invasion was imminent had prompted their return, ensuring the legion was at full strength.

Finally, the signal came to continue and he followed the man in front of him as they scaled the granite crag. When the last soldier had joined the rest of the Century on the plateau, Centurion Severus addressed his men.

'Five minutes rest,' he said. 'Eat some Buccellatum and drink deep. From here on in, there will be little rest.' Within minutes they were formed up in their three ranks and adjusting their kit for maximum comfort.

'Right,' shouted Severus. 'Optio get us moving, we have a standard to obtain.'

'Century,' shouted Remus, 'double time, *Advaaance!*'

The column started down the track in unison at two steps per second, the thud of their steps enhanced by the clank of their armour. The hill soon levelled out and the pace steadied to a regular pattern. Two hundred paces at double time, followed by one hundred at single, repeated over and over again, eating up the miles between them and their destination. They stopped at a stream to refill their water bottles, resting for two minutes to catch their breath.

'How far now, Optio?' asked Montellus between swigs of his water bottle, his two Pilae lying on the floor between his feet.

'An hour!' responded the Optio. 'I reckon we are ten minutes ahead of the nearest Century. If we...'

'Optio!' interrupted Prydain urgently.

Remus stopped mid-sentence, his expression angry at the interruption.

'Did I give you permission to speak?' he asked menacingly.

'No, Optio, but...'

'Shut your slave mouth,' snarled Optio, 'I thought I made it clear you don't talk to me unless I tell you too.'

'Yes, Optio, but you should know something.'

'Nothing you have to say is of interest to me, now get your shit together and move out.'

The soldiers scrambled to form up, ready for the last push to Chabal.

'You never learn, do you?' said Cassus, drawing his sword belt a notch tighter.

'I thought I saw something,' said Prydain. 'Up there on the hill.'

Cassus followed his stare up to the wooded slopes of the valley.

'What did you see?' he asked.

'A reflection.' said Prydain.

'Like a waterfall?' asked Cassus.

'Like a weapon,' said Prydain grimly.

'Double step, Advaaance,' screamed Optio and the column started again down the track.

'What do you mean a weapon?' hissed Cassus between breaths, trotting alongside Prydain.

'Just that,' said Prydain. 'A reflection off a piece of steel, like a sword or helmet.'

'It may just be a local hunter, or something,' said Cassus.

'Maybe, but if it is, there are several of them and they have been following us for the last two miles.' Suddenly Prydain peeled out of the rank and ran back along the column.

'What are you doing?' shouted Cassus, and Optio Remus, who had been leading the Century at the front, spun around to see the commotion.

Prydain ran back along the column toward Centurion Severus who was bringing up the rear, ensuring there were no stragglers.

'Hold fast, soldier.' screamed Remus behind him. 'Get back in line!'

Prydain ignored him and ran back to the Centurion, who was now staring at the disobedient recruit in quiet anger. He ground to a halt before Severus.

'You had better have a good reason for breaking ranks, soldier,' said Severus menacingly.

'Sir,' he began, 'I think…'

Before he could finish, Remus came up behind him and smashed him across the side of his head with his Scutum, knocking Prydain to the floor.

'No one disobeys me, slave-boy,' he spat. 'You need to be taught a lesson.'

'Century halt!' roared Severus and ninety men stopped as one, glad of the unexpected rest break.

'Get up,' said Severus. 'This had better be good, or I'll whip you myself.'

Prydain regained his feet and wiped the blood from his mouth staring at the Optio with loathing.

'Well?' said the Centurion.

'Sir, I think the column is in danger,' he said. 'I think we are walking into an ambush.'

'What?' gasped Remus in disbelief, 'By the Gods, slave-boy I'll have your hide for this.'

'Explain!' snapped Severus interrupting the Optio's imminent tirade.

'We are being followed,' explained Prydain. 'On the hill behind me there's an armed party following us through the valley.'

'I have seen nothing,' said Severus. 'Why do you think this?'

'For the last few miles I have seen the sun reflecting off metal. At first I thought I was mistaken, but it has happened several times, too often to be natural.'

'Have you seen horses?' asked Severus.

'No, but they are keeping pace with us and unless they are legionaries, they have to be mounted. The distance between the first and last suggests at least twenty mounts.'

Severus stared at the hill.

'Why do you think we are at risk?' he asked. 'This area has been in Roman hands for years. There are no tribes that would dare stand against us.'

'If they are friendly, why keep themselves hidden and take a rough road through the forest?' answered Prydain. 'This track is far easier. They hide themselves for a reason.'

Severus continued to sweep the hillside for a sign, pondering whether to trust this man's instincts or beat him with his Vitis for insubordination.

'You are sure of this?' he asked.

'As sure as I can be,' answered Prydain.

'Why haven't you mentioned it before?'

Prydain looked over at Remus who stared back at him with loathing.

'I did not think, Sir,' said Prydain eventually.

'No matter,' said Severus. 'We will investigate.'

'For your sake I hope you are right, slave-boy,' snarled Remus. 'Now get back into line.'

Prydain ran back to his position as Centurion Severus unstrapped his helmet from his chest.

'Actually, Optio,' said Severus quietly, 'I hope he is wrong. This Century has only seen the training ground. Between us, there are only you, me and the eight Tessaria with any battle experience. If there are hostile cavalry out there, we stand little chance.' He fastened his helmet to his head. 'Get them ready,' he said. 'We take no chances.'

The trainees donned their helmets and were fully briefed. The mood had changed and everyone was alert as they scanned the surrounding hills for any threat, their hearts beating with a mix of excitement and fear. Severus had moved to the head of the column and Remus to the rear, ensuring they stayed tight together, their only chance in the event of an attack. Each Tessarius gave words of encouragement to their Contubernia as they marched, ensuring the men stayed alert and disciplined.

'Listen to the Centurion,' instructed Julius. 'And remember your training. When any command comes, act immediately, don't think. He has a greater understanding of tactics and should an attack come, gives no quarter. Your life or theirs, it is as simple as that.'

Just short of the narrow valley exit, Severus brought the column to a halt. Remus came forward alongside the Centurion.

'If you were to lay an ambush, where would you do it?' asked Severus taking a swig from his bottle.

'In the glade to the front,' said Optio. 'Amongst the trees their horses are useless.'

'I agree,' said Severus and lifted his water bottle for another drink but stopped suddenly, the flask only halfway to his lips.

'Looks like the slave-boy was right,' he said and threw the flask to one side.

Over two hundred men emerged from the tree line to their front and trotted across the glade to block the Century's way forward out of the valley. Two dozen horsemen followed them out and formed a single line in front of the foot soldiers, one carrying a white banner emblazoned with an embroidered emblem in the shape of a raven.

'Strange,' said Severus. 'That banner, it is familiar yet doesn't belong around here.'

'This area is settled,' said Remus. 'There is no knowledge of any hostiles for miles around.'

Severus's eyes widened in recognition and he took a single step forward toward the riders.

'That's because they are not from around here, Optio,' he said, 'they are from hundreds of miles away and we are in big trouble.'

'Who are they?' asked the Optio.

'If I am not mistaken, they are Germanic and the one carrying the flag is called Hanzer!'

'You know him?'

'Know him?' said Severus, 'I killed him, or at least I thought I did. Sort out the men; I will see what he wants.' He strode out alone into the middle the glade, seeking parley with the deathly quiet hoard facing him. When he was halfway, he stopped and the rider carrying their flag galloped forward to meet him, reining in his horse at the last minute to kick up dust over the Centurion. The two commanders stared at each other, sizing each other up.

'I know your face,' snarled the rider in broken Latin.

'And I yours, Hanzer,' said Severus.

The horseman straightened up and stared at the Centurion for a long time.

'You were there,' he said eventually in recognition, 'with Gabinius, when he burnt my village to the ground!'

Severus didn't answer but stayed alert as the rider walked his horse slowly around him, speaking as he went.

'You were there when his soldiers raped our women and slaughtered our elders. You were there when they desecrated our shrines and chased our children into the river, laughing as they drowned.' He paused, 'and you were there when they killed my wife took any survivors into slavery!'

When he had completely circled the Centurion, Severus finally spoke.

'Yes I served with Gabinius,' he said, 'and I accept that your tribe was wiped out. But it is no less than what you did to the legions in the Teutoberg. Did your tribe show quarter to our soldiers, our women, our children? Over twenty thousand died that day. None escaped, so when Gabinius led the campaign to find last the eagle, there was no holding our men. The blood is shared, the pain equal.'

'How is it equal?' shouted Hanzer. 'Even now your soldiers butcher my people. Thirty five years after Teutoberg, we are still dying at the point of Roman blades. There is no equality.'

'Then you should be there defending them,' shouted Severus.

'My tribe are all gone, Roman.' he spat. 'Speared at Roman hands or serving as slaves in your death camps digging for salt. We few, are all that remain, and we followed your legions out of the forest when they marched here, to seek final redress.'

'Against a legion,' sneered Severus, 'you will be swatted like a fly?'

'Fear is for those who do not want to die,' said Hanzer, 'we do not fear death, Roman, we only tire. Tire of seeing our people crushed beneath the invading heel. Tire of hiding in the swamps and thickets like scared animals and tire of letting the Roman oppressors carry on with their lives as if nothing has happened. But no more, it is time to join our ancestors around their fires, and if we can take some heads as gifts, then all the better.'

Severus realized this man and his followers were embarked on a one-way mission and there would be no reasoning with him. He tried one last time to avoid the seemingly inevitable confrontation.

'You are in our way,' he said. 'We seek no conflict, let us pass in peace.'

'Peace?' spat Hanzer. 'You don't know the meaning of the word.'

'Let us pass,' said Severus, 'and no one will be hurt. You are no match for a fully armed Century.'

'Perhaps not, but don't take me for a fool, Roman.' came the reply. 'You bear no standard. These are not battle ready troops you lead, but trainees. I have watched your camp from the hills and blessed the Gods when you took the mountain route. It seems I will have my retribution after all and if I die in the process, then so be it.'

Severus cursed under his breath; his bluff had been called. There was nothing left for him to do but square up.

'Have it your way, Hanzer,' he said, 'but, know this; there will be no quarter given. I will personally ensure you meet your ancestors, and this time my Gladius will finish what my Pugio started.'

Hanzer stared in fury at the Roman, realizing this was the actual soldier that had stabbed him in the heat of battle and left him to die in the mud of the river two years ago.

'Prepare yourself, Roman,' he shouted, 'one of us dies today!' He spun his horse around to gallop back to join the remnants of his tribe.

'So be it!' said Severus and turned to join his own troops.

'Discard your Furcas,' roared Severus as he approached the trainees. 'Battle formation, full square facing me, ...*Move!*'

The soldiers dropped their spare kit and formed rapidly into ten ranks of nine, including the instructors.

'Okay, you lot,' he continued, 'listen to me very carefully. This rabble's tribe wiped out the three legions at Teutoberg, slaughtering thousands. Now they want to add you to that list. Make no mistake, they intend to kill every last one of us.'

'But that is not going to happen!' he roared as he paced back and fore. 'You are better than these heathen, you are legionaries. You are well trained, you are disciplined and you are Roman! They seek a fight, but they will be disappointed, for we do not bring a fight, we bring death. They have picked on the wrong army, for they have picked on Rome, and now, Rome will wipe them from the face of the earth.'

The soldiers cheered wildly, their pulses racing from the Centurion's stirring words.

'I have fought against Germanic warriors on many occasions,' he continued, 'and though their assault will be fierce, they lack imagination and rely heavily on the full frontal assault. They will expect us to form a defensive square and will rely on archers and horses before attacking from all sides. This is their weakness, so this is what we are going to do.'

For the next few minutes Severus outlined his strategy to the instructors and the scared men, each listening intently to the Centurion as if their very lives depended on it, as in truth, they most definitely did!

Cassus swallowed heavily, his mouth suddenly dry, and wished he had drained his water bottle as instructed by Julius before discarding it with the rest of his equipment not necessary for the fight. Severus's plan was simple, but relied heavily on the recruits remembering all the moves learned on those tiring drill days back at camp. Cassus's blood was racing as he anticipated his first battle. This was why he had joined, and despite the fact that they were supposed to have at least, another month out in the field before being even considered for battle, his heart drummed in anticipation.

'Ready,' asked Prydain at his side.

'Don't you worry about me,' answered Cassus. 'Just make sure you remember your training. You are covering my left, remember?'

They both returned their concentration to the agitated crowd of warriors to their front. The taunts seemed to go on forever as the opposition built their courage, but each time they came, the warriors edged closer. Finally, their ranks opened, and a group of thirty men ran through to their front, forming a line of their own, each drawing their bows back to their cheeks in unison. Centurion Severus and Optio Remus were stood slightly to one side of the Century and spotted the risk immediately.

'Enemy archers,' roared Severus. 'Century, form Testudo!'

All the soldiers in the outer ranks, presented their shields outwards and crouched down to protect every inch of their own body and of those behind them. Those in the centre ranks lifted their shields above the group's head, each overlapping the next to protect the squad from arrows above. Beneath the shield cover, the tension was enormous as the scared soldiers prepared for their first and possibly last taste of battle.

'*Lift those shields higher!*' screamed Julius. 'Get them off your heads. *Brace!*'

Those holding the shields, eased them upwards to arm's length in confusion, but within seconds, the reasoning was clear, as the points of dozens of arrows thudded into the shields, many smashing through the laminated wood into the gloom of the protected Century beneath. Battle had begun.

Julius peered over the lip of his shield toward the archers.

'Brace! he screamed again, each time a volley was fired. The air within the Testudo was thick with sweat and fear as arrow after arrow rained down, smashing into the legionary shields. A man screamed toward the rear rank as an arrow found a way through the defensive shield.

'Man down!' shouted a voice in panic.

'Silence!' roared an instructor. 'Step up, seal the gap. We will help him later.'

Within minutes, the onslaught eased and Cassus peered over the lip of his own shield. All around him, the ground was a forest of arrow shafts where they had fallen short of the target. The enemy warriors were closer now, having taken advantage of the arrow storm to advance.

Remus and Severus peeled off the side of the Century, and Cassus watched in admiration as Severus casually cut away the dozen arrows piercing his shield with one swipe of his Gladius.

'Report,' shouted Remus.

'Two down, three wounded,' came a reply.

'Better than expected,' murmured Severus to Remus, his eyes never leaving the enemy. 'Here come their cavalry.'

The enemy horsemen charged forward toward the Century, each holding a lance in one hand and brandishing a sword or axe in the other.

'Open order!' screamed Severus and the whole Century exploded into what seemed like chaos, but with speed borne from constant practice on the parade square, over ninety men rapidly reformed into individual Contubernia, each a square of nine men including the Tessarius.

The first Contubernium was positioned at the front, effectively the point of a large wedge with the next two squads, ten paces to either flank and ten paces back. Another two were further back, extending the flanks even wider, and the whole thing was mirrored to the rear, forming a diamond shape over a much larger area of ground. The two remaining Contubernia were positioned close together in the centre, providing a reserve force of twenty men.

The deployment ensured the maximum use of available blades without weakening the Roman strength for close quarter fighting, and ensured a strong element of all-round defence at Century level, as well as individual Contubernia. In addition, the positioning of the groups meant that there were wide channels between them, designed to draw the charging horsemen between them and face spear points from both sides.

'Middle and rear ranks, throwing Pila,' ordered Remus. 'Front rank, heavy Pila, present!'

The soldiers did as they were ordered as the horses thundered over the ground, carrying their screaming riders into battle.

'Here they come;' shouted Julius, 'hold firm!'

The Germanic cavalry reached their lines, and though a dozen throwing axes smashed into raised shields, the expected impact of the war horses never came as they veered into the channels, exactly as Severus had expected.

'Side rank, Pilae!' screamed Severus, and the legionaries launched a lethal assault on the cavalry racing between their ranks.

The effect was devastating, and Germanic blood sprayed everywhere as the Romans slaughtered both men and beasts in a frenzy of aggression and fear. A horse galloped toward Severus, aiming his lance at the Centurion's back. Prydain realized Severus hadn't seen the threat, but before he could call out a warning, Optio Remus appeared from nowhere and launched himself at the rider, knocking him clean off his mount. Both fell to the ground and were winded for a few seconds before the warrior gathered his wits and drew a blade from his waistband. He staggered toward the Optio who was still on hands and knees, but as he raised the blade to administer the killing blow, Prydain charged from the line and drove his heavy Pila through the attacker's spine.

The warrior's head flung back in pain, dropping the sword to the ground in agony, and for a second, Prydain stared in horror at the warrior speared on his Pila, the point of which had carried flesh and bone through the man's back. It was the first man he had ever killed.

Optio Remus stood and barely glanced at the dead man before turning to Prydain.

'Don't just stand there!' he shouted. 'Withdraw your blade and get back in line.'

Three riders broke through the Roman rear ranks and galloped back toward their foot soldiers as Severus screamed the next order.

'*Reform*!' he ordered over the cheering. 'Cuneus formation.'

The soldiers scrambled to form the blunt headed attack wedge.

'Their arrows are used!' shouted Severus. 'Their cavalry lie at our feet.' He looked over at the confused warriors across the glade. 'I estimate there are two hundred of them and ninety of us, that makes it about even in my eyes. We have defended enough, now we advance.'

The attacking wedge marched forward across the grass leaving their casualties behind them. Across the glade, Hanzer rode amongst his infantry, whipping them up to a frenzy. They had not expected their riders to be so easily defeated and had certainly not expected the Romans to advance.

'Prepare Pilae,' called Remus,'

The legionaries changed the overhand grip on their Pila to the underhand throwing grasp, raising them to shoulder level.

The Germanic warriors were screaming in fury and frustration and they finally charged across the grass to meet the oncoming Romans.

'All ranks, loose Pilae,' screamed Severus.
'Century…*Chaaarge!*'

Cassus launched his Pilum as hard as he could, seeing it slam into the neck of a young warrior before him, and with a blood curdling scream, raced forward to crash into the first line of Germanic warriors.

Cassus leapt over the first row of speared men sprawled at his feet. The two ranks had smashed into each other at full speed, each well aware that the first to flinch would lose the advantage. Cassus's whole body shuddered with the impact as he drove his shoulder behind his Scutum to reinforce his assault. At the same time, the two ranks behind added their impetus to the charge, until Cassus and his comrades thought their backs would break under the pressure. The weight from both directions meant he could hardly breathe let alone manoeuvre, though he did manage to thrust his Gladius between his own shield and that of the soldier next to him, unaware if it tasted barbarian flesh or not. Suddenly the pressure eased and he managed to take half a step forward as the opposing ranks gave ground.

'Push!' screamed Julius. 'Break through them!'

Cassus continued to push with all his might, well aware that the whole aim of the impact was to drive an armed wedge through the opposing ranks to divide their strength. Suddenly Cassus realised that the enemy were being forced backwards and at last, he had room to manoeuvre.

'Attack!' screamed Julius. 'Punch and thrust!'

Cassus's training kicked in and he punched his Scutum as hard as he could into the face of a screaming bearded warrior to his front, following it up with a thrust from his Gladius. Steel met bone, and though the German tried to return the blow with one from his own axe, the damage was done, and it was easily deflected by Cassus's Scutum.

He withdrew his Gladius and thrust again, this time having the satisfaction of seeing the man fall to his knees, He smashed the sole of his Caligae into the face of his opponent, using the force to withdraw his Gladius from the dying man's ribs. Strangely, he was more sickened by the feel of smashed teeth and jaw beneath his heel, than the fact he had just cut the man's heart in two.

All around him, Roman was taking on barbarian, and no sooner had Cassus withdrawn his blade from the dead warrior, than another took his place. This time it was easier, and though the Century's ranks were still tight, there was more room to manoeuvre and the superior Roman tactics kicked in.

'Step, punch, thrust!' repeated Cassus to himself as he advanced, repeating the drill commands from the training ground. Time and time again his blade met flesh and a living, breathing man fell at his feet to have his face caved in by hobnailed Caligae. All around, terrified but disciplined men followed the same drills and the result was slaughter.

'Front rank fall back!' roared Remus suddenly. 'Second rank move up!'

Ignoring the command, Cassus carried on advancing, caught up in the blood lust as he delivered blow after blow to the terrified enemy.

'*Fall back, soldier!*' screamed a man behind him.

The command sank in, and Cassus stopped where he was, gasping for breath as the rear ranks barged past him with renewed vigour and fresh muscle. He looked around at the battle taking place all around him. The main thrust was clearly advancing through the weaker lines of warriors, and on the sides, he could see the defensive flanking units protecting the sides of the Century. Everywhere, man killed man without quarter, and though the Romans were taking casualties, they were nothing compared to the undisciplined warriors.

'Change your shield!' shouted Julius by his side. 'Follow me!'

Cassus discarded his shattered shield, and picking up one from a fallen comrade, joined ten others running to the left where the advance was faltering. They ploughed into the fray with renewed vigour, providing the reinforcement needed to the under pressure flank.

As soon as the threat had been extinguished, Cassus paused, breathing deep and flexing the fingers of his right hand to break the sticky seal of drying blood between hand and hilt. He rotated his left arm to ease the stiffening muscles, cramping after the constant strain of wielding his Scutum. Suddenly, he spotted Prydain fighting frantically with Hanzer at the edge of the tree line. Prydain fought with shield and Gladius while Hanzer wielded hand axe and long sword, swinging both alternatively with an aggression borne from ancestral fury. Prydain retreated under the frenzied assault and Cassus started forward to help his comrade.

'Stand still,' ordered Remus, who had also noticed the conflict. 'Leave them be.'

'He needs our help,' said Cassus.

'There are true-blood Romans who need our help first,' snapped Remus. 'He will have to wait. He wants to be a legionnaire, well this is his chance, now re-join the assault.'

'But Optio…'

'Do it!' shouted Remus, and Julius led the ten men including Cassus back to the main fight. As soon as they were gone, Remus turned to watch Prydain and Hanzer fighting furiously at the forest edge. Within moments they disappeared into the undergrowth, and after a moment's pause, he too, turned to re-join the main battle.

Severus's distinctive voice resounded over the battlefield.

'They're turning,' he shouted. 'Rear ranks launch Pila, front ranks hold.' The advance stopped dead in their tracks as the last of the Pila flew over their heads, their lethal points thudding sickeningly in to the retreating warrior's backs. 'Advance!' screamed Severus one more time. 'No prisoners!'

With a renewed roar, the disciplined Century charged after the panicking warriors, striking them down with impunity. Even when some held up their arms in fear and begged for mercy, they found their pleas met with Gladius and Pugio. The slaughter finally stopped at the edge of the forest as any survivors sought refuge in its welcoming density.

Initial cheering was rapidly replaced with silence as the realisation finally dawned on the trainee's that it was over, and many slumped to the floor in relief whilst others stood rooted to the spot, their brains struggling to make sense of the carnage all around them. One or two cried quietly, while others shouted and danced in absolute delight. Everyone reacted differently and Severus wasted no time in regaining order within the shattered Century.

'Optio,' he called, 'take ten men and retrieve the dead. You men there,' he continued, 'gather the water skins, fill them up at the stream and share them out. The rest of you, I want any unused Pila collected. Form a defensive circle. This may not yet be over.'

Julius approached Cassus.

'Are you hurt?' he queried.

'Nothing serious,' said Cassus as he tore a strip of linen with his teeth into a makeshift bandage. 'Have you seen Prydain?'

Julius shook his head.

'We have patrolled the forest edge and there's no sign.'

Cassus's continued wrapping the bandage around the gash in his upper arm.

'You fought well today, Cassus,' said Julius, 'you all did.'

'How many are lost?' asked Cassus.

'Twelve dead, twice as many wounded, and two missing. Both from our Contubernium.'

'What now?'

'We will continue to Chabal,' said Julius. 'The legion will send out the cavalry to hunt down those who escaped.'

'Do you think they will find Prydain?'

'If he is still alive, yes, but I doubt if he is.'

Cassus nodded in acceptance and Julius tied the knot on his bandage before seeking out the other members of his trainee Contubernium. Two hours later, the Century formed up again, carrying twenty makeshift stretchers between them, twelve of which carried corpses. The Centurion walked slowly before them.

'Today you fought well,' he said, 'as well as I could have expected from any battle-hardened Century. You listened to my commands and carried out your drills, that is why many of you are still alive. We will take our fallen to Chabal and bury them with full honours. Until then, there is still a job to be done. Many barbarians escaped and are still at large. If they attack again, I expect the same level of professionalism, nothing less. Now, shoulder your kit, pick up your comrades and stay alert. Optio, move them out.'

'Yes, Severus,' answered Remus. 'Century right turn, single time, *advaaance!'*

The column resumed their initial journey and Cassus took the opportunity to look back one last time at the forest where he last saw Prydain. Despite his initial concerns about Prydain joining the legion, he could not help but feel uneasy about the way he had been abandoned.

The Century marched from the valley, every soldier falling silent as they passed the site of the battle. It was littered with corpses, the remnants of a once proud Germanic clan, left to rot where they fell, their sightless eyes already a beckoning treat for the curious crows that hopped sideways toward the feast.

Cassus wondered if Prydain had suffered the same fate.

Chapter 12

Gwenno woke up on a goose feather mattress and looked around at the opulent surroundings. Thick furs lay both above and beneath her, and a jug of ale stood alongside a plate of fruit and berries on a beautifully crafted table beside the bed. Flowers adorned the walls and a small fire shared its welcoming glow from the central hearth. She had arrived in the village the night before, and after a particularly rough crossing of the strait, had fallen onto the offered bed, too exhausted to eat or drink.

She sat up, leaning on one elbow and looked across toward a young girl tending the fire. Her stirrings attracted the attention of the girl who turned away from the fire to greet her with a beautiful smile.

'Good morning, Miss,' said the girl, 'did you sleep well?'

'Fine, thank you.'

'Good, are you ready for your wash?'

'My wash?'

'Yes, Miss, water to wash the sleep from your eyes. You can't meet the day like that, can you?'

'Oh I see,' said Gwenno. 'How far is the stream?'

'The stream,' asked the girl momentarily confused. 'Oh, I see. You don't need to go to the stream, Miss; I'll have the water brought to you.' She ran to the doorway, and called out to someone outside. 'She's awake, bring the water!'

Gwenno watched in amusement as the pretty girl fussed around the hut.

'I'm sorry,' she said eventually. 'Can we start again, who exactly are you?'

The girl stopped and her hand flew to her mouth.

'Oh, please forgive me, Miss,' she said. 'I get so excited when I meet a new acolyte, my mouth gets carried away before my head thinks things through. I'm Willow and I am here to look after you.'

'Are you a slave?' asked Gwenno.

'Oh no, Miss, not a slave, more of a servant. That's it, an important servant for an important person.' Her face lit up again with her beautiful smile.

'Water!' called a male voice from outside the doorway.

'Leave it there,' answered Willow, and ran over to the doorway, disappearing for a second before re-entering the hut carrying a copper pot, struggling with the weight, and the need to avoid its hot surface from burning her legs.

'Here you are, Miss,' she said. 'Your wash.'

'It's hot,' said Gwenno in surprise, seeing the steam rising from its surface.

'Of course,' said Willow. 'Can't have you washing in cold water, can we?'

'No, of course not!' said Gwenno slowly, though in truth, on the odd occasion she had grudgingly washed, it had always been in cold water.

'Can I have some chicken first?' asked Gwenno, her mouth-watering at the sight of the bird roasting on the spit above the fire.

'Wash first,' said Willow, 'food later.'

'You sound like my mother,' laughed Gwenno, but stopped suddenly as she remembered how far away her mother actually was.

'Oh I hope not,' laughed Willow. 'She's probably a lot older than me. Right now, let's get you done.' She dipped a folded woollen cloth into the hot water, before beckoning Gwenno forward. Gwenno got to her feet, and holding her fur wrap closed with one hand, held out the other to take the cloth.

'Oh no, Miss,' said Willow in shock withdrawing the offered cloth, 'you don't wash yourself, that's my job.'

'Your job?' laughed Gwenno. 'I think not, Willow, I'm quite capable of washing myself, thank you very much.'

'But Miss, you don't understand, that's why I am here, to look after you. Now don't worry, just step out of that wrap so I can purify your body. No need to be shy, I've seen a naked woman before.'

'I don't care what you have done before,' said Gwenno, snatching the cloth from the girls hand with feigned horror, 'I will wash myself, thank you very much!'

Willow looked shocked and hurt.

'I'm sorry, Miss,' she stuttered, 'I didn't mean to offend; it's just that I might get into trouble for not doing my job.'

'I am not offended, Willow,' said Gwenno calmly, 'it's just this place. This is all new to me and well, I'll tell you what, I won't tell anyone if you don't. Now if you really want to help, while I get washed why don't you carve me some of that chicken before I die of hunger?'

Willow smiled again.

'Okay, Miss,' she said, and offered Gwenno the bowl. 'Just for today, but don't you go telling on me.'

'I won't,' said Gwenno, 'now turn around and I'll get started.'

'You'll need this, Miss,' said Willow, and gave her a small jug.

'What is it?'

'Soap, of course,' said Willow, 'scented with herbs and spices.'

'Thank you,' said Gwenno taking the jug hesitatingly, 'I just rub it on my skin, right?'

'Yes, Miss,' said Willow, 'your skin and your hair. It will make you feel as fresh as the first breeze of spring, and when you're ready to have your back washed just...'

'Willow!' chided Gwenno gently, 'I can manage from here, thank you.'

'Sorry, Miss,' said Willow and she turned away to sort out the food.

Gwenno dipped the cloth into the bowl and added some of the liquid soap before rubbing it over her skin. The unfamiliar hot water and tallow soap felt luxurious, and she forgot about her hunger for ten minutes as she washed herself from head to foot. She lathered up her long blonde hair, stacking it up in small piles on her head as she scrubbed the grime from each portion.

Suddenly she cried out in pain.

'Aaah, Willow. Quick, help!'

'What's the matter, Miss?' answered the girl in concern, as she ran over.

'My eyes,' cried Gwenno. 'This devil's potion burns my eyes.'

Willow dipped the bowl into the copper pot, refilling it with clean warm water.

'Tilt your head back!' she commanded and poured the fresh water over Gwenno's face, washing away the burning soapsuds. 'Now, let me finish this.'

'Willow!' shouted Gwenno.

'I'm not taking no for an answer, Miss,' she said. 'I'll just do your hair before you burn your eyes out. Now bend your head forward.'

Gwenno reluctantly did as she was told and gradually relaxed as she enjoyed the sensation of having her hair washed in hot soapy water for the first time in her life.

Chapter 13

Gwenno walked around the village, arm in arm with Willow, enjoying the morning air. She had been at the village for many months, and had settled into a routine. The mornings were her own and after breaking her fast, she often explored the village or the surrounding forest.

After every midday meal, Gwenno and Willow walked together to the grove, a copse of sacred oak trees and met one of the elder Druids for instruction in the ways of the world. However, they were indeed quite old and often white haired, Gwenno soon came to realize, that far from being a group of ancient wizards that lived in caves, the Druids were actually just another tribe encompassing the same values that most other tribes did. Several different clans made up the tribe, and like all others on the mainland, each supplied warriors to a central armed group to defend the island. These armed volunteers were the Druid warriors; an experienced and brutal unit that carried out the Druid's every command, the promise of a heavenly afterlife the only payment sought.

They called themselves the servants of the earth, and talked about reincarnation and the fact that everything around them had spirits. Even the trees, the grass and the rocks had souls according to these strange men, and they showed Gwenno how to meditate in order to converse with their spirits. Gwenno tried and tried but no matter how hard she concentrated, always seemed to fail to make any sort of contact.

'Not to worry,' said the kindly man, 'it will come. The more you learn the easier it will be.'

On other occasions, Gwenno would hide behind the trees and witness the bringing of tribute from the surrounding clans, not just from the island, but from the tribes of the mainland as well. Carts full of wheat, beef or cloth were common gifts, whilst the warrior tribes often sent manacled slaves, for despite their respect for life, it was known that slaves did not possess souls, their destiny was to serve.

It was one such morning when she was walking back to the village with Willow, when Gwenno broached the subject of her purpose there. A fully armed warrior walked a hundred paces behind them, one of many whose job was to protect them from harm when they walked out.

'How big is this island, Willow?' asked Gwenno. 'Can we walk around it?'

'Oh no, Miss,' came the reply, 'I think it is many days across and besides it is not safe.'

'How can it not be safe?' asked Gwenno. 'It is only populated by the Druids and as they went to a lot of trouble to bring me here, why would I be in danger?'

'Well!' said Willow, 'let's see. There are wolves and bears and...'

'Bears!' interrupted Gwenno in alarm. 'No one said anything about bears.'

'Well, I think there are bears,' giggled Willow. 'At least that's what my mother used to say when I was a little girl.'

'And where is your mother?' asked Gwenno. 'I don't think I've met her.'

'No,' said Willow sadly, 'she is not here anymore. She died of the cough when I was in my eighth year.'

'I'm so sorry,' said Gwenno. 'What of your father?'

'He drowned when I was a child. His boat capsized in the strait and the water Gods dragged him down. I never saw him again.'

'Oh how terrible,' said Gwenno. 'So who looks after you now?'

'No one,' said Willow. 'I belong to the elders. My aunt sold me into their service four years ago. She wanted them to take me as an acolyte, but they wouldn't accept me.'

'Why not?' asked Gwenno. 'You're very pretty.'

Willows eyes dropped and her tone became subdued.

'Well, I was pretty enough, but I was sort of, you know, not pure!'

'What do you mean not pure?' asked Gwenno before she realized. 'Oh, I see, but I don't understand, surely you were only a little girl?'

'It was my uncle,' said Willow sadly. 'It wasn't my fault, Miss. He used to sneak to my bed when I was in their hut. He used to say if I made a noise, or tell anyone, he would cast me out to be eaten by bears. So I never did.'

'How old are you, Willow?' asked Gwenno.

'Almost thirteen!'

'And you have been here for four years?'

'Yes,'

'So you must have only been nine when your uncle did those things to you.'

'Yes, Miss.'

'Oh, Willow,' said Gwenno, 'how awful!'

'My aunty didn't care though, she still got a good price,' she said. 'For even at nine I was very pretty and after she sold me, I was brought here. It's a very good life. All I do is serve you and…well, other things, and in return I get a warm hut, food and I get to serve you. I am a very, very lucky girl.'

They walked a few more yards in silence.

'Willow,' ventured Gwenno after a while, 'have you served other girls before me?'

'Yes, Miss, though you are by far the prettiest.'

'Many others?'

'Oh yes, Miss and sometimes we even have princes as well as princesses.'

Gwenno laughed.

'I am no princess, Willow,' she said, 'I am a simple village girl whose father is a clan leader. Nothing more.'

'You look like a princess to me,' blushed Willow and they both laughed in the morning air.

'So tell me, Willow,' said Gwenno, 'all these other acolytes, where are they now?'

'They have gone through the Henge, Miss, to the kingdom of the Gods.'

'The kingdom of the gods?'

'Oh it is a wonderful place,' said Willow, 'where the trees are heavy with the sweetest fruit and no one grows old. A magical place where animals can talk and Gods appear to mortal man.'

'You have been there?' asked Gwenno in awe.

'Oh no, Miss, I'm not important enough, though my cousin's friend has,' she said excitedly. 'And he said, that in the ceremony of the cape, a giant God comes to a sacred glade, and if he looks upon you his blinding gaze can strike you dead.'

'Well!' laughed Gwenno, 'I am sure it is a special place, but even so, your cousin's friend or whoever he is may have exaggerated just a bit.'

'Oh no, Miss,' said Willow, a look of awe in her face, 'it is true, for though I have never been to the Henge, I have seen the cape with my own eyes.'

'You have?' asked Gwenno in amusement. 'What is it like?'

'The most beautiful thing you have ever seen,' said Willow wistfully. 'So beautiful in fact, I don't have the words to describe it. No matter though, you will see it yourself soon enough.'

'And what is it for?'

'When the chosen one is summoned, they are given the cape as a sign of their purity and are given a kingdom of their own,' said Willow. 'A beautiful place, full of grazing and waterfalls as far as the eye can see. You see, Miss, you must be a princess, for only princesses can become queens. And that is what you will soon be, a queen of your own lands.'

Gwenno gasped in astonishment, her heart racing.

'I knew it, 'she said excitedly, 'I always said my destiny was to become a queen.' She grabbed Willows both hands in hers. 'Oh, Willow,' she said, 'I can hardly wait. When do you think my time will come?'

'Soon, Miss,' said Willow. 'Very soon.'

Chapter 14

Prydain swung a high blow toward his opponent's head, easily parried by the German's own blade, and immediately brought down his Gladius to deflect Hanzer's retaliatory thrust. The fight had been equal, and both had fought ferociously until the exhaustion took its toll and the ferociousness of the attacks waned. The two combatants fell apart again, gasping for breath, yet both still equal in skill and intent.

'You fight well, Roman.' gasped Hanzer.

'Not well enough,' replied Prydain, 'for you still breathe, but that is about to change.'

The sound of running men crashing through the undergrowth interrupted the confrontation and both span around, brandishing their weapons in defence. Hanzer lowered his sword in relief as Germanic warriors surrounded their leader and his opponent. Prydain cursed his luck and maintained his defensive stance, spinning around on the spot as they closed in on him.

'I want him alive,' shouted Hanzer in his native language, the strange words not understood by Prydain.

The circle closed even tighter, and as Prydain defended a false attack from a warrior to his front, the haft of a spear smashed him across the head from behind. He dropped to the floor half-conscious as several men fell on him and tied his arms behind his back. Hanzer crouched down next to him.

'It seems you were wrong, Roman.' he said, 'I breathe yet,'

'Just get on with it,' Prydain groaned through gritted teeth, struggling to deal with the pain in his head.

'Don't be in such a hurry, Roman;' said Hanzer, 'you will die soon enough.' He stood up sharply. 'The battle is lost,' he called to the rapidly increasing numbers joining him in the clearing, 'but our ancestors can still be honoured. Get back to the camp.' Prydain was hauled to his feet and forced forward at spear-point, stumbling through the undergrowth as he tried to keep up with the pace of the escaping warriors.

Several hours later, Prydain was sat against a tree in the warrior's camp, his hands tied tightly behind the trunk. Hanzer had made it clear that this was to be his last night in this life and while the warriors had got drunk, Prydain had tried, unsuccessfully to free his bonds. One eye was completely closed and his body ached from the beating he had received when they reached the camp. Night had fallen and a single fire burnt in the centre of the camp, shielded on three sides to minimise the light that may be seen from the valleys below. Warriors lay sleeping around the clearing and the camp was silent except for the occasional crackle from the fire.

Suddenly a familiar voice whispered from the undergrowth.
'Prydain,'
Prydain lifted his head, and strained to hear the voice again.
'Prydain, keep quiet, it is me,' said the voice again.
'Montellus?' quizzed Prydain through his swollen lips. 'What are you doing here?'

'Well, it's not for the intelligent conversation that's for sure, now shut up while I cut your bonds. I have a horse back in the woods. We have to get there as quietly as possible and get the fuck out of here.'

'There's a guard that passes every minute,' whispered Prydain. 'He will notice I'm gone and raise the alarm.'

'Leave him to me,' said Montellus finally cutting through the binds. 'I'll let you know when the coast is clear. Most of them are drunk and I don't fancy your chances much when they sober up.'

'Me neither,' said Prydain before adding, 'Montellus wait, look over there, by the fire.'

Montellus stared in the direction of Prydain's gaze and saw the item attracting his attention. Stuck in the ground was Hanzer's lance and hanging from the shaft was the Germanic standard. Enemy standards were greatly prized by all armies and seldom did a soldier of any country get a chance to obtain one.

'What do you think?' asked Prydain.

'Forget it,' said Montellus, 'let's just get out of here.'

'Like you said, most of them are sleeping; we won't get another chance like this.'

Montellus hesitated but before he could answer, a guard came toward them out of the dark. Silently, the Roman retreated into the undergrowth and Prydain stared up at the German in contempt, his arms still behind the tree but unbound. The old warrior paused for a moment, gave an evil smile and spat in Prydain's face, the globule of spittle running down his cheek. It took all of Prydain's self-control not to jump up immediately now his hands were free, but realising they were far too close to the others and that any noise would bring them running, drunk or not, he stayed still and watched as the man continued his patrol along the perimeter of the camp.

A moment later Prydain heard a muffled sound and saw the warrior struggling quietly in the darkness. Montellus had grabbed him from behind and with one hand over his mouth, sliced open the warrior's throat with his Pugio. The guard fell to the floor and Montellus beckoned Prydain to follow him. Prydain hesitated for a second, but deciding to seize the opportunity, crept between the trees toward the standard, stepping over two drunken bodies as he went. He pulled the spear from the ground, and started back toward the forest edge, holding the weapon in front of him as he went.

Unexpectedly, a second guard came out of nowhere, both he and Prydain as shocked as the other at the unexpected confrontation. Prydain could see the guard was young, nothing more than a teenager, and the inexperienced boy was momentarily paralysed in fear. His terrified eyes opened wide, but before he could utter any sound of warning, Prydain drove the spear straight through his face, and out through the back of his skull. The boy fell backwards to the ground, arms flailing uselessly at the lethal staff.

The very position of the standard behind the spear point meant that it too was driven through the shattered skull and realising it would be too complicated to retrieve the lance, Prydain took the boy's own knife and cut the blood-stained cloth from the pole. He looked around one more time to see if the alert had been given, and when no further movement was evident, he left the camp, making his way as quietly as possible through the thicket to where Montellus was waiting.

'Over here!' hissed a voice and Prydain joined his comrade by the horse. 'You prick,' said Montellus, 'you could have got us both killed.'

'No harm done,' said Prydain, tucking the standard beneath the front of the saddle, 'now let's get out of here, there may be others.'

They crept silently down the track until they were out of earshot and after mounting the horse, made their way quickly down the tree-covered slopes. Neither was familiar with the area, and the only reference they had was the glade where the battle had taken place earlier. Luckily for Prydain, who had been semi-conscious most of the way to the enemy camp, Montellus had had a chance to memorize the route and they made their way there as fast as the poor horse could carry them.

'I think this is it,' said Montellus over his shoulder to Prydain. 'I recognise that stream.' They got off the horse to take a drink. 'The glade is at the base of this mountain,' continued Montellus. 'From there it is another five hours march back to camp, but if we…'

He stopped short, as if suddenly confused and looked down at the arrow head protruding from his own chest. Prydain had heard the thud of the strike, but he too was momentarily confused as to the implications until he saw the blood pouring from the wound. Another arrow slammed into Montellus's back and he fell forward into Prydain's arms, who quickly dragged him down behind the cover of some rocks.

'Shit,' said Prydain. 'It must be a straggler from the battle, hang in there friend, I'll try and sort you out.'

Montellus tried to speak, but no sound came, and Prydain held him in his arms as his comrade descended into oblivion.

'Fuck!' he hissed to himself, realising Montellus was dead. He laid him down gently; fully aware he was still in trouble. The span of time between arrows meant that there was probably only one archer and he must be close due to the strength of the impact, but Prydain had no idea where he was. He peered over the rocks at the upper slope, trying to spot the archers position. He knew he couldn't waste any time, as Hanzer and his men were surely aware of his escape by now and must be in pursuit. He undid the leather strap of Montellus's helmet and placing it on a stick, lifted it slightly above the lip of the rocks, inviting the archer to take another shot.

He peered through the undergrowth at the side of the rocks, watching for the attacker to fall for the ruse. A movement in the bracken caught Prydain's eye and sure enough, an arrow bounced off the rock next to the helmet, revealing the ambusher's position. Prydain immediately sprinted forward into the dead ground directly below the archer, knowing he had seconds before the bow could be re-armed. Now he was in cover, he shuffled sideways along the ground, and crawled up the streambed until he was above the archer's position. He peered over the bank and after a few seconds, saw the back of the archer as he stared nervously down toward Prydain's last known position. As slowly as he could and keeping his body tightly pressed onto a muddy trail, Prydain half crawled and half slid down toward his attacker, who was now kneeling up, his neck stretched to try to see where his target had gone. When he was within ten metres, Prydain realised it was as close as he could get and taking a fresh grip on Montellus's Gladius, got slowly to his feet.

Intending to creep up on the archer, he took a step forward but a resounding crack echoed through the trees as a dead branch gave way beneath his feet. Having no other option, Prydain charged down the slope, and without thinking, hurled his Gladius at the archer. Prydain smashed into the man and they both rolled down the slope onto the track, wrestling with each other, nothing less than their very lives at stake.

The archer was strong, especially in the arms, and he gathered Prydain in a bear hug forcing the breath from the Roman's lungs, his garlic-laden breath overpowering in Prydain's face. With his arms tightly pinned, Prydain realised his options were limited and he had to act quickly. Drawing back his head, he drove his forehead forward into the grinning German's nose, breaking the bone and causing him to loosen his grip. Prydain followed up with a knee to his groin and the warrior fell to his knees in excruciating pain. Prydain took advantage and slammed his foot into his enemy's face before diving onto the prone body in a frenzied follow up. He clamped his arms around the German's body from behind, and holding the German's head tight against his own chest, forced it around until it was almost facing backwards, and he was staring in the man's terrified eyes.

'No, please, no!' gasped the terrified man in accented Latin as the realization of imminent death kicked in.

Gritting his teeth and expending every last ounce of energy, Prydain forced the archer's head past the point of its natural limits, and the terrified scream that had started a few seconds earlier, was instantly silenced by a sickening crunch of vertebrae crushing spinal cord. The archer's body fell limp in Prydain's arms.

Both men fell to the floor, one lifeless, and one gasping for breath. After a few seconds, Prydain became aware of a severe pain and looking down, saw the remains of an arrow shaft sticking out of his shoulder. The archer had managed to get an arrow off before Prydain's assault, but his aim had been affected just enough to miss the killing spot. The shaft had been snapped in the struggle but the arrowhead remained deep inside and though Prydain knew he had to get it out as soon as possible, he couldn't do it on his own. He staggered down to the horse, and despite the pain, managed to wrap Montellus in his cape and lay him across the horse's neck. He pulled himself onto the horses back and taking the captured standard from beneath the saddle, folded it into a pad and placed it against his arrow wound to staunch the bleeding. He leaned forward and patted the horse on the neck.

'Come on, boy,' he said and kicked the horse with his heels to start him going. Prydain knew his life now lay in the ability of the tired horse to get him back to the legion's fort, and gritted his teeth in pain as the horse stumbled down the slope to the plains below.

Two days later, eleven thousand men formed up on the training grounds outside the fort. Across the river, many from the township lined up to see the spectacle of an entire legion on parade.

The legionaries were lined up ten deep, forming two sides of square, while the other two sides were taken up with the Cohorts of the auxiliary units. To one end, the six trainee centuries stood in isolation, their armour gleaming in the morning sun. One Century stood slightly apart from the rest, the gleam of their armour slightly duller, the odd soldier not standing quite as straight as the others, and the ranks not as full as those to either side. Eventually, trumpeters blasted a fanfare from the ramparts of the fort and an honour guard marched out of the gates, closely followed by the standards of the legion.

First, were the Vexillum bearers. Each two-foot square embroidered cloth was suspended from a cross bar fixed atop an eight-foot pole, and carried proudly by a legionary wearing a wolf fur over his armour. Most took up position in front of the Century, whose number was depicted on their Vexillum, but five halted in the centre of the parade.

Then came the Signum bearers. Each had similar sized poles, but this time topped with a clenched fist, and adorned with discs along its length, indicating the names and battle honours of their respective cohorts. When they had taken their place, a solitary figure emerged from the gates carrying the Imaginifer, the sculptured image of Emperor Claudius as a reminder to all, exactly who they served. Finally, to a tumultuous fanfare, came the Aquilifer, a fully armoured legionary, draped in a lion's fur and bearing every legion's sacred standard, the Aquila.

Every pair of eyes stared at the sculptured golden eagle perched on its golden laurel wreath, wings outstretched and grasping a thunderbolt in its talons. It was a potent symbol of power, and every man present would lay down his life to protect it.

The Aquilifer marched to the centre of the parade square and drove the silver staff deep into the ground. A murmur of approval rippled around the gathered legion as it held firm. It would have been a disastrous omen had the Aquila fallen over, especially this close to a campaign.

Finally, a file of six horses rode out; their riders dressed in full ceremonial armour, and formed up behind the Aquila. As one, they dismounted and Caesius Nasica, the Legatus Legionis and overall commander of the legion, stepped forward and waited for the fanfare to end, before addressing the parade.

'Soldiers of Rome,' he called out, his voice resounding around the gathered ranks, 'in a few weeks' time we assault the shores of Britannia. Today we move out into the field for battle training. We will shake out the cobwebs from our armour, sharpen our blunted blades and harden our lazy bodies. When the time comes, we will be ready for the fight and will do justice to our legion's name, the name your predecessors fought and died for, but before we march out, there are honours to bestow.'

One of the five legionaries holding a Vexillum stepped forward and gave his standard to Nasica. He took the standard, marched over to one of the five trainee centuries, and presented it to the Centurion standing to its front.

'Centurion Leonis,' he called out formally, 'take your standard and join your cohort.'

The Centurion saluted Nasica with clenched fist against his chest, and accompanied by huge cheering from the gathered legion, marched his proud trainees to join the Cohort depicted on the Vexillum. Nasica carried out the same ceremony five times until only the Century led by Severus was left on the field.

Centurion Severus and his mauled trainees had arrived back from the final task two days earlier, a full twenty-four hours after their competitors and without one of the prized standards. They had buried their dead and nursed their wounded, but had had little time to rest before the parade. The fact that they had defeated a strong enemy was widely acknowledged and a source of great pride, but tradition dictated that there were only five standards to award. His men were to be dispersed amongst the legion, a shameful outcome for everyone. Nasica approached Severus.

'I feel your pain, Severus,' he said quietly. 'Your action was heroic and your men are a tribute to this legion, but my hands are tied.'

'I understand, Sire,' answered Severus.

'Therefore,' added Nasica, 'I have no option but to disband your Century.' He returned to his position to make the announcement, but before he could bark his commands, his eye was caught by a commotion at the far end of the parade.

'What is going on?' he asked one of the officers at his side.

'A rider approaches, Sire,' said Tribune Mateus.

The horse came into view at the far end of the parade and a nearby Centurion stepped out to grab the horse's reins.

'I'll have him taken away,' said the Tribune.

'No, let him come, I am intrigued. What man rides into the centre of an entire legion with such impunity?'

'Release him!' shouted the Tribune and the Centurion dropped the reins, allowing the horse and its rider to continue its steady journey. Slowly, the lame horse limped closer and Cassus recognised Prydain under the coating of dust and blood. As the horse stopped before the Aquila, Prydain lost consciousness and fell to one side, but before he hit the ground, Severus caught him and lowered him to the floor.

Nasica joined Severus.

'One of your missing men, I assume?' he asked.

'Yes, Sire,' answered Severus.

'And the body?'

'Montellus,' said Cassus, 'our other missing comrade.' Cassus trickled some water between Prydain's cracked lips, causing him to splutter as he regained consciousness.

'How ironic,' said Mateus at Nasica's side. 'Just as your Century is once again complete, it will be disbanded.'

'He is wounded!' said Severus, and removed the blood soaked bandage from Prydain's arrow wound, replacing it with his scarf. 'Two men, take him to the Medicus, quickly!'

Cassus and another soldier carried Prydain through the gates of the fort as Nasica's bent down to pick up the blood sodden bandage from the dirt. He unfolded the scarlet cloth, and looked around at his fellow officers, astonished at how strong an omen he was holding in his hands.

'Have you given tribute to your Gods yet, Severus?' he asked, as the Centurion turned his attention from the disappearing men.

'Not yet, Sire, I haven't had time.'

'Then I suggest you make the time,' he said and gave the fabric to the Centurion. 'I think this belongs to you.'

After a moment, Severus realized the implications. He retrieved his dropped Pila from the floor, and after piercing one corner of the Germanic standard with the point, marched over to his Century and drove the spear into the ground before his men. As it caught the breeze, the fabric unfurled to reveal a blood-stained Raven, the captured standard of Hanzer.

Prydain spent the next few weeks in the hospital while the legion undertook battle training in the surrounding mountains. At first, he had suffered with an infection, but the application of selected herbs by the Medicus meant that the wound soon healed. He was impatient to join the rest of the legion but the weakness in his shoulder meant he was unable to wield a Gladius with any great effect. Finally, he was released from the hospital and put on latrine duty until his shoulder had healed enough for him to re-join the legion. At last, he was given the all clear and sat on his bunk in the quiet bunkhouse, packing his kit. The sound of hobnailed Caligae echoed along the timber decking and he turned to see that a Centurion stood in the doorway. Prydain sprang to attention.

'Are you Prydain Maecilius?' asked the Centurion.

'I am, Sir,' he answered.

'Stand easy,' said the Centurion, and entered the room.

Prydain relaxed slightly but remained wary. The brutality of the Centurions was well known.

'I am Scipio,' said the Centurion, 'and I have been hearing a lot about you, Maecilius.'

'Oh?' said Prydain simply.

'You are the talk of the legion, he said. 'That little escapade with Hanzer's warriors seems to have made you a bit of a hero amongst the ranks.'

'I only did what any other legionary would have done, Sir.'

'Ah, but that's the point,' said Scipio, 'you didn't. Any other legionary wouldn't have left the ranks in the first place. They would have stayed in place, following their training to the letter, fighting as one. But not you, Maecilius,' he continued, 'You had to be different. And I hear it's not the first time. It seems you are always leaning against authority and questioning orders.'

126

'I escaped an enemy camp and captured a standard,' said Prydain defensively.

'And caused the death of a comrade in the process,' shouted the Centurion, smacking his Vitis down hard on the table.

Prydain stared at the Centurion in shock.

'But, Sir,' he started.

'Shut up!' ordered the Centurion. 'I am talking.' He walked around the bunk room, hitting his Vitis into the palm of his hand.

'You are an opinionated, arrogant, individual who, despite all the training invested in you by our glorious Emperor, refuses to conform.' He stopped in front of Prydain, staring into his face. 'I don't know what to make of you Maecilius,' he said. 'Some say you are a hero; others say you are a liability. However, there is no mistaking what you did was quite extraordinary. You spotted the enemy before anyone else did, held your own in a swordfight with Hanzer, which is no mean feat in itself. Captured a standard, killed a man with your bare hands and brought your comrade back to the fort, even though you were wounded. You have the skills of an excellent soldier Maecilius, yet continue to be an individual. And therein lies the problem. Rome doesn't like individuals and the legion has no place for people like you.'

Prydain was dumbstruck.

'You are throwing me out?' he gasped in disbelief.

Scipio stopped and stared at Prydain for a while before continuing.

'That depends on you,' he said.

'I don't understand,' said Prydain

'I have a proposal for you, Maecilius,' he said. 'I am willing to take that streak of defiance and bend it into a form we can use. I command a unit that is made up of men like you. Outsiders, renegades, and insubordinates. But they are also excellent soldiers, and after undertaking training totally different to what you have experienced so far, become the spear point of the Roman army. Interested?'

'Yes, Sir,' said Prydain immediately.

'I thought you would be,' said the Centurion. 'Okay, this is the deal. Your training will start immediately. We don't take any shit, Maecilius, any nonsense and you're out. No second chances, understand?'

'Yes, Sir.'

'Good. Get your kit and come with me,' he said, holding out his hand, 'welcome to the scouts.'

Chapter 15

Two months had passed since the battle with Hanzer, and finally the day had come when the Ninth Hispana's battle training ended and they made their way to the coast to join up with the other legions. Cassus and his comrades were at the peak of fitness and their muscles were hardened from constant exercise. Their kit was packed, weapons sharpened, and every soldier was impatient for the invasion to begin. At last, after several false starts, they finally embarked and the enormous invasion fleet set sail for Britannia.

Cassus listened to the sound of the oars dipping into the gently swelling sea, strangely soothed by the groan of oak against iron. He sat shivering against the walls of the ship, and thanked the Gods that the crossing had been calm. It wasn't just the fact that on the one occasion he had actually been on a ship he had been impossibly sick that worried him, but the knowledge that, as every legionary knew, troop carrying wasn't the strongest skill of the Roman navy and the chances of ending up as fish food were very high in his eyes.

Back in their assembly camp, the sailors had taken great delight in stirring up the soldier's fears with tales of sea monsters, giant waves and how terrible was death by drowning. Fights often ensued when the wine flowed too freely around the Gallic docks, but the sailors gave as good as they got, as, though they were not legionaries, all had trained in the auxiliaries and were used to fighting in the many skirmishes still taking place on seas around the empire. Finally, however, the time had come and all four legions boarded the armada of ships lying at anchor in the port of Gesoriacum.

This was where the sailors came into their own. This was their world and they took command of the situation, instructing the nervous soldiers where to sit in order to balance the ships. The bravado of the famous legionaries diminished as they solemnly took their place in a situation where they had no control whatsoever. Some lost their breakfast as the time drew near and the nerves kicked in, whilst others prayed silently to their personal Gods for protection and courage.

The twelve Triremes brought from the Mare Nostrum, lined up close together in the darkness. The top deck of each triple layered ship had a ballista mounted in the bow, the giant crossbow that could fire their limestone projectiles hundreds of yards across sea or land. Each ship was manned by a team of marines that were permanently stationed on board and supported by twenty Sagittaria, the archers ready to suppress any initial resistance with a hail of iron tipped death.

A Century of fully armed Legionaries from the feared first Cohort, sat shoulder to shoulder in the lead ship, filling every available inch of the open deck ready to disembark at a moment's notice. Below them sat two levels of sweating, heavily muscled rowers. Paid freedmen and just as well trained in their own field as any infantryman and veterans of many conflicts. The lower deck, usually manned by a third layer of rowers had been cleared to allow the carriage of thirty cavalry and their mounts. These were the initial landing troops, tasked to secure the beach before the bulk of the invasion force.

Following the Triremes the troop ships came. Simpler in design with a single hold, and powered by only one bank of rowers, they were packed with the supporting Cohorts of the legion along with the auxiliaries.

Finally, the cargo ships came; a mix of whatever vessels had been sent by Rome or could be sequestered along the shores of Gaul, each filled to the brim with the essential supplies necessary for an expeditionary force of this size.

Even though the commanders were confident of self-sufficiency within days of landing, they still carried enough stores for weeks of unsupported campaign, by when; the huge stockpiles assembled back across the channel would have been brought over by the never-ending relay of cargo ships. The second and third waves would include the camp followers, bribing their way onto merchant ships to follow the soldiers across the sea, for wherever the legions went there was usually coin to be made.

General Aulus Plautius stood in the bow of the lead Trireme looking toward Britannia, the sound of the breaking waves the only indication they were near their objective. The strength of the opposition was unknown on the looming shore, and as the sun had yet to rise, no one could yet see any reception party waiting for them.

Plautius knew that the barbarians would not just roll over and submit. On the contrary, he fully expected a bloody confrontation and knew that Julius Caesar had twice been repelled from these shores. He would not make the same mistakes and had prepared as well as any man could for the expedition. He was confident in his force and had planned for any eventuality, but he was not a stupid man and other preparations had been made. Those preparations were about to come to fruition and he stood in the van of the huge Roman invasion fleet, confident, arrogant, but patient as he awaited the right time to commit his overwhelming force to the annals of history.

A mile away from Plautius on the shores of Britannia, a young boy wrapped himself tighter in his sheepskin wrap as his father added more wood to the fire. The weather was dry but very cold and he would be glad to get back to his family's hut. Their instructions were clear. The minute they saw any sign of any enemy ship, they were to light the bonfire they had prepared on the cliff edge. Many such bonfires were built all along the coastline and should there be an attack, a line of beacons would be lit and over ten thousand warriors could be anywhere along this stretch of Britannia within an hour. He yawned widely but the pleasure of the stretching muscles was interrupted as he saw something far out to sea. He stared again, sure that he had seen something. Suddenly it was there again, a flashing light where no such light should be.

'Father,' he said. 'Look.'

His father threw another few sticks on their campfire and stood up, his eyes taking a few moments to adjust to the darkness after the glow of the flames.

'What do you see?' he asked, and stared out at the inky blackness.

The young boy was not the only one to have seen the light and a legionary scout crawled through the damp grass in the darkness toward him. He wore no armour and his tunic was dyed black, but a Roman soldier nonetheless. He and his colleagues had lain hidden for days, deep in the centre of inaccessible thickets along the coast, eating only Buccellatum and sipping sparingly from their flasks.

The plan was simple. When the fleet was offshore, the signal would be given and the scouts would take out as many of the warning pyres as possible, ensuring that the invasion fleet was guaranteed a secretive landing. Now the long awaited signal had come and the fifty scouts who had landed far down the coastline in the depths of a rainstorm several nights ago, prepared to carry out their lethal orders.

The soldier crawled silently forward alongside his comrade until they were less than five metres away from their target. With his heart racing, he glanced toward the other scout and after receiving a coordinating nod, they both leapt up and raced to the two men alongside the fire. There was no fight, the surprise was absolute and father and son died together, their throats slit before they knew anything was wrong. A few yards away, two more warriors died in their sleep as Pugios were thrust into their wrapped bodies over and over again. For miles down the coastline, the scene was repeated and within minutes, all potential warning fires were thrown over the cliff edges and into the sea below. The mission had been successful and the Centurion in charge of the scouts sent his own signal to the fleet. The way was clear for the invasion to start.

Out at sea, General Plautius gave the order everyone had been waiting for. There was no fanfare, and no special speeches. The order was passed down to double the stroke and the oarsmen bent their backs into their task, all thoughts of subterfuge discarded as they increased the speed to force the ship far up the shingle beach.

Chapter 16

'Stand by!' called the ship's commander, and all the waiting legionaries got to their feet, holding their shields as high as their chins in case of enemy archers. 'Brace!' he shouted and despite gripping the sides, all the soldiers jolted forward as the front of the ship ground to a shuddering halt. 'Marines go!' he shouted and ten of the crew climbed over the side to drop into the surf, each carrying metal stakes and ropes to secure the ship to the beach.

'Shallow water, Sir!' called a voice in the darkness.

The commander nodded to Severus.

'Safe to go,' he said. 'Good luck!'

Severus's voice sounded calmly over the commotion as the oars were stowed by the rowers.

'Raven Century!' he called, referring to them by their own nickname. 'Disembark.'

The men in front of Cassus shuffled forward and climbed over the sides of the ship, lowering themselves by rope into the surf below. Cassus caught his breath as he landed up to his chest in the freezing water.

'Move it!' hissed Remus behind him and the soldiers waded onto the beach. Within a few minutes, the Century was together again and ran to the top of the hill to their front. The night was still relatively quiet despite the hundreds of wet men now racing to take their positions.

At the top of the hill, the front line dropped to their knees and crawled the last few feet to the ridgeline, keen not to present a profile to any unseen watchers on the other side. Centurion Severus and Optio Remus were the first to peer over the crest and into the lands of Britannia.

'See anything?' asked Severus.

'Nothing to worry us,' said Remus, 'though those fires must warm a thousand warriors.' They stared at the looming shape of a mountain in the distance, the base of which was dotted with the fires of an encamped force.

A sudden movement caught Severus's eye and his hand flew to the Pila lying at his side. A group of shadowy figures were approaching along the hilltop, crouching so not to be seen by unwelcome eyes. Suddenly they stopped, dropping to the ground and out of Severus's view.

133

Severus drew his Pugio, and using his shield as a drum, struck three times with the hilt, a full heartbeat between each strike. A second later, a similar sound came out of the darkness, a pre-arranged signal designed to identify friendly troops. Happy that the silhouettes were Roman, Severus called out to them.

'Watchword?' he whispered into the darkness.

'Thunder!' answered the hidden figure, using the name of General Plautius's favourite horse.

A figure crawled out of the darkness.

'Severus!' asked the shadowy figure, 'is that you?'

'Hail, Scipio,' said Severus, 'your mission was successful, I see.'

'Of course!' said the scout Centurion. 'Though you lot took your bloody time. What kept you?'

'We are here now,' said Severus, 'The fleet unloads behind me. What of the enemy?'

'A couple of thousand strong back in the forest,' said Scipio. 'Mainly foot soldiers and some cavalry but nothing worth worrying about. What's the plan?'

'First two Cohorts will advance before dawn,' said Severus. 'We will stand guard while the rest of the legion builds a defensive position. Are there any sentries between us and that river?'

'All guards in this valley have gone to meet their gods,' said Scipio. 'Their arrogance meant that they thought their precious island was easy to defend and that they were safe on top of their cliffs.'

'You've been busy,' said Severus. 'Do you need anything?'

'We could do with some hot food, but apart from that, we are fine.'

'Can you take us to the river edge before you stand down?' asked Severus.

'No problem,' answered Scipio. 'I'll send two men with you.'

He crawled back to his men with the instructions before leading the rest of the group through the friendly lines and down to the beachhead to get some hard-earned rest. The two nominated scouts beckoned Severus forward and word was passed back until well over a thousand heavily armed men followed Severus into the darkness.

Dawn saw two Cohorts of Roman soldiers lined up along the riverbank in a deep defensive formation. Behind them stood hundreds of archers and slingers, shivering in the cold morning mist. A mile behind them, thousands more were hard at work, building their defensive positions.

Severus and Remus stood at the front of their Century staring at the hill in the distance, fully expecting an enemy force to confront them at any time. To one side, the two scouts lay curled up at the base of a tree, fast asleep after their exhausting mission over the last few days.

Remus walked over, his red cloak clinging to his armour in the morning drizzle and stared down at the snoring figure. He frowned as he recognised one of them and he placed his boot on the soldier's shoulder, shoving it forcibly to wake him up. The scout sat up, instantly alert and ready to defend himself. The two stared at each other before Remus broke the silence.

'Hello, slave-boy,' he said, 'it seems our paths cross again.'

Prydain stared up at him in silence, his heart racing at the sight of the man who had left him to die on a field in Gaul. He stood up and adjusted his cape.

'Our fate is no longer linked, Optio,' said Prydain. 'You won, and I have moved on. You can take your bigotry elsewhere.'

'Shame,' said Remus, 'I was just beginning to enjoy myself.'

Prydain stooped to wake his sleeping comrade.

'Come on,' he said, 'let's get back to the unit.'

As they walked away, Remus called out.

'Our paths will cross again, slave-boy,' he shouted. 'I sense it in my bones!'

Prydain span around and reached for his Pugio, but before he could draw it from his scabbard, the point of Remus's Gladius was already at his throat.

'Careful, slave-boy,' he sneered, 'it can get very confusing in the dark when on campaign. I could easily mistake you for a barbarian in that black garb.'

His Gladius hooked under the thong around Prydain's neck and pulled it upwards, revealing the leather pendant he had seen on the first day of the recruit's training many months ago.'

'Still wearing mummy's bauble, I see. Perhaps you should go back to her.'

'She is dead,' snarled Prydain. 'Killed in the arena by bigots such as you.'

'Shame,' said Remus. 'Still, probably for the best I expect.'

Prydain lurched forward but was pulled away by his comrade. Deciding this was a fight he could not win, he turned and strode away over the damp grass, making his way back to the legion's lines. As he went, a memory came flooding back to Remus.

'By the gods,' he said to himself, 'it can't be.'

Chapter 17

On the other side of Britannia, Gwenno walked barefoot through the forest, enjoying the feel of the dew between her toes. The village was only just stirring but Gwenno had been awake for hours, and had watched the sunrise over the vast oak forest that covered the island. To the north, a smaller island dominated by a solitary hill shimmered in the haze. It was a holy place where the main clan of the Druids were based, not only as a spiritual separation from the other tribes, but also to control the flow of Gaelic gold from Ireland to be traded across Britannia, Gaul and beyond.

Willow had explained that though there was only a river separating the holy island from Mona, Druid warriors guarded it jealously, and only those who had undertaken a lifetime of learning and dedication were allowed to live in that special place.

As she walked, she became aware that she was entering a part of the woods she hadn't been to before, and though comfortable she could find her way back, hesitated for a moment as she looked down the well-trodden path in front of her. It was flanked by two rows of standing stones, each covered by strange designs and diagrams. Finally, she made a decision and continued down the track until it opened out into a clearing, cut into the in the depths of the forest.

She hesitated at the edge, staring in fascination at the sight before her. More standing stones surrounded a magnificent hut at the centre of the clearing. The building was far larger than the normal huts in the village, and it's daubed walls were covered with the now familiar Celtic imagery.

Gwenno realised it was probably a religious place and that she should could get into trouble for being there, so she was about to leave when the muffled sound of chanting floated across the clearing. The rhythm was not unlike the poems she had been learning with Lapwing and intrigued, she drew closer to the hut to see if she could hear any more.

The chanting became clearer, though she couldn't understand the words as they were in the ancient language she had heard the Druids use on occasion. She crept around the side of the hut, listening to the strange mantra in fascination, but stopped suddenly as she recognised one word. Her name!

It was too much of a coincidence and Gwenno sidled to the doorway to see if she could see anything. The heavy door was made of split logs braced horizontally with three similar boards, and though hinged with thick leather hinges, it dragged on the ground due to its age and weight. This was lucky for Gwenno, as the bottom of the door had gathered a small pile of soil between its closing edge and the frame, leaving a gap a hand's width wide between them. She placed her face against the gap and peered into the gloom.

At first, she couldn't see was happening, but soon made out the silhouettes of several hooded men forming a circle within the hut. She stared in fascination at the secretive ceremony unfolding before her.

The inside flickered with the light of burning torches, seemingly dancing to the rhythm of the chanting from the circle of men. At the centre of the circle, a stone table was the only fixture and was surrounded by a small moat formed by the stream running through the hut.

The chanting stopped and the room fell into silence. A gap appeared in the circle and two people approached the stone altar. One was a man dressed in a black cape and carrying an oaken staff, the other was obviously a masked young girl, dressed in a hooded blue cape. The girl approached the altar and turned to sit on the edge while the black gowned man recited some strange words, and after dipping his staff into the spring, anointed her head with water. The girl unfastened the ties about her neck and allowing the garment to fall back onto the stone, lay back with her legs still on the floor.

Gwenno stifled a gasp as she realised that apart from the eye mask, the young girl was now naked. The flickering of the surrounding lamps illuminated her pale flesh, and she lay back in submission for the violation that would surely follow. The man disrobed to stand naked before the girl and Gwenno stifled a gasp as she recognised Lapwing, her instructor, his aged white hair falling down the back of his ancient scrawny body.

Gwenno realised what was about to happen and despite her revulsion, her fascination compelled her to stay where she was and witness the sordid scene. The circle of men started to chant again, and as Lapwing approached, the girl lifted her legs to accommodate the violation. The old man paused until finally, the chanting reached a crescendo. This was the moment Lapwing was waiting for and he thrust himself into the recumbent girl shouting her name with a mixture of triumph, ceremony and lust.

Gwenno turned away and stood with her back to the outside wall of the hut, both confused and scared, wondering what that poor girl who shared her name had done to deserve such a fate. It was pointless running for help, for the very fact that Lapwing was a part of the ceremony suggested that the others were probably the other Druids of the village. She had no one to turn to for help and Gwenno wept quietly for the girl.

Finally, Gwenno wiped her eyes and thought about the whole situation. It was not just the name they shared; she also had a blue cape, almost exactly like the one the girl was wearing. She had burned the hem on the fire a few weeks ago and Willow had taken it away for mending. A thought slowly occurred to her, and she returned to the crack in the doorway to check her suspicions.

Once again, her eyes took a few seconds to accustom to the gloom, but eventually they made out the scene. The chanting had restarted, and she could see the scrawny profile of the old man, thrusting himself over and over again into the young girl's body.

Gwenno became even more confused by the girl's involvement in the sick ritual. Far from being upset or scared, she actually seemed to be enjoying the attention, her body moving in unison with the old man and her moans of pleasure audible above the chanting. Gwenno realised that far from being exploited, the girl was a willing and enthusiastic participant, playing a full role in the sordid union.

Gwenno realised that, as the girl was not being held against her will, it was pointless taking any more risks and was about to leave until the victim turned her head slightly in her direction. As their gaze met, the girl's horrified eyes widened in recognition and Gwenno's hand flew to her mouth to stop herself crying out. Despite the darkness of the hut, and the eye mask, the features were unmistakeable. It was Willow!

Gwenno turned away from the sight, gulping draughts of fresh morning air as the full realisation hit home. The chanting stopped and she heard Willow's raised voice arguing with Lapwing. Gwenno ran back into the woods, trying to make sense of everything. The sordid sex, the chanting, the old men, it all could have been just a sick sex ceremony, but it was the final detail that sickened her the most.

Willow had become a close friend, one that she trusted more than anyone in this strange place, but not only was Willow taking a willing part in this sick ritual, she had also stolen Gwenno's cape and was pretending to be her.

Gwenno ran as fast as she could back to the village, sobbing as she went, and bursting through the door of the hut before throwing her few possessions into her woven bag. Willow followed her in, stopping just inside the doorway.

'Oh, Miss,' she cried 'I am so sorry, you weren't supposed to see that.'

'Get away from me!' screamed Gwenno, 'You, you... whore!'

'You don't understand,' cried Willow.

'I understand what I saw and it was revolting. Now get out of my sight while I pack.'

'What do you mean pack? Where do you think you are going?'

'Anywhere away from you,' cried Gwenno. 'I thought we were friends.'

'But I am your friend.'

'You are nothing to me,' said Gwenno. 'Now get out.'

'I am not a whore!' said Willow quietly.

'Not a whore?' laughed Gwenno, wiping tears from her eyes. 'Don't lie to me, Willow, I saw everything. You even wore my clothes to look like me!'

'But you don't understand...' started Willow before she was interrupted.

'I don't want to understand,' shouted Gwenno. 'I've had enough of this place. You go back to your boyfriends if you want to, I am going home.'

'But I did it for you!' screamed Willow.

Gwenno stopped and stared at her in disbelief.

'For me?' she said. 'Don't try to blame me for your lust. You were enjoying yourself at the hands of that old man.'

'Miss, please, just let me explain,' cried Willow, the tears running freely down her face. 'They do what they do to me so you can remain pure.'

'What?' gasped Gwenno.

'You are the chosen one, Miss,' continued Willow wiping her eyes, 'and you have to stay pure, but men are weak and the Druids are but men.'

'What are you saying, Willow?' asked Gwenno.

'You are very beautiful, Miss,' said Willow, 'and every man lusts after you, but your virginity is sacred. That is why I am here. My role is to become your shadow, to absorb your aura, so during the ceremonies and rituals, I can become you and satisfy the lusts of mere mortals. By doing so, I keep you safe and pure.'

'I don't believe you!' stuttered Gwenno.

'But it is true. Ever since you came here that has been my role, to look after you in every way possible, even this one!'

'But you were enjoying it!' gasped Gwenno. 'If what you say is true why did you take pleasure in what those men were doing to you?'

Willow's head looked down in shame.

'I cannot control the way my body reacts, miss. It is true the feelings take control of me, but I am a mere woman. I do not seek their company, but when I am summoned I have no option. I am owned by the Druids and pander to their whims. This is my role and such is my fate.'

'Are you lying to me, Willow? Because if you are...'

'I am telling the truth,' interrupted the young girl quietly, wiping her eyes with part of the cape.

'Oh, Willow, I didn't realise...'

'Why would you? I did not intend to tell you and if you hadn't have come to the clearing, then you would never have known.'

'But why?' asked Gwenno, throwing her bag down in frustration. 'Why is it so important that I stay pure? In fact, what's to stop me going out there right now and dragging the first man I see into my bed? I'm fed up of this so called purity, it's caused me nothing but heartache and I've got a good mind to do just that and end this nonsense.'

'You can't,' said Willow quietly.

'Why not?' snapped Gwenno. 'Was it not you who said I was beautiful and all men are weak? What man would say no?'

'All of them!'

'Why?'

'Because only the pure can speak to the Gods,' said Willow, her head held down.

A silence fell between them as the information sunk in.

'What do you mean speak to the Gods?' asked Gwenno. 'No one can speak to the Gods, they are in the otherworld.'

The young girl continued to stare downward in silence.

'Willow,' said Gwenno in frustration, stepping forward to shake the girls shoulder, 'what do you know, tell me?'

'Oh, Miss I am so sorry,' sobbed Willow looking up, 'I know I should have told you, but I have been warned on pain of death to keep my silence.'

'About what, Willow?' asked Gwenno.

'About your true fate,' wept Willow, her shoulders shuddering in uncontrollable emotion.

Chapter 18

Since leaving the hospital, Prydain had undergone intensive training. The scouts were primarily a mounted unit and tasked with finding out the lay of the land in front of a legion's advance. They were responsible for gathering information about enemy locations, strengths and tactics and were experts in subterfuge, survival and horsemanship. They were also expected to be skilled in the art of murder.

Most of the scouts were accomplished hunters or horsemen back home, and although they had been taught soldiering in the ranks of the legions, had either requested the move or had been recruited after some particular skill had been noticed by those in charge. They kept their distance from the rest of the legion and undertook their special training in secrecy and isolation.

This mission had been different and had been a chance to have a huge impact on the historic invasion. Prydain and fifty other scouts had crossed the channel under the cover of darkness and spread out all along the Britannic coast on a rainy moonless night. They carried only hand weapons, biscuit rations and waterproof cloaks, and as soon as they landed, had disappeared into the undergrowth of the island. It was a tactical masterstroke by Plautius and the success of their mission meant that three legions landed unopposed on the shores of Britannia. By the time the defending tribes became aware of the threat, it was too late, and tens of thousands of heavily armed men already had a foothold in three different locations, safe behind rapidly expanding defensive stockades. Having established a safe beachhead, the Ninth Hispana reinforced the position and cleared the ground for miles around, dealing with minor skirmishes from stubborn locals. As soon as the ground had been secured, the Fourteenth Germina landed and marched through the Hispana's position to establish a fortress ten miles inland, securing any crops or stock animals on the way.

Smaller fortresses were quickly established up and down the coast, protecting their flanks, linking up with the two other legions that had landed on the same momentous night. At last, the order had come to move inland and the invasion force marched into unknown territory. Tens of thousands of heavily armed Legionaries, in full battle dress, led Cohorts of lighter armed auxiliaries through the broad leaved forests, forming several columns, each over ten miles long.

Engineers travelled with their cart mounted Ballistae, ready to be called forward should they encounter any serious resistance and every Century carried a Scorpio, a smaller but still powerful form of the crossbow that could be operated by one man to propel up to four darts a minute with extreme accuracy over a hundred paces.

Hundreds of mules carried the legion's stores ranging from tents and heavy cooking equipment to spare weapons and food. Heavy carts drawn by teams of oxen carried sacks of grain and dried beef in case local supplies were scarce, along with hundreds of amphorae of wine, the essential ingredient of a happy legion. Cavalry protected the Roman's flanks against ambush and also brought up the rear, enabling a quick reaction force to respond to any threat at a moment's notice.

Behind the columns came the camp followers, the traders and prostitutes who made their money from the purses of homesick legionaries. All eager to see to the every whim of any man willing to part with his hard earned coin for a reminder of their homeland, no matter how fleeting.

Twenty miles in front of the legion, Prydain and three of his comrades lay amongst the bracken, hidden from the prying eyes of the enemy in the distance. Their horses were a mile back in the woods, being looked after by the rest of the patrol. They had come upon two isolated riders on the trail, and though at first they had been reluctant to talk, the patrol's interpreter had explained in grisly detail what fate awaited them if they didn't. The resulting information was exactly the sort of thing they needed to know and while four of the patrol took the enemy riders back to the legion to see out the rest of their lives in slavery, the others moved deeper into the forest, and crawled forward to witness the scene below.

The valley to their front was covered with conical tents and crawling with activity. Women tended cooking fires, children played in the dirt and horses were being exercised in mock charges between groups of warriors. Hundreds more were busy seeing to their own tasks for the day, whether it was sharpening their weapons or testing their strength against their comrades by trials of arms.

This was the first substantial enemy encampment the scouts had encountered, and though it was obviously prepared for war, Prydain was surprised to see there were no fortifications defending them. A foolish omission in his eyes.

Centurion Scipio took in the scene with experienced eyes, mentally mapping out the strengths and weaknesses of the position. He quickly realised there was no point in attacking the barbarians in the valley, as there was little room for the legion to manoeuvre into positions of strength. His attention lingered on the lines of chariots for a long time before accepting they were too well defended for any pre-emptive strike. Each of the four scouts memorised as much of the information as they could before crawling back from the edge, and making their way back to the horses and galloping back to the legion.

A few hours later, Plautius stood in his command tent listening carefully to Scipio's report. When he was finished, he dismissed the Centurion before sitting back on his seat and signalled for a servant to pour more wine for the three other commanders present.

'This is irritating news,' said Plautius. 'It would seem that this group isn't the main army, but a sub group that we could well do without.'

'Ignore it!' said Vespasian, commander of the Second Augusta. 'Pass them by and continue to Camulodunum, we can deal with them later.'

'I'm not so sure,' said Plautius. 'We don't want them to suddenly appear at our rear during the midst of battle.' He turned to Nasica.

'Nasica, take the Hispana and sort out this irritation. When you have finished, continue west. Take as many prisoners as possible and find out the locations of their mines and the source of their gold.' He looked over at the casket of bracelets and Torcs already looted from the many villages engulfed so far on the march. 'It would seem that they have a never ending supply and the majority of it comes from the west. When we have taken Camulodunum, I will send for you.'

'Yes, General,' said Nasica.

'The rest of us will find this Caratacus they speak of and send him in chains back to Rome. Tomorrow we will make our plans, but tonight, we will relax and toast Nasica, for it would seem his legion is to be the first into battle on Britannia.' He raised his silver goblet high. 'Nasica,' he said, 'may you wade through streams of Celtic blood.'

'Nasica!' laughed the other officers and drank to the coming campaign.

Nasica didn't stay late in Plautius's tent but he could hear the sound of revelry for a long time as he rode back toward his own legion's lines. As he approached, a voice called out in the darkness, halting the mounted party. Nasica could see dozens of helmets peering over the staked ramparts of the temporary camp.

'Draw close!' came the command and one of the guards rode up to the gate so he could be recognized in the burning torchlight and say the watchword without being overheard. The guards opened the gate and allowed the party in, saluting as the Legatus passed, secretly relieved that they had carried out their drills impeccably. Any slacking on duty incurred strict punishment ranging from loss of pay to decimation for the more serious offences. As he passed the guard commander, Nasica stopped and called out to him from his horse.

'Tessarius,' he called, 'find Centurion Scipio and bring him to my tent.'

'Yes, Sir!' answered the soldier and ran into the darkness.

Nasica continued between the perfectly aligned rows of tents, passing the pyramids of Pilae that were stacked outside each entrance flap. His legion was at full strength and was as ready as they could be. As he rode, he listened to the underlying sound of the sleeping camp. Sounds of snoring from within the tents, and the gentle murmur of those who could not sleep as they sat around campfires mixed with the distant restlessness of the horses in their pens. He reached his tent and stripped his armour before donning a warm cape over his tunic. A few moments later, Scipio entered, wrapped in his own cape, his eyes still red from being awakened.

'Hail, Nasica,' said Scipio.

'Come in,' said the Legatus, 'make yourself comfortable.'

Scipio sat at the central table and waited patiently as Nasica poured him a glass of warm wine.

'Right, Centurion,' he said passing him the tankard, 'about this enemy force, I want you to tell me everything about what you saw. Start from the beginning and leave nothing out.'

By the time they were finished, the sun was halfway over the horizon and the camp was coming to life. Scipio returned to the scouts and Nasica finalized his strategy. The order was given to strike camp and the Ninth Hispana marched westward into the unknown. Behind them, the ditch had been filled in and what was left of the temporary camp burned in the morning light, the black smoke reaching high into the clear sky. Marching legions left nothing behind that could be used by the enemy.

Chapter 19

'What do you mean landed?' shouted Caratacus. 'I gave orders that I was to be informed as soon as they were sighted.'

'They killed the lookouts, Sire,' said Bragus, the clan leader who had brought the bad news. 'By the time we knew any different, their ships had landed thousands of troops along the coast and in the lagoon of Thanet.'

'And why did you not strike?' shouted Caratacus. 'You have the men and the chariots; you should have attacked before they had time to reorganise.'

'By the time we realised what had happened,' answered Bragus, 'they had built a palisade across the valley and dominated the high ground with archers and cavalry.'

'A palisade, how can they build a defence in less than a day?' asked Caratacus. 'It is not possible.'

'They brought ships loaded with prepared timbers, lord.' said the captain. 'An army of men dug a trench and pre-made walls were dropped into the holes. I have never seen such organisation. I watched from a nearby hill and the wall was twice the size of a man right by the time night fell.'

'I care not about wooden walls,' snarled Caratacus, 'wooden walls burn as easily as men bleed. We have not assembled all these clans to sit back and let the Romans walk into our lands without as much as an arrow in return.'

'What would you have me do, lord?' asked Bragus.

'I'll tell you what I would have you do,' said Caratacus. 'First of all; you will have all the families of the watchers who failed me at the signal fires killed. Throw them from the very cliffs their men failed to defend. Wipe their seed from the face of the earth.' He turned to his brother. 'Togodumnus, you will call the clans to gather at the Medway, I will coordinate our defence there. As for you, Bragus,' he said turning to the warrior, 'I trusted you with defending this island. You have failed me.'

Bragus drew his long sword and presented it hilt first to his King before dropping to one knee.

'My shame burns like fire, lord,' he said, 'my head is yours.' He removed his helmet and bent his head to expose his neck, inviting the strike that would end his shame.

Caratacus stared down at the warrior for a long time. He had been a faithful follower and a feared warrior, but he had been in charge of the defences and Caratacus could not allow him to get away with failure. He placed the tip of Bragus's sword beneath the warrior's chin and lifted his head up to meet his gaze.

'You will have the chance to rectify your failure, Bragus,' he said. 'You will take your chariots and your people and slow up the Roman's advance. Gain us some time to gather our army at the Medway.'

Bragus got to his feet; grateful for the chance he had been given.

'How long do you need, lord?' he asked.

Caratacus stared at Bragus for a few moments.

'The Druids will write your clan's name in the standing stones of Afallon,' he said eventually and with a nod, dismissed the warrior without another word.

Bragus exited the tent and paused in the open air, looking up at the stars as the devastating implications sank in. Only the names of Kings, or clans long dead to the memory of the tribe were immortalised by Druidic inscriptions. He had expected to lose his own life, but Caratacus's adjudication was catastrophic to his people. The condemnation of his clan's name to the Afallon stones meant that the King had written them off and expected every man, woman, and child of his clan to confront the Romans, fighting with everything at their disposal. A collective suicidal mission from which there would be no return.

It took the rest of the night for Bragus to ride back to his village, and dismounting at the outskirts, he walked amongst the huts on the wooded slopes of the river valley, taking in the familiar evening sounds of those he knew so well. As he led his horse back to his family's hut, he received greeting after greeting from familiar faces. He felt alien pangs of emotion, as he realised the respect in the eyes of those who trusted him would soon be replaced with accusation and disappointment when they found out his failure had condemned them to die at the end of a Roman blade.

Bragus's loyalty knew no limits and the thought of not carrying out Caratacus's orders didn't cross his mind. It was his fate to die in the service of his King and he accepted that it was the duty of every tribe to protect their homeland to the death, but for the first time in his life, he doubted the King's instructions. As a young man, he would not have thought twice about leading the whole tribe into the jaws of death, but since his wife had died in childbirth five years ago, leaving him two beautiful children, the burden of fatherhood had softened his heart and opened his eyes. He looked up at the skies as if seeking guidance from his dead wife's spirit, his face screwing up as he remembered all the heart wrenching pain that she endured to deliver the babies, knowing full well that she would not survive to see them grow up.

'Was it all in vain?' he whispered in anguish, remembering Mira's weak smile, the pain of her ravaged body forgotten as she held the babies for the first and last time. 'Did the Gods really want you to suffer so much to produce two beautiful children, just to take them away again so soon?' He lifted his hands to cover his face, remembering the last conversation he had had with the woman who had given her life to bear him both a son and daughter.

'Look after them,' she had said weakly as her life ebbed, and as she had died, he had made a solemn promise.

'I will, Mira,' he had vowed through his tears. 'By the Gods, I promise I will!'

With a heavy heart, he continued to his hut to arrange for his tribe to face the might of the Roman army, unaware that even as he walked, the time and place of the conflict had already been taken out of his hands by the men from across the seas.

149

Chapter 20

Gwydion sat on his horse near to the King's tent. They had received instruction to be ready to ride at dawn and head west to the Medway River. Caratacus was livid that the choice of battlefield had been denied to him, due to the surprise landings, but had hastily reorganized his forces to best use his strengths. He needed wide-open space to deploy his chariots and needed to take his army beyond both the river Medway, and the river Tamesas if he was to have any chance against the enemy cavalry. Subsequently, over sixty thousand warriors made their way westward toward the ford across the Medway with orders to reform on the far side.

Caratacus emerged from his tent and mounted his own horse alongside Idwal and Togodumnus. Gwydion and the rest of the King's bodyguard followed close behind as the whole entourage headed north. Togodumnus rode just behind the two Kings, but soon dropped back amongst the following men, much happier to be amongst warriors rather than politicians. He manoeuvred his horse until he rode alongside Gwydion.

'Well,' said Togodumnus, 'it seems that you will have to wait a while longer for your first full scale battle.'

'We are patient, Sire,' said Gwydion. 'Our weapons will be as good tomorrow as they are today.'

'Ah yes, your weapons,' he said. 'As I recall, I lost one of my best warriors over a squabble over some bow. Enlighten me why it was worth the life of a good man.'

'He brought on his own death, Sire; the bow was but an excuse.'

'That may be so, but humour me. What is so special about this weapon you carry?'

'It is a gift from my father, Sire,' said Gwydion, 'and has been in my family for countless generations.'

'I understand it is a heathen bow,' said Togodumnus.

'It is in the Parthenian style, Sire, but was made locally by ancient artisans.'

'Ancient artisans?'

'Yes, Sire, it is said that this bow will change the course of history.'

'Can I see it?'

Gwydion considered for a moment before withdrawing the unstrung bow from its leather pouch hanging alongside his leg. Togodumnus examined the weapon with interest.

'It is a beautiful piece of workmanship, admittedly,' he said, 'but I have seen others as good. Tell me, Deceangli,' he said, 'what is to stop me from taking this bow from you right now?'

Gwydion stared at the King's brother in concern.

'I can't let you do that, Sire,' he said.

'And how would you stop me? You have ten men, I have sixty thousand. The odds are a little uneven, wouldn't you say?'

'You would have to kill both me and my men, Sire,' said Gwydion. 'To kill the Deceangli King's bodyguard would be seen as a great insult to our tribe and the last thing you want is a war with the Deceangli and the Romans on two different fronts.'

Togodumnus laughed.

'Fret not, Deceangli,' he said, 'you can keep your bow. I will stick to my broadsword.'

He gave the weapon back and rode forward to re-join his brother.

That evening Gwydion and his comrades camped under a clear sky, eating the last of their food, but were interrupted when Idwal approached. He joined them at the fire, refusing a share of their meagre meal.

'Worrying times, Sire?' ventured Gwydion.

'They are,' said the King.

'Do you think Caratacus can turn this around?'

'I don't know,' said Idwal. 'These Romans are better than I expected. Our people need to be put on a war footing in case he fails. That is why I am here. I need to return to the Cerrig to call our tribe to arms.'

'I agree,' said Gwydion. 'Our worth here is limited, we need to worry about our own people.'

'You are not coming, Gwydion,' interrupted Idwal. 'I want you to stay here and watch what unfolds.'

'Stay here, Sire?' said Gwydion. 'Surely my sword would be better off defending our own lands.'

'It is just as important that we get information,' countered Idwal. 'You speak both the Catuvellauni tongue and that of the Romans, so you are the best person for the job. You and your men will stay with Caratacus as long as possible, the rest of us leave immediately.'

'But, Sire…' started Gwydion.

'But nothing,' answered Idwal. 'Avoid getting drawn in to the battle, but wait as long as possible before returning to the Khymru.' He stood up to leave. 'Make no mistake, Gwydion, this is a very important task, I will await your report in the Cerrig.'

'Yes, Sire,' said Gwydion and watched Idwal disappear into the darkness.

Gwydion and his men travelled with the retreating army for two days until they reached the Medway and waited patiently for the tidal river to reduce in level until their turn came to cross the ford. Over the next few days, the land between the rivers became crowded with the throng of the Catuvellauni and their families. Every day, thousands of warriors waited for orders as news filtered through about the rear-guard action being fought by Caratacus's cavalry until eventually, the monotony was broken when a rider rode into Gwydion's camp.

'Who is the one known as Gwydion?' asked the warrior.

'I am.'

'It is said you speak the Roman tongue.'

'I do.'

'Then come with me, your services are required.'

Gwydion followed him through the encampment and was ushered into the King's tent, quickly taking in the smoky scene before him. Several bloodied warriors were scattered around the interior, tending their wounds and Caratacus himself was sat in the corner, being bandaged by a female slave. In the centre of the tent, Togodumnus paced the floor like a rabid dog.

Everyone looked stressed, but in the centre was the reason Gwydion had been summoned. A figure lay in a foetal position on the floor, his hands bound so tightly that his wrists bled and his hair was matted where a club had knocked him from his horse when he had been taken prisoner.

'At last!' said Togodumnus and turning to one of his warriors, indicated the man on the floor. 'Pick him up.'

The warrior grabbed the captive's hair and pulled him onto his knees, his head yanked backward until he faced Togodumnus, his face caked with dried blood. Gwydion was summoned forward by the King's brother.

'Right, Deceangli,' he said, 'time to earn your rations. Tell this shit who I am and that his life is about to get a whole lot worse.'

Gwydion stared at Togodumnus for a few seconds before turning to the miserable wreck of a man and translated his words into broken Latin. The man looked at him in abject misery, though didn't answer.

'Ask him how many men the Romans have,' continued Togodumnus.

Again, Gwydion translated and again there was no answer.

'Why doesn't he answer?' screamed Togodumnus, 'he's Roman, isn't he?'

'I know you understand me,' said Gwydion. 'If you do, just nod your head, or the pain you now suffer will increase tenfold.'

The captive nodded slowly.

'Good!' said Togodumnus, recognizing the gesture. 'Ask him about their strengths and their plans. I need to know what they intend.'

Gwydion relayed the questions and after a few seconds, the man mumbled something through his smashed teeth. Gwydion bent to hear better before reporting back to Togodumnus.

'He says he is not Roman, Sire, he is a Syrian archer who has no knowledge of the plans of the Roman Generals.'

'Horseshit,' exclaimed Togodumnus. 'Archer or not, he must know something, ask him again.'

Gwydion did so and again relayed the answer.

'He says all he knows is that the army is enormous and no one can stop the might of the Romans.'

'Stand him up!' said Togodumnus and two warriors dragged the man to his feet. He stood directly in front of the captive and stared into his face.

'Tell him this!' he said. 'And make sure you repeat exactly what I say. You are already a dead man. All that you have left is the manner of dying. If you tell me what you know, the death will be quick and your head will hang on a chieftain's saddle, a sign to your Gods that you were a worthy opponent. If you don't talk, you will die slowly and your flesh fed to the pigs of the forest. Make your choice!'

The man's head sagged a little as if he was deep in thought before he looked up again at Togodumnus and answered through his shattered mouth.

'Unlike your barbarian Gods, mine will greet me whatever my fate,' he said. 'Death is death and pain is fleeting. Do your worst barbarian, you have your answer.'

Silence fell as Gwydion translated and everyone looked toward Togodumnus waiting for the explosion of rage that would surely follow.

'Burn him,' he said, and the two warriors dragged him out of the tent into the darkness.

Outside, the archer was stripped naked and tied spread eagled to a wooden frame. A rope was thrown over an overhanging limb and the frame was hoisted upright in front of a low fire, tilting forward until the smell of singing body hair told them he was close enough. They secured the rope in position, watching the man bake slowly above the fire.

It was only a few minutes before they heard his first cry of pain in the King's tent, though it seemed to Gwydion that he was the only one to find the sound disturbing. He had seen many men die and this was just another enemy, but the manner of death was repugnant to him. The man's cries turned to screams as his flesh roasted, begging his God's for death and release from his torment. Gwydion's discomfort was suddenly interrupted, when another of Caratacus's warriors ran into the tent in obvious panic and looking around the interior for the King.

'What is it?' asked Caratacus standing up quickly.

'The Romans, Sire,' he cried between gasps of breath, 'they are here!'

'Here, what do you mean here?' he said. 'They are miles away.'

'No, Sire, their advance units have reached the far banks of the river. Our warriors are fighting them as we speak.'

'How many?'

'About five hundred, Sire, the Romans are trying to take the bridge.'

'They cannot take the bridge,' said Togodumnus. 'Our forces are disorganized, we will stand no chance. We must send more warriors across.'

'No!' said Caratacus. 'They will be concentrated in too small an area.' He paused for a few seconds before adding 'burn the bridge!'

'Sire, we still have men on the other side,' said the messenger.

'It's too late for them,' said Caratacus. 'They will buy us some valuable time. Fire the bridge and cut the lines, they must not take the crossing. The rest of you, mobilize your clans along the bank. Togodumnus, get me spear throwers in case they take the bridge. We have to hold them while the rest of our people cross the Tamesas.'

Gwydion turned to leave the command tent, but paused as he heard the next sentence from the King's brother.

'Let's hope your people are better at being sacrificed than you are at intelligence gathering.'

Gwydion turned.

'Sorry, Sire,' he said, 'I don't understand.'

Togodumnus ignored him, but the ever-present Druid stationed just inside the tent flaps explained.

'Caratacus's armies will be aided by the strength of the God's in just under three weeks' time,' he said. 'At the celebration of the solstice, the elders will make a sacrifice.'

'What type of sacrifice?' asked Gwydion, already dreading the answer.

'The most powerful,' said the Druid. 'And your tribe have the honour of supplying the chosen one.'

'I thought the chosen one had to be taught the ways of the Gods,' said Gwydion. 'The solstice is in fifteen days, surely this is too short a time for the instruction to be given.'

'We already have someone,' said the Druid. 'She was given freely by the Blaidd many months ago, a pure girl with extraordinary golden hair as I understand. The Gods can't fail to be impressed.'

'Be gone!' shouted Togodumnus and Gwydion fell through the entrance to the tent, his mind racing as he struggled with the implications. He stood outside the tent for several minutes, watching the chaotic scenes as men ran everywhere, organizing their arms and defences. In amongst the mayhem, Gwydion again heard the pitiful cries of the dying Syrian as his charred skin peeled from his flesh. Everyone was preoccupied with preparing for the forthcoming battle and the area quickly cleared of warriors leaving only Gwydion and the dying archer. The victim turned his charred and sightless face toward Gwydion.

'Please,' he begged in broken Latin, 'help me!'

Gwydion looked around the clearing and realizing they were alone, approached the dying captive. He was the enemy and deserved to die, but he was also a warrior who had only been doing his duty.

There was no honour here and no man warranted such a fate. He withdrew his sword and placed the tip under the rib cage of the tormented man. The Syrian felt the point of the blade against his flesh and realised relief was at hand.

'Do it!' he said through blistered lips and Gwydion thrust his sword upwards into the Syrian's heart.

The archer's head flung back and his mouth fell open as the pain ripped through his body and as he died, Gwydion cut the rope with a swipe of his blade, releasing the body to fall into the flames. He looked around and wiped his blade on the wall of the tent before running off to find his own men.

Gwydion raced through the woods to the camp, his hands fending the branches away from his face as he took a shortcut through the thicket and burst into the clearing where his troops were bivouacked. All around, women and children were making their way northwards to the Tamesas, eager to reach the ferries and bridges that would carry them to the safety of the other side and the road to Camulodunum. Warriors raced in the opposite direction, toward the banks of the Medway to face the Roman army.

Gwydion's followers span around at the noise, their hands reaching for their swords, their instincts sharpened by the sudden downturn in events.

'Gwydion,' shouted Cody, 'where have you been?'

'No time for that,' answered Gwydion brushing past him. 'Gather your things, we are getting out of here.'

'What?' asked Cody incredulously, 'surely we are needed here?'

Gwydion started to saddle his horse.

'We were sent here to help Caratacus throw the invaders back into the sea,' he said. 'So far, the Romans have landed tens of thousands of heavily armed soldiers, built a string of fortresses along the coast and we haven't fired an arrow in anger. Even as we speak, they are in the process of slaughtering Catuvellauni on the other side of the river while Caratacus's chariots lie idle.'

'But Caratacus's army outnumber the Romans tenfold. The invaders stand no chance.'

Gwydion grabbed Cody by the tunic and dragged him close.

'You listen to me, Cody,' he said. 'When I was in Caratacus's tent, I heard the reports from his clan leaders. Thousands of Romans are marching toward Camulodunum. They have hundreds of cavalry, thousands of heavily armoured men and machines that throw fire across the sky. They have wiped out dozens of villages on the way here, receiving only a handful of casualties in return. When there were no more men to kill, they turned on the women and the children, slaughtering everyone they could ride down. No-one was spared, do you hear me, no one!'

'That may be so,' said Cody pulling himself free from Gwydion's grasp, 'but if everyone runs, then the Romans will walk unopposed to Camulodunum.'

'We are but ten men, Cody,' said Gwydion. 'We will make no difference to the outcome of this fight. I cannot make you leave, but you have your own families back in the hills to defend and when the Romans turn their face to the Khymru, you should be there to defend your own kin. There is no honour in a futile death here. If your blood must spill, then let it enrich the soil of our youth, not Catuvellauni soil'

'You speak like you are not coming with us,' said Cody.

'I am also leaving,' said Gwydion turning his attention back to the securing of his saddle, 'but not back to the Blaidd, I ride to Mona.'

'Why Mona?'

'I believe Gwenno is to be offered in sacrifice by the Druids. I will not let that happen.'

The men fell silent. Gwydion's love for Gwenno was common knowledge and they all had a soft spot for the girl.

'When?' asked Cody.

'Solstice,' said Gwydion simply and ducked into his tent to retrieve his few possessions. When he emerged, the whole group were waiting for him.

'We can't let you do this,' said Cody. 'Even if you are successful, what will you do? They won't let you settle down anywhere, you will be branded a coward and an outlaw. The Druids will send word around Britannia and you will be hunted down like an animal. There will be nowhere you can hide.'

'I'll worry about that when it happens,' said Gwydion, tying the final knots on the fastenings securing his equipment to his fidgeting horse. ' I will not stand by and let Gwenno be sacrificed to avoid that which cannot be avoided.' He vaulted onto his horse. 'I am leaving.' he said. 'My fate is written. Stay and fight, or leave and defend your families, the choice is yours, now get out of my way!'

'Wait!' said Cody. 'A few more minutes will not make any difference.'

The group walked a little distance from the mounted Gwydion and talked rapidly discussing the options, eventually coming back into the fire-lit clearing.

'We are split, Gwydion,' said Cody, 'so every man will follow his own heart. Some swords ache to taste Roman blood and will fight alongside the Catuvellauni. The family men will return to the Blaidd and will defend their clans. I have no ties back home and have no wish to die defending Catuvellauni lands, so I will ride with you and meet my fate alongside yours.'

'I cannot ask you to do that,' said Gwydion, 'the cause is mine and mine alone.'

'You forget that I also grew up alongside Gwenno,' said Cody. 'She deserves a better fate than the axe-man's blade.'

Gwydion stared at the man who was willing to live the life of an outlaw and suffer a probable early death to help him in his quest.

'My mind is set,' said Cody. 'I ride with you!'

'Thank you,' said Gwydion, simply.

'Didn't have a choice,' said Cody. 'You wouldn't cope without me to hold your hand, now get lost; I have a horse to load.'

Chapter 21

Willow sat on the edge of the bed, wiping her eyes between sentences as she explained what she knew about Gwenno's fate.

'All the poems and stories you have been learning,' she said, 'they are all messages to the Gods. Usually they are chanted at the gatherings of the Druids, but sometimes they are taken in person by the chosen ones.'

'How, Willow?' asked Gwenno earnestly, 'how can someone speak to the Gods when they live in the otherworld?'

'It is possible, Miss,' she said, 'but only those who have remained pure can enter the gates of Afallon.'

Gwenno wracked her mind. Although women in the clan had little to do with spiritual matters, she had overheard the name Afallon mentioned occasionally back in the Blaidd, when the warriors were drunk around the fires.

'But isn't Afallon just a small island of the coast to the west?'

'All I know, Miss, is that all the messengers are taken there by the Druids after they have gone through the Henge. There lies their new kingdom, the lands that are your birth right as the chosen one. You will take your rightful place alongside those who have travelled before.'

'But that cannot be,' said Gwenno. 'The island is too small, much smaller than even this one. How can so many people be given lands? There will not be enough to go around.'

'You must be wrong, Miss; many have travelled the path before you.'

Gwenno's mind was racing. None of this added up and the more she heard, the more worried she became.

'This Henge, you told me about,' she said, 'tell me again what happens there.'

'Well, Miss; there is a great ceremony where the Druids pay tribute to the chosen one. You will wear the cape and travel through the stone gateway before you are taken to Afallon.'

'And you have seen this?'

'Like I said before, Miss, my cousin...'

'What exactly did your cousin say, Willow?' she asked, interrupting the girl. 'Think back, and try to remember everything he said.'

'Just what I said, Miss,' stuttered Willow, 'about the Druids, and the cape and the stone gate, that's all I know, really.'

'Okay,' said Gwenno standing up and pacing back and fore. 'About this Henge, do you know where it is?'

'No, miss.'

'You have not taken any other acolytes there before?'

'No, Miss, you will be my first.'

'Did your cousin describe where this place is?'

'No, Miss, though he said the ceremony looks over the water toward Afallon.'

'It must be on the west coast.' She said before taking Willow's hands in hers. 'Willow, we have to go there.'

'But we can't,' said Willow, 'they will capture us and we will be punished.'

'They won't know,' said Gwenno. 'We can sneak away tonight and be long gone before we are missed.'

'The guards will see us,' said Willow.

'There are no guards,' said Gwenno. 'They have been removed.'

'The Druids know you saw the ceremony, Miss, and have instructed that you are guarded once more.'

Gwenno ran to the door and peered through the gaps between the planks. Sure enough, an armed guard stood across the clearing watching Gwenno's hut. She returned to the bed and sat next to Willow.

'So I am no better than a captive,' she said.

'I don't think it is like that, Miss,' said Willow. 'It's for your own protection.'

Gwenno turned to Willow slowly, and suddenly everything made sense.

'Protection has nothing to do with it,' she said. 'Afallon is a small island and there is little room for the smallest of clans, let alone lands of beasts and forests. The Druids are not being truthful with you, Willow, there is no way the chosen ones live on Afallon. It is just not possible.'

'But it is common knowledge, Miss, and even Lapwing has told me it is so.'

'Oh, I have no doubt the chosen ones are taken there,' said Gwenno, with tears welling up in her eyes, 'but not to live in peace amongst lands of plenty, but to lie amongst the ancestors as an offering

160

to the Gods. Oh, Willow,' she said bursting into tears,' I think I am going to be sacrificed!'

Chapter 22

Prydain stood alongside his horse waiting for Centurion Scipio to return from the ridge overlooking the enemy camp. He wondered how the other three legions were faring on their march northward and felt a little aggrieved that they would get to conquer a city while the Ninth had been sent to sort out a minor tribe. Glory lay northward not westward.

The whole Century of scouts were together for this action, a rare event for them as usually they were split up on different missions. They had cleared the slopes of lookouts overnight with a mixture of stealth and blade, and prepared the way for the diversionary tactics that would conclude their part in the action. At last Scipio scrambled back down from his vantage point.

'Mount up,' he said. 'It is time.'

The scouts mounted their horses and looked to their leader.

'Move fast and strike quick,' said Scipio. 'Do not get sucked in to combat, that is not our role. Spare their horses; we want them to follow with as much strength as possible. Okay, let's go.' He turned his horse and led the troop out of the gorge, taking the enemy encampment by surprise as they stormed into the valley without warning.

They galloped along the fringes loosing a hail of arrows into the huts as they passed, screaming insults and challenges as they passed. They span around at the end of their run and galloped back up the valley, though this time; many warriors had gathered their wits and raced from their huts, picking up their spears and swords to attack the horsemen with a fanaticism borne from fearless belief in the afterlife.

'The hornet's nest has been shaken!' shouted Scipio, 'let's get out of here!'

Prydain and the rest of the scouts galloped out of the valley with Scipio bringing up the rear. Hundreds of mounted barbarians, all armed with spear or sword followed a few hundred metres behind them as they sought to bring down the invaders.

The scouts neared the exit to the valley and were almost clear when Scipio's mount placed a galloping hoof in a pothole and tumbled forward, its leg snapping with a resounding crack and catapulting his rider forward to land face down in the dust. The Centurion regained his feet groggily, his left arm hanging uselessly by his side, blood pouring down from the severed bone that protruded angrily from his upper arm. The barbarians were closing fast and Scipio looked to his retreating scouts, and realising there could be no rescue; he turned to his horse to see if he could remount and escape. The horse had regained his feet, but one foreleg hung loosely from its sinews, broken in two places and Scipio patted the horse on the neck to reassure him, whispering in its ear.

'Looks like it's our time, old friend,' he said. 'At least we will go together.' Scipio drew his Gladius and started to hobble forward toward the screaming hoard less than a hundred metres away. He picked up the pace, ignoring the pain from his broken body until he was running as fast as he could toward the thousand-strong enemy, raising his sword above his head and screaming the final challenge of his life.

Two hundred yards away, one of the retreating scouts glanced back and reined in suddenly as he witnessed their leader being engulfed by the barbarians.

'Stop!' screamed Prydain and two of the nearby scouts pulled up to find out the problem.

'What's the matter?' panted one of the Decurions, pulling up alongside Prydain.

'Scipio has fallen,' shouted Prydain. 'He's in amongst that lot.'

The Decurion struggled to control his horse as he calculated the risks. Finally, he gave his orders.

'There's nothing we can do for him,' he said. 'It's too late.'

'We can't just leave him,' said Prydain.

'What would you have me do?' shouted the Decurion. 'There are thousands of them and eighty of us. He is gone, Prydain, we have to finish our mission.' They looked at the swarming tribe now within a hundred metres before the Decurion added finally, 'Scipio was a fine man, but he is only one, we have a legion to think of. Now move out!' He turned his horse and galloped after the distant scouts, closely followed by Prydain and his comrade.

Two miles away, Cassus lined up in the third rank of the assembled soldiers, looking between the first two ranks and across the empty plain to his front. Behind him, the heavily wooded hills formed a semi-circle of protection, though also presenting a barrier, which could not be quickly climbed, should they need to retreat. The legion had assumed a linear deployment and two Cohorts stretched across the flood plain from hill to hill. The ground was perfectly flat, eroded from the attentions of the spring floods and ideal ground for manoeuvring both infantry and cavalry.

Legatus Nasica peered down from one of the flanking hills at his deployed forces. It was a typical Roman deployment with two auxiliary cavalry units on the flanks, slingers and archers to the rear and over a thousand legionaries stretched across the plain in three ranks. It looked impressive and any enemy spies couldn't fail to be impressed.

But it wasn't a good impression that Nasica wanted to achieve, and if he was being honest with himself, he had to admit that the lines did stretch quite a long way and seemed somewhat weak with no heavy infantry back up. In addition, the archers, whilst deadly, would be far more effective had there been at least four times as many. As for the slingers, everyone knew flood plains were notoriously sparse of sling sized stones and when their pouches of lead projectiles had been used, there was not much in the way of natural ammunition lying around.

He turned his gaze to the ground to the front of the formed up Cohorts. Yes, it was ideal for infantry to manoeuvre, but it was also ideal for chariots. Nasica knew that whilst there were the two units of cavalry deployed, any sizeable force being faced with the stretched Roman deployment and perfectly flat battleground would think they were there for the taking which was exactly what Nasica hoped!

Cassus shivered slightly in the early morning breeze, flexing his fingers around the haft of his Pilum to get the blood flowing. This would be his third action since landing in Britannia, but still his stomach turned in anticipation. Over the last two weeks, the legion had encountered some resistance as they made their way westward and had laid waste to several villages en-route. Those who had welcomed the Romans and had met their demands with little resistance got off relatively lightly. Those villages that argued or showed any resistance were dealt with mercilessly, and their occupants either slaughtered or taken as slaves before the provisions were taken anyway.

However, this was different. This was the first time Cassus had formed up with his legion in classic battle formation on an open field, ready to meet an enemy at least of equal strength. Every man was fully aware that their somewhat weak deployment was a deliberate ploy and not a tactical gaffe by their commanders. If this worked, Nasica would enjoy a great victory, and though defeat was not envisaged, a tactical

164

miscalculation could cost an awful lot of Roman lives. Cassus's reverie was interrupted by the shout of the Primus Pilus standing ten metres to their front.

'Legion!' he roared, 'present Pilae!'

Cassus re-gripped his stabbing spear, all thoughts of cold or discomfort forgotten as he focussed on the dust cloud on the horizon. As he was in the rear rank, the butt of his Pila rested on the ground with the blade pointing straight up in the air, unlikely to be needed in the first encounter. The middle rank rested their heavier spears on the shoulders of the front rank, who in turn, gripped theirs firmly in two hands at waist level, their left feet slightly forward of their right in the classic thrusting stance used as a defence against cavalry or chariots.

Nasica strained his eyes as the scouts raced back to the legion and even though he was pleased to see a strong force of barbarian cavalry in hot pursuit, was unable to see if they were backed up by the main threat to the legion, chariots. The scouts thundered close to the legions lines, heading for the centre, and as they approached, the ranks pivoted backwards, opening up a large gap in a well-rehearsed move that allowed them to disappear behind the infantry lines. At the same time, the flanking cavalry raced in from the sides of the plain to engage the pursuing horsemen in the first clash of the battle.

The mounted units crashed into each other in the centre of the plain, the barbarians equalling the auxiliaries in number, ferocity and skill. Men and beasts screamed as the initial exchange of hardened spears tore into the flesh of those unlucky enough to be in the initial impact, and as the momentum of both forces ground to a halt, swords were drawn on both to engage in close quarter battle.

High above on the hill, Nasica watched closely and considered sending the scouts back into the fray to strengthen the auxiliaries, but resisted the temptation when it became apparent that his forces had started to get the upper hand. Finally the surviving enemy warriors broke free from the conflict and raced back the way they came to meet up with the bulk of their force entering the plain far behind.

The cavalry started to pursue the retreating barbarians, but a long blast on the horn from Nasica's signaller stopped them in their tracks and they returned behind the infantry lines to reform and sort out their wounds. Dozens of lightweight infantry ran forward to cut the throats of any surviving enemy wounded before carrying the legion's own casualties back to the tree line and the waiting medical orderlies.

The excitement died down as the dust settled and the chatter in the ranks increased until the Centurion's voice once again echoed across the position.

'Silence!' he roared, and the plain fell quiet as everyone's ears strained to hear what the Centurion had obviously heard.

'Listen,' whispered a voice to Cassus's side, 'can you hear it?'

'I can't hear anything,' said another.

Slowly, a distant hum reached the ears of the legion, borne on the morning breeze.

'What is it?' asked the soldier.

'I don't know,' said Cassus, 'but whatever it is, it doesn't sound happy.'

In the distance, the settling dust revealed an army flowing onto the flood plain like a cloud of black smoke blown across the land, their weapons glinting across the battlefield as they reflected the morning sunlight. Armoured warriors roared their challenges and beat their shields with their weapons while others, draped in cloaks of varying colours, blew into unrecognisable horns producing the melancholy tones rebounding off the hills. Women and children wailed their laments into the air, their hands held aloft as they implored their Gods for aid in defeating the invader and even the aged were amongst the throng, adding their screaming voices to the deafening and terrifying din. Suddenly the advancing army stopped dead in their tracks and everyone stared across the plain as if waiting for a sign.

High up above the valley, Nasica turned his attention from the warrior tribe and toward the entrance to the flood plain, eventually rewarded with the sight of two hundred chariots riding slowly into view. Each was manned by two heavily armed warriors and pulled by a pair of the strong, but small horses that were native to these lands.

'There they are, Mateus,' said Nasica, 'like flies into a web.'

Cassus swallowed dryly. There was no way their thin lines could repel an assault from such an army. Even at this distance, he could see the variety of their weapons, ranging from swords and spears to clubs, maces and huge hammers. There were even some weapons that he had never seen before that looked well capable of smashing the Roman shields with ease.

A solitary warrior stood to the front of the tribe, his stature and regalia easily marking him out as the leader. Around him stood the half-naked Shamen, their bodies heavily tattooed with Celtic designs etched into their skin with blue wode. Druids of the tribe, each invoking the support of their Gods walked up and down the lines of chariots, blessing the horses with bowls of human blood, their white cloaks blowing in the breeze.

One man, standing silently alongside the chief, wore a black cloak from neck to ankles, a sharp contrast to the long white hair that fell down past his shoulders. As if his appearance wasn't distinctive enough, he wore a belt of human skulls around his waist and held a two metre staff in his hand, topped with a human head, still wearing a Roman helmet. Though it was accepted that some tribes would take and display the heads of captured enemies, this one was different. It had a crest atop the helmet but instead of lying front to back as was usual in some units, its dyed red horsehair crest swept side to side, an honour reserved for only one rank in the Roman army, Centurions. It was the head of Scipio!

Nasica watched as the enemy tribe moved further into the valley and leaned over to a messenger standing at his side to give an instruction. The messenger nodded and ran down the hill to the line of Scorpios hidden in the undergrowth, passing the instruction to the Decurion in charge, who in turn approached one of the Scorpio operators. When everything was ready, the Decurion stared up at Nasica, waiting for the signal.

The General waited until the warriors had totally entered the plain and when he was happy they were committed, raised his Gladius above his head, before dropping it sharply to give the signal. The Decurion turned to the Scorpio operator.

'Okay, soldier,' he said, 'this is your chance of glory. Make this shot and when this is over, I will personally ensure every man of your unit gets an amphora of wine.'

'Yes, Sir,' said the legionary, and leaned into the post-mounted crossbow, aiming carefully at his target over a hundred yards away.

Cassus stared at the army of warriors now stationary and eerily silent to his front. The priest dressed in black walked forward from the enemy ranks and held up the head of Scipio, cursing the Romans and imploring the Gods for support in the impending battle. He held his arms out wide, chanting his mantras to the heavens, watched by the barbarians, who were totally entranced by his magic.

Cassus too was entranced by the mystical figure, until his mantra was suddenly interrupted by the thud of iron as it smashed through bone. Even from this distance, the sound was sickening and for a second, Cassus didn't understand what had happened until the barbarian priest fell slowly forward, his neck skewered by an iron bolt shot from the nearby Scorpio. As the Druid's body hit the floor, Scipio's head fell from the staff and rolled forward in the dust, coming to rest facing the barbarians as if in a final gesture of defiance.

High above, Nasica smiled in satisfaction, and ordered his trumpeter to give the signal. A deep tone resounded around the valley, being copied by other strategically placed trumpeters until the valley was echoing with the sound.

The barbarians looked around in fear, unaware what the sounds were or where they were coming from. Their leaders quickly regained order, and realising there was no turning back, led over five thousand warriors into battle with only a thousand thinly stretched Romans.

At the last moment, Nasica gave the order everyone had been waiting for and a waiting Ballista launched a flaming projectile high above the battlefield, signalling the battle to commence. Instantly, bushes on the slopes of the flanking hills fell aside and five hundred archers sprung up, darkening the sky as they fired thousands of arrows into the massed ranks of barbarian warriors. Despite their casualties, the barbarians raced forward, still screaming their war cries, keen to engage the invaders in close quarter battle.

'Ready,' shouted the Primus Pilus as the enemy closed in, 'Now!'

All three ranks of the Roman lines dropped to one knee presenting their stabbing Pila forward in defence. The manoeuvre was completely unexpected by the attackers and revealed thousands more infantry behind the first three lines, each jumping to their feet from the prone position they had been in for the last two hours.

Again, hundreds of missiles filled the air as the spear throwers hurled their Pila into the front ranks of the charging tribe, slowing the advance of those behind, as charging men tripped over the dying bodies of their comrades. As the charge faltered, The Primus Pilus raised his Gladius and commanded the Cohort to their feet.

'First Cohort,' he roared, 'Advance!'

The previously kneeling heavy infantry rose to their feet and took the attack to the decimated ranks of the barbarian army, each screaming their own challenge as they closed the hundred paces between them.

The front rank smashed into the confused enemy, punching the bronze bosses of their shields into snarling faces before following up the assault with the devastating thrusts of their Gladii. Forced into close order, the long swords, axes and maces of the barbarians were of little use and even when one did manage to cut deep into a legionary shield, they had no time to withdraw it before a Gladius was thrust deep into their torso from around the edge of an expertly wielded Scutum. The Romans were disciplined and ruthless, as systematically they forced the attacking lines backwards.

Within minutes, Cassus found himself in the front rank, stepping over wounded comrades to join the fray and found himself caught up in the blood lust again, killing anything to his front in a controlled frenzy of drilled manoeuvres. He worked alongside the men next to him, each covering each other and knowing instinctively how their comrades would act. The skills had been drilled into them over and over again, and though almost every soldier hated the daily drills during peacetime, the repetitive training became priceless when their lives became dependant on the ruthless efficiency of the killing machine that was the Roman army.

'Chariots, lord,' said Tribune Mateus, though Nasica had already seen them racing down the flood plain to attack the flanks of the Roman position. Another signal was relayed across the valley and five hundred auxiliary cavalry raced out of cover to confront the chariots.

The initial exchange went far better for the Celts than the Romans as spinning blades on the wheels cut mercilessly through the legs of the horses, causing man and beast to fall in a screaming mess of flesh.

Two distinct battles were now taking place on the plains. The infantry battle where man faced man in a conflict of arms and the other where the chariot riders had now dismounted and were despatching horses and men with axe and blade.

'Sire, the first wave is lost,' said the Tribune.

For the first time, Nasica's face showed concern, not so much for the men, but horses were hard to come by.

'Tell the Scorpios to wipe them out,' he said, 'and send in the third and fourth Cohorts to the flanks.'

The necessary orders were relayed and the temporary Century of Scorpio operators ran along the forest edge to get within range of the cavalry battle, each carrying their heavy weapons over their shoulders.

The charioteers were almost rabid in their battle fever and hacked every living thing apart until there was none left to kill. They remounted their chariots, elated at the initial success and turned their attentions to the infantry battle to their front, but before they could move forward, a hail of crossbow bolts slammed into riders and horses alike.

The remaining chariots spun to race headlong toward the line of Scorpio operators lining the edge of the woods. One more volley hit the chariots, though this time it was not as devastating, as nerves affected many operators' aims.

'Retreat!' shouted the Tribune and every operator shouldered their Scorpio to run up the wooded hill as fast as their heavy weapons allowed.

Seeing their flight, the euphoric warriors dismounted from their chariots and raced after them, sensing an easy victory over the unit that had decimated their ranks. Only twenty paces lay between the labouring Roman's and the pursuing warriors when the odds swung massively in the legion's favour.

From behind what seemed like every tree sprung an auxiliary light infantryman, each armed with a curved sword and round shield and the whole Cohort swarmed down through the forest to meet the stalled charioteers in close conflict, outnumbering their enemy two to one. Though the charioteers were fearless, they had already fought one battle and had climbed up the steep hill during the pursuit, tiring themselves out in the process. The light infantry, by comparison, were fresh, dominated the high ground and had the momentum of the downhill charge to aid the impact of their assault. There was no contest and warriors fell like hay before the scythe at the ferocity of the auxiliary assault. The few warriors that managed to regain their chariots only managed to get a few hundred yards back up the plain before the cavalry ran them down and the last of the charioteers fell beneath Roman blades.

Back on the plain, Cassus gasped for breath as he recovered from his exertions. He was covered with blood and whilst most of it was Britannic, there was some of his own running down his face, the result of a glancing blow from a barbarian club. He was lucky. A full blow would have crushed his skull like an egg.

170

A comrade tended to his wound as he drunk deeply from his flask. The first three ranks had been withdrawn as the rear troops had come through their lines to provide fresh impetus in the battle, and at last, the superior numbers and discipline of the legion started to take its toll on the enemy.

Bodies lay everywhere and the natural barrier of dead and dying human flesh piled high across the battlefield, meant that there were lulls in the conflict as either side scrambled over the corpses to fight their opponent. Eventually the signal sounded across the valley, and the surrounding Cohorts stopped the attack on the few hundred survivors that were left in the centre of the plain. Many were women and children, and they formed a screaming protective circle around their leader who lay wounded in the centre of the throng. Though the killing had stopped, stabbing Pilae were held against the outer circle to hold back the barbarians and gradually the furore died down as the tribe realised they were beaten. Translators recruited from local tribes instructed the survivors to sit down and eventually over two hundred men, women, and children sat or squatted on the floor in despair as they awaited their fate.

Nasica rode slowly out of the woods on his charger, dressed in full military regalia accompanied by the other officers of the legion. The ranks of the surrounding auxiliaries opened to let the group through and they stopped their horses, fifty metres from the prisoners.

'Casualties?' asked Nasica simply.

'Still counting, Sire,' said the Tribune, 'but we estimate sixty auxiliary cavalry and a dozen legionaries dead, including Centurion Scipio from the Scouts. About twice as many wounded.'

Nasica grimaced. The casualties were higher than he had anticipated and stained the victory.

'The blades on the chariots took us by surprise,' said the Tribune. 'They will not do so again.'

'How many charioteers survived?'

'None, Sire,' replied the Tribune, 'though their chief lies wounded amongst this lot!'

'Instruct the legion to build a camp,' continued Nasica. 'We will stay here until our wounded are ready to march. I will send instructions as to the prisoner's fate shortly.' He turned and rode back to the formed up lines of the legion.

The engineers quickly identified a suitable location for the fort where the ground was dry enough to ensure suitable conditions, but soft enough to be able to dig. The fresher Cohorts started to dig the ditches, using the soil to build a high bank on the inner edge and topped with the sharpened stakes that every legionary carried.

Nasica sat in his tent, receiving updates about the battle from his commanders. He sent the scout unit out to retrieve Scipio's corpse and to burn the enemy village while a Cohort of light infantry were sent into the forests to winkle out any stragglers that may have escaped. In addition, he sent messengers to General Plautius, updating him about the situation and in particular the tactics used by their enemy. This was the first pitched battle against any Britannic tribe and information regarding the way they fought was priceless, especially the chariots. When the most pressing jobs had been done, and the wounded had been tended to, he turned his attention to the fate of the prisoners.

'We have to send a message to these heathen,' he said to the gathered officers, 'one that will spread like wildfire. I have made my decision. The women will be sent back to serve as slaves in Rome. The chief will join them, for his fate will be decided by the senate.'

A murmur of agreement rippled through the officers. It was usual for captured chiefs to be paraded through the streets of Rome before being executed by the Praetorian Guard, usually by throttling.

'The hags and the female children,' continued Nasica 'will be released to spread the news about the folly of opposing Rome, but not before they witness the fate of the men.' He paused, looking around the group of hardened soldiers and the lesser experienced officers. 'At dawn tomorrow, every male barbarian will be crucified along the river bank as retribution for the casualties inflicted by their chariots. Tribune, you will make the arrangements. Ensure they are in full view of the surviving prisoners, and only when the crows have plucked the eyes of the last rotting corpse, will you release the hags to return to their clans.'

The scouts retrieved the head and corpse of their revered Centurion and built a funeral pyre on the edge of the river. Nasica had given them a frightened captive to accompany Scipio to the afterlife and Prydain had to hold back the nausea as the boy was thrown alive into the inferno, his screams and thrashing lasting only seconds before the flames took their toll. Scipio had been honoured and now his soul had a slave to see to his every need. The scouts were issued wine to celebrate the life and death of their leader, and though they were

172

allowed to join with the rest of the cavalry in the rape of the prisoner women, they preferred to sit around the funeral pyre, drinking themselves into oblivion. One however, sat slightly separate from the rest, staring across the slow moving water to the setting sun, sipping his wine slowly as he contemplated the day's events.

Cassus approached the Scout's camp, clutching his own flask of wine. He spotted Prydain sat leaning against the trunk of the tree.

'Hail, Prydain,' he said, 'I heard you had joined the scouts. How are you?'

'I don't know,' sighed Prydain. 'Something doesn't seem right. All this killing and raping, I just feel sick at the futility of it all.'

'What do you mean?' asked Cassus. 'You knew what we were letting ourselves in for when we signed up. What's made you change your mind?'

'It's not the fighting I have a problem with,' said Prydain, 'but the aftermath. Did you hear they are going to crucify the men tomorrow?'

'We have to lay down a marker to the barbarians,' said Cassus. 'By doing this, we will save many Roman lives.'

'Or cause their deaths,' answered Prydain before taking a swig from his amphora.

'What do you mean?' asked Cassus.

Prydain looked up.

'Warriors expect to die in battle!' he said. 'We expect to die in battle. I can even understand the crucifixion of the men, but in the name of the Gods, Cassus, why the children?'

'Some of those boys were armed with knives,' said Cassus, 'and would slit your throat given half a chance.'

'Yes and others are only just off their mother's breast. I joined up to fight for Rome and take my chances against barbarian warriors, not to murder babies. Nasica has gone too far this time and I am beginning to wonder who the barbarians are here, us or them?'

'You don't mean that, Prydain,' said Cassus, 'it's the wine talking. Why don't you come with me and have some fun with some of the women? Take your mind off it for a while.'

'These are not the willing girls of back home, or even whores who will accept your coin for their services,' said Prydain. 'They are mothers and wives who would rather die than give themselves to you. I know you have a lot of faults Cassus, but I never had you down as a rapist?'

173

'Spoils of war, Prydain,' said Cassus getting annoyed. 'It is our right as conquerors.'

'Well, don't be surprised if you get your throat ripped out,' snapped Prydain.

'I've thought of that,' answered Cassus. 'I'll pick one with a child and ensure the mother understands that if she doesn't participate enthusiastically, then her child will join the men on the crosses.'

Prydain stared in disbelief.

'Cassus, what have you become? Where are the compassion and the mercy?'

'I am a legionary,' shouted Cassus. 'And today I fought for my life alongside my comrades. Some of them didn't make it, Prydain; some of them will never again see the slopes of home. Where was their compassion? Where was their mercy? No, the barbarian men deserve their fate and the women are nothing more than spoils of war. The quicker you learn that, the better.' He threw down his flask in disgust and stomped away into the darkness.

'I don't know who you are any more, Cassus,' shouted Prydain after the retreating figure. 'You shame your father's name.'

Cassus had disappeared and Prydain sat back against the tree contemplating the outburst.

'Oh shit!' he said eventually, realising he had over reacted. Despite his arrogance, Cassus had been in the front line, facing barbarian blades only hours before and the last thing he needed was a fellow soldier judging him on his morals. Realising he had been too harsh, Prydain followed Cassus into the darkness, walking toward the burning village.

There was nothing left of the barbarian encampment except for piles of glowing embers, their glow reflected in the eyes of the occasional scavenging dog skulking in the darkness. Prydain walked toward one of the fires before a sudden movement in the bushes caught his eye and he turned to face the unknown.

'Cassus, is that you?' he asked.

There was no answer.

'Cassus don't be a prick,' said Prydain, 'if it's you, say so.'

When there was still no answer, Prydain drew his Gladius and walked slowly toward the bushes. Although the auxiliaries had swept the area there was always the possibility that the odd warrior had escaped the search and lay hidden in the undergrowth. He reached the tree line and leant forward to move a suspect bush with his left hand, whilst raising his Gladius with his right, ready to strike, but stopped in surprise as he stared down at the sight before him. It wasn't a hiding enemy warrior gazing back up at him but the wide tearful eyes of a boy and a girl, each no more than five years old, staring up at him in absolute terror and clinging tightly to each other for mutual assurance.

For what seemed an age, Prydain stared down at the children in confusion until the little girl lifted up her tiny arm, offering Prydain something she had clenched in her fist. Prydain looked at the offered gift in confusion, not realising what it was until the firelight gleamed on its surface. It was a Torc, beautifully braided from the finest golden cords and its pendant engraved with a bird of prey with tiny green stones for its eyes. It was a beautiful ornament and had obviously belonged to someone of very high status within the tribe, perhaps even the chief.

Prydain's mind was spinning. Here he was, standing in the remnants of a burning enemy village, being offered a priceless Torc by a couple of tiny children, obviously in a pathetic attempt to buy their lives from this terrifying invader. They must have been given this ornament by the owner and instructed what to do if they were found. The girl still held the ornament up and let out a quiet whimper, struggling to control her fear as she stared up at the raised sword. Prydain lowered his Gladius and took the Torc, placing it in the inner pocket of his tunic.

'Shhh,' he said, quickly putting his finger to his lips in the universal gesture for silence and looked around to see if he was being watched. The sky was now pitch black and the two semi naked children were shivering in the biting cold of the night. Prydain undid his cape and wrapped it around them while reassuring them quietly.

'Stay here and be quiet,' he said, though knowing full well that they didn't understand him. He pointed at the ground and repeated himself.

'You stay here, understand? You must be quiet.' He smiled gently in reassurance and placed his finger gently on either of the children's mouths in turn indicating the need for silence. The boy nodded his understanding and mimicked the gesture with his own hand.

'Good,' said Prydain, and he reached inside his tunic to retrieve some Buccellatum biscuit, snapping it in half to give some to each of the twins. He thought quickly. He should turn them in, but if he did, the girl, despite her age would probably fall victim to the disgusting carnal desires of the Batavian cavalry units, while the boy's fate surely lay on the cross.

Prydain watched the famished children devouring the hard biscuit. Whether it was the wine or his conscience kicking in, he made his decision. He may not be able to do anything for the hundred or so children whose fate had already been decided, but he could certainly save these two.

'Stay here!' he said for the last time and walked back out of the bushes, leaving the siblings huddled under his black cape. What he was about to do, was stupid, ill thought out and would probably cost the lives of him and the children, but his decision was made. He ran back into the darkness toward the tented camp.

Chapter 23

Whilst the Ninth were wiping out Bragus's clan, the three remaining legions made their way northward with ruthless efficiency. The aim was to take on the might of Caratacus and close in on Britannia's capital, Camulodunum, but though they had faced small pockets of resistance, the vast bulk of the barbarian army had retreated before them in confusion. However, as they approached the Medway, it became apparent that the Catuvellauni were reorganising and making their plans to retaliate.

Plautius called a war council and was deep in conversation with a scout Centurion when the officers arrived. They waited patiently, making small talk until the Centurion finally saluted the General, and left the tent to return to his unit. The waiting officers moved out of the way as the commander approached the central table to unroll the parchment given to him by the departed Centurion, weighing each corner down with a wine tankard.

'Right, gentlemen,' announced Plautius, 'we have a problem. As you are aware, the advance has stalled due to this cursed river.' He indicated the feature on the recently drawn map. 'Our lines are strong; however this is as far as we can go at the moment. Caratacus and his barbarians are entrenched on the far side, and while we listen to the taunts of his warriors, he gathers his strength.'

'We have nothing to fear from the barbarians,' said Vespasian, 'they are disorganised and have presented little problem to our legions to date.'

'That may be so,' said Plautius, 'but so far, we have had the advantage of surprise. They now know we are here and how we operate. With this river holding us up, they can chose the manner and place in which to take us on.'

'The carpenters are felling trees as we speak to make the extra boats,' said Geta. 'We have a hundred assault boats being brought up from the rear but they will not be enough. We need a full month before we can storm the far bank in any strength.'

'We do not have a month,' said Plautius. 'We need to take them on tomorrow or the next day at the latest, while they are still disorganised and still trapped between the rivers.'

'The river can be forded here,' said Vespasian. 'The bridge is burnt, but a column may be able to cross at low tide.'

'Our men would be slaughtered,' said Plautius, 'the far bank at that point is heavily defended.'

'Then we must take steps to weaken that defence,' said Vespasian, 'my men hold no fear of these inbreeds.'

'I have no doubt about the bravery or ability of your men, Vespasian,' said Plautius, 'but it's not the spears that concern me or indeed whether we can cross, but that which awaits us on the other side.' He went on to describe the landscape on the far side of the river that he had witnessed from a nearby hilltop earlier in the day.

'First, there is the river,' he said, 'the flow is fast at low tide and too deep when the tide is high. The boats will take only ten men each, a total force of just a thousand and with the bank being covered by enemy spears, our men would be sitting ducks as they founder in the mire. Even if we succeed, the ground then opens up to perfect chariot country and they have over a thousand waiting to fall on our exhausted men!' He straightened up, and for the next hour, the officers discussed the assault options. Finally, Plautius called for quiet.

'Okay,' he said, 'I have heard enough. Vespasian, I believe your Batavian Cohorts have a particular skill when it comes to river crossings.'

'Yes, Sire,' said Vespasian beginning to realise the essence of the plan. 'They are well rested and eager to enter the fray.'

'Good,' said Plautius. 'They will have their day, as will the rest of the Augusta.' He turned to the other legion commander. 'Geta, bring up your boats but send them five miles upstream. Ensure they are not seen until needed.' He turned to the remaining officers. 'Gentlemen,' he said, 'at dawn tomorrow, I want both of your legions formed up on this side of the river in full battle kit. We will drill the men and give Caratacus a show of strength he will never forget. Assemble the Onagers and send over a constant hail of missiles to keep them on their toes. Let them think that our armies are going to assault them head on.' He turned to Vespasian. 'In the meantime, this is what I want you and the Augusta to do.'

For the rest of the evening they made their plans until every officer knew their role in detail and each left to brief his men. The battle of the Medway was about to begin.

Caratacus and Togodumnus stood high on their vantage point overlooking the legions formed up on the other side of the river. Rank after rank of heavily armed men stared back across the water and had done so since first light. Troops of cavalry galloped around the edges and dozens of lighter armed units were strategically placed at the edges of the legion. The King and his brother were particularly fascinated at the giant wooden machines that catapulted stones across the river, and though they were easily dodged and landed harmlessly in the marshland, their potential was obviously huge.

Below the two brothers, their own warriors were formed up in their separate clans, waiting on the hard ground to meet any force crossing the river, and the King knew that any Romans managing to reach the harder surface would be mercilessly cut down by his men. Should his front line be taken, his chariots would sweep down and wipe the invaders from the field. The bulk of his forces were deployed across the wooded slopes between the Medway and the Tamesas, while most of the women and children had already crossed the second river and were well on their way to Camulodunum.

Caratacus had expected better from the Romans. Their reputation was formidable but he could see nothing to worry him here and was impatient for the assault to start. He did not have the slightest idea that the manoeuvres to his front were a diversion, and the actual assault had started many hours earlier.

In the darkness of the early hours, over four thousand Batavian auxiliaries, experts in river crossings back in their native Germania, had already swum across the river five miles downstream and taken up positions in the bracken and undergrowth of the enemy hills. Similarly, five miles upstream, the engineers had floated the assault boats in the darkness and tied them side by side until they stretched across the river from bank to bank. Under normal circumstances, the boats would have been boarded out with planks to make a solid bridge, but as the noise would have alerted any nearby sentries, over five thousand men crossed barefoot from boat to bobbing boat, until eventually, the entire Augustan legion lay hidden on the northernmost bank of the Medway. When Plautius received the runners telling him the crossings had been successful, he sent the message to start and eight Cohorts of Batavian light infantry arose silently from their positions to start the advance on the enemy positions deep in the forests.

The outer positions of Caratacus's warriors were taken completely by surprise, and as the silent attackers picked up momentum; their overwhelming force carried them deep into the enemy positions. They fell on the sentries and rampaged throughout the lines of chariots, targeting the horse's legs as they passed, hamstringing the panicking animals to prevent them from being of any use in the harnesses. Man and beast fell beneath the initial onslaught and they decimated over half of Caratacus's animals before the defending warriors realised the danger. Caratacus heard the news from a runner and though he was initially shocked, refused to panic. He turned to Togodumnus.

'Take the northern clans and wipe them out,' he said. 'I will face the frontal assault when it comes.'

Togodumnus turned his horse and galloped to the council of northern leaders gathered half a mile away. Twenty minutes later, over two thousand warriors were storming through the woods to confront the threat from the Batavians.

Within the hour, the Roman offensive faltered and the Batavians, having achieved their mission, retreated eastwards along the river before forming a defensive line across the valley. They strung their bows and waited patiently as the counter offensive drew closer. Within minutes, the expected throng of warriors emerged screaming from the forest and descended on the Batavian lines. The first few hundred fell beneath the hail of arrows, but such was the impetus of the assault, the Batavians only managed to get three volleys off before the barbarians were upon them, man against man in a straightforward battle to the death.

To the west, the waiting Vespasian received the order to advance and led his legion down-stream to assault Caratacus's west flank, but due to the delay in communication, this time found the barbarian army ready and waiting. With over half of his chariots out of use, Caratacus deployed the centre bulk of his forces to meet Vespasian's legion, outnumbering them two to one. With little time, the Romans formed up into classic battle lines and Centurions raced amongst their forces barking their orders and encouraging their nervous men.

'At fifty metres,' screamed the Primus Pilus, 'launch all remaining Pilae, they will be no use to you at close range. At ten metres, we will charge. Do not falter; strike with as much aggression as you can muster. This will be a battle like no other. If the man to your front falls, then step over him. There will be no relief, each man will fight until we prevail or fall.'

A roar from above threatened to drown out his voice as their opponents streamed from the wooded hill.

'Look to your Gods, men,' shouted Vespasian drawing his Gladius, 'for today we make history.'

Again, two massive and ferocious forces smashed into each other on the banks of the Medway and though he had sent seasoned warriors to face Vespasian, Caratacus knew he had been outthought by the Roman General. Across the river he could see his opposite number on a hill and realised the display had been a diversion.

'Very clever, Roman,' he said to himself, 'but your forces are still outnumbered. By the time you ford the river, your men will be nothing but meat for the wolves.' Even though he was aware that the Batavians to the east had been contained, he knew that the legion attacking him from the west had to be repelled to stand any chance of victory. He gave the order for the remainder of his force to be deployed westward, to back up those already confronting Vespasian's legion, leaving only a thousand men to repel any frontal assault from Plautius.

Plautius watched what he could of the battles across the river and received runner after runner bringing news from the two fronts. Throughout the day, dozens of separate conflicts took place between the rivers, with both forces equally matched and the battles ebbed and flowed as each side took the initiative, only to be beaten back by their opponents.

To the east, the Batavians had repelled the first onslaught of the barbarians and were holding their own in their defensive positions, benefiting from the advantage of having hundreds of archers, a luxury Togodumnus did not enjoy.

To the west, Vespasian was in trouble, and though his legion fought bravely, by the time nightfall came they had lost the ground previously gained throughout the bloody battles of the day. Caratacus had managed to deploy some of his remaining chariots and though Pila had brought many of the horses down, they inflicted terrible casualties on the legion before they fell.

At last, darkness fell and as the legion was so close to the enemy, there was no possibility of building a camp. Instead, they formed defensive lines, ten men deep with every other man allowed to sleep for an hour at a time.

A few hundred yards away, the barbarians also slept with their weapons and though they were unwilling to fight in the dark, Caratacus knew that with a final push, they would overwhelm the legion the following morning. The barbarians were by far the happier force throughout the night and the taunts of their warriors echoed across the battlefield, ringing in the ears of the silent Romans, unaware that even as they celebrated, Plautius had taken steps to ensure the following day went better than the first.

Caratacus had left his position above the ford, knowing that he had another twelve hours before the tidal river would be low enough for Plautius to bring his legion across. He joined the tribes facing the threat to the west and reinforced their numbers with even more men, determined to shatter Vespasian's numbers with overwhelming force. He held a war council with the clan leaders and his tribes moved onto the slope above Vespasian's position, waiting for the dawn to light his historic victory. As the darkness eased, the chanting started and Caratacus was joined by Togodumnus to stare over the battlefield, fully expecting to see lines of terrified Romans facing certain death.

What he saw chilled him to the bone. Vespasian's legion had already mustered in the darkness and stood in their Cohorts, impatient for the conflict to begin. They had reorganised after the battle the day before and though their numbers were somewhat smaller, they had managed to reform into recognisable units. Banners and standards flew from each Cohort, and in the centre, Caratacus could see the famed Roman eagle he had heard so much about. However, it was not the reorganised legion that caused his doubt, but what lay beyond.

Behind Vespasian, stood thousands of extra troops sent by Plautius to reinforce the beleaguered legion. Heavy infantry, archers and spear throwers stood in their units and detachments of cavalry lurked on the fringes like predators at a killing, waiting for their swift and lethal skills to be called upon. A unit of over five hundred men littered the forward slope of a small hill, their leather slings hanging from their muscular right arms, while their left hands played with the lethal lead shot stored in their pouches.

Geta had brought his legion across the same pontoon bridge during the night and not only had they managed to form up in support of Vespasian in time for the dawn, but behind their lines, Caratacus could see something else, a line of wooden structures that filled him with dread.

'Ready!' roared Geta and over fifty artillery pieces were loaded with an assortment of ammunition. Some of the Onagers were loaded with limestone rocks, their fragile structure designed to shatter on impact with the hard ground to send flint sharp shards amongst the enemy, whilst others were loaded with oil filled clay pots, their narrow necks plugged with wax around a protruding wick. When the pots smashed amongst an enemy force, the burning wicks would ignite the oil, and spread flaming death amongst flesh and bone.

Teams of operators loaded Ballistae with iron tipped arrows, standing ready to re-arm the crossbows as fast as they could be fired, and rank upon rank of Scorpio operators loaded their smaller tripod based crossbows with their own heavy bolts. Every legionary in the front two ranks drew their swords, and the spear throwers ran forward to form up before the lines, each armed with a dozen Pilae.

It was an awesome sight and Caratacus couldn't fail to be impressed. He looked around his army and though he realised the risk, his forces were now almost frantic with blood lust and impatient to attack the Romans. He knew the outcome was now far from certain, but there was no way he could stop his forces from engaging the enemy, for even if he had given the order to withdraw, he would be ignored. Realising he had no choice; he drew his longsword and held it above his head. All around, his forces stared up at the King, awaiting the final order.

'Catuvellauni!' he roared. 'They have raped our women and killed our children. Now is the time for revenge. Before the sun sets, your belts will be heavy with Roman heads.'

Those within earshot cheered their King and the roar was taken up all the way along the lines of warriors.

'Are you ready?' he shouted.

The crescendo of screaming peaked at an unbelievable level.

'Spare no one,' he roared. 'Drive them back into the sea,' and Caratacus dropped his sword to point toward the enemy before finally screaming the battle charge.

'Britannia!'

'Britannia!' echoed the thousands of warriors and the whole army descended on the two waiting legions like a swarm of locusts.

Caratacus had never seen anything like it. Before his men were within a hundred yards, they were being decimated by exploding stones and balls of flame. A hail of arrows and lead shot brought those who dodged the missiles down before they had to run the gauntlet of the spear throwers. His men fell in their hundreds, but despite this, their sheer numbers and the impetus of their downhill charge, meant that his warriors crashed into the Roman lines with lethal force. The deep lines of opposing men surged back and fore like a swell on the sea, the front lines unable to deploy their personal weapons with much effect, due to the pressure from those in front and of those behind. As natural lulls took place and the lines disengaged, individual conflict broke out between hundreds of combatants, and though the skill and training of the Romans meant they were far more efficient at killing, the overall weight of numbers started to tell, and Vespasian's legion was forced to fall back.

Caratacus suddenly spotted an opportunity to deal a devastating blow to his enemy. A clan of his warriors had broken through the Roman lines, and were closing in on the legion's standard bearer. Vespasian, had quickly reformed his defences to protect the eagle, but was under severe pressure. Caratacus turned to his brother.

'Take the remaining chariots,' he said. 'Bring me their eagle.'

Togodumnus signalled the chariot leader and led them in a breakneck charge toward the battle taking place around the legion's standard.

Across the valley, Legatus Geta saw the danger. There was nothing more devastating to any force than the loss of their eagle, and though it was not his own, he would not stand back and watch a comrade suffer the ultimate humiliation. He signalled for a Cohort to follow him and charged across the valley to help his comrade.

Vespasian and a hundred of his men were fighting desperately to defend their eagle, outnumbered four to one by screaming warriors, and was relieved to see Geta's Cohort smash into the flanks of the enemy. Again, the battle swung as sword cleaved flesh and club smashed skull. The screaming of man and beast echoed across the plain and Caratacus deployed even more men, knowing that the whole battle could revolve around this smaller conflict. Geta had lost his helmet to a glancing blow from a sword and stood atop a crashed chariot surrounded by his Cohort, exhorting his men to greater efforts against the overwhelming numbers.

Caratacus looked down at the battle, picking out the bright red hair of his brother as his chariot closed in on Vespasian's standard. Togodumnus was within a few metres of his prize and Caratacus knew that the Romans would falter with the fall of one of their leaders. The hill was now swarming with his warriors and the two sides were indistinguishable amongst the fray. Caratacus knew this was the moment he would fulfil his destiny.

Suddenly, he looked up at the sky, the light seemingly darker and for a second, he frowned as he wondered what was happening. The air was thick with death, as thousands of missiles soared across the valley. Caratacus was shocked. Surely the enemy risked the death of their own men with such a volley.

As if to answer his unspoken question, a division of Roman horns bellowed a distinctly different tone across the battlefield and hundreds of legionaries dropped to their knees, each covering themselves with their shields.

The effect was devastating. Arrows, spears and lead shot fell on the ranks of Roman and Celt alike, but being aware of the tactic, the attackers had reacted instantly to the risk from their own forces and protected themselves from the hail of death. During the battle, Geta's legion had advanced in support of their Legatus and the supporting Cohorts had brought their weapons within range to provide the devastating onslaught, and though some legionaries were killed in the assault, their numbers were minimal whilst the Catuvellauni on the other hand, fell in their thousands. Caratacus's attention turned to his brother. There was still hope. If they could only seize a standard, they could hold it to ransom.

Togodumnus had left his chariot and along with the last of his warriors, had managed to get within a few paces of the legion's eagle, when a red cloaked Roman ran across to block his way.

'Over my dead body, heathen,' hissed Vespasian in Latin and he launched into a straight sword battle with the brother of the King. Togodumnus had the advantage with the larger sword and forced Vespasian backwards, the Roman's shorter sword deflecting the larger one frantically and without time to respond with a strike of his own. Seeing an opportunity, Vespasian ducked a blow aimed at his head and ran into Togodumnus, tackling him to the floor, but though he had the momentum, the larger warrior got the better of the Roman and rolled on top of him, grabbing him around the throat to cut off his airway.

Vespasian's strength was fading and he knew he was losing the fight, but as his consciousness started to ebb, the clamp around his airway suddenly eased and the look of hatred on his opponent's face was replaced with one of painful surprise, as Vespasian slowly pushed his Pugio deep between the Celt's ribs and into his lungs. Togodumnus released his opponent and got to his feet before staggering a few yards and falling to his knees. He held the wound closed with his blood-stained hands as he struggled to draw breath. Vespasian stood up and grabbed the legion's standard from the Aquilifer. He turned to Togodumnus.

'Is this what you want barbarian?' he asked as the mortally wounded warrior looked up at him.

'Well here it is,' he snarled and thrust the iron tipped staff bearing the golden eagle deep into his opponents chest, forcing his body to arch backwards and pinning him to the ground.

All around him Geta's reinforcing cavalry were pouring into the fray, followed up by Cohorts of infantry slaughtering everything in their path. Caratacus knew the battle was lost, for though there were still thousands of his warriors fighting the Romans, the momentum had finally turned his enemy's way and the fresh troops were wiping out his exhausted men with impunity.

Caratacus looked one more time down at his brother's body, impaled by the legion's standard. His limp body was bent backwards at the knees and his head hung unnaturally back, his flaming red hair dangling to the floor, exposing his throat to the sky.

Vespasian picked up his Gladius and looked up at Caratacus astride his war horse on the rise.

'Caratacus!' he screamed, 'thus lays the fate of Britannia!'

He turned back to Togodumnus and with a single stroke, cleaved his head from his shoulders.

A nearby soldier picked up the rolling head and thrust it onto the end of his spear before planting the shaft deep into the ground.

Caratacus turned his horse away from the grisly scene and rode hard back into the forest, welcoming the slap of the thin branches across his face as he tried to wipe out the picture of his brothers head, impaled atop a staff alongside the golden eagle of the Romans.

Chapter 24

Prydain reached the scout's camp and gave the watchword before entering the perimeter. The scouts did not camp within the stockade of the legion, but had formed their own bivouac near the river. It was patrolled by those unlucky to be on guard duty whilst their comrades celebrated the life and death of their leader.

He made his way to his tent and gathered some dried food and extra water skins, placing them into a pair of saddlebags. He took an extra cape from someone else's bed space and made his way to the paddock. He approached the horses and was relieved to recognise the scout on guard.

'Hail, Seppus!' said Prydain brazenly without breaking his stride.

'Where are you going this time of night?' asked Seppus, as Prydain started to saddle his own horse.

'I'm wanted up at the fort,' Prydain lied. 'Something about an early morning patrol with my old unit.'

'Bad luck!' said Seppus. 'I hear there's quite a party going on down there.'

'Yeah!' said Prydain, concentrating on his task. 'Never mind, perhaps next time.'

'Why two horses?' continued Seppus, looking at the extra tack.

Prydain thought quickly.

'They have a lame mount,' he said. 'They need to borrow a horse.'

'Here, let me help you,' said Seppus and started to saddle the second animal.

'Thanks!' said Prydain and mounted his horse before taking the bridle of the second animal and riding casually out of the paddock. The guard watched him disappear into the darkness and returned to his post, completely unaware of the plan Prydain was unfolding.

When Prydain was certain he was out of sight, he turned back toward the burnt out village and had almost crossed the plain without any drama, when a figure approached out of the darkness, obviously the worse for wear with wine.

'Prydain!' called Cassus drunkenly, 'there you are. You should have come with me, these barbarian women are something special.' He drunk from his flask and grabbed Prydain's arm. 'Come on, get off your horse, I've got one over here, you can have her, I'm done!'

187

Prydain dismounted and after tying the horses to a tree, allowed himself to be led into the undergrowth. Within seconds, they came across a naked woman curled up on the bracken, her face swollen and mouth bleeding from the beating she had obviously received.

'Go on,' said Cassus. 'She's worth it, trust me.'

The woman looked up in despair, fully expecting another beating at the hands of these monsters, before being raped again. Prydain hid his disgust well, not for the girl, but for Cassus.

'No!' said, Prydain coldly, 'I like my women willing.' He turned to his friend. 'Let her go Cassus, you've had your fun, now take her back to her people. She faces a life of slavery anyway; at least allow her some dignity now.'

Cassus's shoulders slumped before he finally answered.

'You just don't understand do you?' he snarled. 'She is my prize, my reward and I will take her back when I am good and ready. In the name of the God's, Prydain, what is the matter with you?'

'Believe me,' said Prydain, 'the problem is with you, Cassus. Have some compassion and let her go.'

'No!'

'Then you leave me no option.'

Before Cassus could react, Prydain punched him as hard as he could on the jaw, knocking him to the floor. Cassus was stunned and tried to get up.

'Sorry, friend,' said Prydain, 'but I have had enough of this madness.' He drew his Gladius and using the hilt, knocked Cassus out cold. The woman looked up in fear, struggling to understand the implications before Prydain indicated she should get dressed.

'Come on,' he said beckoning her, 'come with me.'

She donned her clothes nervously and followed him toward the nearby remains of her former home. When they reached the hiding place, he pulled back the cape beneath to reveal the sleeping children.

'I know you don't understand me,' he said to the woman, 'but somehow I need you to help.' He picked up the little boy and indicated she should do the same with the girl. 'Come on,' he said, 'we don't have much time,' and led her back to where he had left the horses.

Prydain knew that when Cassus recovered, he would raise the alarm and a search would be instigated. The legion wouldn't stand for deserters and would move heaven and earth to find him.

Within minutes, both Prydain and the barbarian woman were each sat on a horse with a frightened child wrapped under a cape, and riding as hard as they dared away from the legion. By midmorning, they had forded the river and Prydain led the way into unknown territory, knowing only that he couldn't go east due to the continued saturation of the coast by Rome and her allies. Nightfall found them encamped deep in the centre of a forest and at last, Prydain felt safe enough to light a fire. He dug out some dried fruit and Buccellatum from his pouches and shared it out among the group.

When they had all eaten, they stared at each other in silence. Prydain was starting to wonder whether he had done the right thing. Here he was, in a strange land, with a woman and two children who no doubt hated him with a vengeance. He was exhausted and knew that he had to rest, but was also aware that the woman was more than capable of killing him while he slept. He could tie her up, but the children would probably release her and there was no way he would tie them up as well. They all sat around the fire and despite his best efforts, the warmth finally got to him and he fell into the dreamless sleep of the exhausted.

Prydain struggled into consciousness, aware of strange voices within their small encampment. Realising he could be in danger, his hand reached slowly to his belt to retrieve his Gladius, only to find the weapon missing. He took a deep breath and spun off his stomach to sit up with his back against the tree trunk and stared at the scene before him. The previous night there had been only him, the children and the woman. Now, with the sun only just over the horizon, their number had increased to over twenty people and most worryingly, there were armed men. There was a heated argument going on between them and Prydain suspected his fate would hang on the outcome.

Though there was no sign of the children, Prydain could see the woman near the fire. She looked up and after a moment's hesitation, got to her feet before retrieving something from the embers and walked toward Prydain, gently pushing her way between the men. She knelt down before him, and with a smile, offered him a leaf package, scorched from the heat of the fire. Prydain opened the parcel, and as it came open, his taste buds flared with the enticing aroma of the roasted fish within. He looked at the woman again, returning her smile before carefully picking the flesh off the bones of the trout, hope growing that they were hardly going to feed him, if they intended to kill him.

He finished the fish, a bit disappointed that there wasn't any more, but the hot food made him feel much better and he realised things were looking up. The old men seemed to have reached an agreement and they stood silently as he finished his meal. Finally, one of the older men stepped forward.

'Come!' he said and beckoned Prydain to follow. Though he didn't understand the word, the gesture was recognisable and Prydain got to his feet to follow the group, but as he stood, the golden Torc with the bird of prey pendant fell from within his tunic and landed at the feet of the warrior. Both men stared at the ornament for a few seconds before Prydain looked again into the warrior's face, this time seeing only anger and rage. Before he had even the slightest chance to explain, he was smashed across the head from behind and as he sunk into unconsciousness, the last thing he heard was the sound of the woman screaming at his assaulter before the darkness mercifully took him from the pain.

Chapter 25

Gwydion and Cody had ridden all day from Caratacus's camp, following the trail that led back toward Khymru. He had heard tell of the slaughter of Bragus's tribe several days earlier and knew that somewhere behind him Caratacus's army was locked in battle with the Roman invasion force. As they rode, a village appeared in the distance and the two men decided to stop and rest. Hopefully, they could trade for some food as there was still two days travel left before they reached the isle of Mona. They rode up to the palisade and approached the closed wooden gate. An old man's face looked over the wall and Gwydion addressed him in the Catuvellauni tongue.

'Greetings, old man,' he said. 'We would talk with your chief.'

'He fights alongside Caratacus,' answered the man. 'State your business.'

'We seek shelter for the night and some food if you can spare any.'

'I know your accent, stranger,' he said, 'what tribe are you?'

'Deceangli!' answered Gwydion, 'but we come in peace and share a common enemy.'

'These are dangerous times, Deceangli,' said the man. 'Our gates remain closed to all who are not of our clan, and there is not enough grain for our own children. I fear we cannot help.'

'Understandable,' said Gwydion. 'We will be on our way.'

'Wait!' shouted the old man. 'I see you have two spare horses.'

'What of it?' asked Gwydion.

'We could do with the meat,' answered the old man, 'and we have something to trade that you may be interested in.'

'Which is?'

'A Roman!'

Inside the fort, Prydain turned his head away from the glaring sunlight streaming through the door of the empty stone granary that had been his prison since his capture. The unexpected glare hurt his eyes and after days of darkness, was as painful as the many punches he had received from his captors. Usually they came at night, two or more and often took great pleasure in using their fists or boots to remind him of his position. He squinted at the silhouettes of the two men striding toward him and cried out as they grabbed the bindings on his wrists to

191

lift him to his feet, almost wrenching his arms out of his sockets in the process.

'Shut up, Roman,' snarled the man in his strange language. 'It looks like your Gods smile on you this day.'

They dragged him out of the granary and over to the stockade gate where a group of old men gathered around a horse. The leader looked at Prydain and then to the horse.

'It is a fair deal,' he said, 'let him go.'

'I say we keep him.' said another. 'We will get more for him from Caratacus.'

'No, we need the meat,' said the old man indicating the animal. 'This will feed our children for a week. Open the gates, the deal is done.'

Two men lifted the bar and eased the gate open just enough for a man to step through.

'Go!' said the old man and pushed Prydain to the gap. Though confused, Prydain needed no second invitation and stumbled quickly through the gate and away from his captors.

Gwydion watched as the prisoner stumbled toward him. He was unshaven and his clothes were soiled, but apart from that, he wasn't in too bad a shape. Prydain stopped short of the mounted men, waiting for something to happen.

'Water,' gasped Prydain, 'do you have any water?' He pointed at the skin hanging from Gwydion's saddle.

Gwydion unfastened the skin and threw it to Prydain who unfastened the neck and drank the sweet contents as fast as he was able. The warriors waited patiently, staring at the wreck of a man.

'Food,' ventured Prydain when he finished, 'I don't suppose you have any food.' He mimed putting food into his mouth.

'Don't push your luck, Roman,' said Gwydion.

Prydain stopped in surprise.

'You speak Latin,' he stated.

Gwydion didn't answer.

'Are you going to kill me?' asked Prydain eventually.

'Why would I kill you, when I have just saved your life?' answered Gwydion.

'Saved my life, how?'

'How long do you think your captors would have kept you alive before getting bored and feeding you to the pigs?'

Prydain shrugged.

192

'They have not killed me yet, perhaps I am worth more alive than dead.'

'I agree there,' said Gwydion, 'but it is only the fact that you apparently saved a chieftain's children that has kept you alive this long. Now they are fed up and want rid of you, so at great personal cost, you now belong to me.'

Prydain sneered.

'From imprisonment into slavery,' he said. 'Perhaps I was better off as I was.'

'No, not a slave, Roman,' he said. 'Something far more valuable than that.'

Gwydion unwrapped Angau from its leather wrap and after stringing the bow, removed an arrow from his quiver. He looked around carefully before selecting his target. Without speaking, he caught Prydain's eye and indicated the nearby tree line. Prydain followed his gaze, not understanding the point of the exercise. Gwydion drew back the bowstring before letting the arrow fly toward the trees. Two seconds later, a wood pigeon fell from a limb, speared by the arrow. Prydain was amazed; he had never seen such a shot.

'You are a much easier target, Roman,' he said, 'and worth more to me alive than dead, but if you try to escape, then you are of no more value than that bird. Do you understand?'

Prydain nodded his head slowly, the warning was clear.

Gwydion nodded toward Cody who threw a noose around Prydain's head and pulled the slip-knot tight around his neck. Gwydion rode toward the tree line and without dismounting, stooped low from the back of his horse to retrieve the speared pigeon. He extracted the arrow and threw the bird to Prydain.

'Eat sparingly, Roman.' he said. 'We will be moving fast and will have little time to hunt.'

Prydain stuffed the bird under his tunic before Cody tugged at the tether and forced him to trot behind the Celt's horse as the group sought a campsite for the night.

Chapter 26

'Miss, you must eat something,' pleaded Willow, stirring the bowl of broth she had prepared. 'Please, just a little.'

Gwenno stayed where she was, curled into a foetal position on her mattress, scrunching her cape beneath her chin and staring blankly at the wall. She had been there for the last two days, since the guards had caught her in the woods, trying to escape for the third time in a week.

'I don't care,' she said.

'But you must eat, Miss,' encouraged Willow, 'or you will make yourself ill.'

Gwenno turned her head to look at the girl kneeling at her bedside.

'Make myself ill?' she asked. 'We wouldn't want that would we, Willow? Perhaps I would become so ill I might die, then what would the Druids do? What would they do for entertainment then, Willow?'

'Perhaps it would be for the best if I was dead,' she continued. 'That way there would be no need for you to take part in their sick rituals and I wouldn't have to relive the terror filled nightmares every night.'

'Don't say that, Miss,' said Willow, 'don't wish yourself dead.'

'Why not?' asked Gwenno raising her voice. 'Because that is what I will be soon enough, and do you know what?' She grabbed the girl's arm, making her look at her. 'Do you know what, Willow? I don't care anymore; I've had enough of dying a thousand times before waking up every morning and realising that I have to relive it for another day. Why don't they get it over with, Willow? Why do they torture me with the waiting?' Tears flowed from Gwenno's eyes as she looked pleadingly at the younger girl, as if waiting for an answer.

Willow looked back at her through tears of her own.

'Oh, Miss,' she said, 'I wish I could help, but since you ran away again, they have posted guards around the whole village. There's no way through anymore, we would be caught in a few minutes.'

Gwenno placed her head in her hands and sobbed quietly as Willow looked on, distraught at the anguish she was suffering. Willow was confused, as though she fully understood that sacrifice meant the end of this life, everyone knew it was simply a gateway to the next. A place of beauty and plenty, living alongside the Gods where hunger and pain were unheard of, and everyone lived forever. She struggled to understand why Gwenno was so upset, for only the royal and the sacred were even given the chance to undertake the great journey. Had she been lucky enough to be of high birth, she would have welcomed the chance with open arms. Willow gently stroked Gwenno's hair until the sobs finally fell silent. She sat back, her sleeping mistress's head lying in her lap and for the next hour she considered her options, until finally, she formed an idea.

Gwenno woke into the silence of the hut and looked around the fire lit gloom for Willow. The hut was obviously empty, but she could see the handmaiden had left a small cauldron of the broth in the embers at the side of the fire. She made her way over to the pot and ladled a few spoons of the soup into a wooden bowl, before walking to the door to peer between the slats. Outside, there were three guards around the clearing, each watching the hut to ensure she could not escape. She sipped on the soup as she watched and soon the monotony was broken when she saw Willow approaching, carrying a bundle in her arms. The girl was allowed past and ducked into the hut, slightly surprised to see Gwenno on her feet.

'Hello, Miss,' she said, 'I am so glad you're feeling better.'
She swerved around Gwenno and made her way across to the corner to place her package on the table, indicating for Gwenno to join her.

'Come and see,' she said excitedly, 'I have a present for you.'
Gwenno sighed, before joining Willow at the table.
'What is it?' she asked.
'It's beautiful, Miss,' she said, 'and very, very precious.'
Willow untied the hemp wrapping and unfolded the flaps to unveil one of the most beautiful things Gwenno had ever seen.

'Oh, Willow!' gasped Gwenno, 'it is beautiful.' She reached down and gently picked up the fabric with both hands, lifting it up to feel the luxury against her cheek.

'I have never seen such a thing,' she said and held the garment up to examine the finery. The silk fabric shone in the firelight, its royal purple colour providing a perfect backdrop for the golden thread piping that trimmed the edges, and decorated with the finest embroidery she had ever seen, each intricate design depicting the beasts and flowers of the forest. The patterns were embellished with threads of gold and silver, bordering panels of silk in a rainbow of colours, but most of all, it was the eyes of the animals that caught her breath, tiny precious jewels that reflected the flames of the fire with a life of their very own.

'Is this for me, Willow?' she asked.

'Yes, Miss, it is yours.'

'Can I try it on?'

'Yes, Miss, but I guarantee it will fit.'

Gwenno swung the cape around her shoulders and fastened it at her chest with the built in broach of exquisite jade. Despite its embroidery, it felt as light as a feather and fell snugly around her shoulders. The hem hung down to her calves and she spun around, making the robe flare outwards.

'Wait a minute, Miss,' said Willow, and ran to her bed space to retrieve a polished brass mirror. She quickly returned and held it up for Gwenno to see the effect.

Gwenno stared at her reflection, her troubles momentarily forgotten and raised the ermine trimmed hood to frame her face before teasing out her long blonde hair to fall over her chest.

'It's beautiful,' she whispered.

'Wait, Miss, there's more,' said Willow, and she returned to the table to retrieve another object from the parcel. She handed over a moulded eye mask, studded with exquisite tiny stones of ruby and sapphire.

Gwenno lowered the hood and placed the mask gently on the bridge of her nose. Willow tied it at the back of her head before Gwenno looked again into the brass mirror. Staring back at her was the gilded and bejewelled mask of a mountain cat, pierced by the sparkle of her deep blue eyes. The fringe of ermine around the hood framed her face beautifully, and the overall effect was an apparition of half human, half cat, enhanced by the thick golden hair falling about her face. Her eyes shifted slightly and she focussed on Willow in the mirror.

'Truly you are the chosen one, Miss,' whispered Willow.

Gwenno's gaze hardened and suddenly she tore the mask from her face, spinning to face the girl.

'Why would they give me this, Willow?' she snapped, 'all this finery, all these precious stones. I'll tell you why, shall I? These are ceremonial clothes, designed for my journey into the next world. This is nothing more than my shroud.'

She ripped off the cloak and stormed back to her bed, throwing herself face down onto the mattress, bursting into tears again.

Willow paused to collect a hair brush before following her to the mattress. She gently started to brush Gwenno's hair until the sobs eased.

'Miss,' she said eventually, 'do you trust me?'

'What?' came a muffled reply.

'I said, do you trust me?'

Gwenno turned her head slightly and wiped some tears from her eyes.

'Trust you? I don't understand.'

Willow kept brushing her hair before answering, her voice, whimsical in tone.

'Well, Miss,' she said, 'If you trust me, I can help you. But you must do as I say for the next few days before the solstice.'

Gwenno sat up.

'Help me, how?'

'I can't say, Miss,' said Willow gently, 'but if you do exactly as I say before the ceremony, there's a chance, just a slight chance mind you, that I can help you escape.'

Gwenno grasped Willow by the hands.

'I don't understand, Willow,' she said, blinking away the tears. 'What would you have me do?'

'I can't tell you, Miss,' said Willow again, 'for if you knew, the plan would fail. All I ask is that you do everything I tell you.'

Gwenno stared back for what seemed an age.

'Okay, Willow,' she said, 'you seem to be my only friend at the moment, I will trust you. What do I have to do?'

Willow repositioned herself behind Gwenno and resumed the brushing.

'First of all, Miss, you must resume the training with the Druids,' she said. 'The solstice is in seven days' time and they need to be assured that the ceremony will go ahead as planned. Attend all the teachings and the rehearsals. You must convince them that you have had a change of heart. From now on, you must wear the robe and carry yourself in a manner appropriate to the Gods chosen one. Show everyone that you accept your fate and are willing to embrace your destiny. Give them no cause to doubt your intentions.'

'How long must I carry on the pretence?' asked Gwenno.

'Right up until the last moment, and if the Gods are on our side, everyone will achieve their desired outcome.'

'I will live?' asked Gwenno, a hint of hope in her voice.

197

'I hope so, Miss,' said Willow.

'And if it goes wrong?' asked Gwenno.

'Then you will die,' stated Willow bluntly. 'We both will.' She shuffled around to face Gwenno. 'I know I ask a lot, Miss,' she said, 'but it is your only chance.'

'I don't understand, Willow,' whispered Gwenno. 'Why can't you tell me? Surely if I knew the plan, I could help.'

'Not this one, Miss,' answered Willow. 'If you knew, it would fail. So will you trust me?'

Gwenno nodded grimly and Willow resumed her place behind her. Despite her excitement, Gwenno finally relaxed, hypnotised by Willows gentle tones as she brushed her hair.

'Such beautiful hair, Miss,' she said, 'you are so lucky.'

Chapter 27

Once again, Gwydion stood in the hall of King Idwal in the heart of the Cerrig. There were no council members this time, and passage up to the hall was much easier due to so many men having been sent to support Caratacus. Gwydion and Cody stood side by side, and between them stood the bedraggled Roman prisoner. Finally a door crashed open and Idwal strode into the chamber. He circled around the giant table and sat on the edge before his visitors.

'Gwydion!' he announced, 'you have returned sooner than I expected. What news of the battle?'

'I am afraid it does not bode well, Sire,' said Gwydion. 'Caratacus was routed at Medway and fled into the hills. Thousands have fallen and the rest of the army is scattered across the land.'

'How can this be?' asked Idwal. 'Caratacus had the largest army ever assembled. I even sent him a thousand of our best men.'

'The Romans fight like nothing I have ever seen.' said Gwydion. 'They stand tightly side by side and act as one, each protecting each other.'

'Nothing a good horseman couldn't break through,' said Idwal.

'Our horses are torn apart before they reach their lines,' said Gwydion. 'Balls of fire fall like hail and explode amongst our men before they are within range of our spears. The skies darken with countless arrows and slingshot cuts down our warriors like hay. For every Roman that falls, a hundred of ours are killed. We cannot beat this foe.'

Idwal was silent as he absorbed the news, his face grey as the implications sank in. Finally, his gaze fell on the prisoner.

'Who is this?' he asked eventually.

'This is the Roman.' said Gwydion. 'He is a deserter and I have brought him to you as a payment.'

'Payment?'

'Yes, Sire, I seek a favour.' For the next few minutes, Gwydion explained the news he had received about Gwenno and the fate that lay before her on Mona.

'And what is it you expect of me?' asked Idwal.

'Sire, with a troop of armed men and your seal, I could ride to Isla Mona and free her. I could be back within days.'

'Why would I do that?' asked Idwal bemusedly.

'Sire, this Roman has knowledge of the enemy. The way they fight, their strengths, and their weaknesses. All this information is of value to you and our people.' He paused. 'Sire, I was to marry this girl and I have little gold to pay for the favour I seek, but the Roman's knowledge is worth a cart full of gold. If you cannot spare the troop, I ask only for your seal to instruct the Druids to release her.'

'Tell me something,' said Idwal, 'even if I wanted to, what makes you think that I hold sway over the Druids?'

'You are their King, sire. They will listen to you.'

'I fear you hold me in too high esteem, young man,' said Idwal. 'The Druids are the real power holders in these lands. I am King in name only, as is Caratacus or any other tribal leader. The Druids do what the Druids want. If they wish to sacrifice this girl, then I have no power to stop it or indeed the inclination. They have their reasons, and if by this act they strengthen our warrior's sword arms, then it can only be for the good. By your own words, it would seem that we will need all the help we can get, if we are to defeat these Romans. Your favour is denied. Over the next few days, I intend to gather the clans to defend our lands against the invader. Take my advice, go back to your kin, find another girl and make the most of her while you still can. This other one will be remembered as she whose sacrifice helped repel the invader.'

'But, Sire!'

'The decision is made and I have work to do. I will send for you in ten days' time.' Idwal turned and left the hall leaving the three men staring after him.

'What now?' asked Cody.

'There are still three days to the solstice,' said Gwydion, 'I can still get to her in time.'

'The King has forbidden it, Gwydion, you have to stop this folly.'

'No,' said Gwydion, 'he didn't forbid it; he just denied me his support. You go back to the clan, Cody. I will continue alone.'

'You can't do this,' said Cody, 'It is suicide.'

'You have stayed with me long enough, friend,' said Gwydion. 'This is now my fight. Go and see your family, for when the Romans come, you may not get another chance.'

Cody held out his arm in friendship.

'May the Gods protect you, Gwydion,' he said.

'And you, Cody,' said Gwydion grasping his comrade's forearm.

Cody turned and strode out of the hall leaving Gwydion and his prisoner alone in the silence.

'What's happening?' asked Prydain in Latin.

Gwydion turned to his prisoner, staring at him for a long time.

'It would seem you have no value to me, Roman.' he said. 'Begone before the King returns and realises your worth.'

'Where lies your fate?' asked Prydain.

'Mine?' laughed Gwydion sarcastically. 'My fate is to try to rescue a beautiful girl from a well-armed warrior tribe, and very probably die in the process. But that is no concern of yours. Go home, Roman. Go back from whence you came. This place will soon be dripping with blood.'

Gwydion strode toward the door before Prydain called out to him one last time.

'A quest, you say, to save a pretty girl with death almost a certainty. I like the sound of it. Cut me loose and I will help.'

Gwydion stopped and turned back.

'Why would you help?'

'Why not?' shrugged Prydain, 'I have nowhere else to go. If I flee, how long would I last in these strange lands speaking only Latin? At least with you I have a chance, no matter how small.'

Gwydion walked up directly in front of Prydain.

'And if I cut you loose, how do I know you would not kill me in my sleep?'

Prydain thought for a moment before replying.

'You don't!' he said simply, and raised his tethered hands.

Gwydion nodded.

'That's probably the only answer I would have believed,' he said. 'Welcome to life as an outlaw, Roman,' and with a single swipe, he cut through Prydain's bonds with his sword.

Chapter 28

The battle of Medway was over! Plautius gazed over the plains, calculating the cost in terms of life lost. As far as he could see, was a bloody carpet of Britannic and Roman flesh. The end game had been savage and the outcome had been in doubt for a long time, but despite the enemies overwhelming numbers, the legion's superior training and devastating technology had finally won through.

Wave after wave of barbarians had assaulted the advancing Roman lines despite catastrophic losses. Even when cut down, they were a risk, and his soldiers soon learned the meaning of the order 'Kill them twice,' a command designed to remind the legions of the need to ensure any fallen foe was definitely dead before advancing.

Plautius was full of admiration for his foe. They knew no fear and fought to the bitter end. If they had been better trained, then the battle could well have had a different outcome, but such was the will of the Gods. He now had to deal with the aftermath.

The surviving members of two legions stood scattered around the battlefield, exhausted by the relentless hand-to-hand conflict. Many sat in the blood coloured mud, tending their wounds or simply staring across the carnage, unable to grasp that they still lived. Many more lay in the filth, crying out for help as their blood drained into the foreign soil. Plautius noted grimly that few Britannic voices called out, and wondered whether the reason was there were fewer enemy survivors, or that they were made of sterner stuff. He suspected the latter.

Horns started to sound and rallying calls made, summoning the able-bodied back to their units. Centurions and Optios rallied their charges, doing the headcounts that Roman efficiency demanded. The day had seen the blurring of the edges between the two legion's heavy infantry, and for the first time, Vespasian's legionaries had fought shoulder to shoulder with those of Geta's, until each unit's colours merged into a uniform muddy brown.

Survivors staggered toward their standards, and troops of cavalry galloped from the legion arriving from the rear to chase down any enemy survivors. Hundreds of trained slaves swarmed onto the battlefield to tend to the wounded, or decant cool water from huge skins slung over their soldiers, a benefit gratefully received by survivors and dying alike. Auxiliary light infantry wandered through the enemy fallen, despatching any wounded with their spears as they found them, and medics erected tents at the edge of the carnage to receive the injured and treat their wounds.

Plautius despatched three Cohorts to the forward edge of the battlefield to provide a defensive line, while the rest of the Germania was tasked with building a marching camp on a nearby hill. The General walked amongst the wounded with his entourage, giving comforting words or compliments on particular acts of bravery. Eventually he spied Vespasian, sat against a tree, having a knife wound to his side tended by a medic. He was sipping on a flask of water.

'Vespasian!' stated Plautius, 'you are wounded.'

'Nothing more than a scratch, General,' replied Vespasian, grimacing as the bandages were pulled tight.

'The front line is no place for a Legate,' said Plautius.

Vespasian laughed wryly.

'For an age, there were no lines of any sort.' he said. 'They seemed to be everywhere and we fought whoever was within reach of our blades.' He swigged from the flask again. 'How is Geta?' he asked eventually, 'Did he prevail?'

'Geta is fine and is busy making his men's life hell,' laughed Plautius, 'That man has the lives of a cat.'

'I suppose I had better do the same,' Vespasian winced and struggled to his feet, 'We still have a way to go to the heathen city.'

'No rush,' said Plautius, 'We will make a stronghold here and lick our wounds.'

'But we should press home the advantage,' said Vespasian, 'take their city before they can regroup.'

'There will be no further assault,' said Plautius. 'The bulk of their army is dead or soon will be. Our cavalry units are chasing them down as they run and our Batavians scour the forests seeking retribution for their dead comrades. We will consolidate here and send deputations to the local tribes, demanding their surrender. In the meantime, the Germania will lay waste to the surrounding area. By the time the Emperor arrives, the barbarians will be begging for peace.'

'The Emperor?' queried Vespasian. 'What do you mean?'

'Didn't I tell you, Legatus?' said the General. 'Even as we speak, Claudius travels through Gaul, fully expecting to claim Britannia as a province of Rome.'

'Claudius is coming here?' asked Vespasian in amazement.

'He is, and will take the surrender of Caratacus personally. All we have to do now is find him. Anyway, enough politics, we have funeral pyres to build and wounded to tend. Get yourself sorted out and see to your men. The area is defended well, but it will take a few days to build the camp. Get them fed, watered, and ensure they are well rested. Who knows what these heathen may throw at us next?'

'Yes Sir!' said Vespasian and saluted as the General returned to his tour of the battlefield.

A hundred miles away, Legate Nasica was holding his own briefing in his command tent.

'What was the name of this deserter?' he asked.

'Prydain Maecilius Sire', answered Optio Remus, 'from the province of Picenum.'

'What was his unit?'

'Second Century,' said Remus, 'but he was seconded to the scouts.'

'One of your own, then?' said Nasica in slight surprise.

'Yes, Sire and I take full responsibility for his treachery. I should have beaten it out of him when I had the chance.'

'You knew he was a problem?'

'He is a son of a slave with ideas of grandeur,' answered Remus. 'I should have posted him to the auxiliaries back in Gaul.'

'Ah yes, I recall you have a particularly strong view of freedmen in the legions.'

'No place for them here Sire,' said Remus. 'There's plenty of room in the auxiliaries.'

'Hmm, interesting,' said Nasica, 'the point is, Optio, what are we going to do about it? He is only one man, yet it would seem he is a bit of a hero within the Cohort. Something to do with capturing a Germanic flag back in Gaul.'

'He did, Sire, the second Century's standard.'

'Shame!' said Nasica. 'Still, hero or not, we can't allow desertion.'

'No Sire!' agreed Remus. 'We have to set an example. Give me a Century of men and I will bring him back here alive. Let the legion witness what befalls traitors on campaign.'

Nasica stared at Remus, flipping a Claudian coin repeatedly as he thought. Finally, he slammed the coin down on the table and looked up, his decision made.

'We are in dangerous territory' he said, 'and the task is too big for a single Century.' He turned to one of the officers present. 'Tribune Mateus,' he said. 'you have been itching to lead an operation. Do you think you can handle this?'

'Yes, Sire!' said Mateus instantly, his chest expanding at the chance of glory at last.

'Good,' said Nasica. 'The legion is staying here while we await news from Medway. Take a Cohort and campaign westwards. Find this traitor and bring him back. In addition, you will make intensive enquiries as to the source of their gold.'

'Sire,' interrupted Remus, 'this man has brought shame on my Century. I request permission to accompany Tribune Mateus and bring him back.'

'Granted,' said Nasica and turned to the Tribune. 'Optio Remus is a veteran of many campaigns, seek his advice first and heed it well.'

'What about the other Centurions, Sire?' asked Mateus. 'It would not bode well for an Optio to be seen as outranking them.'

Nasica thought for a while.

'You are right, Mateus,' he said, 'and despite Optio Remus's credentials, it would nurture unrest amongst the men, but there is a solution. As you know Centurion Scipio was killed in the raiding party on the enemy village.'

'Yes Sire.'

'The scouts need an experienced leader to command them, so I have been thinking about redeploying Centurion Severus to the Scouts.'

Mateus nodded, it made sense, as the scouts were a very individual unit and needed strong and talented leadership.

'That leaves a vacancy for a Centurion in the second Century,' continued Nasica, and turned to Remus. 'How about it, Optio?' he said. 'You have turned down the post of Centurion many times in the past; and it's about time you carried the vine stick. What do you say; do you think you can command a Century?'

Remus looked back at the Legatus and considered carefully.

'In my time I have served under many Centurions,' he said, 'some were brave men and inspired leaders; others seemed more interested in the privileges the rank carries. Most of the second type are now dead. However, I concur that my rank could be an issue on this expedition, so I will accept until the task is done. Then I request that I am returned to the role of Optio.'

'Good!' said Nasica and threw him a vine stick, the badge of a Centurion's authority before turning to the Tribune.

'You have until the next full moon,' he said. 'Your task is twofold. I want the location of the gold mines and the traitor Maecilius. Make sure you return with at least one. Dismissed!'

'Yes, Sire!' answered Mateus and saluted in unison with the newly promoted Remus before ducking out of the tent. When they were outside, Mateus turned to the new Centurion.

'We will take the third Cohort,' he said. 'How long before you can have them ready?'

'First light,' answered Remus, but I would rather take my own cohort.'

'Agreed, said the Tribune, but leave the Ravens behind, they are too closely linked to the deserter.'

'Sire, there is one Decurion who I recommend we take. He grew up alongside the traitor and knows the way he thinks.'

'See to it' said the Tribune, 'we leave at dawn.' He turned and walked away, leaving the Centurion staring after him, pondering the hand the Gods had dealt him. There was no doubt that Tribune Mateus was a donkey's arse, however his weakness could work to Remus's advantage. Remus was not interested in gold or any other material goods. As far as he was concerned, he would focus on one thing and one thing only, the capture and subsequent killing of the slave-boy, Prydain Maecilius.

Chapter 29

Gwenno and Willow walked up the track, flanked by six warriors. Despite Gwenno's new found enthusiasm, the Druids had learnt their lesson and still guarded her closely. They were making their way up to a low stone building overlooking the vale of the Henge that was to be their new home until the ceremony the following morning.

The procession stopped as they neared the hut and Gwenno stared at the reception committee that awaited her. All around the perimeter stood a throng of Druid acolytes dressed in robes of vibrant colours. In the centre stood Lapwing, his own midnight black cloak stark contrast to the long white hair that blew gently in the breeze. In his hand was an unpolished staff of plain Oak, the symbol of his clan since their ancestors had walked these lands during the time of the ice, many thousands of years ago.

He waited until Gwenno approached before turning around and leading her into the hut. Gwenno expected the inside to be dark, but was surprised to see the circular room brightly lit with hundreds of candles, warming the entire room with their combined heat. The room was sparsely furnished with only a bed and a single chair, and opposite the doorway hung a pair of heavy drapes, each flanked by a Druid guard. Lapwing called Gwenno forward and manoeuvred himself to stand behind her, his hands resting on her shoulders as they both faced the curtains.

'Be not afraid, Gwenno of the Blaidd,' said Lapwing, 'you carry the pleadings of our tribes to the hearts of the Gods. Your purity enhances the songs of our people and the journey you take tomorrow is both glorious and breath-taking. Only a few are ever selected and you are one of those few, Gwenno, you are the chosen one. Behold your path, Gwenno of the Blaidd, behold the gateway.'

The two guards drew back the curtains revealing an opening in the wall and Gwenno walked forward to stare at the vista before her. A paved pathway fell away from the hut and through a small valley toward a ring of enormous standing stones. Gwenno stared around the wooded valley with mixed emotions. Rows upon rows of oak trees flanked the sides of the valley, interspersed with carefully positioned waterfalls that tumbled down the slopes to feed the tranquil moat surrounding the Henge, and a carved wooden bridge spanned the water leading to the centrepiece of the whole scene, the altar.

Despite the surrounding beauty, Gwenno was transfixed by this final stone and could see the farthest end blackened from the spilt blood of those who had travelled before her. This was to be the last place from which she would be aware of this world, the place where she would be laid on her back and see the sky for the last time. For a few seconds, she wanted to scream, to lash out and run from this place, but remembering Willow's instructions, managed to keep her emotions in check.

'It is beautiful,' she whispered.

'Tomorrow,' said Lapwing, 'you will take the path down to the Henge. Be brave and pay tribute to the awaiting Gods. Walk with your head held high, Gwenno, you will be walking into immortality.'

The two guards walked out of the hut, followed by Lapwing, leaving the girls alone in the candlelit room. Willow joined Gwenno in front of the window and stared down at the sacrificial altar.

'I told you it was beautiful, Miss,' she said quietly.

'How many have there been, Willow?' asked Gwenno.

'You are the second this year, Miss,' she said.

'And there have been others before that?'

'Yes, miss. Many.'

'Then what is the point?' asked Gwenno. 'They send so many, yet still there is a need for more. You would think that if this ceremony is of any use, then the Gods would have taken notice by now. I fear there are no Gods, Willow. And even if I am wrong, then they will not heed our representations of peace and love. They are bloodthirsty and evil Gods who revel in pain and suffering.'

'Miss, don't say that,' said Willow shocked.

'Why not, Willow?' asked Gwenno. 'What are they going to do, kill me?'

There was an awkward silence as they both continued to stare down at the Henge. Finally Gwenno turned to her companion.

'There is no escape plan is there, Willow?'

'Sorry, Miss?'

'Your plan to save me, it was just a ploy to get me up here with the minimum amount of fuss, wasn't it?'

'No, Miss, it's just...'

'It's okay, Willow,' said Gwenno, gently touching her cheek with the back of her hand, 'I understand. Don't worry, I realise now it's pointless to try to avoid my fate. I promise I will do as expected. I may not believe, Willow, but there are thousands that do. I will do it for them.'

Gwenno walked to the bed and picked up the beautiful cloak. She smoothed the fabric lovingly.

'It is very beautiful,' she said wistfully, 'I hope I don't get blood on it.' She looked up at Willow and smiled. 'Your cape is beautiful too,' she said. 'We will make a very regal pair, you and I, as we walk through the valley tomorrow.'

'I won't be there,' whispered Willow.

'Won't be there?' asked Gwenno, 'Why not?'

'The path is yours and yours alone, Miss,' answered Willow, 'I am not allowed to walk with you. My role is to care for you tonight and prepare you in the morning. I will be watching from here.'

Gwenno stared at the younger girl and tears welled in her eyes once more.

'I will be alone then,' she said, 'not even the touch of a friend's hand for comfort.'

Willow rushed forward and threw her arms around Gwenno.

'You can do this, Miss,' she whispered through her own tears, 'I may be stuck up here, but I will be with you every step of the way, I promise.'

It was still dark when Willow woke Gwenno with a gentle shake of her shoulders.

Gwenno opened her eyes, momentarily confused as to where she was. Willow stood before her resplendent in her red gown, already prepared for the day's events.

'It's time, Miss,' she said, stroking Gwenno's hair.

Gwenno sat up and looked around, surprised that she had actually fallen asleep.

'How long have we got?' she asked.

'A couple of hours, Miss,' said Willow. 'Here, drink this.'

'What is it?'

'I've made you a drink. It will warm you up.'

Gwenno sipped on the warm wine, resigned to her fate. Willow brought a bowl of warm water from the fire and put it on the table for Gwenno to bathe.

'Miss, there is something you should know,' said Willow as she started to brush Gwenno's hair.

'Which is?'

'Before your time comes, something will happen and you may yet have a chance to live.'

'What do you mean?' asked Gwenno.

'I can't tell you, Miss,' she said, 'all I can say is that when it does, you will know, and when that time comes, you must run. Run as fast as you can.'

'I don't understand, Willow,' she said. 'Even if I get the chance, what is the point? Guards surround us. Surely I would be caught within minutes.'

'There will be a short time when their attention will be elsewhere. When that happens, run for your life, like you have never run before.'

'And what about you?' asked Gwenno, her pulse rate increasing as she realised it was not yet all over.

'I will be fine,' said Willow. 'You just concentrate on getting away.'

Gwenno was silent for a while until Willow finished brushing her hair. The younger girl passed her the bowl of warm water.

'You should bathe now, Miss,' she said, 'it's almost time.'

'Willow,' said Gwenno gently, 'will you do it for me?'

Willows eyes moistened.

'Of course, Miss,' she said, and Gwenno stood up while Willow washed her body with the rose scented water.

Chapter 30

The warrior sat in the midst of a reed bed, wrapped in his muddy cloak. It was still wet but at least it kept the worst of the biting wind from his freezing body. He had lain in the mud for hours, feigning death as the invaders had rampaged through the forests. He heard a rustle to his right and an old man carrying a woven sack came scuttling through the reeds, keeping as low as possible to avoid any unwanted attention. He opened the bag and started pulling the contents onto a rock.

'I've got water,' he said, 'cloth for a bandage and look,' he held up the last item, proud of his prize, 'horse meat,' he said. 'Can't have been dead more than a couple of days. We'll have to eat it raw of course, can't risk a fire, but it's meat nonetheless.'

The wounded warrior stared at the older man as he busied himself stripping the cloth into bandages with his knife.

'Why, Holler?' asked the wounded warrior weakly.

'We need food, Sire,' said the old man 'and we have to clean that wound before...'

'No,' interrupted the warrior. 'Why did you return?'

'Why wouldn't I?' asked the man, without taking his eyes from the task in hand.

'You could have made good your escape.'

'Escape, Sire?'

'From me of course,' came the reply. 'The Gods have forsaken me, Holler, you should too.'

'I have known nothing else but service to you since a boy,' said the servant. 'I have been told what to do, how to do it and when to do it. I have been fed, clothed and have had a roof over my head. I know no other way.'

'But you would be free,' said the warrior. 'There is no one left to hunt you down or administer the whip. You could see out the rest of your days as a freeman.'

'And what sort of freedom would that be?' he asked. 'Whether I serve in a household or wander unfettered through the forests, I will never be free while they echo to the step of the Romans. I am still a Briton and I will never be free as long as one invader remains in these lands. Don't forget, Sire, I too have witnessed their brutality. I have also held my hands over my ears at night to block out the screams of the crucified. I have thought of running, but I stayed, and have done so

211

for one reason only.' He lowered his eyes; suddenly aware of whom he was talking too.

'Some speech for a servant,' said the warrior. 'Probably the most I have ever heard you say.'

'I know my place,' said the old man, 'I was born into servitude and will die the same. Every man should follow the fate the God's intended, servants, brigands or Kings.'

'Holler, you old scoundrel,' said the warrior, 'your words wound me more than my enemy's sword, yet I see their intent is to shame me into action, but don't you see, it is too late. The battle is lost, the army is slaughtered or scattered across the country.'

The old man grabbed the warriors arm causing him to wince as he jarred the wound in his chest.

'No, Sire, it's not too late. Yes, the battle is lost and yes, the army is scattered to the four winds, but this country is worth fighting for. This time we were but one tribe that stood against the Roman boot and we came so close. If one tribe can do that, imagine what an army made from all the tribes from across Britannia could do. If someone could unite us under one banner, then the invaders will be little more than ants beneath our heel.'

'The tribes spend most of their time fighting each other,' said the warrior. 'No one has ever united them.'

'But this is different, Sire,' said Holler. 'We have never faced a common enemy before. I believe the right man can unite us all and take the fight back to them. It may take years, but it can be done.'

'And where will we find this man?' asked the warrior.

'I am talking to him,' said Holler.

'What makes you think they will listen to me?'

'Why wouldn't they? You alone have faced the invader. Your tribe, the mighty Catuvellauni came close to defeating them. Many lesser men bent their knee to the Romans and took their coin even before they had stepped foot off their cursed ships. You alone faced them down and spat in their face.'

'And you think I can do this?'

'I know you can, Sire,' answered Holler, 'and so do many others.'

'Others?'

'Stand up, Sire,' he said, 'and look to the trees.'

The warrior struggled to his feet and stared across the reed beds. Over a hundred men stood at the forest edge, many wounded but all standing tall and proud.

'Who are they?' he asked.

'Survivors,' said Holler. 'Stragglers from many different clans. Only a few but there are many such groups and they seek a leader. They seek their King.'

They stared for a long time before the warrior spoke again.

'Bandage me up, Holler,' he said, 'we have work to do.'

'Yes, Sire!' said the servant and hastened to the task. This was the man he knew, the leader that the country needed. King Caratacus, son of the great Cunobelinus.

Chapter 31

Gwydion and Prydain had ridden their horses hard from the Cerrig and paid a fisherman to take them across the narrow straits of water between the mainland and the island of Mona. They left the horses back in the fisherman's stables, and it was only when they were out in the middle of the strait that Gwydion offered further payment to the fisherman to take them around the headland and nearer to the Henge.

Since leaving the mainland, the musical tinkling of a row of tiny bells hanging from the mast had accompanied them, and as they neared the shore, Gwydion turned to the fisherman.

'Can't you shut that noise up,' he asked, 'someone will hear us.'

'Can't do that,' said the fisherman. 'Them's my fairy bells, keeps the evil spirits away they do. A witch from the emerald isle gave them to me many years ago.'

'Oh for God's sake,' mumbled Gwydion.

It was dark when they landed on a pebbly beach. Nearby a stream emptied its fresh water into the sea.

'Follow that stream,' said the fisherman, 'it will take you right into the Henge.'

'Are you sure?' asked Gwydion.

'Sure as I can be,' said the fisherman. 'It runs blood red often enough.'

'Can you wait for us?' asked Gwydion.

'I am already risking execution,' he said. 'This is a holy place. If I am found, it would be my blood that colours the stream.'

'I will pay you extra!' said Gwydion.

'I will not stay,' said the fisherman, 'but for the right price, I will return tomorrow night when the moon is at its highest.'

'Name it.'

'That Torc you wear around your neck.'

Gwydion's fingers crept subconsciously to his necklace. It was the symbol of his clan given to him by Erwyn, the first time he had visited the Cerrig.

'How do I know you will return?' he asked.

'If I don't, and you still live, then you know where to find me.'

'Okay, I will trust you,' said Gwydion, 'but if you betray me, then know this. Before I cut your throat you will watch me burn your wife and children.'

The fisherman swallowed nervously.

'Understood!' he said.

'Midnight tomorrow,' confirmed Gwydion.

'I will be here,' said the fisherman, 'but will lay off shore. If you are successful, light a flame and I will come in to get you. I will wait no longer than sunrise.'

Gwydion unfastened the Torc and gave it to the fisherman.

'Until tomorrow,' he said.

The fisherman climbed back into his boat as the two men ran toward the nearby tree line.

Prydain was still weakened from his imprisonment, and he struggled to keep up. He stopped to catch his breath, leaning against a tree.

'You okay?' asked Gwydion.

'Just need a minute,' answered Prydain.

Gwydion removed a leather water flask from beneath his tunic and offered it to the Roman.

'We have to push on,' he said, 'the solstice is in a few hours and the Druids like to conduct their grisly business at the rising of the sun.'

'What do you intend to do when we get there?' asked Prydain.

'I don't know,' answered Gwydion, 'but I haven't ridden two hundred miles to give up now. Are you ready?'

Prydain nodded and forced himself away from the tree trunk. They started to run again, following the stream inland. Suddenly, Gwydion stopped dead in his tracks, causing Prydain to walk into him.'

'Shhh,' he said, holding up his hand and they both fell silent, listening to the ethereal drumming that echoed faintly through the forest. 'Must be getting near,' said Gwydion and they continued at a slower pace.

To their front, the darkened sky was glowing from unseen fires and the two men slowed their pace even more. Eventually they peered through the forest edge and saw a ring of braziers around a stone circle. Rows of robed men and women chanted strange incantations and a drum beat permeated the air as more robed people filed into the clearing, each carrying a flaming torch.

'This must be it,' whispered Gwydion. 'But where is Gwenno?'

Prydain pointed up the slope at the far end of the valley to a stone hut, surrounded by armed warriors.

'I'll wager she's in there,' he said.

'We have to get up there,' said Gwydion, 'there's only an hour until dawn.'

They retreated into the undergrowth and circled the Henge, staying well away from the hive of activity.

The going was much slower than they expected due to the amount of human traffic making their way to the Henge in the pre-dawn gloom. They stayed in amongst the thicker undergrowth around the outer edge of the copse, crawling on their bellies to remain unseen in the darkness. Finally, they reached the edge opposite the hut door and were dismayed to see there was still a guard on duty. They waited for an age, listening to the hypnotic chanting of thousands of voices permeating the surrounding hills and forests. Suddenly, Gwydion grabbed Prydain's arm.

'Look!' he said.

Prydain followed his pointing finger and could see the shutters being opened from the inside. Though it was still dark outside, the two men could see the profile of a girl, illuminated by the light of candles.

'Is it her?' asked Prydain, staring at the shorthaired girl wrapped in a scarlet cape.

'No!' said Gwydion, the disappointment evident in his voice, 'I don't understand. The messenger in Caratacus's camp described her clearly.'

'Perhaps, he was mistaken,' said Prydain. 'Perhaps she is safe at home while you have travelled all this way for nothing.'

'I hope you're right, Roman,' said Gwydion.

Suddenly another figure joined the red caped girl at the window, her long blond hair reflecting the candlelight in a golden glow that beautifully matched the astonishing bejewelled cloak she was wearing.

'There she is,' stuttered Gwydion. 'By the Gods, I have never seen a vision so entrancing.'

'Are you sure it is her?'

'I grew up with her, Roman, I would recognise her anywhere. Who else in the whole of these Britannic islands has hair such as she?'

'What do we do now?' asked Prydain.

'We have a little time,' said Gwydion. 'I hope that guard will be distracted long enough for us to get inside and bring her out.'

Prydain pointed at another three guards around the edge of the thicket, each keeping an eye on the hut entrance.

'What about those?'

Gwydion evaluated the situation over and over again, finally realising that there was no way he could approach the hut without being seen. The drums and chanting grew louder and he was conscious that the horizon was getting lighter. They had to act now. He turned to Prydain.

'I hardly know you, Roman.' he said. 'Our people are at war and I have imprisoned you with the full intention of selling you into slavery for my own ends. Yet now, I find myself asking you to do something that I have no right to ask.'

Prydain stared back in silence as Gwydion drew his knife and offered it to him handle first.

'Have you ever murdered a man, Roman?' he asked.

'No,' answered Prydain eventually. 'But I have killed many in a cause designed to make a rich man richer. Is that not the same?'

'Only the Gods can judge,' said Gwydion and nodded toward the furthest guard.

'If you can take care of him, I will take the other three.'

'Three for you and one for me,' smiled Prydain, 'you think a lot of yourself.'

'I know my own skills, Roman.' he said. 'Wait two hundred heartbeats and I will slay the first. When he falls, you take your man. The rest are mine.'

Prydain paused before taking the knife and without another word, crawled back into the undergrowth to circle his way toward his target.

Gwydion unpacked Angau from its leather wrap and strung the bow, grimacing as its ancient frame creaked under the strain. He withdrew three arrows and placed them on the ground before him, calculating the order of the kills. He needed to take the one facing him first so there would be a delay before the alarm was raised. After that, he would take the nearest and finally, if he had been successful with the first two kills, he should have enough time to take the third. He placed an arrow in the string of Angau and as the beats of his heart reached two hundred, took a step into the clearing in full view of the guard facing him.

The guard's eyes suddenly widened as he saw the threat and reached for his sword, but his hand's journey suddenly changed direction and rose to his throat in confusion. There was no arrow sticking out of his neck, only a feather-lined hole rapidly filling with arterial blood where the shaft had passed clean through.

He fell to his knees in shock and tried to call out a warning to his comrades. His efforts were in vain as he choked on his own blood and as the pain kicked in, he dropped writhing to the floor. A second guard looked over, attracted by the noise. More alert than the first victim, he immediately recognised the danger and called out as he ran toward Gwydion.

Gwydion reloaded Angau and sent an arrow straight into the middle of the warrior's chest, killing him instantly, but as good as he was, he knew that he could take only one more before the last warrior reached him.

'Blast the Roman.' he thought, 'this one should already be dead.'

His third arrow missed completely as the warrior ducked at the last moment and Gwydion discarded Angau to draw his sword. He knew there was no way he could defeat the two attacking warriors, but he would go down fighting. He raised his sword to deflect the strike of the warrior's larger blade being brought down to cleave his skull in two, shuddering under the impact. Pain shot through his arm and it was all he could do to lift it up again to deflect the second strike. The remaining warrior closed in to finish him off and Gwydion knew he his chances were minimal.

Suddenly Prydain came crashing out of the undergrowth and flew at the second warrior, knocking him off his feet. Gwydion's strength was momentarily refreshed by the unexpected arrival of the Roman, and as the other two antagonists grappled in the dirt, he renewed his efforts against the heavier swordsman.

Both Prydain's knife and the warrior's sword had been dislodged in the collision, and though Prydain was weaker than his enemy, he had managed to cut through the man's upper arm muscle before he lost his blade. With one arm now useless, the odds were even and they rolled around the clearing, each seeking an advantage over the other. They got to their feet before Prydain managed to get his hands around his opponent's throat to throttle him, but the man responded by smashing his forehead into the Roman's nose, spreading it across his face.

Prydain staggered backwards, momentarily stunned as the warrior closed in for the kill. He realised he was close to losing the fight and placed all his strength into one last effort. He allowed the man to come in close and as his opponent reached back to wind up an enormous punch, Prydain stepped in toward him, and using every last ounce of strength, drove the heel of his hand upwards onto his opponents chin, instantly shattering both sides of his jaw at the joints and driving the bones up into his brain. The warrior fell back in excruciating pain and as the brain cells struggled to make sense of the damage, he fell to the floor before thrashing uncontrollably in a final painful death throe.

Gwydion had also bettered his man and was forcing him backwards despite the warrior's larger sword. He knew he was the better swordsman and kept the pressure on. Finally, the opportunity he had been waiting for materialized and as the tired warrior swung a wild horizontal blow, intended to decapitate him, Gwydion ducked inside and drove the point of his sword upwards through his opponent's stomach and deep into his chest. The warrior stopped suddenly and gripped Gwydion's throat, but the sword was deep inside his body and Gwydion savagely twisted the blade, slicing the man's heart in two. The warrior's grip fell away and Gwydion pushed the dying warrior backwards to withdraw his blade.

Gwydion took a step backwards gasping for breath, but seeing a movement out of the corner of his eye, span around to defend himself.

Prydain stood in front of him, and as Gwydion watched in horror, the Roman reached back and threw his knife directly at Gwydion's head. The spinning blade passed close enough for him to hear the rush of air, and realised the Roman had missed.

Prydain stood across from Gwydion, each staring at each other in silence. Although he didn't understand the reason for the betrayal, Gwydion resolved to finish the situation once and for all. He re-gripped the hilt of his sword, but before he moved, another sound from behind him caused him to spin around.

A final, previously unseen guard had fallen to his knees a few paces behind Gwydion. He had sneaked up to kill him from behind, the threat obvious by the sword hanging limply from his hand, but his mission had been cut short by Prydain's blade sticking angrily from between his eyes. As Gwydion watched, the warrior toppled forward into the dirt and Gwydion span back around to stare in gratitude at the Roman.

'I thought that was meant for me!' he said.

'Perhaps it was,' said Prydain, 'maybe I killed the wrong man.'

'Perhaps,' answered Gwydion. 'Anyway you were late!'

'You count too fast!' answered Prydain.

'Come on,' said Gwydion, 'there is little time!' and he ran across the clearing and into the hut.

Chapter 32

On the northern coast of Khymru, a stranger sat on a grassy bank at the side of the road leading through Treforum, hungrily eating a bowl of soup from the same trader that Gwydion had patronised over a year earlier. The nosey old woman gave up trying to engage him in conversation when he had indicated he couldn't understand, but though he looked a bit rough, his money was as good as any and she had happily ladled two heaped spoons of broth into a wooden bowl in return for a copper coin. The stranger's common clothing was well worn and dirty. His black hair was unkempt and droplets of soup ran through his week old beard. The woman's partner joined them and tried to make conversation.

'Come far?' he asked.

The man shrugged his shoulders and mumbled something in a strange language.

'I've tried that!' said the woman. 'Can't you see he's a foreigner?'

The old man stared at the stranger wolfing down the food.

'Hasn't had a meal in days by the look of him,' he said before trying again. 'Gaul?' he asked pointing at the man's chest. 'Are you from Gaul?'

The man looked puzzled for a moment and then nodded in agreement.

'Oui,' he said, 'Gaul.'

'I knew it,' said the old man, 'another refugee from the Romans, I'll wager.'

The man looked up again, spoon halfway to his mouth seemingly alarmed at the familiar word and he sprang up, drawing his knife and looking around him nervously.

'*Roomans*?' he repeated in his strange language and looked quizzically at the old man.

'Don't worry,' laughed the old man, 'no *Roomans* around here. Well, not yet anyway.'

'Poor thing!' said his wife. 'Must have had some bad experiences.'

'What's your name, friend?' asked the old man slowly, trying to break through the language barrier, 'I am Owen,' he continued pointing at his own chest, 'You?'

The man looked puzzled but then realisation dawned.

'Jeanne,' he answered, 'Jeanne.'

Owen laughed.

'See,' he called to his wife, 'the smelly brute isn't so stupid after all; he understands me.'

'Owen, Jeanne!' repeated the stranger again.

'Well, Jeanne,' said Owen, 'we may not be able to understand each other, but anyone who has faced the Romans and survived is welcome here. Wife!' he called, 'bring our friend a tankard of beer.'

As the old woman poured the ale, a commotion appeared further down the track and a troop of horses appeared from around the bend to gallop past the hut in a cloud of dust. The old woman came out carrying the ale and watched the warriors passing.

'Where are they going?' she asked.

'Out to the clans,' said the old man. 'Idwal is calling them to arms.'

Jeanne looked at the riders and then quizzically at Owen, the unspoken question obvious on his face.

'Warriors!' said Owen slowly. 'From the Cerrig,' he pointed up toward the nearby mountain, 'The King's fort up in the hills.'

Jeanne shrugged and smiled simply, his demeanour displaying his lack of understanding.

'Never you mind, Jeanne,' said Owen. 'here's your ale.'

Jeanne took the drink and sat back down on the grass verge before picking up the bowl once again. His eyes were focussed on the soup, but underneath, his mind was racing. Not only did he understand everything the old couple were saying, but he had only been in the village an hour and already he had learned vital intelligence. Jeanne of Gaul, otherwise known as Andronicus of Rome and scout of the General Plautius's personal elite, put down his empty bowl and finished his ale. He had to admit, despite their backward ways, they certainly knew how to treat a guest.

Andronicus wandered through Treforum, careful not to be too conspicuous, yet taking in everything he could about the people. He had learnt the Britannic languages back in Gaul, taught by prisoners who had been sent to Rome by minor Britannic kings. He had learnt the particularly difficult Khymric tongue, and whilst he would never pass as a local, could understand enough to gather the intelligence he sought. He had landed secretly on the shoreline many months ago in anticipation of the invasion and had spent the time embedding himself in the locality as the harmless foreign buffoon he portrayed. Others of his unit were undertaking similar tasks in villages across the country and the time was fast approaching when he would be expected to rendezvous with Plautius.

Chapter 33

Fifty miles away, over a hundred men, women and children who had not been required by Caratacus, stood nervously behind the pointed logs of a small stockade, brandishing a range of old weapons and field implements in defiance of the force to their front.

Before them, grassland that less than an hour ago had held only a few scrawny goats, now held almost five hundred heavy infantry in battle formation, supported by twenty cavalry and two centuries of Germanic archers.

A few yards to their front, Tribune Mateus sat astride his horse alongside Centurion Remus, both amused at the feeble defences of the stockade. A bruised and bleeding prisoner lay in a heap at their feet, clinging onto life. It was his testimony that had brought them to the stockade, the severe beating finally convincing him that his only chance was to let the Romans know what they wanted to hear. They were looking for a deserter and at first, the boy had denied any knowledge, but after the brutal attention of Remus, realised he had no choice and told them of the prisoner taken by his people a few days earlier. He looked up in misery. He had given in to the pain and betrayed his people by bringing the enemy here, and was surely dammed. Mateus spoke to his interpreter who called out to the defenders on the wall, relaying the answers back to the Tribune.

'Who speaks for your people?' he called.

'I do!' said an old man, brandishing a pitchfork above the palisade. 'There is nothing for you here, be on your way,'

'On the contrary,' said Mateus. 'You have something I value very much, a Roman prisoner. We would have him back.'

'We have no prisoners,' said the old man.'

'Don't waste my time, old man,' said Mateus. 'If you value the lives of all within your quaint little stockade, you would hand him over or suffer our wrath.'

'I've already told you, there is no Roman here,' repeated the old man.

Centurion Remus gave a signal and a moment later, a long metal arrow slammed into the chest of the old man, surprising both the defenders and the Tribune who turned suddenly to stare at the Scorpio operator.

'Who ordered that?' he barked.

'I did!' said Remus. 'We waste time and it is the only language they understand.'

Mateus grunted and decided to let it go. He couldn't afford an argument with his Centurion in front of the men. Panic was ensuing on the wall and confusion reigned for a few moments before Mateus called out again.

'Silence!' he shouted. 'I will ask one more time, hand over the prisoner.'

A woman screamed back at him in rage.

'He told you he is not here,' she shouted, 'but you Romans never listen. There was a prisoner, but he was sold to a man named Gwydion many days ago.'

'Where will we find this Gwydion?' shouted Remus, frustrated at the response.

'He is of the Blaidd, a Khymric clan of the Deceangli tribe to the west,' spat the woman. 'If it's a fight you seek, take your tyranny to them. I promise you their warriors will give you a far warmer welcome than we can, or would you take pleasure in killing a handful of old men and women?'

'Cease your rant, woman,' answered Mateus. 'You are lucky that my sword has no taste for barbarian blood today. We will leave you to rot in your own filth.'

They turned their horses to return to the Cohort, but before they took a few paces, Remus's mount screamed and reared upwards, throwing the Centurion to the floor. He jumped up instantly and saw the Tribune frantically holding on to the horse's reins as it bucked and reared in pain, an arrow sticking out of its side. An order rang out from another Centurion and a Contubernium of men ran forward, using their shields to form one wall of a defensive Testudo.

Behind the shield, Remus helped restrain the horse, realising that the frothy blood meant the beast's lungs had been pierced. There was nothing he could do for him. He put his arms around the horse's neck and held its head against his chest, whispering soothing words to calm it down. The horses frenzy eased and finally stood still, though his breath was laboured.

'Goodbye, old friend,' said Remus as he petted the animal's head, 'I'll seek you out in the next world.' With a sudden thrust, Remus drove his Gladius up through the horse's throat and into its brain, killing him instantly. The horse dropped at his feet and Remus stared up at the stockade, and in particular, the frightened face of a young boy, no more than ten years old who had sent the arrow at his back.

'Well, sir?' asked Remus without taking his eyes of the wall.

'What?'

'They tried to kill one of us,' he said. 'Are you going to let them get away with it?'

'He is only a boy,' answered Mateus. 'He made a mistake.'

Remus bent over, and placing his foot on the body of his dead horse, wrenched the arrow free, ripping out flesh and fur as it came.

'This was meant for you or me,' snapped Remus under his breath, 'If you don't do something now, they will feel free to send arrows at the next Roman that passes. Next time, he might not miss!'

'But...'

'But nothing,' said Remus. 'You have a Cohort behind you expecting you to do something. Fail this, and you will lose them.'

'You're right,' said Mateus, 'we cannot allow them to threaten the glory of Rome, do what you have to do.'

Remus turned away and walked back to the Roman lines, cursing under his breath.

'Glory of Rome!' he thought. 'Who the fuck does he think he is?' He called his Optio to him. 'Pass the order to the cavalry,' he said. 'Collect as much deadwood and dry brush as they can and pile it up against the gate under the protection of full Testudo.'

'We are going in then?' asked the Optio, his manner displaying the rising excitement at the thought of battle.

'We are,' said Remus. 'Over the ashes of their puny gates. First two centuries only, shouldn't need much more than that. Pass the command, relinquish Pila, we are going in with swords only. No prisoners!'

'Yes, Sir,' answered the soldier and barked out the necessary commands.

Remus called to one of the attendants to bring his armour and a fresh horse. He faced the fort once more as he fastened his helmet under his chin, preparing for the assault. Up on the palisade, panic started to set in as the elderly defenders realised what was going to happen.

Remus walked to the young prisoner still sprawled in the dirt by the dead horse. Grabbing him by the hair, he tilted his head back and held his Pugio to the boy's throat. The captive's eyes widened in fear as Remus's intention became clear.

'No!' he pleaded in his own language. 'Please, don't...'

Both his thin arms grasped Remus's battle hardened arm in a desperate, yet futile attempt to pull the knife away from his throat.

'Centurion no!' shouted Tribune Mateus. Remus paused, and looked at his Tribune before dragging his Pugio deep across the boy's neck to open his throat.

The boy released the Centurion's arms and clutched desperately at the wound in a vain attempt to stem the bleeding. Picking himself up off the floor, he staggered across the pasture toward the wall of the palisade, desperate to reach his home and the help within. He managed to get within ten yards of the gate before collapsing to the floor, his strength failing as his life spurted out between his fingers. The Tribune's face drained of colour as he watched the boy die.

'Was there any need of that?' he hissed.

'Every need,' said Remus. 'You have to shock them into realising what they are dealing with. Let them know the futility of their actions.'

'Won't that make them fight all the harder?' asked Mateus, a look of nervousness on his face.

'Some will, but most will hide, shitting themselves in fear,' answered Remus scornfully. 'Anyway, you don't think any of that filth is a match for your sword, do you, Sire?'

'Of course not!' blustered the Tribune. 'I was only asking so I could understand the threat.'

'Oh there will be a threat' said Remus, 'a small one, but a threat nonetheless. I am sure you will deal with it admirably.'

'Me?'

'Yes, Sire,' said Remus, 'this is your chance. You are leading us in.'

Chapter 34

Back at the Henge, Gwydion kicked in the door and raced inside to find Gwenno, but stopped in the doorway, momentarily confused. There was no sign of life and Gwydion called out in the Gloom.

'Gwenno!' he hissed, 'where are you?'

There was no reply, but seeing the silhouette of a girl laying still on the bed, he lurched forward fearing the worst. He stopped dead in his tracks when he saw it was the short-haired girl in the red cape, face down in a pool of blood.

'By the Gods, Roman.' he swore, 'what's happened here? Where is she?'

'I fear we are too late,' said Prydain quietly. He was at the back wall, holding open one of the heavy drapes.

'What do you mean?' asked Gwydion and joined Prydain at the wall, pulling open the second drape to see what lay beyond.

The flanks of the valley below were populated by countless onlookers and resonated with the sound of a thousand voices chanting in unison. In the distance, the rays of the sun were starting to creep over the horizon, illuminating the stones of the Henge in all its glory.

Before them, a procession walked serenely through the valley, two lines of Druids walking side by side, their white robes in stark contrast to the vibrant colours of the onlookers. An armed guard of honour lined each side of the path, resplendent in their leather armour polished to a high shine that mirrored the glint of their iron tipped spears.

Yet all this splendour was eclipsed by the lone figure that walked at the very centre. Even from this distance, the luxurious cape positively glowed in the pre-dawn light, its glorious colours only interrupted by the long blond hair that hung down as far as the girl's waist.

'Gwenno,' whispered Gwydion, distraught as he watched the girl walk to her death. He lurched forward to run down the path, but was grabbed by Prydain before he managed to pass the curtains.

'What do you think you're doing?' hissed Prydain pinning him to the wall.

'I can't leave her to die like this,' said Gwydion, 'I'm going down there.'

'And how far do you think you'll get?'

'I don't care, I can't just leave her.'

'That's exactly what you can do,' insisted Prydain. 'It's too late. You have done everything you can and will achieve nothing by dying here. Honour her by living your life to the full and remembering her sacrifice. She would not want you to die.'

Gwydion stared back down the hill, tears in his eyes. He knew the Roman was right and he wouldn't get twenty paces before he would be cut down. He would die for nothing.

The procession reached the Henge and the white clad escorts took their places around the stone circle. Each stood in front of a pillar as the girl walked forward alone to stand before the black cloaked Druid waiting for her.

'She does your tribe proud,' said Prydain as they watched her dignified approach.

Gwydion mumbled an answer through his tears but Prydain's attention was distracted by a sound behind him. He span around, poised to defend himself but the room was still empty. The sound came again and Prydain realised it came from the girl in the red cloak. They had forgotten about her and Prydain suddenly realised that she may still be alive. He crossed the room quickly and stared down at the body.

Something was wrong. If this Gwenno was so virtuous, why did she try to kill this girl before she left the hut?' He lifted the wounded girl's head gently from the pool of blood, trying not to hurt her but immediately realised something else didn't add up.

'Gwydion,' he called, 'come here, quickly!'

The Celt reluctantly dragged his eyes away from the scene and looked at the Roman.

'What is it?' he asked.

'This girl,' said Prydain, 'who is she?'

'I don't know and care less,' answered Gwydion, 'and by the look of all that blood, she won't be here much longer anyway.'

'That's just it,' said Prydain, 'it's not blood, it's wine!'

Gwydion stared uncomprehendingly.

'What do you mean wine?'

'This liquid, it's red wine,' said Prydain. 'In the darkness, we mistook it for blood.'

Gwydion walked over.

'Is she not wounded?' he asked.

229

'I don't think so,' said Prydain. 'Though I don't understand the purpose of the knife.' He indicated the weapon on the floor. He shifted slightly and Gwydion got a close look at the girl's face. His eyes opened wide in astonishment.

'By the Gods, Roman,' he said, 'it's Gwenno.' He staggered forward and took the girl in his arms. 'I don't understand,' he gasped. 'How can this be, and her hair, where is her beautiful hair?'

Prydain picked up the knife and studied it closely before taking a few strands of blonde hair from the blade. He looked again around the bed and spied the empty wine goblet lying on the floor. He picked it up and sniffed the dregs.

'Where am I?' moaned Gwenno, returning to consciousness. 'Gwydion, what are you doing here and where is Willow?'

'We don't have much time, we'll talk later,' said Gwydion, 'but who is Willow?'

'My handmaiden,' answered Gwenno. 'She promised to help me escape. Where is she?'

'I know where she is,' interrupted Prydain from the curtains. 'She is fulfilling her promise.'

Willow stood before Lapwing holding her breath, praying he would not see through her subterfuge. She was sweating heavily, not just through nervousness, but the cape was far heavier than she had imagined and she had tied the mask a little too tightly around her head. It was uncomfortable but necessary to secure the long golden tresses carefully arranged only ten minutes earlier. Lapwing was concentrating on his mantra and anointed Willow with water before indicating she should lie on the altar. Willow breathed again as she realised she had got away with it. She sat on the edge of the stone before laying back as she had done many times before, though this time, it wasn't for the sexual gratification of old men, but for the ultimate sacrifice and the chance to travel to the otherworld.

Gwenno and Gwydion were alone in the hut while Prydain checked that there were no more guards. Gwydion explained what had happened.

'What do you mean?' cried Gwenno. 'What has she done?'

'She drugged you with the wine,' said Gwydion gently, 'and took your place in the ceremony.'

'But my hair,' said Gwenno feeling her head, 'I don't understand.'

'It would seem she needed to make herself look like you,' answered Gwydion. 'The one thing that makes you stand out, even from behind golden capes and bejewelled masks was your hair. If she had that, then perhaps no one would look too closely.'

'Oh no,' cried Gwenno. 'That poor girl.'

'She is very brave,' said Gwydion. 'She must think an awful lot of you.'

Prydain came back into the hut.

'I have got the guard's horses,' he said. 'Come on we have to leave.'

'We can't just leave her,' said Gwenno.

'It is too late,' said Gwydion. 'We have to go now; there is nothing more we can do.'

Down in the Henge, Willow lay serenely on the altar looking up at the sky. Some female acolytes had arranged her gown around her, and Gwenno's golden locks hung magnificently from her head and over the sides of the stone slab. A skein of geese flew overhead and she realised it would be the last thing she would see in this life. As her eyes followed the geese, they came to rest on the hut where she had spent her last night and for a split second, she thought she saw the face of Gwenno peering from behind the drapes. Willow smiled. The carefully measured drug had worked and Gwenno had woken.

The chanting reached a crescendo as the sun's rays reached down to the altar and as they fell on Willow's golden mask, she closed her eyes, not wanting to see the Druid's raised axe.

The chanting suddenly ended and in the silence, some of the acolytes heard the girl's last words.

'I love you, Miss!' she whispered quietly.

Lapwing brought the axe swinging down and Willow's world went dark forever.

The three fugitives rode hard away from the Henge, heading inland until they reached the ruins of a hut on the edge of a trading village. They stopped to rest while Gwydion walked into the village to seek a particular type of person, and had only been there for half an hour when he spied a suitable target, a teenage boy who seemed to have too much time on his hands. Gwydion beckoned him over.

'Boy, come here,' he said.

The teenager looked up with suspicion.

'Why?' he said. 'I haven't done anything wrong.'

'I'm sure you haven't,' said Gwydion. 'How would you like to earn two coins?'

An hour later, Gwydion returned to the ruined hut where Gwenno and Prydain were waiting.

'There you are,' said Gwenno jumping up and giving him a hug, 'I was getting worried.'

'I'm back now,' said Gwydion, 'and I've got some food.' He pulled a loaf of bread from beneath his cloak and handed it over.

'Eat quickly,' he said, 'we have a long way to go.'

'Where are the horses?' asked Prydain through a mouthful of bread.

'Gone!' answered Gwydion. 'I've given them away.'

'Why?' asked Gwenno.

'We are leaving a trail too easy to follow. A farm boy is going to take all three eastward until dusk. Their saddles have been weighted down to simulate riders so hopefully, the trail they leave will give us a few extra hours to make our escape.'

'Why would he do that?' asked Prydain

'I told him that he is to meet someone at the next village who would pay him well, and if they are not there, he can keep the horses.'

'What now?' asked Gwenno.

'Now we walk,' answered Gwydion.

'Where to?'

'Back the way we came,' interrupted Prydain, guessing the answer.

Gwydion explained to Gwenno the reason for the subterfuge, and after they had finished the meal, they started walking back the way they had come but circling far enough south to avoid coming into contact with any pursuers.

At last they reached the isolated beach where the two men had been dropped off by the fisherman the previous day. They lay in a bramble thicket at the edge of the beach. Gwenno was fast asleep wrapped in Gwydion's cloak while Prydain sat alongside her, his back against a piece of driftwood. He stared out through the cover to the open sea, hoping that the fisherman would return early.

232

Gwydion lay at the top of a sand dune keeping watch for any pursuit. The sun was setting when he crawled back down to their hiding place.

'Any sign?' he asked.

'None,' answered Prydain. 'I don't believe he will come.'

'He will be here,' said Gwydion.

They sat quietly as they waited, watching the sun set into the sea. Finally, it was pitch dark, with only the stars to light the beach.

'What's that?' asked Prydain sitting up suddenly.

'What?'

'Listen, I heard something.'

They fell silent, listening for anything out of the ordinary. A faint voice carried to them in the night air.

'Is it the fisherman?' asked Prydain.

'I don't think so,' said Gwydion. He turned to Prydain, a look of concern on his face, 'it's coming from inland!'

'Wake Gwenno!' snapped Gwydion, 'I'll see what's happening.'

Gwydion ran up the dune again and crawled the last few feet to peer into the darkness. A few hundred yards away, two men walked slowly out of the tree line, crouching low as they examined the ground for any signs of tracks. They each held a flaming torch to light their way and behind them, Gwydion could make out the shapes of mounted men stretching back into the darkness.

'Shit!' he mumbled and scrambled back down the dune. 'They've found our trail,' he said, 'We have to go.'

'Where exactly?' asked Prydain, 'If they found us this quickly, how long would it be until they caught us anyway?'

'I can't run anymore,' cried Gwenno, 'I am exhausted.'

'We have to,' pleaded Gwydion, 'if we stay here we will be caught within the hour.'

'There is one place they won't look,' said Prydain.

'Where?' asked Gwydion.

'Out there!' said Prydain, and pointed out to sea.

'What do you mean out there?' asked Gwydion. 'We don't have a boat?'

'What choice do we have?' asked Prydain. 'Our way inland is blocked. The only place they would not expect us to go is out there.'

'Where would we go?' asked Gwydion. 'It's too far to swim to the mainland.'

'That's the beauty of it,' said Prydain. 'We only have to go far enough out so they don't see us and as soon as they've gone, we can return; half an hour at the most!'

Gwydion considered carefully.

'It is a calm night,' he said, 'I suppose we would only need to be out there until they cleared this area. It is worth trying I suppose.'

'I can't,' said Gwenno suddenly.

'It is our only chance,' said Prydain, 'we have no other choice.'

'No,' she continued, 'you don't understand!' She looked at him with fear in her eyes, 'I can't swim.'

There was an awkward silence as each realised the implications.

'You two must go,' she said. 'It is me they seek. There is no need for us all to be caught. You swim out, I will tell them you left me alone hours ago.'

'I gave you up once,' said Gwydion, 'I will not make the same mistake again. Either we escape together or we die together.' He walked over and held Gwenno tightly in his arms, her head resting on his shoulder.

'It's not over yet,' said Prydain suddenly, 'I have an idea!' He ran toward the bramble thicket, returning a few minutes later dragging the driftwood they had used as a backrest. Out in the open it was obviously the remains of a plank, a remnant of an ill-fated ship that had gone down somewhere out at sea.

'We'll use this,' he said. 'Gwenno can lie on top while we swim alongside.'

Both men looked at Gwenno in anticipation.

'Well,' said Gwydion, 'what do you think, can you do it?'

Gwenno looked at the plank and back at Gwydion.

'It's our only chance isn't it!' she said.

'That's the spirit,' said Prydain. 'Come on; help me get it to the water.'

They dragged the plank to the water's edge before the two men stripped off their clothes to avoid the weight dragging them under. Gwenno watched surreptitiously as they tied their bundles of clothes on to the plank.

'Gwenno, you will need to take off your clothes as well,' said Prydain.

'Why?' interrupted Gwydion defensively. 'She will be on the plank, there is no need for her to strip.'

234

'If she falls off, the weight of her cloak will send her straight to the bottom,' said Prydain, 'she can lay her tunic over her, but has to be able to discard it quickly if needed.'

'There's no need...' started Gwydion.

'Oh, Gwydion,' interrupted Gwenno, 'in the name of the Gods, don't be such a prude. This man has helped save my life; I have nothing to hide from him.'

'But...' started Gwydion.

'Shut up, Gwydion,' said Gwenno already starting to disrobe, 'our lives are in the balance here.' She gave the cape to Prydain and paused before lifting Willow's red tunic over her head.

'Right!' she said, holding the garment in front of her. 'Let's go swimming.'

The two naked men dragged the plank into waist deep water closely followed by Gwenno, gasping as the cold water crept up her body. They guided it over the swell and held the board steady while Gwenno hauled herself up. For a few moments, her naked body was fully exposed in the moonlight, and modesty forgotten, both men stared in awe at her natural beauty before she steadied herself and laid face down on the wood. Gwydion spread the tunic the best he could over her back to help her maintain some semblance of warmth. The board sunk a little lower in the water as it took Gwenno's weight, but as soon as the load distributed evenly, it floated well enough.

'Time to go!' said Prydain and indicated the light of the burning torches coming over the dunes.

The two men kicked out, propelling themselves and the raft further out to sea, conscious that they not only had to be out of range of the torchlight, but also far enough out that they couldn't be picked out in the moonlight. They swam gently, keeping the splashes to a minimum. For ten minutes they continued before Prydain called a halt.

'I think this is far enough,' he said and they each held onto the raft as they trod water, getting their breath back.

'You okay?' asked Gwydion to Gwenno.

'I'm fine,' she answered, her voice shaking with the cold. 'How about you two?'

The two men looked at each other, each knowing how the other felt. While they were swimming, it wasn't so bad, but now they had stopped, the cold was beginning to bite deeply.

'I'm good,' Gwydion lied. 'How about you, Roman?'

'Never better!' said Prydain through chattering teeth and they all floated in silence as they waited for the distant burning torches to disappear.

They lasted ten more minutes before Prydain knew they couldn't wait much longer.

'I think they are leaving,' he said, 'their torches are further away.'

'There is only one torch,' said Gwydion, 'the rest must have already gone.'

Prydain's brow furrowed as he stared at the shoreline. He swam around to Gwydion and whispered quietly, so as not to alarm Gwenno who had the tunic over her head.

'We have to go back,' he said. 'Now!'

'What's the problem,' asked Gwydion, 'they are leaving anyway. A few more minutes won't hurt.'

'They are not leaving,' said Prydain. 'That light you see is not a torch but a fire. They have made camp on the beach.'

'Can't have,' said Gwydion, 'it is too far away. They must have retreated into the dunes.'

'They are still on the beach,' said Prydain. 'It is us who have retreated. The tide must have turned and we are drifting out to sea. We have to get back in right now.'

Realising the danger, they kicked out as hard as they could toward the shadowy land, half-numb with cold and silently terrified at the thought of drifting out to sea. Though some feeling came back to their limbs, it was soon obvious that they were making little headway. Their strength left them and they finally stopped their exertions, clinging on to the raft as they drifted in the darkness, the fire a mere pinprick in the distance.

Gwenno lay still on the board, soaked through with the wash of the swell. She had heard the explanations and despite her own fears, she didn't want to add to the men's distress and shame at failing her. Her hand crept forward and her fingers intertwined with those of Gwydion. They drifted aimlessly and Gwydion knew he could not hold on much longer. His head lay in the crux of his arm, which rested on the board, and he had lost all feeling in his lower body. He heard a mumble from Gwenno.

'What did you say?' he asked lifting his head.

'Horses!' murmured Gwenno weakly through salt encrusted lips.

'Horses?' queried Gwydion. 'There are no horses out here Gwenno.'

'I can hear their harnesses,' she said weakly. 'Perhaps, we are nearing death and the horses await us in the next life.'

Gwydion smiled weakly.

'You will ride a white stallion my love,' he said, 'as befits a princess.'

'Wait!' said Prydain lifting his head. 'I hear them too - listen.'

'It sounds like bells,' said Gwenno. 'Tiny little bells.'

Gwydion suddenly looked at Prydain, realising the source of the sound.

'Fairy bells,' confirmed Prydain and they both started laughing.

'Fairy bells?' asked Gwenno. 'I don't understand.'

'Fairy bells!' confirmed Gwydion through his laughter. 'We are saved Gwenno; our fisherman is here.'

Without any more explanation, both men started calling out across the water. Gwenno watched for a few moments in bemusement before, without quite realising why, raised her voice to join the others.

Chapter 35

Caratacus stood at the mouth of a cave contemplating the scene below him. The stream pouring through the gulley had carved this feature in the landscape over tens of thousands of years and the water fell angrily from the inaccessible gorges above. For years, it had been the hiding place of fugitives and brigands, but the sight of five hundred battle weary warriors descending on their hideout had persuaded the incumbents it was probably in their interests to move out, and Caratacus had taken over the gorge with little argument.

They had been on the move for weeks and their numbers had increased to over a thousand men, women and children with more arriving by the day. He looked down at the makeshift camp with growing concern and turned to his servant.

'How much food do we have, Holler?' he asked.

'The meat is gone, the grain runs short and the people eat the frogs and creatures that live at the water's edge,' he said.

'How fare the hunting parties?' asked Caratacus.

'No matter how successful the hunt, Sire, there is never enough. We send riders to the local clans but they fear the Romans and know that any village caught helping us, will be slaughtered to the last child.'

'How many fit men do we have?' asked the King.

'About five hundred, Sire,'

'Bring me the leaders,' said Caratacus. 'We cannot continue like this.'

Ten minutes later, ten battle hardened warriors sat in a circle around the small fire Holler kept burning outside the cave. Caratacus emerged from the cave and joined the surviving leaders of his decimated army.

'I will get straight to the point,' said Caratacus. 'Three weeks ago we came here with the aim of raising an army and taking the fight back to the Romans, but we have become distracted. It was never my intention to carry women and children with us, especially refugees. While they are here, our time is taken up foraging to keep them fed. This is not the way of warriors.'

Everyone looked at him in silence.

'Every day we spend here,' he continued, 'the people get hungrier and we are one more day away from spilling Roman blood. We have to take action.'

'But what?' said one of the warriors. 'We hide like rats from dogs but if we leave, the Romans will catch us in days.'

'Yet, if we stay,' interrupted another, 'it is only a matter of time before they find us anyway. We will be trapped and killed like fish in a pool.'

'We are safe here,' replied the first warrior. 'This place is almost impossible to find unless you know of its existence. Only the locals know how to find it.'

'And how long do you think it will be before someone shares the information in return for a crust of stale bread?' interrupted Caratacus.

'They are your people, lord,' said the warrior. 'They will not betray you.'

'They are loyal, I agree,' said Caratacus, 'but loyalty doesn't feed the stomach twisted in starvation and the point of a blade is very efficient at loosening a loyal tongue. No, we cannot stay. Even as we speak, my people are suffering through their silence. The sooner this Plautius thinks I have gone, the sooner our people can get on with their lives. We have to leave tonight.'

The first man spoke up again.

'It is impossible,' he said, 'our people are too weak and our wounded still need to heal. They cannot travel and we cannot leave them here.'

'That is exactly what we must do,' said Caratacus. 'We aim to rebuild an army in order to help our people, yet it is they who are our greatest threat. The longer we stay the more likely it is that we are discovered. We must seek other tribes to join our cause.'

'We cannot leave our people to starve!' shouted the first warrior, jumping to his feet. 'What sort of King are you?'

'Blennus,' said Caratacus calmly, 'your concern is admirable, but you are still a young man. Sometimes the benefits of leadership are great, but they are countered by the weight of responsibility. This is such a time. We have to leave them for the greater good.'

'You would see them starve to death?'

'We will leave them what food we can and draw off the Romans so they can escape to the villages. The foreign devils seek me, and if they know I have been unearthed, they will take up our trail leaving our people time to escape.'

'And where would we go?' asked another chieftain. 'This area is swarming with Romans and more arrive by the day. Already they send envoys into the villages preaching cooperation or annihilation. Our source of recruits grows smaller by the day.'

'There is one place where the arm of Plautius has yet to reach,' said the King, 'the land of the Deceangli.'

The warrior spat on the floor and many voices were raised in anger.

'Seek union with our enemies,' shouted one, 'I would attack the Roman legions alone before sharing their campfires.'

'Do you think they see us as different tribes?' shouted Caratacus. 'To them, we are but a single barbarian race to be killed, raped or sold into slavery as they see fit, the name of the tribe is irrelevant. We share a common purpose and need to stand shoulder to shoulder against the invader. At last light, we will leave this valley and make speed to the land of the Deceangli. Those who would follow me will need a horse and enough bread for one meal. Leave everything else for those we leave behind. If we travel hard and the Gods are with us, we can be in the camp of Idwal by tomorrow night.' He turned to Holler. 'You will check each man who steps forward,' he said, 'I only want fit men who can ride and can still wield a sword.'

'Yes, Sire,' said Holler.

'You would give a servant sway over a warrior,' sneered Blennus. 'I don't recognise his authority or come to think of it, yours!' He stepped forward and drew his sword, but before he could assault Caratacus, the King flew across the clearing and charged into Blennus, driving him to the floor. Holler leapt forward to aid his King, but was held back by another warrior.

'Leave him!' he said.

'But the King is already wounded,' said Holler. 'He can't win.'

'He is Caratacus,' said the warrior, 'and Caratacus does not lose.'

The two men wrestled on the floor, Blennus's sword lying in the dust, having been dislodged in the fight. Caratacus got the upper hand, managed to twist himself on top of Blennus, and gripped his throat, cutting of his airway. Blennus's hand crept down to his waist band and drew his knife. He drove it into Caratacus's side and the King rolled off in agony. Blennus staggered to his feet, coughing and spluttering as he caught his breath.

Caratacus withdrew the knife and scrunched his tunic against the wound in pain. Both men looked at the sword and they both staggered toward it, each determined to gain the advantage. Caratacus got to the blade first, but as he bent to pick it up, Blennus kicked him in the face sending the King flying backwards. Caratacus sprawled in the dirt, his hands clawing at the earth.

Blennus picked up the sword and stood over him panting for breath.

'Stand up!' he said.

'Finish it,' said Caratacus.

'I will not kill you while you grovel in the dirt,' said Blennus. 'Stand up and die like a King.'

Caratacus stood up and stared at the young warrior chief.

'You were a great King, Caratacus,' said Blennus, 'but your time is over.'

'You are wrong,' said Caratacus, 'it only just begins.' Suddenly he threw a handful of gravel he had picked up whilst he was on the floor into Blennus's face, causing him to flinch for half a second, but it was all Caratacus needed. He launched himself forward and punched the warrior as hard as he could with a swinging right arm. Blennus's jaw was smashed sideways and though he staggered back, he did not fall. He turned his head back toward the King, his lower jaw completely wrecked and hanging loose by the tendons, blood pouring from his mouth as he stood there in shock.

Caratacus drove the flat of his foot forward onto Blennus's knee, smashing it backwards and tearing the ligaments causing the man to collapse in agony. The King stepped forward, still nursing his side before half collapsing on top of the younger man. He sat astride his chest and stared into the young warrior's terrified eyes.

'You have balls, Blennus,' he said through gritted teeth, 'I'll give you that.'

Without another word, he grabbed the warrior's hair and drove the back of his head down onto the rocky ground, over and over again until his shattered skull spewed its contents over the valley floor. The rest of the warriors looked on in silence until the King's rage abated and he hung his head in exhaustion. Holler ran over and helped him to his feet, examining the wound as he did. Caratacus turned to the chieftains.

'Does anyone else challenge my authority?' he asked. When no answer was forthcoming, he continued.

'Then nothing has changed,' he said, 'I am still King and we ride at dusk'.

The group split up and Holler led the King back into the cave to see to the wound.

'You are lucky, Sire,' he said, 'it is but a flesh wound.'

'Sew me up, Holler,' he said,' we have a long ride ahead of us.'

Chapter 36

After being rescued from the sea, Gwenno, Prydain and Gwydion had been taken to the fisherman's home. They sat huddled around the fire, exhausted and weakened from the freezing sea, desperate to feel the heat on their skin and scooping spoons of hot stew greedily into their mouths. They were given a heavy blanket each and shown into the attached barn where their horses had been stabled for the past two days. After stripping out of their wet clothes, they wrapped themselves in the warm blankets before laying down on the hayrick to rest, and within minutes, all three fugitives were fast asleep.

Gwydion woke reluctantly from his dreamless sleep, his shoulders shaken by someone in the darkness.

'Gwydion!' called a voice gently, 'wake up, I have some food.'

Gwydion opened his eyes slowly and looked around, momentarily confused as to his whereabouts, but as he became accustomed to the gloom, the memories soon came flooding back.

'Gwenno,' he said, 'you're awake!'

'I have been for hours,' she said. 'Sit up; Hivel has provided us with food.'

'Hivel?'

'The fisherman's wife, she has been really helpful.'

Gwydion sat up and looked around the stable. Across from him, Prydain sat on a hay bale concentrating on his own plate of food, his blanket draped over his shoulders. A freshly baked loaf of bread lay between them, along with a flask of ale and a couple of simple wooden cups. His mouth watered at the aromas and he took the bowl eagerly from Gwenno. Two pieces of fish lay steaming at the bottom, surrounded by a mixture of tiny beet and turnips. Gwydion was surprised, as despite the family's meagre means, the meal was a relative feast. Ignoring the supplied knife, he dipped his fingers into the food and ate hungrily.

'Where's yours?' he asked.

'I have already eaten,' she said, 'hours ago.'

'You'll need more than just that soup,' said Gwydion, 'we have a long way to go before dawn.'

'I have had two meals since the broth,' said Gwenno. 'At breakfast and midday.'

'I don't understand,' said Gwydion.

'The sun has risen and set since we fell asleep,' she said, 'you have slept the day through.'

Gwydion stopped eating and stared incredulously.

'We can't have,' he said.

'She's right,' said Prydain, 'I have checked.'

'We have to get moving,' said Gwydion, 'where's my clothes?'

'There,' said Gwenno, 'washed and dried. Like I said, Hivel has been great.'

Gwydion put his food aside and got dressed quickly.

'Why did you let me sleep?' he asked, untying his horse from the rail. 'They will be coming after us and we need as much distance between us as we can.'

'The need is not so urgent,' said Gwenno. 'Hivel has been to the village and the talk is that there is a large search going on around the coastline of Mona. I don't think they believe we have crossed the strait.'

'Still,' said Gwydion, reaching for his saddle, 'we should take advantage of the lull.'

Prydain joined Gwydion at the horses.

'Finish your food,' he said.

'We have to go!' he answered.

'Gwydion,' said Prydain, 'eat. We don't know when we will next have the chance, I will saddle the horses. Five more minutes won't make a difference.'

Gwydion relented and returned to his food.

'We have to take advantage of the dark,' he said. 'If we ride hard, we can be back by dawn.'

'Back where?' asked Gwenno.

'Back to the Blaidd,' said Gwydion. 'We need fresh horses and supplies.'

'Don't you think the Druids will look there?' asked Gwenno.

'Probably,' said Gwydion, 'but if we ride hard we may get there before them. I can get horses from my father and Erwyn will give us provisions and coin, I'm sure he will.'

'Okay,' said Gwenno. 'Give me a few minutes, I want to say goodbye to Hivel.' She walked to the nearby hut just as the fisherman's wife was coming out of the door.

'We're leaving now,' said Gwenno, 'I just want to say thank you for what you have done for us.'

'It is nothing,' said Hivel,' and after some hesitation held out a small parcel wrapped in Hessian. 'Take it!' she said, 'But don't open it until you have cleared the mountains.'

'What is it?' asked Gwenno.

'You will see,' she laughed, 'my husband doesn't know, but by the time he realises, you will be days away.'

'It should be us giving you gifts,' she said, 'not the other way around. How can we ever repay you?'

Hivel took a deep breath before replying, tears welling in her eyes.

'Many years ago, my daughter was also chosen,' she said, 'but there was no one to help her. Aiding you has been a great comfort to me. Waste no more time on ritual or ceremony Gwenno, life is for living. Grasp every breath and live every minute as if it is your last. Do this and your debt to me will be repaid.'

'I have known you but one day, Hivel,' said Gwenno, 'yet already I love you as I do my own mother. Take care, and one day I will return to thank you properly.'

'Live well, Gwenno,' said Hivel and retreated into her humble hut.

'Ready?' asked Gwydion.

Gwenno nodded and joined the two men at the horses. Within minutes, they were riding hard toward the mountain range separating them from the lands of the Deceangli.

Chapter 37

Plautius sat at his table with his officers. His headquarters had been established and a secure stockade built to house the legion. Vespasian had taken his legion north and he was busy imposing Roman will on the local villages while Geta's legion had retuned south to meet the Emperor. They had consolidated their victory and extra guards had been posted, not just on the fort walls, but throughout the surrounding countryside to ensure any rogue bands of warriors thought twice about any foolhardy attacks on their positions.

Camulodunum was an hour's march away and though it was still intact, it was poorly defended and ripe for the taking. Plautius had held his army back from the final sacking of the city. Claudius was on his way and the Emperor had given strict instructions that he and he alone, would take the surrender of the capital of Britannia. Messengers had kept Plautius informed about the progress of the Emperor and the last week had been hectic, whilst the preparations were being made. But, despite the honour and the total domination of the enemy by Plautius and his forces, the insistence of the Emperor to place himself in the front line placed the General in a quandary.

He had sent envoys into Camulodunum and had received assurances that the collective tribal Kings would surrender to the Emperor in return for continued local governance of their own people. Plautius was happy with this arrangement, as peaceful domination was always preferable to military might. The problem was, it only took one rogue warrior to take the chance to strike a blow against Rome, and the Emperor could be wounded or even killed. Plautius knew that all the security arrangements in the world could be undone by a fanatic intent on glory, and while Claudius was in his protection, his own life depended on his safety. He needed an unbreakable guarantee that the chieftains would behave, and to that end, he had called a meeting with his staff.

'Claudius is two days away,' said Plautius. 'He and his entourage are being escorted by a Cohort of Praetorian Guard, but worry not; I have sent Geta to ensure his safety.'

A ripple of laughter rippled around the gathered officers. Every one of them despised the Praetorian Guard. They seldom left the safety of Rome, served lesser periods than regular troops and were far better paid than the average legionary.

'Claudius will take the surrender of the city three days from now,' he continued. 'Most of the lesser chieftains are already here, but we lack the main man. Any news on Caratacus?'

'There was rumour of him gathering an army, Sire,' said a Tribune, 'but it has come to naught. He has fled westward with less than five hundred men. Do you want to send a Cohort in pursuit?'

'No,' said Plautius. 'We can deal with him later, though his head would have been a great prize for Claudius. What of the rest of the prisoners?'

'We have over a thousand, Sire,' answered the Tribune, 'but most are women and children. Camulodunum have sent envoys asking for their release.'

'What is their worth?' asked Plautius, an idea beginning to form.

'Slavery mostly, but a few men for the mines. Most decided to fight to the death and those who are left are not worth wasting rations on.'

Plautius thought a while before answering.

'Isolate the women from the children,' he said. 'Send the fit men to the mines, kill any too weak to travel. Now, let's get down to the business I called you here for. I have to ensure the Emperor's safety,' he explained, 'and I do not trust these Britannic animals further than I can hurl them, so this is what I want you to do.' He outlined his idea and within the hour had formed a plan to ensure the safety of the Emperor.

Two days later, a troop of cavalry escorted a representation from the city across the fields of corn to an open plain, and ushered them forward to see what lay beyond the mounds of excavated soil in the centre. The leader of the group scrambled over the spoil and looked down into long trench that had been dug over the previous two days. His face dropped as he looked into the gaze of several hundred pairs of children's eyes, each looking up at him pleadingly, as they realised their fate lay in this man's hands.

'What is this?' he asked over his shoulder. 'Why are they down there? Release them immediately.'

A Tribune stepped forward.

'You forget yourself, barbarian,' he said, 'you are in no position to make demands. Your city still stands, only because Plautius

247

wills it so. These children only live because I will it so. Both decisions are easily reversed.'

'What is it that you want?' asked the envoy.

'Simple, really,' said the Tribune, 'tomorrow Claudius will take the surrender of Camulodunum. If the ceremony goes well, he will lose no time in returning to Rome and our lives, both yours and mine, will become a lot less stressful. These children will be released and your city will be spared to trade with us.'

'However,' he continued, 'should anyone be foolish enough to make an attempt on the Emperor's safety, then things will be quite different.' He nodded to a group of slaves who immediately started shovelling earth down onto the upturned faces of the unsuspecting children below. Many started screaming as they realised what was happening, and tried to scramble up the steep muddy sides.

'Stop!' shouted the envoy. 'What are you doing?'

The Tribune held up his hand and the shovelling stopped.

'I have two hundred men waiting to fill in this hole,' said the Tribune. 'It will take less than ten minutes to fill, burying everyone in it alive. Give Plautius cause for concern tomorrow and there will be corn planted over these children before they have struggled for their last breath. You will be able to contemplate their suffering as we slaughter every living thing in your city before burning it to the ground. There will be no trace of Camulodunum or its people. We will wipe you off the face of the Earth.'

'They are but children,' shouted the envoy, 'what have they done to you?'

'Children today become warriors tomorrow,' came the answer. 'It would be a sensible military strategy.'

'Not even you are that heartless,' spat the envoy. 'Children are children the world over and are innocent in the eyes of the Gods.'

'And we will do nothing to them,' said the Tribune, 'as long as you control your warriors. Take our message back to your chieftains. The choice is clear. Accept your fate graciously, or get wiped from the pages of history.'

As the entourage was led back to the city to relay the message, the Tribune returned to the legion's fort and rode through the stockade to Plautius's tent. The General was outside and stripped to the waist as he washed in a bucket of water. He spied the approaching Tribune and dismissed the servant before towelling the remaining soap from his chin.

'Well,' he asked, 'how did they react?'

'I think we can safely say there will be no trouble tomorrow,' answered the Tribune.

'Good,' said Plautius. 'The quicker Claudius returns to Rome, the quicker we can get on with business.'

The Tribune agreed and joined Plautius as he entered the tent to make the final arrangements.

Chapter 38

Gwenno had wanted to ride straight into the village, but had heeded Gwydion's words of caution. They left the horses with Prydain in the forest and approached via the hidden paths of their youth, peering carefully down at the village. Life seemed to be going on as normal and teenage boys guarded the herds in the valley, whilst younger children of both sexes looked after the flocks of geese that wandered through the outskirts of the woods. Gwydion could see the occasional mounted warrior guarding the village.

'Are they looking for us?' whispered Gwenno.

'I don't think so,' answered Gwydion. 'They fear fellow Khymric raiders, though it's not the plaid of Ordovices they should be worried about, but the scarlet of the Romans.'

'Surely they will not come here,' said Gwenno. 'It is too far away and besides, if Camulodunum falls, they may just take the Catuvellauni gold and return to Rome?'

'You have not seen them, Gwenno,' said Gwydion. 'Their army is one of invasion. Nowhere in Britannia is safe and it is simply a matter of time before these mountains echo to the sound of their marching feet.'

'Then we must warn our people,' said Gwenno. 'Come on, why are we waiting?'

'I'm not sure,' said Gwydion, 'something's not right.'

Gwenno grabbed Gwydion's arm and pointed at the fort.

'Look,' she said, 'there's Hammer.'

Gwydion's heart leapt at the sight of his father exiting the gate pulling a hand drawn cart.

'Going to get wood for the furnace,' smiled Gwydion. 'Some things never change, come on, this is one man I trust with my life, keep low.'

They crouched down and made their way down the slope using the thorny hedge as cover until they reached the edge of the path. Finally, as the cart drew alongside, Gwydion called out as loud as he dared.

'Hammer,' he said in a loud whisper.

The blacksmith stopped and looked around.

'Who's there?' he asked, somewhat startled.

'Hammer, it's me, Gwydion.'

The blacksmith stared at the source of the voice through the thicket.

'I know no Gwydion,' he said. 'Be on your way before I call the guards.'

'Hammer,' said Gwydion, 'it is me your son, truly it is.' He took a chance and stood up for his father to see him.

The old man's face fell.

'Get down!' he hissed. 'What are you doing here?'

'We need help,' said Gwydion, shocked at Hammer's reaction.

'We?' asked Hammer. 'Who else is here?'

'I am here also,' said Gwenno. 'Why are you so angry, Hammer? Where is the welcome?'

Hammer walked around the cart and fussed with the wheel, a pretence to pacify any prying eyes.

'You will find no welcome here, Gwenno,' he said. 'Nor you, Gwydion. The news that you have betrayed the Gods has preceded you and you are hunted by the Druids.'

'I feared this,' said Gwydion, 'but we seek only food and some fresh horses. A night's stay is all we ask. Surely Erwyn would grant his only daughter this.'

'Erwyn is no longer chief here,' said Hammer, 'Robbus overthrew him many months ago.'

Gwenno gasped in shock.

'Is he alright?' she asked eventually.

'He was killed,' said Hammer somewhat abruptly, 'as were most of his men. Those that survived were banished along with their families. The Blaidd is a different place now. Robbus rules with a fist of iron and all fear his wrath.'

'What about my mother?' asked Gwenno. 'Does she still live?'

'Oh yes!' spat Hammer, 'she still lives. The whore warms Robbus's bed at night. It is her hand that drugged the wine that dulled your father's senses. Only thus, could Robbus better him.'

Gwenno cried out before Gwydion grabbed her and buried her face into his chest.

'Is there no one to help us, Hammer?' he asked.

'They are all Robbus's men here,' said Hammer, 'I only stay to look after your mother.'

'Is she ill?' asked Gwydion.

'During the fight, I took up arms with Erwyn,' said Hammer. 'Robbus's blacksmith was killed but I was only wounded. In the

251

aftermath, when the others were banished, Robbus made certain that I stayed to serve him.'

'How?'

'He hamstrung your mother,' said Hammer simply.

It was Gwydion's turn to stifle a cry and he looked to the heavens in pain as he imagined his mother unable to walk.

'So you see,' said Hammer, 'I cannot help you. If I do, they will kill her.'

'Then you should both come with us,' said Gwydion. 'Bring a team of horses and a cart. We can escape together.'

'How far do you think we will get, Gwydion?' snapped Hammer. 'Robbus is a brutal man and is not stupid. He knows you are in the area and if we flee, it would take but a moment to realize what is happening. We would be dead by nightfall and that girl would be back in Mona by morning. No, you must escape while you can.'

'Is there anyone else who I can turn to?' asked Gwydion.

'I love you dearly, son,' he said 'but I will not risk the life of your mother. If circumstances were different, I would challenge Robbus directly, but she needs me.'

'I understand,' said Gwydion. 'Fear not, father, I will not put her or you at risk. We will leave this place forthwith, but know this, before I draw my last breath, I will one day wipe Robbus's blood from my blade. This I swear by all the Gods.'

'One more thing, Gwydion,' said Hammer, 'the Druids know you are here. You were seen crossing the mountains. Every tribe has been warned they will be cursed if they offer you succour. Even now, two Druid warriors drink wine with Robbus. I don't know where you are going and don't want to know, but wherever it is, make haste. Get out of these lands while you still can. Now someone is coming, I have to go.'

Gwenno had stopped crying.

'I don't believe it,' she mumbled. 'How could she do it?'

Gwydion didn't answer for a while, but just held her close as he thought of the available options.

'Come on,' he said eventually. 'We have to go, Prydain awaits.'

'Where?' asked Gwenno. 'There is nowhere else to go. You heard Hammer, even the Durotriges and the Ordovices have been warned against us. No one can help; they are all terrified of the Druid's wrath.'

'There is one place,' said Gwydion quietly, 'where even the Druids fear to tread.'

'Where?' asked Gwenno again.

Gwydion looked deep into her eyes.

'We have to travel to the lands of the Silures.'

Chapter 39

Remus rode at the head of the Cohort as they travelled westward. They were flanked ether side by the cavalry units and the trail was being blazed to his front by a mounted section of scouts. Far behind the marching Cohort, a plume of black smoke rose lazily to the sky. Remus had no compassion for those they had slaughtered back in the fort; on the contrary, he had led the charge through the burning gates with ruthless enthusiasm. What had concerned him was the fact that the Tribune had faltered in the decision to burn it down, and as overall commander, had needed to act swiftly and decisively if he was to earn the respect of his men. What was more worrying was despite all his bluster and parading outside the stockade, when it came to the combat inside, Mateus had held back from any situation where he had to face an armed opponent.

Remus had quickly taken control and as soon as the gate had fallen, two centuries had charged through with a ferocity that crushed the few stubborn defenders who thought they could make a difference with their scythes and pitchforks. All resistance was wiped out and the Cohort only received one fatality and two wounded in the one sided battle. All adult men had been killed on the spot and any surviving old women or children had been placed in the absent chieftain's thatched hut, with the doors barred from the outside.

The younger women and teenage girls had been rounded up and though the quality of the women had been admittedly poor, the two hundred or so men involved in the assault had been rewarded with an hour's freedom to do as they liked before putting them to the blade. Two hours later, the Cohort were once again assembled in marching order, ready to continue their campaign, and they watched in silence as the archers prepared for the final grisly task of the day.

'Archers!' shouted Remus. 'Prepare arrows!'

The one hundred and sixty archers dipped their arrows into prepared fires and aimed them high into the air. The trajectory was designed to rain a hail of fiery arrows onto the thatch of the chieftain's hut, visible through the charred embers where the gates had once stood.

'Release!' roared Remus, and the sky was lined with smoky trails as the fire arrows soared into the air. Remus knew there was no need for a second salvo. More than enough arrows would find their target and the extra brushwood they had placed around the hut would ensure the place would be an inferno in seconds. He turned away from the scene.

'Ready when you are, Sire,' he called.

'Cohort, advance!' called the Tribune and the column marched away from the fort toward the west. They hadn't gone fifty paces before the first screams were carried to them on the wind, but not one man's head turned in concern. This was war and such was the God's will.

Two nights later, Tribune Mateus stood alongside Remus looking over a slow moving river. Behind them, the Cohort was busy building the marching camp.

'The camp is almost finished, Sire,' said Remus as he broke some Buccellatum biscuit and offered it to the Tribune.

'What do you think, Centurion?' asked Mateus. 'Have we come far enough?'

'I have seen nothing that persuades me these heathen are anywhere near the quality of warriors to be found in Germania,' he said. 'We have a full Cohort of battle hardened infantry supported by archers, cavalry and scouts. It would take a number twenty times that to cause us a problem, if the last rabble were anything to go by.' Despite his own assurances, Remus himself harboured some doubts but his determination to catch up with Prydain drove any uncertainties from his mind.

'Okay,' said Mateus. 'We will continue, but send a rider to Nasica to inform him of our progress. I will prepare a briefing about our magnificent defeat of the heathen back in their palisade.'

Remus returned to the Cohort to oversee the camp's completion, and after the men were settled and the guards posted, he withdrew to his own tent to get some sleep.

Several hours later, someone banged on the wet canvas.

'What is it?' asked Remus, instantly awake beneath his heavy cape.

'Someone is approaching the camp,' said Cassus, the guard commander.

Remus threw back his cape and pulled on his Caligae before crawling out of the tent.

'How many?' he asked, as he belted on his Gladius.

'We can see only one, Sire, but there may be others.'

255

'Where is he?'

'Outside the south rampart,' said Cassus. 'He has made camp. Shall we sound the alarm?'

'No,' said Remus, 'no need to wake the Cohort for one man.' He ran between the tents to the earthen wall that had been erected just hours before. The duty Contubernia was peering between the pointed stakes, and into the darkness beyond.

'Show me!' whispered Remus to the nearest guard, and his gaze followed the pointing finger into a nearby copse. At first, he could see nothing, but as his vision became accustomed to the darkness, he made out the shape of a horse and the figure of a man sat against a tree trunk.

'I see him, are there any more?'

'We haven't seen any,' said the legionary. 'He has been there for at least half an hour.'

'Wake the translator,' he said, 'and bring your shield.'

When Cassus returned with the translator, Remus stood up and beckoned the two men.

'Follow me,' he said and walked over the top of the bank and down toward the copse. They walked slowly, holding their shields as a defence against any sudden arrow or spear out of the dark. When they were within twenty paces, they stopped, and Remus told the translator what to say.

'Declare yourself, stranger!' he called, causing the silhouette to jump up suddenly and grab the unseen reins of his horse.

'Hold your weapons,' answered the lone rider, 'I am no threat!'

'Declare your business,' responded the Centurion.

'I am but a simple traveller,' came the answer in his strange accent. 'I will move on in peace.'

'Step forward.' ordered Remus and the man approached slowly.

'Are you Roman?' he asked nervously, staring hard into the darkness, unable to make out the shapes of the men. Centurion Remus drew his sword quietly as did Cassus. The traveller heard the unmistakable sound, and realising the danger, took a chance.

'I hear Claudius scratches his arse while his legionaries die to fill his coffers,' he said in perfect Latin. Remus and Cassus straightened up and stared in disbelief. It was a classic Roman curse.

'Who are you stranger?' asked Remus in his own language.

'I am Andronicus of the Exploratores,' he replied, 'and I am seeking the armies of Plautius.' All three men from the camp breathed a collective sigh of relief.

'Well, Andronicus,' said Remus, 'step forward and be recognised, it would seem you have found us.'

Back in the camp, Remus and Cassus sat around a tiny fire and shared a flask of warm watered wine with the scout. They waited patiently as he devoured some dried meat from their supplies. His hair was long and dirty and he smelled to high heaven.

'How long have you been out there?' asked Remus.

'Three months altogether,' said Andronicus, 'gathering information for Plautius.'

'Why are you in such a state?' asked Cassus.

'When you sleep with pigs, you live like a pig,' he said before taking another slurp from his tankard.

'You were actually living amongst the barbarians?'

'Sleeping, eating and shitting,' he confirmed between mouthfuls of meat. Andronicus let out a huge belch and looked around. 'Seems there's no more than a Cohort here,' he said. 'Where are the legions?'

'About ten days march,' said Remus. 'You are welcome to stay with us; I could use someone who has local knowledge.'

'Better not,' said Andronicus, 'Plautius himself awaits my report. I have information that will be useful when the he decides to march into the Khymru. What are you doing so far west anyway?'

'We are seeking a deserter,' said Cassus, 'I don't suppose you have come across him?'

'Can't say I have,' said Andronicus, his brow knitted in thought, 'though there was a rumour that a local had kidnapped a girl from the Druids and was heading south. Could that be your man?'

'I doubt it,' said Remus.

'Shame!' said Andronicus. 'If you should come across him, ensure you take his colleague alive. The Druids have placed a huge price on his head. Apparently he goes by the name of Gwydion.'

Both Cassus and Remus looked up sharply.

'That's our man,' said Cassus excitedly, 'Prydain was bought by Gwydion as a slave.'

'Don't know about slave,' said Andronicus. 'Last I heard, they rode as comrades.'

257

'Where did you say they went?' asked Cassus

'I didn't,' said Andronicus. 'I only know that they were last seen heading for the land of the Silures.'

'And how do we get there?' asked Remus.

'What exactly has this Prydain done?' asked Andronicus. 'To send a Cohort after one man, what did he do, kill the Emperor?'

'It is personal,' said Remus. 'Now how do we get to these Silures?'

'You don't,' said Andronicus, 'they will kill you.'

'We'll take our chances.'

'They are not like the others,' said Andronicus. 'They are savages with no compassion. Your Cohort will be annihilated.'

'I'll worry about that,' said Remus, his patience wearing thin. 'Now, I'll ask again, do you know how I will find them.'

'Your funeral pyre,' said Andronicus, 'but yes I do.' He pointed in the direction of the river, hidden in the darkness.

'Cross the river and head west until you reach a well-marked road,' he said. 'When you reach the road, head south but keep your wits about you. The Silures are not ordinary men. They are feared by all the other tribes of Britannia and will eat your heart without a second thought. Don't say you haven't been warned.'

They talked deep into the night before Andronicus curled up under his heavy cape to grab a few hours' sleep. Remus and Cassus talked some more before they too retired, though Remus didn't sleep. He knew he was close. A few more days and the slave-boy Prydain Maecilius would be within his grasp.

The following day, Centurion Remus and Tribune Mateus sat astride their horses staring across the river. Andronicus had given them detailed directions before resuming his journey eastward several hours earlier and the Cohort had travelled downstream to find a ford in the river. While the rest of the Cohort took advantage of the overdue break, they rode forward to join the scouts at the water's edge and assessed the grisly situation in front of them.

On the far bank of the river and on either side of the natural path that led from the water's edge, a thicket of over a hundred stakes had been driven into the soft riverside ground, each topped with a human head in different stages of decay, ranging from aged bare skulls to those freshly decapitated. Many were still adorned with the helmets their wearers had foolishly thought would protect them. Though there were no written words, the message was obvious; it said 'Keep out!'

'What do you think?' asked the Tribune nervously.

'Meaningless drama,' said Remus in contempt, 'I have seen it a hundred times in a hundred different places. I see nothing here to prevent us continuing.'

'Do you think it's wise?' asked Mateus.

'We are so close,' said Remus, 'it would be foolish to return now. Our quarry lies within reach as does the location of the gold mines. Nasica wants either, but bring back both and your name will be known to Claudius himself. Think how quickly the political career of the man who delivers the Khymric gold would advance.'

Mateus stared across the water, his nerves easing as Remus massaged his ego. Already he could see himself taking his senatorial seat in Rome.

'The matter is decided,' he said, 'we will complete our mission. Assemble the men, we push on immediately.'

'Yes, Sire,' said Remus and returned to the Cohort. Twenty minutes later, they waded through the river in silence as they passed the macabre warning and when they were safely assembled on the far side, Tribune Mateus addressed the entire Cohort.

'Today you men have made history as the first Roman unit to enter the Khymru,' he said. 'Heed not those childish warnings at the river; they are designed to frighten the weak. But we are not weak, we are Roman and they know not what they are dealing with. Thirty miles west lays a route that runs north to south through this land. Before the sun sets tonight, I want to be on that road, so take a moment to secure your kit, for we will not rest until we reach it.'

'This is what you joined for!' interjected Remus, 'for adventure, for glory and for gold. All three lie there.' He waived his hand toward the distant rolling hills. 'All we have to do is go and get it.'

They took the chance to eat some Buccellatum and dried meat before securing their equipment. As they were in enemy territory, Remus insisted they wear helmets and armour on the march and the scouts were deployed to the front and flanks of the column. They stood in a double column waiting to start; a heavily armed and highly trained unit of experienced legionaries. A cog in the greatest military machine that ever existed.

'Cohort ready,' roared Remus, 'double speed, advaaance!

As one, the column stepped forward, their pace designed to eat up the miles before them and as long as they did not meet any problems on the way, would see them reach the road in less than eight hours.

Chapter 40

The fugitives had ridden the horses to exhaustion in a bid to get as far away from the village as possible, and at last, Gwydion called a halt before their mounts died beneath them. They turned off the path to seek protection of the deeper parts of the flanking wood and finally settled into an overgrown thicket of ash. Their food was almost gone, as was the grain for the horses, and Prydain went with the nose bags to find grass on the outskirts of the wood. Gwenno sat hunched against a tree wrapped in her blanket, her eyes closed in misery. When Gwydion had finished with the horses, he sat down alongside her, stroking her arm gently.

'Gwenno,' he said, 'are you okay?'

The girl didn't answer.

'Here, eat something,' he continued, offering her a strip of dried beef.

'I'm not hungry,' she said.

'You can't go on like this, Gwenno,' said Gwydion. 'I know you are upset, but what is done, is done. You have to think of yourself now and be strong. We haven't gone through all this to give up now.'

'What's the point, Gwydion?' she asked. 'Erwyn is dead, Hammer is forced to serve a tyrant, your mother mutilated, and as for mine, she betrayed her own family to whore herself with a murderer. Why should I go on when I have nothing to live for?'

'We have each other,' said Gwydion. 'I know it's hard at the moment, but it will soon get better. Once we pass into the lands of the Silures we can take it easy and perhaps join up with a friendly clan.'

'Is there such a thing with the Silures?' she asked with a sneer.

'There may be clans in the south that do not follow the ways of the warrior,' said Gwydion. 'We can talk to them and ask for shelter. We are young, strong, and we would prove a valuable asset to any clan. If we can convince them we come in peace and have something to offer, then I think there is every chance.'

'How far away are we?' asked the girl.

'Half a day,' said Gwydion, 'but we are stuck here until tomorrow. The horses are weak and need to feed, as do you.' He offered her the meat again.

'What about you?' she asked.

'I have already eaten,' he lied, 'this is your share.'

261

She took the last of the meat and started to chew, surprised at how hungry she actually was.

Gwydion unwrapped his bundle and sorted out his equipment. He had two quivers of arrows left along with his bow, knife and sword. He hoped he didn't have to use them over the next few days, but wasn't optimistic. He gazed in the direction Prydain had taken, his brow creasing in concern. The Roman had been gone for over an hour, far longer than had been expected.

'I'll be back in a while,' he said to Gwenno.

'Where are you going?'

'To find the Roman,' he said. 'We need as much forage as possible for the next few days. While I'm there I'll refill the water pouch.'

'Don't be long,' she answered and pulled her blanket closer around her. Night was falling and there was a chill in the air.

It didn't take Gwydion long to find the trail and he paused at the forest edge, looking for any sign of the Roman. His eyes fell on something half hidden in the undergrowth and he approached cautiously.

A nosebag lay discarded in the scrub and Gwydion recognised the unmistakeable signs of a struggle. He searched the surrounding area and to his horror, came across the bodies of two recently killed men. He realised that neither was Prydain, but any thoughts that the Roman had escaped the conflict faded when he saw the signs of countless horses that had been in the area less than an hour earlier. Gwydion came to the conclusion that either his body lay further afield, or he had been taken prisoner by the horsemen.

He glimpsed something in the grass and bent to pick up a vicious looking knife with a curved blade. Its design was unfamiliar to him and he tucked it into his belt before returning to the temporary camp via a circuitous route, careful to avoid leaving any trail back to their hiding place.

When he arrived, Gwenno was fast asleep and Gwydion decided to stay awake for the rest of the night to guard her against any revisit of the unknown warriors. He knew he had to change his plans. They couldn't realistically continue south, for if the unknown attackers were Silures, it was obvious that they weren't welcome and he didn't want to place Gwenno in any more danger. He would let her sleep tonight and tomorrow he would explain, but he knew deep down inside, their chances of survival were minimal.

He watched the darkness creep into the forest until finally, with his overtired body giving in to the demands of exhaustion, his breathing slowed and he fell into a deep sleep.

The following morning, the first thing to reach into Gwydion's consciousness was the birdsong echoing around the forest. He shuddered as his body registered the coldness of the dew on his skin and his mind struggled to comprehend the strange sound that interrupted the birds. It was familiar, but out of place, and he tried to focus on its origin. It sounded like the bark of a fox or a cough. Yes that was it, a throaty cough. He hoped Gwenno hadn't caught a chill, but he quickly dismissed that idea for it was far too deep for a female; it was obviously a man's cough.

A second later as the implications dawned, his eyes flew open and he reached for the sword he had left at his side hours earlier, but his hand fell on nothing but space where his weapon had lay. The point of a spear hovered inches from his chest held by the looming figure of an unknown warrior. For a second, he contemplated knocking the spear aside and taking his chances with the man, but soon realised the futility of the idea when he saw at least a dozen more men standing guard. Across the clearing, Gwenno was gagged and tied to a tree. Gwydion stared around the camp and cursed himself for falling asleep, realising that if these men were Silures or Druid warriors, then his incompetence had probably cost them their lives.

'Gwenno, are you all right?' he asked.

She nodded her head. The spear holder lifted his weapon, the blood stained point tilting Gwydion's chin upwards, forcing him to look at the man.

'Shut your mouth,' he snarled.

'Who are you?' asked Gwydion. 'Have you been sent by the Druids, because if you have, surely you can see it is too late? The Romans are already here and no amount of sacrifice will make any difference.'

'What do you know of the Romans?' asked the warrior suddenly interested.

'I know they defeated Caratacus at the Medway,' he said, 'and if they can do that, the life of one girl won't make any difference one way or another. Why don't you let her go? I will take her place.'

'Hold your tongue,' snapped the warrior. 'You fret like a woman. We are not of the Druids.'

Gwydion breathed a sigh of relief.

'Who are you then?' he asked. 'You are obviously not Silures.'

'If I was, your head would already adorn my saddle, but I am interested about what you know of the Romans. Who told you about Medway?'

'I was there,' said Gwydion, 'I saw it with my own eyes.'

'You are not of the Catuvellauni!'

'I am Deceangli,' answered Gwydion.

'There were no Deceangli at Medway.'

'I accompanied Idwal as one of his guard and to translate for Caratacus,' explained Gwydion.

The warrior withdrew his spear slightly.

'Stand up!' he ordered. 'There is someone who you should meet. If you tell the truth, your life may be spared, however if you lie, the crows will be pecking at your eyes within the hour. Bring the girl,' he barked and marched Gwydion out of the camp toward the road at spear point, closely followed by the rest of the armed party.

They emerged near the base of a hill and Gwydion was astonished to see several hundred men dispersed across the slope, talking in subdued tones within their small groups. The prisoners were marched toward a ragged tent situated in the centre of the small army.

'Wait here!' said the warrior and ducked inside. Gwenno was brought up besides Gwydion, her gag now removed and her bonds cut.

'Who are they?' she asked nervously.

'I don't know,' answered Gwydion, 'though they speak the Catuvellaunian tongue.'

'Have they been sent by the Druids?'

'I don't think so,' he answered, 'this group is far too big to have been sent after two runaways.'

'Where is Prydain?' she asked suddenly noticing his absence.

'I'm not sure,' said Gwydion, 'I'm hoping these people may be able to give us some answers.'

Gwenno's face fell, but before her concern could develop, the warrior emerged from the tent, closely followed by a giant bearded man. He walked slowly up to Gwydion and stared at him for several moments.

'Do I know you?' he asked. 'Your face is familiar to me.'

'I was with Idwal prior to the battle of Medway,' said Gwydion. 'I had cause to speak to you once.'

'Who is he?' interrupted Gwenno.

The bearded man turned to the girl.

'Allow me to introduce myself, pretty one,' he said. 'My name is Caratacus, King of the Catuvellauni.'

Chapter 41

Remus and Mateus rode side by side as they led the column further west. The Centurion had forced the pace all day, stopping for five minutes every hour to allow the men to drink and catch their breath. Their armour was heavy and not designed to be worn for long periods of marching. That was what the following mule train was for, but this was unknown territory and neither Mateus nor Remus wanted to take any risks with this so called Silures tribe.

The rolling landscape was thick with broad-leafed forestry interspersed with manmade clearings, obviously formed for the grazing of cattle, but strangely unoccupied by man or beast. They neared a stream and called a halt to enable the men to refill their water skins.

The ground was muddied and trampled near the water, a sign that animals often drank at this point. Remus dismounted and allowed his horse to drink his fill from the cool stream. Mateus removed his helmet and dipped it into the water before pouring it over his head, gasping at its refreshing coolness.

Remus crouched and put his fingers into a cowpat before looking up thoughtfully.

'That's disgusting,' said Mateus looking down at the squatting Centurion.

'Cow shit,' said Remus simply.

'So what?' asked Mateus.

'Still fresh, yet no cattle to be seen.'

'Perhaps they wandered off?'

'It's still warm,' said Remus standing up and wading into the stream to wash his hands. 'They were here less than an hour ago and cows don't move that fast unless they are a being driven by men'

'They can't be that far away,' said Mateus. 'Perhaps, we should pursue them; we could do with fresh meat.'

'I think not,' said Remus. 'What worries me more is that if these herdsmen knew we were coming, then who else knows?' He looked around at the surrounding hills. 'My guess is that we have been watched since we crossed the river this morning.'

'This concerns you?'

'Not unduly, it would take quite an army to take on a full Cohort, and armies take a while to assemble. We should be gone long before anyone can assemble the sort of strength needed to cause us any problems.'

'Riders coming!' called one of the sentries and everyone reached for their weapons.

Remus stepped forward and peered at the dust trail being kicked up by the fast approaching horses.

'It's two of the scouts.' said Remus, 'and they look as if they are in a hurry.' The horses reined in before him. One of the scouts dismounted and saluted him

'Hail, Remus,' he said, 'we have important news for the Tribune.'

'Report,' answered Remus simply.

'Sire, there is a large band of barbarians encamped on the other side of the hills to the front.'

'Do they know we are here?'

'No, Sire,' answered the scout. 'Their route follows the road we seek and takes them south.'

'Then it is of no concern of ours,' he said. 'Keep an eye on them but we will allow them to pass. We have more important things to do.'

'Sire, there is something important you should know,' said the scout. 'The group is led by Caratacus himself.'

'Caratacus,' gasped Mateus, 'you must be mistaken; he faces Plautius in the east.'

'It would seem Plautius was victorious and routed the Britons at Medway,' said the scout, 'Caratacus flees south to seek refuge with the southern tribes.'

'How do you know this?' interrupted Remus.

'While he was hunting, we took one of them as prisoner,' said the scout, 'he told us everything.'

'You are sure of this?' snapped Mateus.

'Why would he lie? We did not suspect they were led by Caratacus, he volunteered the information as he thought it would save his life.'

'And did it?' asked Remus.

'No, Sire,' answered the scout.

Mateus turned to Remus.

'Do you realise what this means?' he said. 'The King of Britannia lies within our grasp. This is an opportunity that can't be missed.'

'It is not our mission,' said Remus.

'Forget the mission, Remus,' said Mateus, 'this is far bigger. If we can deliver the head of Caratacus to Plautius, Claudius himself would bestow honour and riches on us. Think about it. How many Centurions have the chance to deliver the King of an entire country to their Emperor? Our names would be whispered in awe.'

Remus considered carefully. Although he had never sought glory or riches, this would probably be his last campaign, and the capture of Caratacus could ensure his retirement would be spent in luxury. The Gods knew he had earned it. He turned to the scout and interrogated him for more information.

'How many are there?' he asked.

'About five hundred, Sire,' he said. 'Half of them mounted.'

'What state are they in?'

'Battle weary,' said the scout, 'many carry wounds and all seem tired.'

'Are they aware of us?'

'No Sire, my men watch from a nearby hill. We have not been seen.'

'Are they currently on the march?'

'No, it seems that they are licking their wounds. No doubt they feel safe here for they have set up a temporary camp.'

'Fortifications?'

'None.'

The Centurion looked at the Tribune. It sounded too good to be true, yet still he hesitated until the scout's next words made his mind up for him.

'Sire, there is one more thing,' he said. 'Yesterday, they brought in two prisoners. One man and one girl. It may be our quarry.'

'You saw the deserter?' snapped Remus, suddenly focussed.

'It was too far to be sure, Sire, but one of the prisoners is definitely a woman.'

'Do you think it is them?' asked Mateus.

'No way of knowing,' said Remus, but there is one way to find out.'

'You think we should take them?'

'Like you said,' said Remus, 'this is an opportunity too good to miss.'

'Good,' said Mateus, 'I will go forward with the scouts to view the enemy camp, you sort out the men. Make sure they eat well and get some rest. If the land lies good, we will attack at dawn.'

'Yes, Sire,' said Remus, slightly amused at the Tribune's newly found assertiveness. He wondered if he would be so confident during the inevitable battle. Somehow, he doubted it.

Chapter 42

Gwydion and Gwenno sat cross-legged in Caratacus's tent, sharing the roasted haunch of a boar that had been caught earlier in the day. They ate ravenously, and Gwenno was slightly disappointed when Caratacus ordered the rest of the beast to be taken away to be shared out between his men. Food was scarce and every morsel counted for the remnants of the army.

'So,' said Caratacus, after wiping the grease from his beard, 'tell me about yourselves. How come you are so far west yet not a few weeks back, you faced the invaders at Medway?'

Gwydion started to tell the lies he and Gwenno had carefully prepared the night before.

'Not much to tell, really,' he said, 'I was split from my unit during the battle and amongst the confusion, managed to make my way back to the land of my fathers, only to find there had been a coup while we were away, so we decided to seek our future in the south.'

Caratacus stared at the two fugitives as Gwenno fidgeted nervously.

'And have you seen anyone else on your journey?' he asked.

'No, it's been quiet.'

'Just the two of you?' asked Caratacus.

'No Sire, we had a comrade from my clan,' he lied. It was pointless trying to explain the Roman to the king; it would just complicate things.

'And where is he now?'

'I don't know,' said Gwydion, 'I thought perhaps your men may have some information.'

'Why would you think this?'

'Your warriors are the only others we have seen.'

Caratacus picked up a curved knife and placed it on the floor between them.

'Do you recognise this?'

'It is the knife I found at the scene of the fight,' confirmed Gwydion.

'It is a Silures blade,' said the King, picking it up and turning the bone carved handle over in his hands. 'Your friend's head probably hangs from one of their saddles by now.'

Gwenno's head dropped as she contemplated the death of one of her rescuers.

'The thing is, Gwydion' continued Caratacus, 'I have a problem.'

'Problem?' queried Gwydion, 'I don't understand.'

'You see,' said the King, 'a few days ago we were approached by two riders on the road. They were warriors from the Druids. It would seem that they are seeking a group of three people, two men and one woman. Apparently, the girl was to be a sacred sacrifice, but was stolen from them by the two men. Now, you wouldn't know anything about this would you?'

'Coincidence?' said Gwydion nervously. 'Must be hundreds of people on the road like that.'

'Even so,' said Caratacus, 'how many women wear their hair as short as your pretty companion?'

An awkward silence fell and Gwydion knew that the game was up.

'Enough of this nonsense,' said the King, 'I jest at your expense. I have known who you are since before my men took you prisoner.'

Gwenno's heart sank

'Are you going to take us back?' she asked quietly.

Caratacus stared back at her for a long time and took a deep breath before answering.

'I think not,' said the King eventually, 'I owe the Druids no favours. Over the years, I have sent them enough tribute for several lifetimes, yet, when I needed the support of the Gods, where were they? No, as far as I am concerned, their loss is no business of mine. Tomorrow we continue south to the land of the Silures.'

'And what of us?' asked Gwydion.

'You are free to leave,' said Caratacus. 'Call it payment for your service at Medway.'

'Thank you, Sire,' said Gwydion and stood up to leave, but as they went, Gwenno turned back around.

'Sire,' she said. 'One more thing.'

'Yes?'

'You say you are going to join the Silures?'

'We are.'

'We are also going south,' she said glancing at Gwydion, 'perhaps we could join you.'

'Gwenno!' interrupted Gwydion. 'We have taken enough of the King's hospitality, we should go.'

'It's okay,' said Caratacus, 'the girl makes sense. On your own, you are easy targets. With me, at least you will have the strength of my army to protect you, modest as it is.'

'Are you sure?' asked Gwydion. 'We would not want to put you out.'

'You won't be putting us out,' said Caratacus. 'You will hunt for yourself and look after your own horses. All I ask is that you keep away from my men.' He glanced at Gwenno before adding, 'they have not had the pleasure of a woman's company for a long time. I will warn them off, but give no guarantees.'

'I understand,' said Gwenno, 'we will be no problem.'

'Wait outside,' said Caratacus, 'I will send my servant to find a tent for you. Get some sleep, for tomorrow we enter the lands of the Silures'

Chapter 43

The sky was still dark when the Roman attack started. It wasn't the full frontal ranks of armoured legionaries that were so typical of Roman battles, but a silent and deadly act of subterfuge. First of all, the sentries were taken one by one in silence, their throats slashed before they were lowered gently to the ground, their blood flowing through the hands of their assassins.

Once all the outlying guards were taken, the scouts stripped them of their heavy woollen capes and donned them over their own tunics. Suitably disguised, the scouts wandered unnoticed through the encampment, taking the opportunity to kill as many men as possible without being seen, and many Catuvellauni died where they slept, without even knowing they were in danger.

One of the scouts walked quietly amongst the smouldering camp fires, the fresh blood on his spear unnoticed in the darkness. An armed guard walking amongst the tribe at this time of the night was hardly unusual. He noticed a tent over on the edge of the camp and made his way over to see if there was a better opportunity there.

As he approached, he could see he was in luck. An older man lay wrapped in a fur cape, snoring heavily. The scout stood alongside the sleeping man and adjusted the grip on his spear before placing the point over the man's chest, bracing to plunge the weapon deep into his heart.

'Stop!' screamed Gwydion, emerging from behind a nearby tree where he had gone to urinate. 'What do you think you're doing?'

The scout spun around at the shout, realising that this was the point of the assault that was inevitable. Below him, the sleeping man woke up, alerted by the shouting. The scout continued to stare at Gwydion and without as much as a flinch, drove his spear down into the terrified man's chest.

Gwydion's confusion lasted only seconds, but was enough time to allow the assassin to withdraw his spear and hurl it at him with full force. Instinctively, Gwydion ducked, causing the spear to miss his head by inches. The scout disappeared into the darkness as Gwydion realised the danger.

'Alarm!' he screamed at the top of his voice waking everyone in the camp. 'To arms!'

The camp erupted into life as the warriors rushed to their weapons and many more lost their lives as the scouts took advantage of the confusion to inflict death in the darkness. Gwydion crouched at the speared man on the floor.

'Holler,' he said gently, 'don't worry, I'll get help.'

'No!' gasped the King's servant weakly. 'It's too late, my life is done. Bury me deep, Deceangli. None of this burning nonsense, I want to be wrapped in the earth's blanket.' He coughed violently, blood spurting from his mouth. 'Promise me,' he continued grabbing Gwydion's arm, 'a grave, not a fire.'

Gwydion stared at the dying man, realising how close he himself had come to death. Holler had given up his tent for Gwenno to have privacy and a few moments ago, Gwydion had been lying alongside the King's servant outside her tent. If he hadn't risen to answer the call of nature, it could be him lying there, gasping his last breath.

'I promise, Holler,' he said, 'I will dig it myself.'

'Thank you,' whispered Holler, 'I guess not all Deceangli are bad.' He coughed again and with a last gasp, the light left his eyes as his body gave up its impossible struggle.

Caratacus ran out of the darkness, carrying his broad sword.

'Explain,' he demanded coldly.

'There is an assassin in the camp,' said Gwydion. 'Maybe more than one. I saw him kill Holler.'

'Bring your weapon,' said Caratacus, 'Let's find this man.'

Gwenno crawled out of her tent, wrapped in her cape against the cold.

'Gwydion,' she called, 'what's happening?'

'Gwenno, get back inside,' he ordered and retrieved his sword from his sheath. 'Stay hidden,' he added, 'I will be back as soon as I can.' He followed Caratacus into the camp, alarmed at the sound of conflict in the darkness. It was obvious that however many there were, they were causing havoc amongst the Catuvellauni.

By the time the sun had risen, over thirty men lay dead or dying across the Catuvellauni camp. Four of the attackers also lay dead and were thrown in a pile outside Caratacus's tent. The leaders of the tribe gathered around and Caratacus called for silence.

'Is that the last?' he asked.

'As far as we know,' said one of the warriors, 'though many escaped in the confusion.'

'They wear familiar clothing,' said Caratacus. 'Who are they?'

'They wear the cloaks of our own people,' said the warrior, 'taken from their dead bodies.'

Gwydion looked down at the bodies, noticing something familiar. He bent down and lifted one of the legs for a better look.

'Caligae,' he said simply.

'What?' asked Caratacus.

'Caligae.' repeated Gwydion standing up. 'Military sandals!' He looked at Caratacus, 'Roman!'

'Roman?' questioned Caratacus in astonishment. 'How can this be?'

'I don't know,' said Gwydion, 'but there is no mistake, look at their weapons.'

'They must have followed us,' said Caratacus. 'We can waste no more time. Gather the men, we move out immediately.'

The leaders left to assemble the rest of the army and Caratacus turned to Gwydion.

'You have my gratitude,' he said. 'If it wasn't for your alarm, many more of our men would lie dead.'

'Luck,' said Gwydion, 'I just happened to be awake at the right time.'

'Nevertheless, I am grateful. Gather your things. For the rest of the journey, you and your woman will travel close to me.'

'How long do we have?' asked Gwydion.

'About an hour,' said Caratacus. 'Why?'

Gwydion looked across at the wrapped corpse of Holler.

'I have a promise to keep,' he said. 'Where can I get a shovel?'

An hour later, the remnants of Caratacus's army were riding south into the lands of the Silures. High on a nearby hill, a lone Roman soldier pulled out a small mirror from his cape and focused the suns reflection on the raised finger of his outstretched arm, pointing its beam southward. The signal was repeated along a line of hills and within minutes, ten miles away, a runner crashed through the woods to address a waiting officer.

'Sire,' he said, 'the signal has been received, they're on their way.'

'Good,' said Mateus and turned to Remus, 'is everything ready?'

'The trap is set,' said Remus, 'let them come.'

Gwydion rode alongside Caratacus at the head of the column. They had ridden hard for an hour before easing the pace to rest the horses. Gwenno had been given Holler's horse and rode just behind the two men.

'What is your plan when you find the Silures?' asked Gwydion.

'Try to convince them to join with me to face the Romans,' said Caratacus. 'They have a feared reputation and shouldn't take much convincing.'

'You have to find them first,' said Gwydion. 'I understand they hide their villages deep in the forests and move often, depending on the season.'

'They will find us,' said Caratacus. 'I wouldn't be surprised if we were being watched even as we speak.' They rode for another ten minutes before the King reined in his horse and held up his hand to halt the column.

'What's that?' he asked and Gwydion stared down the valley following the King's stare. At the centre of the valley, two freshly cut tree limbs had been lashed together to form a cross over ten foot high. Suspended from the cross bar, hung a naked man, his head hanging down and his chest covered with blood. They stared in fascination and behind them Gwenno stifled a gasp of horror.

'Is this the work of the Silures?' she asked.

'I have never heard of them using crucifixion as a means of execution,' said Caratacus, 'only one people favour the method.'

'Who?' asked Gwenno.

'Romans,' answered Gwydion.

'Who do you think it is?' asked Gwenno.

'It is one of my men,' said Caratacus. 'He must have been taken in the confusion last night.'

'But why do this? Why didn't they just kill him?'

Before any of the men could answer, the crucified man raised his head and let out an unintelligible scream.

'By the God's, he's still alive,' said Gwenno, 'we have to help him,' and before anyone could stop her, she dug her heels into her horses flank.

'Gwenno stop!' called Gwydion, but she was already on her way.

'Leave her go,' ordered the King sharply, 'it may be a trap.'

'I am aware of the risk,' said Gwydion, 'but I've lost her once, I won't do so again.' He galloped down the field to join Gwenno at the base of the cross. As he reined in his horse, he realised why the man's chest was covered with blood. Not only had his eyes been gouged out, but his nose and ears had been cut off along with his lips. The whole effect was horrific and whilst it hadn't been fatal, the pain the mutilation had caused was obvious.

'Cut him down!' cried Gwenno.

'It is too late,' said Gwydion, 'he is as good as dead.'

'Gwydion,' she shouted, 'cut him down!'

Gwydion drew his sword and positioned his horse to catch the man's body before cutting the bindings. He lowered him to the ground and Gwenno dismounted to comfort him.

'They have torn out his tongue,' she sobbed. 'Oh Gwydion, what manner of beasts are these?'

Gwydion ignored her, and stared at a deer that had bolted from the cover of the forest to race across the clearing not fifty yards away.

'Gwenno, get up,' he said.

'What's the matter with you?' she hissed. 'Have some pity, Gwydion. Give me your flask, the least we can do is give this man some water before he dies.'

'Gwenno,' said Gwydion slowly, 'listen very carefully. Stand up and get on your horse. We have to get out of here, right now.'

Gwenno recognised the seriousness of his voice and stood up.

'What's the matter?' she asked.

'That tree line,' he said, 'there's someone in there.'

'How do you know?'

'There is no way that deer would risk passing a man unless there was a greater risk behind it.'

'What sort of risk?'

'The worst kind,' he said. 'Another man!'

Gwenno spun around to the sound of galloping horses, but was relieved to see it was just Caratacus and his warriors closing in on them.

'It's okay,' shouted Gwydion. 'I've seen it, we're coming now.'

'Too late!' boomed Caratacus. 'There is nowhere to go.'

'What do you mean?' asked Gwydion.

'Listen!' said Caratacus, and Gwydion strained to hear anything above the noise of the horses. Eventually he heard the sound of drums, increasing in volume as it got louder. Suddenly he spun around as he realised it was coming from the far end of the valley and as he watched, four lines of Roman infantry, line abreast marched up the valley toward them, beating their swords against their shields as they marched.

'That way?' asked Gwydion pointing back the way they had come.

'The valley is blocked by archers,' said Caratacus. 'To go that way would be suicide, the only way out is there,' he pointed at the advancing infantry. 'If we ride hard we can break their lines, some of us will die, but many will get through.'

Suddenly the drumming stopped and silence fell. The Roman ranks had stopped and Caratacus could see the mounted Centurion to the front of the infantry staring at him across the plain. The Centurion raised his right hand and after a few seconds, dropped it down sharply. Hundreds more infantry ran from the forest, reinforcing the Roman lines and Caratacus knew they were trapped.

'Dismount!' he roared. 'We will make our stand here. Our swords are as keen as theirs. It will be a fair battle.'

However, Caratacus was wrong. They weren't in the centre of a battlefield; they were in a killing zone carefully selected by Remus for maximum effect. A hundred yards away, Mateus gave his own signal and two Centuries of archers drew back their bows, aiming high into the sky.

'Loose arrows!' roared Mateus and one hundred and sixty bowstrings propelled death from the flanking hills. Even before the first volley landed, the second lethal volley was airborne. As expected, most of the warriors survived by using their round shields to protect them from the hail of death, but the horses had no such protection. When Remus gave the order to stop less than a minute later, most were lying on the ground already dead or dying.

The Centurion was satisfied. The only advantage Caratacus's army had held over his Cohort was the number of horses, and now that threat had been eliminated, the enemy were isolated and had no choice but to face them.

Remus dismounted and gave the reins to an auxiliary to take away. He fastened the chinstrap of his helmet before drawing his Gladius. Raising it in the air, he gave the command.

'Cohort ready,' he shouted before levelling it toward the shocked Catuvellauni warriors. *Advaaance!*'

'Are you alright?' shouted Gwydion at Gwenno over the din.

'I think so,' said Gwenno and raised herself up from her grisly refuge. If it wasn't for Gwydion's horse they would be dead, but the beast had taken the first hail of arrows even as they were wondering what was happening. After the initial panic the horse had collapsed in pain and as it lay dying on the floor, Gwydion had dragged Gwenno down to lie tight against its body, a still breathing shelter against the hail of death.

Gwydion knew they had been lucky to survive. All around him, men were screaming in rage and pain and responding to the Roman challenge with their own battle cries. Already some individuals had charged forward down the slope to launch a futile lone attack on the solid wall of armour approaching Caratacus's army.

'Gwydion,' cried Gwenno, 'what are we going to do?'

He turned to the girl and grabbed her by the shoulders.

'Gwenno, listen to me,' he ordered. 'Whatever happens, stay close to the King, do you understand? Stay by his side at all times.'

'But why?' cried Gwenno.

'There is no chance we can win this battle,' he said, retrieving his shield from the dead horse. 'Our only hope is that they will want to take Caratacus alive and will hold back from killing him when the end comes. If you are close to him, they may spare you as well.'

'What about you?' asked Gwenno grabbing his arm.

'I cannot stand by while my countrymen die,' he said, 'I will take my place alongside them. '

'What do you mean countrymen?' she asked. 'They are Catuvellauni not Deceangli.'

'They are Britons,' snapped Gwydion, 'as are we.'

The anger in his voice shocked her, and she released his arm.

'I'm sorry, Gwenno,' he said, 'but there is no other way. One more sword may make all the difference. He turned away and ran to join the assembling warriors preparing to defend themselves against the approaching Romans. He barged his way through to join the front row, his voice soon joining those of his new comrades as they roared their defiance.

Within minutes, the sound of a horn sounded above the din and the marching Romans broke into a run as the final assault started. The sound of the charge was answered by the screaming of the warriors as

279

they surged forward to meet the attack in a melee of blood, flesh and bone.

Cassus was part of the second rank of Romans and added his weight to the man in front to repel the initial clash. For a few moments, the killing stalled as bodies were rammed against each other, but as was normal in these situations, the pressure inevitably eased and weapons were brought to bear. The Catuvellauni's ferocious onslaught made some initial headway, but despite some casualties, the Romans took the initiative, stabbing at opportune moments from behind the safety of the body length shields. The relentless pressure took its toll and warriors started to fall before the Roman wall of steel.

The legionary in front of Cassus dropped to the ground, his skull cleaved clean in two by a huge axe that had smashed through his helmet as if it was parchment. Cassus stepped over his body and drove his Gladius into the warrior's face who had wielded the axe. The training kicked in and he joined in the advance, killing ruthlessly alongside his comrades. In the centre of the front line, Centurion Remus fought like a madman. His skill with a sword was unmatched and his manic style belied the technical ability that he wielded with such lethal efficiency. A path of dead warriors fell before him and a dozen Romans joined Remus as he made his way toward Caratacus.

Gwydion fought ferociously, but knew it was only a matter of time before the battle was lost. He looked around frantically for Gwenno hoping that perhaps they could make a last attempt to escape, but was shocked to see how few of the Catuvellauni were still standing. He ducked a blow from his opponent and swung his sword below the shield, cutting into the ankle, and as the Roman fell in agony, disengaged to run back toward the King.

'Gwydion!' screamed Gwenno as he arrived and threw her arms around him as he addressed the King.

'The day is lost, Sire,' he said. 'If we fight our way to the trees, we may yet escape.'

'There is no escape,' said Caratacus. 'Our last stand will be here.'

'Then we will all die,' said Gwydion.

'Perhaps not,' said Caratacus. 'I recall you speak their tongue, translate for me.'

He stepped up onto a boulder and addressed the fighting men directly to his front.

'Romans,' he screamed, at the top of his voice, 'hear my words.'

Remus stepped back from the man he had just slain and looked up at the impressive King. He held up his hand to halt the attack, both sides taking welcome respite from the slaughter

'Who speaks for you?' continued Caratacus.

Remus stepped forward but before he could speak, a voice rang out from behind the ranks.

'I do!' shouted a voice, and Tribune Mateus rode his horse through the carnage to stop alongside Remus.

'Sire, leave this to me,' said Remus quietly.

'I am in command here,' said Mateus, 'and it is I who will take this so called King back to Rome. Do not forget yourself, Centurion, I am a Tribune and this is my birth right.'

Remus stared at him in disgust. The Tribune had once again stayed well back during the fight and now intended to claim the glory.

'So be it,' said Remus eventually, and stepped back from the horse.

'I am Tribune Gaius Mateus,' he called, 'and I am in command here. Do you lead these barbarians?'

'I am Caratacus, King of the Catuvellauni,' he answered. 'You have come into my lands and slaughtered my people. Camulodunum is now probably in Roman hands, yet still you pursue me. What is it that you want from us?'

Mateus sat up straight in his saddle.

'I want you, Caratacus,' he said. 'Bend your knee to me and I will spare your people. Fight on, and none of your men will see this sunset.'

'You obviously do not know me, Mateus,' said Caratacus .'I bend my knee to no man, yet I have no desire for any more of my people to die in my name. I have an offer for you.'

'State it?' said Mateus.

'Meet one on one,' he said. 'Two leaders in mortal combat before the sight of their Gods. If I win, you let my people go, but I will give myself up. If I lose, then nothing has changed. Either way your Emperor will have his prize.'

Mateus's face fell. He was in a situation he could not easily get out of. There was no way he would win a fight with this warrior King, yet could not escape the challenge with any respect intact.

'There is no merit in this challenge,' he stated, looking around, hoping to see support in the faces of the legionaries at his back. 'Your army is defeated. If you don't surrender, your head will adorn my spear within the hour.'

'It is a fair challenge,' called Caratacus, 'is the leader of such wolves, little more than a sheep.'

Remus hid a smirk. This King had talked to Mateus for only a few minutes but already had his measure. Yet he knew that Caratacus wasted his breath. There was no way Mateus would fight him.

'Enough of this folly,' shouted an enraged Mateus. 'This is your last chance barbarian, 'Either you surrender to me now, or I will crucify every last one of you.'

Silence fell as Caratacus stared at the Tribune. Gwydion drew his sword and stepped forward.

'Let them come, Sire,' he said. 'We will sell our blood dearly and for every cross they make, they will dig twice as many graves for their own men.'

Caratacus looked back at the two hundred or so men that still survived.

'Do not dishonour us, Sire,' shouted one of his warriors, 'I would rather die here than live a slave of the Romans.' The remainder of his men took up his shout and all started screaming their challenges at the enemy. Caratacus held up his hand for silence and addressed Mateus.

'It would seem you have your answer, Roman,' he called. 'Look to your weapons.'

'So be it!' answered Mateus and turned to ride back through the legionary ranks. As he passed Remus, he turned to speak to him.

'Kill them all,' he said, 'and bring me his head.'

Remus's gaze didn't leave the face of Caratacus as he answered.

'You had the opportunity to take it yourself,' he said.

'I could have lost my own,' hissed Mateus.

'You have lost more than that,' spat Remus, 'you have lost the men.'

Mateus looked around at the legionary ranks. Most stared at him in disgust. He turned back to Remus.

'You just do what you are paid to do, Centurion,' he said. 'Leave the men to me. When we get back to the legion, I will have them dispersed amongst all the shit postings from here to Rome. Now

I gave you an order and I expect you to carry it out. Do you understand?'

'Perfectly,' said Remus. 'But you should know this. After I take this King's head,' he paused before looking up to the officer, 'I will be coming for yours.'

Tribune Mateus's face fell.

'You dare to threaten me, Centurion?' he gasped.

Remus looked over at the waiting warriors.

'Within the hour, those men will be dead,' he said, 'yet every one of them is more of a man than you can ever hope to be.'

Mateus's face contorted with rage.

'I will have you crucified for this,' he screamed.

'You have till dawn,' came the answer. 'Now, get from my sight or I'll kill you where you stand.'

Mateus wheeled his horse and rode back down the clearing toward the wood line. He knew if he could just get to the legion, he could let Nasica know about Remus's treachery. Nasica would back him up, after all, he was a fellow officer and their families were close friends back in Rome.

Remus estimated the enemy numbers and ordered the Cohort to surround those who were left. The six hundred men who were under his command encircled Caratacus's two hundred survivors to prepare for the final assault.

The Romans started to bang their shields again, building up the tension before the final assault. Gwydion held Gwenno in his arms, staring at the front rank as they started to close in. A sudden movement caught his eye and he spun around to stare in confusion as a lone horse galloped out from the forest edge.

The rider galloped hard toward the rear ranks of the Romans, his long black hair streaming behind him in the wind. The man was naked, yet tattooed from head to foot in multiple designs of blue wode. In either hand, he brandished a lethal double-edged sword and raised them high as he closed on the unsuspecting Cohort. A few legionaries heard the galloping hooves and turned to see the cause, but their shouts of warning were too late, as at the last moment, the rider screamed a terrifying war cry and launched himself from his horse and deep into their ranks. In amongst the confusion, he managed to kill several legionaries before he was cut down. For a second, Gwydion was unsure what had been the point of this lone assault by the strange man, but any uncertainty was quickly cleared up, when another war cry came from the forest edge. The sound was repeated from all directions and soon the valley was echoing with terrifying screams from throats of unseen men. Roman heads were turning in confusion at the deafening sound and suddenly, over five hundred horses galloped out from the forest to bear down on the Cohort of legionaries.

'Who are they?' shouted Gwenno, hope beginning to rise in her voice.

'I'm not sure,' shouted Gwydion 'but I would guess Silures.'

The riders smashed into the unorganised rear of the Cohort, closely followed by hundreds of tattooed foot soldiers. Caratacus realised this was an opportunity and seized the chance.

'Catuvellauni,' he shouted 'this is our time, pay them back for every drop of Britannic blood that stains their hands.' He held up his sword. 'For Britannia,' he screamed.

With a deafening roar, the remaining Catuvellauni fell upon the Romans to their front squeezing them between themselves and the Silures.

The Romans were immediately at a disadvantage and the fighting broke down into a widespread melee of individual hand-to-hand conflict. Cassus fought furiously, slashing and hacking at anything that moved. The enemy were manic, yet skilled with their weapons. On and on they came and as soon as he cut one down, another took his place, snarling and spitting their defiance as they pressed their assault. All around him men screamed as flesh was hewn apart, both sides uncompromising in their brutality. Cassus lost count of the men who fell before his blade, but eventually realised that they were losing the fight as he and his fellow legionaries became isolated . Remus spotted the risk and called out in Latin.

'Cohort, to the outcrop,' he screamed and all who heard fought their way to a rocky mound to one side of the clearing.

Finally, Cassus found himself alongside Remus and fifty other survivors standing on a rocky knoll, surrounded by thousands of screaming warriors and realised that there was no way out. Death was inevitable.

A haunting tone from an unseen horn echoed over the valley and the assault from the Silures eased. The lines of blue painted warriors retreated a few yards back from the bedraggled Roman survivors. To one side, Gwydion and Caratacus stood alongside each other amazed at the turnaround in their fortunes.

'Why have they stopped?' asked Gwenno. 'Why don't they finish it?'

'Look!' said Caratacus, and pointed down the vale.

A column of horses rode slowly through the battlefield carrying more warriors toward them. Their long black hair fell down around their shoulders and they were obviously of the same tribe. Gwydion's eyes narrowed as they got closer, focussing on the two lead riders. One was an older man wearing a multi coloured cape and obviously, a chieftain of some sort, but the focus of his attention was the second man. He was stripped to the waist, but his hair was much shorter and his skin was clear of any markings. Gwydion's eyes opened suddenly as he recognised the rider.

'By the Gods,' he said quietly. 'It can't be!'

'What's the matter?' asked Gwenno

'Look,' he said, 'alongside their chief, it's the Roman.'

The massed warrior infantry opened up to allow the column through and they pulled up fifty yards short of the isolated Romans on the knoll. Prydain dismounted and walked forward.

'Cassus Maecilius!' he called out in Latin.

Centurion Remus made his way to stand alongside Cassus.

'It's him!' he spat, 'the slave-boy. Look at him; he's even sided with the barbarians. I always knew he was filth. Find out what he wants.'

'I am here!' shouted Cassus. 'What do you want, Prydain?'

'I would talk with you,' he said, 'leave your Gladius and step forward.'

'I command here,' interrupted Remus, 'you can talk to me.'

'My words are for Cassus alone,' answered Prydain.

Cassus looked at Remus.

'What would you have me do?' he asked.

Remus considered for a moment before answering.

'Go and talk,' he said, 'but don't be fooled by his traitorous words. Remember he deserted his comrades and joined the enemy.'

Cassus walked forward and waited for the mounted Prydain between the two lines of opposing combatants.

'Drop your sword, Cassus,' shouted Prydain.

'You come with an army of thousands yet are worried about a single Gladius,' stated Cassus.

'It is no secret I am no match for your sword,' said Prydain. 'I am just ensuring I live long enough for you to hear me.'

'You have nothing to say that interests me,' spat Cassus. 'The boy I grew up with is dead to me.'

'Perhaps so,' said Prydain, 'but before we are finished here, you will at least know the truth.'

'Then speak quickly,' said Cassus. 'There is killing to be done.'

'Your sword,' reminded Prydain.

Cassus made a show of unfastening his belt and casting it away to one side. Prydain dismounted and walked to meet Cassus on one of the few patches of bare earth that wasn't covered with the dead or dying.

'And your Pugio,' added Prydain.

'It is on my belt.'

Prydain closed within two metres and held out his hand in greeting. Cassus stared at it and looked into Prydain's eyes.

'You jest with me,' he said, 'I take the hand of no traitor.'

'Traitor?' asked Prydain. 'Traitor to whom, Cassus, my family, my people, my comrades?'

'Everyone,' replied Cassus, 'You have turned your back on your very country.'

'My country,' said Prydain. 'Let's take that one first. I was born to a slave who was destined to die in the arena for nothing else but being unfortunate enough to be in the wrong place at the wrong time. Rome is not my country and the Romans are not my people.'

'My father brought you up and put food in your belly,' snapped Cassus.

'Karim brought me up,' answered Prydain, 'and it is he who grafted to feed me. Yes, your father's intervention in the arena all those years ago saved my life, and I will always respect him for that, but I have always known that I didn't belong.'

'Yet you joined up with me,' said Cassus, 'to serve in the Emperor's name. You were as keen as I to seek glory across the empire.'

'A boyhood dream,' said Prydain. 'The reality is much different and since we have been in Britannia, the endless killing of innocent people has sickened me.'

'You have killed men in the past.'

'Men yes, even women when the need was great, but the slaughter of countless innocents in the name of one man lies heavy on my conscience. To slay children who have done no more than stand alongside their parents is not what I joined up for. Marcus was right. These so-called barbarians that we grew up despising have culture, families, hopes and dreams, just like you or I.'

'Then your comrades,' answered Cassus, 'you have turned your back on those who have fought alongside you in other battles. How could you betray them?'

'I have killed no Roman.' snapped Prydain. 'Throughout all this, I have not killed a single one of those I called comrade.'

'Then what do you call this?' laughed Cassus, spinning around and indicating the carnage around him. 'It may not be your blade Prydain, but you ride with them, your hands are as soiled as theirs.'

'We rode into their country!' shouted Prydain. 'They are defending their lands and their families. You would do the same to anyone riding on Rome.'

'And you,' snapped Cassus, 'what is your excuse? What do you defend, Prydain?'

Prydain paused before answering.

'My home, Cassus,' he said eventually. 'These hills are the lands of my fathers.'

Cassus stared for a long time in confusion.

'I don't understand,' he said, 'you were born in Rome.'

'I may have been born on the back of a slave trader's cart,' said Prydain, 'but my mother was brought up here, amongst these hills. This is the place I belong, and these,' he indicated the warriors, 'are my people.'

'You don't know that is true.'

'I have never been surer of anything,' said Prydain.

'How?'

'My mother told me.'

'But you were just a baby when she died.'

'I was, but she left me a sign, one that lasted through all these years.' He lifted the leather pendant that still hung around his neck.

'Remember this, Cassus?' he asked, 'This was the only possession that my mother owned and she gave it to Karim when she handed me over. Look at the design.'

'I am familiar with the design,' said Cassus, 'It means nothing to me.'

'Look around you, Cassus,' said Prydain. 'and open your eyes.'

Cassus stared at the warrior nearest him, suddenly realising that the exact design was tattooed on his chest. He quickly scanned anyone else in range, only to see that the same design was borne by every man.

'You see, Cassus,' said Prydain, 'these are my people. Many years ago, a Cornovii raiding party took my mother. The Silures pursued, but by the time they caught up with them, she had been sold to a Gallic trader who then sold her in the slave markets of Rome.'

'I don't understand,' said Cassus. 'How can they be sure you didn't just pick this up from some random body?'

'You are right,' said Prydain, 'the pendant stopped me from being killed, but did not prove who I was. But there was one more gift that my mother left me before she died.'

'What gift?' asked Cassus.

'My name!'

'What has your name to do with it?'

'Before she was dragged off to her death, my mother made sure Karim understood the name by which I was to be called,' said Prydain.

'And I assume that your name is Khymric in origin,' guessed Cassus. 'Hardly proof of your identity.'

'Perhaps not,' said Prydain, 'but it is reserved for someone special, the first born in line to the tribal chief.'

'Don't tell me you also lead these people,' Cassus sneered.

'No, and I never will, for there are others of pure blood before me, but at the time, my mother was the chief's only child and she bestowed the name on me as was the custom for the first born male child.'

'This is too far a stretch for my imagination,' said Cassus, 'the coincidence is too great.'

Prydain pointed at the old man waiting patiently on his horse.

'That man there,' he said, 'is the chief of the Silures. They do not recognise the rule of Caratacus as King of Britannia, for they have hunted these lands long before the Catuvellauni even had a name. Even the name of these islands descends from Silures culture and has been changed over the years from its original.'

'This was the gift of my mother Cassus,' he continued, 'as the chief's first child, only she was allowed to use the ancient name of this country for her son. The name Britannia is taken from the Silures original. Its true name is Prydain!'

288

Chapter 44

Centurion Remus was getting impatient at the wait, and deciding to take matters into his own hands, walked forward to join the two men. Four armed Silures warriors stopped him in his tracks.

'What do you want, Remus?' called Prydain.

'I command these men,' said Remus indicating the last of the Cohort. 'If there are any decisions to be made regarding their future, then those decisions are mine to make.'

Prydain considered before answering.

'Drop your Gladius and draw near,' he said.

Remus did as he was asked, and he submitted to a search by one of the warriors, before advancing to stand alongside Cassus.

'So, finally gone native have you, slave-boy?' he sneered. 'Why doesn't that surprise me?'

'You would do well to hold your taunts, Remus,' said Prydain, 'your life lies in my hands.'

'I speak as I like to a slave,' said Remus.

'I am no slave,' said Prydain.

'You were born to a slave,' said Remus, 'and does not a rat give birth to a rat? You were a slave at birth and will be a slave when you die.'

'I don't understand you,' said Prydain. 'All through my time with the legion you made my life hell. Why is that? Even if I was once a slave, there must be thousands of other freedmen serving in Rome's legion. Surely you do not persecute them as much as you do me?'

'You are right,' said Remus. 'There are many, and I despise them all for soiling the true blood of the legions, but you, Prydain, you are something special. You are blight upon this earth and a stain on my very soul.'

Cassus looked on in confusion, unable to comprehend why there was so much venom in Remus's voice.

'Is this what all this is about?' asked Prydain, 'all this persecution, all these deaths, just because I am a freedman in the ranks of Rome?'

Remus tilted back his head and laughed briefly.

'Oh no, Prydain, this is much more personal. I was brought up in a time when Romans were Romans, barbarians were barbarians and slaves were slaves. Everyone knew their place. It was a good time. Gladiators, slaves, life, death, all in our hands and for a young man like me at the time; life was intoxicating. Wine, gambling, fighting, and as for the women, oh I had my choice of those. Rich girls, poor girls,' he paused and looked at Prydain, 'slave girls.'

'You surprise me, Remus,' said Prydain, 'you, who have such a low opinion of slaves, soiling yourself with our women.'

'Oh no,' said Remus, 'I have no problem abusing slave girls, and when I grew bored with them, I could always earn myself a few coins by selling them as entertainment in the arena.'

Prydain's face hardened as he realised what Remus was getting at, his mind racing as he watched the Centurion undo the chinstrap of the bronze helmet crested with the magnificent red horsehair plume.

'You see,' continued Remus, 'you and I have a lot in common, slave-boy. We grew up not far from each other, albeit twenty years apart. Even before you were born, I was fornicating amongst the slave girls. In fact, I remember one in particular; pretty little thing she was. Oh how we used that girl. Passed her around the garrison like a wash towel, and when we got bored of her, sent her to the arena.'

Cassus's eyes widened as he realised the implications and stared at Prydain.

'There must have been thousands of slave women who were sent to the arenas,' said Prydain, 'it means nothing. '

'Perhaps so,' said Remus. 'But there was something else, a pendant similar to the one you now wear. Hang on,' he said screwing up his eyes as if in recognition, 'I would say exactly the same.'

'You lie,' said Prydain, his anger rising, 'anyone could make up this story.'

'Tell me,' said Remus, 'how many of these pendants are there and more importantly, how would I know you got it from your mother?'

Silence fell and the two men stared at each other.

'Don't listen to him, Prydain,'' said Cassus, 'it could have been anyone.'

Prydain didn't take his eyes off the smirking Centurion. Remus removed his helmet and stared up at the sky for a few seconds before he answered.

'But there was only one pendant wasn't there, slave-boy?' he said. 'I'm sure your new found friends over there explained the importance of that pathetic necklace. Oh, how we laughed when she cried that she was some sort of princess and showed us that pathetic symbol as evidence. In fact, we found it so funny we allowed her to keep it. After all, it was something to hold on to as we screwed her from behind.'

'It was you,' said Prydain. 'You sent my mother to her death. You sent her to be slaughtered in the name of entertainment.'

'Oh don't worry;' continued Remus,' I didn't lose out on the deal. If I recall, I had six copper coins for her. They paid good money for women and children in the arenas back then. It made for a fascinating spectacle to watch their deaths, especially slave babies and stinking barbarian whores.'

Remus's deliberate goading had the desired effect and a roaring Prydain hurled himself at the soldier, his face contorted with rage, exactly as Remus had hoped. The Centurion threw himself to one side while at the same time swinging his helmet up to smash Prydain across the side of the head. The shock of the impact and his own momentum resulted in Prydain sprawling face down into the dirt and before he could re-gather his senses, Remus dived onto his back and jerked back the warriors head to expose his neck. Remus pulled out a hidden Pugio from his tunic and held the blade against Prydain's throat.

'Have you learnt nothing, slave boy? It was easier this time than the first day I met you. Remember that day, slave-boy, when I put you in your place? It was then that I first recognised the pendant. That was the day that you brought back memories that I wanted to forget and since then, I knew there would be a reckoning?'

'Remus, leave him,' shouted Cassus. 'If you kill him we will all die.'

'We are already dead,' barked Remus, 'but before I go, I will feel his blood running through my fingers.'

'You see, slave-boy,' he said, returning his attention to Prydain, 'there was one more thing I didn't tell you. It is true I used your mother, and yes, it was I who sent her to the arena, but it wasn't immediately. After the bitch had gone and got herself pregnant, she was no use to me and as soon as I found out, I sold her on to a whorehouse and as far as I was concerned, she no longer existed.'

'But it was after she whelped her brat the rumours started,' he continued, 'the sneers from those I grew up with. All the sidelong glances that spoke silently of their condemnation and eventually I went to the whorehouse to see for myself. To my disgust, the rumours were right. The hair colour was right, the nose was the same, but most importantly, the eyes said it all. You see, slave-boy, you are not the only one to have the devil's stare. I may have had one smashed out in Africa, but unlike this brown one that will soon witness your death, that one was blue. You have the same eyes as your father slave-boy, the same eyes as me!'

Silence fell between the three men, eventually broken by Cassus.

'You are his father!' he gasped. 'Surely that is impossible,' yet even as he spoke, he could see the resemblance and wondered how he hadn't noticed before. 'Remus for God's sake stop this,' he said. 'Even if this is true, you can't kill your own son!'

'Son of my loins only, not of my heart,' shouted Remus, ' he should have died in the arena, or better still, never have been born. Because of him, I left my family in disgrace and spent all my life fighting in godforsaken lands in the name of Rome. If it wasn't for him, I would have lived my life in luxury. Now it is payback time.'

He spun Prydain around to face the Silures, kneeling up and yanking his son's bleeding head back to expose his throat'

'I said goodbye to my family twenty years ago,' he snarled, 'now, say goodbye to yours!'

'Noooo!' screamed Gwenno, but before the sound had died, a metallic thud rang out and Remus's body shuddered with an unexpected impact. He looked shocked, but still held his knife against Prydain's throat, even though a black arrowhead protruded from his chest armour.

He looked over at Cassus and shuddered again as a second arrow smashed into his back, yet still the blade lay against his son's neck.

Cassus shook his head slowly from side to side.

'Don't do it,' he whispered.

Remus released his grip and staggered to his feet, still grasping the knife.

Prydain scrambled forward away from him and stood up before turning to face his would be killer. The two men stared at each other before Prydain broke the silence.

'You are my father?' he asked still shocked at the news.

A trickle of blood ran from Remus's mouth.

'So now you know the truth, slave-boy,' gasped Remus, 'the burden that the Gods placed upon me; to have been cast out by my fellows and to sire a coward.' He stumbled in pain and Prydain stepped forward to catch him before he fell.

Prydain held the wounded man in his arms as the news sunk in and even though he hated the thought, it all made sense. Remus opened his eyes and spoke weakly.

'So what happens now, slave-boy?' he whispered. 'How ends this tragedy?'

'I don't know,' answered Prydain, 'it is too much to take in.'

'Then prove me wrong,' gasped Remus. 'Show me you are not a coward, prove to me you are truly my son.' He pressed something into Prydain's hand.

'I need to know one thing,' whispered Prydain. 'What you just said about my mother; is that the way it really was?'

'Every word,' said Remus weakly.

Tears ran freely down Prydain's face as he answered.

'Then I will do as you ask,' he said, 'but not for you…for her!'

Prydain plunged the Pugio Remus had placed in his hand, deep into his father's heart and as the light faded in the Centurion's eyes, Remus silently formed his son's name, 'Prydain!'

Across the clearing, Gwydion lowered Angau, the third arrow no longer needed.

Chapter 45

The funeral pyres were still burning two days later when Prydain approached the closely guarded Romans that still survived. Cassus watched him draw near and when a Silures warrior indicated he should follow him, left his comrades to meet with Prydain.

'Well,' said Cassus, 'has our fate been decided?'

'It has,' said Prydain.

'Spit it out then,' said Cassus, 'I tire of the waiting.'

'I have managed to secure your release,' said Prydain. 'You will have one day to make good your escape before they pursue you. If you are caught, you will be killed.'

'Are we to be given horses?' asked Cassus

'You misunderstand,' answered Prydain. 'You alone will be allowed to leave.'

'Just me, but what will become of the rest of the men?'

'Do not ask what you do not want to hear,' said Prydain.

'You can't just murder fifty men,' hissed Cassus. 'They were only doing what they were ordered to do. You are a soldier, Prydain, for God's sake; can't you get them to change their minds?'

'It was all I could do to get them to spare you,' said Prydain. 'There is nothing more I can do.'

'They were your comrades,' spat Cassus. 'Does that not mean anything to you?'

'Be grateful you are to live,' answered Prydain. 'Go back to Rome, Cassus, leave this place to those who belong here. Caratacus is to join with the Silures and take the fight to the Romans. Get out while you still can.'

'You can't do this, Prydain,' shouted Cassus. 'For Jupiter's sake man, you are a Roman.'

'No, Cassus,' answered Prydain, 'I am a Briton.'

He held out his horses reins and after a moment's pause, Cassus mounted and rode a few paces before spinning around to face Prydain one last time.

'I will not be caught, Prydain,' he said, 'neither will I forget this day. Were it not for my desire for revenge, I would die alongside my comrades, but you should know this. I will ride and I will survive. My future lies not back in Rome, but here in this country, serving my Emperor. I will continue to take my place in the ranks of the legions and continue to kill barbarians, taking strength from the knowledge that every one that falls beneath my blade, brings the day closer when we will meet again. For meet again we will Prydain, before the Gods I swear it. I will not rest until the day when my Gladius takes the head from your shoulders in payment for your part in this.'

'So be it,' said Prydain.

Cassus stared in loathing at his boyhood friend before spinning the horse around, and after riding through the assembled warriors, headed back toward where he knew the legions of Rome were encamped far to the east. The lines of Silures closed behind him and before he had rode a few hundred yards, the sounds of shouting and screaming echoed once again around the valley, as the Silures closed in on the surrounded Romans to carry out their final act of savagery.

Cassus dug his heels into the flanks of the horse and galloped hard away from the slaughter, his eyes full of tears for the first time in his life, but as he crested the first hill, he pulled up and stared at something that chilled him to the bone. High on the next hill stood another cross, but unlike any that Cassus had ever seen.

First of all, it was obviously carved from a single slab of stone and stood thrice the height of the tallest man. Secondly, though the basic cruciform shape was there, the junction of upright and crossbar was intersected by an integral stone circle. For a second, Cassus struggled to remember where he had seen the design before, but suddenly it came back to him. It was the design on Prydain's leather amulet. The sign of the Silures, the Celtic cross.

He pushed the thought from his mind as he neared the shrine and paused for the last time to take in the grisly scene. Another crucified man was attached to the cross, but this time the victim was obviously Roman, as evidenced by the red cape hanging from his shoulders. Unlike any other crucifixion, the man had been hung upside down, his limbs spread-eagled across the central circle on the cross, and despite the empty eye sockets that had already received the attention of the crows, Cassus recognised the corpse of Tribune Mateus.

'You will pay for this, Prydain,' swore Cassus under his breath, 'if it is the last thing I do, I swear there will be retribution.' He spurred his horse and rode east, back to the legions of Rome.

Chapter 46

Gwydion was putting up the tent, while Gwenno was starting a fire to cook the small deer Gwydion had brought down with his bow. They were in a stream fed clearing in a small glade deep within the forest, many miles away from the scene of the battle three days earlier. A rider approached and Gwydion looked for his sword before Gwenno put his mind to rest.

'It's okay,' she said, 'it's Prydain.'

'Hail, Gwydion,' called Prydain.

'A Roman greeting,' said Gwydion, 'you surprise me.'

Prydain laughed at his own mistake.

'Some habits die hard,' he said, 'we are ready to leave for the homes of the Silures in the south. Are you sure you will not come?'

'We are sure,' said Gwydion. 'We have seen enough blood to last a dozen lifetimes. It is time for some peace and quiet.'

'I understand,' said Prydain. 'I wish you were coming with me, but at least you should be safe enough here. We are far enough south to deter anyone else coming after you.'

'What about you, Prydain?' asked Gwenno, 'what will you do?'

'I will go with Caratacus,' he answered 'and meet my fate alongside my brethren.'

'Yes, I heard about that,' said Gwydion, 'though I still can't believe you are alive. I thought you had died weeks ago when you disappeared from the woods. It's a shame you had to kill two of them before you realised they were your own people.'

'Killed two?' quizzed Prydain, 'I don't understand.'

'The two men you killed back in the forest when you were first captured,' said Gwydion, 'I found their bodies.'

'Oh those,' answered Prydain, 'they weren't Silures.'

'Who were they?' asked Gwenno'

'Druids,' answered Prydain. 'The two they sent after you and the only ones who knew where you are.'

'Then we are safe?' asked Gwenno.

'Should be!' said Prydain. 'You won't be troubled by the Silures and apparently the nearby clans are friendly.' He looked around. 'The forest is full of deer, and the rivers are full of fish. With a bit of hard work, a man could raise a strong family around here.'

'I am counting on it,' said Gwydion putting his arm around Gwenno.

'What about your clan back in the north,' asked Prydain, 'don't you have some unfinished business there?'

'I do,' said Gwydion, 'but it can wait. There is more important business here.'

'Then I will leave you in peace,' said Prydain. 'Good luck both, I will call in as the chance arises.'

'You will always be welcome,' said Gwenno and tiptoed up to kiss him goodbye.

Without another word, Prydain turned his horse and rode away. Gwydion and Gwenno watched him go until he disappeared from view.

'Did you mean it, Gwydion?' asked Gwenno eventually.

'Mean what?' he asked.

'What you said about unfinished business. Will you return to the Blaidd?'

'I gave my word to my father,' said Gwydion. 'I will gain revenge for both my family and yours, if is the last thing I do.'

'Then there is something you should have,' said Gwenno, 'wait there.'

She ducked into the tent, quickly returning a moment later with the Hessian parcel given to her weeks earlier by the fisherman's wife.

'When you go back,' she said, 'you will need this.'

'What is it?' he asked as he opened the package.

'It is the sign of our clan, Gwydion,' she said, 'the proof of who you are.'

The wrap fell away revealing the golden Wolf's head Torc he had paid the fisherman with.

'How did you get this?' he asked holding it up reverently.

'The fisherman's wife gave it back before we left,' she said, 'in honour of her daughter. Put it on.'

'No Gwenno,' he said. 'At this moment, I am not of the Blaidd. This Torc will not adorn any neck until the true clan leader once again sits in council. Until then, it will remain in my pack as a reminder of an unfulfilled promise.'

'But Erwyn is dead,' she said. 'He cannot return.'

'But his daughter still lives,' interrupted Gwydion, 'and will one day take her place as leader of the Blaidd.'

'Me?' asked Gwenno incredulously, 'But…'

'But nothing,' said Gwydion, 'it is your birth right. Erwyn had no sons, so you are his rightful successor. One day I will place this Torc around your neck as a sign of your authority.'

'What do I know about leadership?' she asked.

'Nothing that I cannot teach you,' he said, 'but the time for such things is later. Until then, there is unfinished business to be addressed here.'

'What business?'

He swept her up into his arms and kissed her deeply.

Gwenno returned the kiss until she finally broke away to catch her breath.

'I suppose,' she said, 'that this means that within the very near future, I will not be such an attraction to the Druids.'

'What do you mean?' asked Gwydion.

'Well, all their sacrifices need to be pure of body,' she said with a mischievous smile. 'Am I right in assuming that label will be denied me very soon?'

He smiled.

'Your assumption is correct,' he said and carried her over to the stream, laying her gently on a patch of lush grass lit by the sun's rays as it streamed through the ancient oaks.

'Make it special Gwydion,' whispered Gwenno as he disrobed before her. 'We will remember this moment forever.'

Chapter 47

The twelve surviving leaders of the Catuvellauni clans lined up outside the gates of Camulodunum. They were dressed in their finest armour and flanked by five hundred horsemen as they awaited the arrival of the Romans. Behind them, two thousand infantry warriors stood in disciplined ranks, each bearing their tribal shields and standards. Behind them, the entire population of the city had gathered to watch the ceremony.

Rebellon looked around at the remainder of the mighty Catuvellauni tribe and realised that it was still an awesome sight.

'Who knows?' he thought. 'When they see this show of strength, the Romans may even realise that they are out of their depth and retreat to the safety of their boats.'

Whatever happened, the tribal leaders had decided that they would not accept any terms that disadvantaged the Catuvellauni, and if necessary, would take them on in battle before the gates of the city. Rebellion's reverie was suddenly shattered by the long drawn out sound of a horn as it blasted across the valley from a lone rider high on a hill, and the gathering of over ten thousand Britons fell quiet. For a few seconds, nothing changed until someone shouted out from the gathered people.

'Over there, look, horses are coming.'

At first Rebellon was unimpressed, but as events unfolded, his jaw dropped in awe.

First, were the Batavian cavalry, galloping from the tree line and lining the vale on either side. They formed a perimeter three deep and as soon as they were settled, the auxiliary Cohorts, dressed in their finest armour, ran into position, resplendent in their finery.

A deep rhythm echoed around the open expanse and the heavy infantry of the legions marched into the centre, to the beat of a thousand drums. Ten thousand men in all formed a half-mile long honour guard, every inch of their uniform spotlessly clean and gleaming in the sun.

Again, the sound of horns rang out though this time magnified a hundred fold as the combined horns of three legions trumpeted their fanfare.

Rebellon stared, expecting to see the Roman leader approach, but was confused when he saw only a dozen men emerge from the tree line, running toward the Catuvellauni, each with a large dog on the end of a leash. He looked in interest, but suddenly realised they were not dogs, but giant cats.

The leopard handlers ran the full length of the escort and spread out along the front of the Catuvellauni leaders. Rebellon and his fellow tribesmen were astonished. The snarling beasts wore collars of gleaming gold while the jet-black skin of every handler was draped in the brilliant white furs of animals unknown to the Celts. Every member of the watching tribe was in awe of the display, but what came next blew their minds.

A cacophony of sound erupted from the trees causing every Briton to stare in fright at the unseen terror. Even the leopards pulled nervously at their gilded chains, as the unearthly bellowing reached a crescendo, and when it seemed that, there could be no more surprises, the source of the bellowing revealed itself.

From beneath the canopy of the surrounding woods emerged the most terrifying beast Rebellon had ever seen. The enormous animal plodded forward into the clearing, his tusks swooping low to the floor as he swung his head from side to side. Draped in a chain mail coat, the male tusker had lethal, multi pointed tips attached to his tusks and within a walled platform high on the animals back, four African warriors brandished their spears and bows in a display of awesome might, the Britons could never have dreamed of. If this was not enough, a further thirty African elephants followed behind, each as magnificent as the first and adding their trumpeting calls to the cacophony.

A Cohort of Praetorian Guard followed and lined the avenue of soldiers, their bronze ceremonial armour, almost blinding in the morning sunlight, and as the noise finally died down a column of young girls dressed in pure white robes followed them in, scattering rose petals along the path.

At last came the moment they had been waiting for, and to a final fanfare of trumpets, one more elephant entered the field, but this was unlike any that had come previously. Though it was smaller, it was twice as striking, and even though the blanket that hung from the platform was royal purple, it could not take away the effect of the pure white skin of the albino elephant.

One man sat alone upon within the canopied platform upon the elephants back, and the awe inspiring display of strength, designed to install shock and awe into any that witnessed it, served its purpose as the leaders of the Catuvellauni finally realised that resistance of any sort was futile.

The man descended from the kneeling elephant via a gilded stairway, carried especially for this purpose by a dozen slaves and sat on an ornate carved chair surrounded by a unit of Praetorian Guard. At a signal from an accompanying senator, the Catuvellauni leaders were summoned forward one by one to bend their knee before the most powerful man in the world, Claudius, Emperor of Rome.

Within the hour, the ceremony had ended, the Catuvellauni subjugated and the country absorbed into the mighty Roman Empire.

Epilogue

The year was 43 AD, and to all intents and purposes, Britannia had fallen, but despite the celebrations, General Plautius was subdued. Already he was hearing of other tribes right across this strange country, gathering their warriors and sharpening their weapons to confront his four legions.

Claudius could crow all he liked, and no doubt would soak up the plaudits back in Rome for conquering a complete country in her name, but Plautius knew different. He knew that a lot more Roman blood would stain this country's soil before they could even begin to believe they were the victors. There were no doubt, treasures to be uncovered, the tribute already paid was evidence of that, but he knew that they would not be surrendered easily. The barbarians were ill disciplined, but they were also fearless, and should anyone take the initiative to forge them into a united army, then Rome's occupation of Britannia could be very short lived.

He knew it was his job to ensure that did not happen and was impatient for Claudius to leave so he could start his campaign in earnest. He needed to find the missing Caratacus and kill him if necessary and there was the matter of those troublesome Druids that he had been hearing about. They seemed to have an influence over everything and everyone in this cold and misty land and could provide a dangerous focal point for barbarian resistance given the chance. Both threats had to be dealt with and he would make it his personal mission to deal with them once and for all, but despite his focus there were two other facts unknown to him at that time.

One was that a little known tribe called the Silures in a strange area of Britannia called the Khymru had just slaughtered a complete Cohort. The second fact, and one he could never have imagined, was that less than a hundred miles to the north was a far greater threat than Caratacus had ever been.

This was no six-foot battle hardened warrior; this was an unassuming mother of two with no intention of opposing the Romans. On the contrary, she wanted a quiet life in which to bring up her two beautiful daughters and as wife to Prasatagus, chief of one of the smaller tribes was happy, along with her husband to accept the presence of the Romans.

However, unbeknownst to her or indeed anyone else, fate would intervene and make this woman a pivotal figure around which the entire Roman occupation of Britannia would revolve. Her name was Boudicca, queen of the Iceni.

This was not an end for Plautius, but just the beginning.

****

The End

Author's Notes

The Roman Invasion of Britain
Rome did indeed successfully invade Britain in 43 AD after two previously unsuccessful attempts by Julius Caesar.

The battles
Though there were many battles two of the most famous and strategically important were the battles of the river Medway and the battle of the river Thames. Caratacus and his army were taken by surprise when the Batavian auxiliaries fell on them from the rear, having swam the river with full weapons and equipment, a skill they were famed for. Eventually after winning both battles, the Romans took Colchester (Camulodunum) the capital of Britannia at the time.

The defending tribes
It is believed that the Romans initially fought the Catuvellauni and it is thought that Togodumnus may have been killed at the battle of Medway, while his brother King Caratacus, escaped westward into Wales where he travelled south to join the Silures tribe.

Roman Life
All training methods, weapons and tactics depicted in this book are typical for the time.

Claudius
Claudius himself came to Britannia to ceremoniously accept the surrender of Britannia and there is evidence that war elephants were present on British soil at that time, either in battle or possibly for ceremonial duties.

See more of Kevin's work at
http://kevin-ashman.blogspot.com

Contact Kevin direct at:
KMAshman@Silverbackbooks.co.uk

Book List
The Dead Virgins
The Treasures of Suleiman
The Mummies of the Reich
Savage Eden
The Last Citadel
Vampire

CPSIA information can be obtained at www.ICGtesting.com
Printed in the USA
BVOW070427030513

319788BV00002B/245/P